"Can I help you up?"

Cassie Lynn blinked, coming back to herself, and quickly nodded. "Yes, thank you." Hoping there was no visible sign of the warmth she felt climbing in her cheeks, she held out her hand.

He took it in his larger, work-calloused one and placed his other hand behind her back. With surprisingly little effort, the green-eyed stranger had her on her feet in no time. He stepped away once he was certain she was steady, and she found herself missing the gentle strength of his touch.

He continued to eye her cautiously. "Are you sure you're okay?"

Cassie Lynn nodded as she busied herself dusting her skirt. It wasn't often she found herself flustered this way. "Please don't worry. I've taken worse falls tripping over my own feet."

She studied him while trying not to appear to be nosy. There was something about the man that intrigued her. It wasn't his vivid eyes, or his appearance, though that was appealing enough in a rugged, well-muscled sort of way.

No, it was something about his demeanor and bearing that commanded her attention.

Winnie Griggs
and
Regina Scott

Texas Cinderella
&
Would-Be Wilderness Wife

LOVE INSPIRED
INSPIRATIONAL ROMANCE

LOVE INSPIRED®

INSPIRATIONAL ROMANCE

Recycling programs
for this product may
not exist in your area.

ISBN-13: 978-1-335-52998-5

Texas Cinderella and Would-Be Wilderness Wife

Copyright © 2022 by Harlequin Enterprises ULC

Texas Cinderella
First published in 2016. This edition published in 2022.
Copyright © 2016 by Winnie Griggs

Would-Be Wilderness Wife
First published in 2015. This edition published in 2022.
Copyright © 2015 by Regina Lundgren

For questions and comments about the quality of this book, please contact us
at CustomerService@Harlequin.com.

Love Inspired
22 Adelaide St. West, 41st Floor
Toronto, Ontario M5H 4E3, Canada
www.LoveInspired.com

Printed in U.S.A.

CONTENTS

Winnie Griggs is the multipublished, award-winning author of historical (and occasionally contemporary) romances that focus on small towns, big hearts and amazing grace. She is also a list maker and a lover of dragonflies, and holds an advanced degree in the art of procrastination. Winnie loves to hear from readers—you can connect with her on Facebook at Facebook.com/winniegriggs.author or email her at winnie@winniegriggs.com.

Books by Winnie Griggs

Love Inspired Historical

Texas Grooms

Visit the Author Profile page
at LoveInspired.com for more titles.

TEXAS CINDERELLA

Winnie Griggs

Live in harmony with one another; be sympathetic,
love as brothers, be compassionate and humble.
—*1 Peter* 3:8

Dedicated to my fabulous agent, Michelle Grajkowski,
who is always there for me
and who never loses faith in me.

And to my wonderful writer friends who are always
willing to help me brainstorm my way out of sticky
plot scenarios—Amy, Christopher, Dustin and Renee.

Chapter One

Turnabout, Texas
August 1898

Cassie Lynn Vickers stopped at the doorway to the parlor and smiled at the woman seated in her wheelchair. "Mrs. Flanagan, I'm about to head out for my afternoon walk. I left a pitcher of lemonade and a slice of pie on the kitchen table. Is there anything else you need before I go?"

Her employer waved a hand dismissively. "Go on with you. You know I hate being fussed over."

Cassie Lynn hid a smile. Mrs. Flanagan detested any reminder that she could no longer do for herself, at least not for the near future. She'd injured her leg in a fall two weeks ago and had been confined to a wheelchair ever since. That's when the cantankerous widow had hired Cassie Lynn to act as her housekeeper and personal attendant.

"Yes, ma'am," she said meekly. "And I'll try not to tarry today. I have extra baking to do tonight."

Cheered by the thought of her new enterprise, Cassie Lynn gave a final wave and headed for the front door.

But as soon as she stepped out on the porch and closed the door behind her, she paused. There was someone striding up the walk. That was odd—Mrs. Flanagan rarely received callers.

Cassie Lynn's eyes widened in recognition. She'd know that slight limp and stiff-backed posture anywhere. It was her father. What was he doing here?

Although she'd seen him from time to time since she'd moved to town last December, it was the first time he'd deliberately sought her out. Fearing something was wrong, she quickly descended the porch steps, meeting her father halfway down the front walk.

"Hello, Pa." She was breathless and tried to calm herself. "Is something the matter? Did something happen to one of the boys?" She had four brothers, three of them younger than her, and all still living with her father out on the remote farm.

He frowned disapprovingly. "Goodness, girl, there's no need to get all in a fret. Your brothers are just fine."

She let out a relieved breath, then gave her father a smile. Perhaps he'd come especially to check on her, after all. She set her market basket down and gave him a quick hug. "You're looking well," she said as she stepped back.

He hooked a thumb under his suspenders. "Comes from living a simple life filled with honest labor."

"Yes, sir." He'd always been a no-nonsense, unsentimental sort of man. Trying to ignore the little pinch of yearning for a softer greeting, she offered him a tentative smile. "I have some news."

His brow went up at that and he gave her a keen glance. "And what might that be?"

To her surprise he seemed truly interested. Buoyed by that, she rushed to explain. "I'm going to start a bakery business. Mrs. Fulton over at the restaurant and Mrs. Dawson over at the sweet shop are both going to try my wares. And Mrs. Flanagan here is talking about partnering with me." It was a modest start, but if things worked out, by the time Mrs. Flanagan no longer needed her help, Cassie Lynn might actually be able to make a go of this bakery idea. And then she would truly have established herself as part of the town, something she'd been striving for since she'd escaped her father's farm nine months ago.

Her father was no longer smiling, though, and she found herself almost apologizing. "I know it's not a lot, but in time it could grow to something big enough for me to make a good living from."

Her voice trailed off as she saw the disappointment deepen on his face.

"I thought you might be wanting to tell me you'd found yourself a beau." His tone made it clear she'd failed in some significant way. "I figured that was why you left home in the first place. After things didn't work out with Hank Chandler, I assumed you were setting your sights on some other bachelor."

When Verne, Cassie Lynn's oldest brother, had married and brought his bride home to take over as lady of the house, Cassie Lynn had made her escape from the isolation and drudgery of her father's farm and moved to town. At the time, Hank Chandler had been looking for a wife to help him raise the two children in his charge. For a while it had looked like she might just be that woman, but then she realized Mr. Chandler had fallen in love with the schoolteacher, and Cassie Lynn had pulled herself out of the running.

Not that she had really minded. Finding a husband had never been her reason for leaving the farm.

"I didn't move to town to find a husband, Pa." She struggled to keep her tone matter-of-fact. "I moved here to be around other people and to make a new life for myself."

Her father dismissed her statement with an impatient wave of his hand. "And just what kind of life can a girl make for herself without a husband and young'uns?"

Cassie Lynn's chest tightened as she realized that trying to explain her dreams to him was useless, that he would never understand. So instead of responding to his statement, she changed the subject. "Was there something you came here to see me about?"

Her father nodded. "Verne bought himself some land of his own to farm, and he and Dinah are planning to build a house on it and move out."

Cassie Lynn smiled, genuinely pleased for her older brother. "Verne always loved working the land. He'll do well."

"That he will. But once he and his wife move away, that leaves me and your other brothers on our own."

Her stomach clenched. She knew what was coming next, and she frantically searched her mind for a way to stave it off.

But her father pressed on. "I want you to come back home and take your place as lady of the house. Since it doesn't look like you're going to have a home and family of your own to care for anytime soon, that shouldn't be a problem."

No! She'd already escaped that life. She couldn't return to that lonely drudgery. "I've made a commitment to take care of Mrs. Flanagan," she protested, "and I can't go back on my word. Surely you wouldn't expect me to."

"No, I suppose not. A Vickers's word is never given lightly." Her father rubbed his chin thoughtfully. "How long does Doc Pratt say she's gonna be stuck in that chair?"

"Probably another four or five weeks."

He nodded in satisfaction. "Well then, that shouldn't be a problem. Even if Verne is ready to move out sooner, I'm sure I can convince him to stay that long."

Cassie Lynn steeled herself to take a stand. Her father couldn't *force* her to return to the farm. "I didn't say I would come home when I'm done here. I told you, I'm starting a bakery business."

He frowned. "Of course you'll come home. This town doesn't need a baker—any housewife worth her salt can do her own baking. So there's nothing here in town to hold you." He eyed her sternly. "Me and your brothers work hard keeping that farm going—sunup to sundown most days. You don't want us to have to cook our own meals and do all the housework, too, do you?"

"No, of course not. But—"

He gave a decisive nod. "Good. Then it's agreed. I'll expect you back when your work here is done." And with a quick pat to her shoulder, her father departed, apparently assuming the subject was closed.

Cassie Lynn's fists tightened at her sides as she watched him walk away. If her father had his way, she'd have only four or five weeks before her world drew in once more to the narrow confines of the isolated farm—the world she thought she'd escaped for good. She *couldn't* let that happen.

How could her father expect her to meekly return home, as if she had no ambitions for her life? So what if she didn't yet have a husband? She was only twenty-two! It wasn't as if she was past marriageable age. Besides, what chance did she ever have of finding a man if she returned to the farm?

But how could she refuse her father when he was so determined? Especially when it was her fault that her mother was no longer around to fill that role.

Cassie Lynn picked up the basket and began to slowly walk down the sidewalk, trying to tamp down her panic and focus on finding a solution to this problem. She'd tried to reason with her father and she'd tried to stand against him, and neither tactic had been very effective. What did that leave?

The Good Lord commanded that children should honor their parents, and she certainly didn't want to *dishonor* her father, but surely there was a way out of this without having to outright stand against him.

She wasn't surprised that her father thought a woman's only goal should be to look after the men in her life. It was how he'd treated her mother, after all. Cassie Lynn had never heard him, or her brothers, for that matter, utter a word of thanks for all her mother had done. And they'd certainly never extended her that courtesy, either, after her mother had passed.

She paused as an idea occurred to her. According to her father's own words, if she had a husband, or at least a serious suitor, he wouldn't have asked her to come home. So, perhaps that was her answer.

She just had to get herself a beau before her commitment to Mrs. Flanagan was completed.

Riley Walker stepped out of the Turnabout train depot, ushering his niece and nephew before him. This hadn't been a planned stop, but the kids had gotten restless and a bit cranky after three days of travel, so he figured it wouldn't hurt to lay over here for a few days. After all, the meeting in Tyler wasn't until next Wednesday morning, a whole week away.

Besides, his horse, River, was no doubt ready to escape the livestock car and have a chance to get some freedom to move about, as well. A quick look to his left showed Riley that the gray gelding was already being led off the train.

He turned to the kids and pointed to a bench near the depot door. "Sit over there while I see to River. Don't move from this spot, understand?"

Ten-year-old Pru nodded and took her seven-year-old brother's hand. Riley watched until she and Noah were seated, once again feeling his own inadequacy as guardian to these children. But they'd needed a protector when their mother died and so they'd been stuck with him.

He turned and quickly took possession of his horse, checking the animal carefully for any injuries he might have sustained on the trip. Satisfied, Riley led him to where the kids were seated.

"Ready? Let's get River settled at the livery and then we'll head over to the hotel." He'd gotten directions to both establishments when he'd stepped inside the depot to make arrangements for their bags to be delivered to the hotel.

"How long can we stay here, Uncle Riley?" Noah asked.

Riley heard the hopeful note in the boy's voice, and made a quick decision. "What do you say we stay through Sunday so we can all attend church service here? Would you like that?"

Noah nodded enthusiastically.

Riley turned to his niece. "What about you, Pru?"

She nodded, as well, though with more reserve than her brother. Pru was normally quiet and shy, but this listlessness was unusual. Was all the traveling they were doing starting to wear on her?

Fortunately, the livery stable was near the train station so they reached it quickly.

Cassie Lynn placed her now full shopping basket at her feet and leaned against the corral fence behind the livery stable.

She dug the apple slices from her pocket. Already the two resident horses were trotting over to see what she'd brought them today.

"Here you go, Duchess," she crooned as she held out her hand and let the black mare lip two slices from her palm.

She laughed as a reddish brown mare tried to push Duchess aside. "Mind your manners, Scarlett, I have some for you, too."

She gave Scarlett her treat. "I've had some excitement today, both good and bad," she confided to the two mares as she stroked Scarlett's muzzle. "The good news is that I'm moving forward on my bakery business."

Cassie Lynn shifted to give Duchess her share of attention. "The bad news is that Pa wants me to go back to the farm and take care of him and my brothers." She breathed a sigh. "I don't want to do that, of course. So now I need to find me a husband."

She gave both horses a final pat, then crossed her arms on the top rail and leaned into it. "I sure wish you gals could speak. I bet you'd be able to give me some good insights. I figure the way a man treats his animals is a good measure of his character."

"Are you talking to the horses?"

Cassie Lynn turned her head to see a freckle-faced boy of six or seven eyeing her curiously.

"Of course. They're friends of mine." Then she smiled and stepped back from the corral fence. "I don't think we've met before, have we?"

The boy shook his head. "We just got to town a little while ago. I'm Noah." As he stepped out of the shade of the livery, the sun highlighted a bit of copper mixed in with his blond hair.

"Glad to meet you, Noah. I'm Cassie Lynn."

"My uncle Riley likes to talk to horses, too."

"Sounds like a smart man." She held out her last few apple slices and nodded toward the two mares. "Would you like to feed them?"

The boy smiled, displaying a gap where one of his front teeth should be, and took the slices. He eagerly stepped up on the second-from-the-bottom board of the fence so he could lean over the top rail. Fearlessly holding his hand out just as she had, Noah smiled as the black mare happily took the offering. "What's her name?" he asked.

"Duchess." Cassie Lynn moved beside the boy and propped a foot on the bottom board, concerned by his precarious perch. She rubbed the other mare's neck. "And this here is Scarlett."

She smiled as the boy stroked the mare's muzzle. "I see you've done this before," she said.

The boy nodded. "Uncle Riley has a real fine horse— a gray named River. He's inside right now talking to Mr. Humphries about stabling him here."

Well, at least she knew the boy wasn't alone. Cassie Lynn patted Scarlett's muzzle so the animal wouldn't feel left out, then she leaned her elbows on the top rail again. "Are you visiting someone here or do you and your folks plan to settle down in Turnabout?"

The boy shook his head. "We don't know anyone here. And I don't have folks anymore. It's just me, Pru and Uncle Riley."

She absorbed the words, as well as his matter-of-fact tone. Before she could form a response, though, they were interrupted.

"Noah, what are you doing out here?"

At the sharply uttered question, Noah quickly turned, and in the process lost his footing. Cassie Lynn moved swiftly to stop his fall and ended up landing in the dirt on her backside with Noah on her lap.

"Are you all right?"

She looked up to see a man she didn't know helping Noah stand up. But the concerned frown on his face was focused on her.

"I'm a bit dusty, but otherwise fine," she said with a rueful smile.

He stooped down, studying her as if he didn't quite believe her reassurances.

She met his gaze and found herself looking into the deepest, greenest eyes she'd ever seen.

Chapter Two

Cassie Lynn found herself entranced by the genuine concern and intelligence reflected in the newcomer's expression. It made her temporarily forget that she was sitting in the dust and dirt of the livery yard.

"Can I help you up?"

She blinked, coming back to herself, and quickly nodded. "Yes, thank you." Hoping there was no visible sign of the warmth she felt climbing in her cheeks, Cassie Lynn held out her hand.

He took it in his larger, work-callused one and she had the strangest feeling that she could hold on to that hand forever.

Then he placed his other hand behind her back, and with surprisingly little effort, the green-eyed stranger had her on her feet in no time. He stepped away once he was certain she was steady, and she found herself missing the protective strength of his touch.

He continued to eye her cautiously. "Are you sure you're okay?"

Cassie Lynn nodded as she busied herself dusting off her skirt.

What was wrong with her? It wasn't often she found herself flustered this way. "Please, don't worry. I've taken worse falls tripping over my own feet." She quickly turned to Noah. "How about you? Are you all right?"

"Yes, ma'am. Thanks for catching me."

She ruffled his hair. "Glad to help." For the first time she noticed a young girl standing slightly behind the man, chewing her lip as if she didn't want to be here. Before Cassie Lynn could introduce herself, however, the man spoke up again.

"I've told you before not to wander off without telling me." His tone was stern.

Noah's expression turned defensive. "I just wanted to get out in the sunshine. We've been cooped up *forever.*" The boy scuffed the ground with the toe of his shoe. "Besides, you were right inside, and I didn't go far."

The man didn't seem the least bit appeased. "That's no excuse."

Noah's shoulders slumped. Then he gave his uncle a hopeful look. "But you found me right away. And I knew Pru saw where I was going."

Watching the interplay between the two of them, Cassie Lynn could detect genuine concern behind the man's scolding. This, of course, must be the Uncle Riley that Noah had mentioned.

She studied the boy's uncle while trying not to appear to be nosy. There was something about the man that intrigued her. It wasn't just his vivid eyes, or his appearance, though that was appealing enough in a rugged, well-muscled sort of way. No, it was something about his bearing that commanded her attention, an air of self-confidence and strength, balanced with a concern for his nephew, which lent just a hint of vulnerability. It all came together in a way that she found compelling.

The man gave his nephew a final exasperated look, then turned to face her.

She quickly schooled her features, hoping she hadn't given away any hint of her rather inappropriate thoughts. To her relief, his expression was merely polite.

"My apologies, miss, for any trouble Noah might have caused you."

"No need to apologize." She gave the boy a companionable smile, then held out her hand to the man beside him. "I'm Cassie Lynn Vickers, by the way."

He took her hand and gave it a perfunctory shake before releasing it. "Glad to meet you, Miss Vickers. I'm Riley Walker. And I appreciate you coming to Noah's rescue the way you did."

She dipped her head in acknowledgment. "Glad to help." Then she turned to the little girl. "And I assume you are Noah's sister, Pru?"

The girl, who looked to be no older than ten or eleven, nodded.

Cassie Lynn turned to the children's uncle. "I understand you folks are new to town. I hope you enjoy your stay here."

"I'm sure we will." Mr. Walker touched the brim of his hat, and she thought for a moment he would make his exit. But instead he hesitated a moment and then nodded toward the corral. "Which one of these horses is yours?"

"None, I'm afraid. We're just good friends." She rested an arm on the fence. "I understand from Noah you've brought your own horse to town with you."

He nodded. "River goes everywhere I do." He waved toward the livery end of the corral, where Mr. Humphries was leading what was presumably Mr. Walker's horse through the gate. "That's him now."

She heard the pride in his voice and turned to study the animal more closely. His coat was silvery-gray with a few darker flecks on his flank and a charcoal colored mane and tail. The animal appeared spirited and well cared for.

"He looks to be a fine horse."

Mr. Walker's smile had a touch of affection in it. "He is that." Then he turned serious again. "It was nice meeting you, Miss Vickers, but if you'll excuse us, I need to get us checked in at the hotel."

"Of course." As he moved away, she called out to them. "Mr. Walker?"

He paused and turned back, his expression one of polite inquiry. "Ma'am?"

She felt foolish for her impulsive act. "I just wanted to say if you have questions about any of the local establishments, or need directions of any sort, I'd be glad to help you."

"That's very kind of you, but not necessary at the moment."

They resumed their exit and this time she let them. But she overheard another snippet of their conversation before they moved out of hearing range.

"Are you really going to work here, Uncle Riley?" Noah asked.

His uncle nodded. "I am. But just for a few hours each day."

Were the Walkers going to settle here then? She certainly hoped so. It would give her a chance to see that sweet little Noah again.

And his uncle.

She watched them until they disappeared around the corner of the livery. Then she dusted the back of her skirt with her hands and turned to the horses. "Well, now, wasn't that an interesting little encounter? I must say, I found Mr. Walker and his charges to be quite fascinating." She stroked Scarlett's muzzle again. Given that Cassie Lynn was looking for a husband, she couldn't help but think that Mr. Walker would be a not unpleasant choice.

Ridiculous, of course, since she didn't really know him. Then again, she didn't know any of the local gents very well, either. It certainly couldn't hurt to put the newcomer on her list while she tried to learn more about him. For instance, learning if he was even planning to settle down in Turnabout or was just passing through.

She grinned at her own silliness. Then the reminder of just why she was making her husband candidate list came flooding back, and she no longer had any desire to smile.

It was time to stop her foolish daydreaming and get down to business. Cassie Lynn picked up her shopping basket and walked away from the corral.

Finding a husband wouldn't be easy, but it wasn't altogether impossible.

Please, God, if this plan be in Your will, prepare the man You have in mind for me so that he is open to my proposal.

Feeling somewhat better now that she had a direction, Cassie Lynn straightened and moved forward with a lighter step.

But there was one big problem with her plan. She didn't know the men in town well enough to evaluate them against her requirements. Which meant she needed an advisor, someone who could help her make those comparisons and who would perhaps think of candidates she might not be aware of. There were only a few people she felt comfortable turning to for that kind of assistance.

There was Janell Chandler, the former schoolteacher who had eventually won the hand of Hank Chandler.

Then there was Daisy Fulton, the restaurant owner Cassie Lynn had worked for for six months.

And of course there was her current employer, Mrs. Flanagan. Daisy and Janell were closer to her own age, and both had moved to Turnabout from elsewhere, so they would know something of her situation. On the other hand, Mrs. Flanagan had grown up here and knew just about everything there was to know about her fellow townsfolk.

But did she really want her employer involved in her dilemma that way?

Better to turn her thoughts to what she would prepare for Mrs. Flanagan's evening meal and let the other matter simmer a bit.

A simple vegetable soup, perhaps, or a potpie could be prepared with very little thought and would leave her mind free to ponder her situation…

What would Mr. Walker and his two charges be doing for supper tonight? Maybe she could convince Mrs. Flanagan to invite the Walker family to dine with them one night soon. Having company to ease the monotony of the widow's days would be good for her, whether she would be willing to admit it or not.

And it would, after all, be the neighborly thing to do.

Riley hurried Pru and Noah along. There were several things he still had to do this afternoon, and the sooner he settled the children at the hotel the better.

The most pressing matter was to get a telegraph off to Mr. Claypool. He always made a point of letting the Pinkerton detective know where to reach him when he arrived in a new town.

Then he wanted to take River for a run. The horse had been cooped up in that train car for much too long and would be ready for some exercise. And truth to tell, Riley was, too. He missed being on horseback—there hadn't been nearly enough opportunity for him to turn loose and ride lately.

His mind drifted back to Miss Vickers. She was an interesting lady. At first glance he'd thought her a tomboyish adolescent. The way she'd stood so casually at the corral fence, elbows on the top rail, laughing with Noah—no wonder he'd gotten the wrong idea. And her slight build had only reinforced that impression.

Rushing to Noah's aid with such disregard for her own well-being or dignity as she had, and then taking her fall with a touch of humor rather than dismay— there weren't many grown ladies who would have done such a thing.

It was only when he'd stooped down to check on her that he'd realized his mistake. That engagingly rueful smile had most definitely belonged to a woman, not a child.

It was when their gazes first met, though, that he'd

found himself thrown off balance. He'd never encountered quite that combination of innocence and humor before, especially mixed as it was with an air of maturity and resolve.

It was such a curious mix he wondered if he'd really seen all that in one quick glance. Still, the impression had remained with him. Of course, her cheery smile, and the dimple that kept appearing near the left corner of her lip, had contributed to the unexpected air that seemed to surround her. It bestowed on her a kind of unconventional attractiveness, even when she was sitting in the dust with a chagrinned look on her face. He hadn't been so taken by a woman in quite some time. For just a heartbeat he'd been tempted to linger, to get to know her better.

And that had brought him up short. Because he couldn't afford to let himself be diverted by such fetching distractions now, no matter how intriguing. Especially when there was no chance it could go anywhere. In another few days he and the kids would be moving on again.

"Uncle Riley?"

Noah's words brought his thoughts back to the present. "Yes?"

"That Miss Vickers lady seems nice, don't you think?"

It appeared he and Noah were thinking along similar lines. "I suppose." Actually, "nice" seemed inadequate. Not everyone would have gone to such lengths to come to the aid of a stranger and then brushed off his thanks so modestly.

"And there are probably lots of other nice folks in

this town, too, don't you think?" Noah's tone had taken on a cajoling quality.

"Could be." Riley had an idea where this was headed and tried to cut it off. "But there are nice people everywhere." He gave his nephew a little nudge. "Besides, who wouldn't be nice to a great kid like you?"

Noah grinned up at him, then pressed on. "Anyway, since there are such nice folks here, don't you think it would be okay for us to stay longer than a few days?"

There it was. "We've talked about this before. We don't stay very long in small towns. Big towns are better for long stays." Places where it was easier to disappear and not stand out so starkly. The only reason he'd stopped here in the first place was because the kids, especially Pru, had seemed unusually restless. It would do them good to get out and move around and get some fresh air and sunshine. "Besides, I have to be in Tyler for a meeting by Wednesday morning."

Riley could tell Noah wasn't satisfied with his answer. "I promise I'll find us a nice big town to spend some time in real soon. Maybe you two could even go to school for a while." He gave his niece's shoulder a nudge. "You'd like that, wouldn't you, Pru?"

The girl nodded. "I miss going to school."

"That's settled then. By the time school starts next month, we'll be someplace where we can stay put for a while." Assuming they could keep their relentless pursuer off their trail.

To Riley's relief, they'd reached the hotel by this time and it ended the need for further conversation.

This whole business of moving from town to town, never staying in one place for long, was taking its toll on all of them. If only there was some other way. But he couldn't afford the luxury of letting them set down permanent roots anywhere.

The well-being of the children depended on his keeping them several steps ahead of Guy.

His stepbrother.

The kids' father.

Chapter Three

Cassie Lynn pushed open the door to Mrs. Flanagan's home, her mood considerably different from the cheery one she'd had when she'd left here just one short hour ago. So much had happened in such a short period of time.

Dapple sat just inside the door, tail swishing impatiently. Seeming to sense her mood, the normally imperious tortoiseshell cat stropped against Cassie Lynn's legs with a sympathetic purr.

She bent down and stroked the animal's back. "Thanks, Dapple. You can be really sweet sometimes."

That was apparently too much for the feline. He gave Cassie Lynn a baleful look, then turned and stalked down the hall, the very picture of affronted dignity.

With a smile, Cassie Lynn headed for the kitchen. "I'm back," she called out as she set her shopping basket on the kitchen table. "Sorry I took so long."

Mrs. Flanagan wheeled her chair into the kitchen. "Rather than apologizing," the widow said acerbically, "tell me what that father of yours wanted."

Cassie Lynn should have realized her employer had

known he was there. How much should she say? "He wanted to give me some news about Verne and Dinah."

Mrs. Flanagan raised a brow. "They're expecting a new young'un, are they?"

"No, at least not that I know of." She started putting away the items she'd purchased at the mercantile. "But they *are* moving out and planning to set up their own place."

There was a moment of silence, but even with her back turned, Cassie Lynn could feel the keen stare the widow had focused on her.

"I've known Alvin Vickers most of his life," Mrs. Flanagan finally said, "so I know he didn't come all the way into town just to deliver news like that. He wants you to move back to his place and take care of him, doesn't he?"

Cassie Lynn reluctantly glanced back over her shoulder and nodded.

"You didn't agree to go, did you?"

"Not exactly."

The widow's eyes narrowed. "What does *not exactly* mean?"

Rather than give a direct answer, she hedged. "He was very insistent."

"You mean he tried to roll right over your objections!"

Cassie Lynn gave her a tight smile that was part grimace. "I appreciate you're concerned about me, but—"

"Ha! Who said I was concerned about you?"

When she'd first come to work here, Cassie Lynn had been taken aback by Mrs. Flanagan's vinegary tongue, but it hadn't taken her long to see behind the woman's facade to the soft heart beneath. So she didn't take offense at the words.

The woman settled back in her chair with a determined frown. "I've got a stake in that bakery business you're trying to start, remember? And you can't run it from that back-of-beyond farm."

Cassie Lynn felt compelled to defend her father. "He's my pa. I owe him—"

Mrs. Flanagan actually wagged a finger at her. "Cassie Lynn Vickers, you're twenty-two years old, a grown woman by anyone's reckoning. You need to grow some backbone and make that father of yours listen to you."

Cassie Lynn grimaced, then turned away. Mrs. Flanagan might not say that if she knew the whole story. "At any rate, I told him I wasn't leaving here as long as you needed my help."

"Well, that's something." The widow gave a decisive snort. "And I have a feeling that I may need your help for much longer than we first expected."

Startled, Cassie Lynn shot her a quick glance. Then, making up her mind, she decided to share her plan. "I do have an idea about how I might get around this."

Mrs. Flanagan straightened. "Well, bless my soul, you do have some gumption, after all." She leaned back with a satisfied nod. "Let's hear it."

Cassie Lynn took a deep breath. "It appears the only excuse my father will accept is if I was spoken for. So that's what I intend to do—find a man to marry."

The widow's brow went up. "Just like that, you're going to go out and find yourself a suitor?"

"I didn't say it would be easy." Cassie Lynn tried to keep the defensiveness from her tone. "And it's not as if I expect anything romantic." She didn't have any notions of finding a fairy-tale prince who would look at her, fall instantly in love and whisk her away.

After all, she'd already contemplated a businesslike marriage with Mr. Chandler when she'd first come to town. So she'd already come to terms with that kind of arrangement.

But Mrs. Flanagan was frowning at her. "You're much too young to be giving up on love. Don't you want at least a touch of romance in your life?"

"Romance is no guarantee of happiness. And even if that was something I wanted, in this case there's no time for such schoolgirl notions. So a more practical approach is called for."

"I see." Mrs. Flanagan crossed her arms, clearly not in agreement with Cassie Lynn's argument, but willing to move on. "Is there a particular bachelor you've set your sights on?"

"I've been pondering on that and I have a couple of ideas. The main thing, though, is I've decided what requirements the gents need to meet." She'd given that a lot of thought on her walk home.

"And those are?"

"Well, for one, since I want to continue pursuing my goal of opening a bakery, the candidate will need to be okay with having a wife who does more than just keep his house. And it would also require that he live here in town so I can be close to my customers, for delivery purposes."

"Surely you also want to consider his character."

"Of course. He should be honest, kind and God-fearing." She didn't expect affection—after all, this would be a businesslike arrangement—but she did hope for mutual respect.

"And his appearance?"

Cassie Lynn shrugged. "That's of less importance. Though naturally, I wouldn't mind if he's pleasant to look at." Like Mr. Walker, for example.

She shook off that thought and returned to the discussion at hand. "But none of that matters unless I can find someone who's also open to my proposal."

"And you've thought of someone who meets this list of qualifications?"

"Two. But I don't really know the men here very well, so I was hoping that perhaps you could give me some suggestions."

"Humph! I've always thought of matchmakers as busybodies, so I never aspired to become one."

"Oh, I don't want a matchmaker—I intend to make up my own mind on who I marry. I'd just like to have the benefit of advice from someone who knows the townsfolk better than I do. And who has experienced what a marriage involves."

"Well, then, much as I'm not sure I approve of this plan of yours, I don't suppose I can just let you go through it without guidance of some sort."

"Thank you so much, Mrs. Flanagan. I can't tell you what a relief that is."

"Now don't go getting all emotional on me. I said I'd help and I will. Tell me who these two gents are that you're considering."

"The first name that occurred to me was Morris Hilburn."

"The butcher?"

Cassie Lynn nodded. "From what I can tell, he meets

most of my criteria. Of course, I won't know how he feels about having a wife who runs a bakery until I talk to him."

"Morris Hilburn is a God-fearing man with a good heart, all right. But he is not the smartest of men and he's not much of a talker."

"Book learning and good conversation are not requirements."

"Think about that before you rule them out. Do you *really* want to spend the rest of your life with a man whose idea of conversation is single syllable responses?"

Cassie Lynn paused. Then she remembered the fate her father had in mind for her. "There are worse things." She moved on before her employer could comment. "The other gentleman I thought of was Mr. Gilbert Drummond."

"The undertaker? Well, I suppose he might be someone to look at. Then again, he strikes me as being a bit finicky."

"There are worse qualities one could find in a man. Besides, a woman in my position doesn't have the luxury of being choosy." More's the pity. "But I'm open to other suggestions if you have any."

"I'll need to ponder on this awhile."

"Unfortunately, my time is short." She hesitated a heartbeat, then spoke up again, keeping her voice oh-so-casual. "There's actually a third candidate I'm considering."

"And who might that be?"

"I met a newcomer to town while I was at the livery. He just arrived on today's train."

"A newcomer? And you're just now telling me about

this? You know good and well part of the reason I hired you is to have someone to bring me the latest bits of news."

Cassie Lynn laughed. "And here I thought it was for my cooking."

"Don't be impertinent. I want to hear everything. How did you meet him? Is he a young man or more mature? Is he handsome? Is he traveling alone." She waved impatiently. "Come on, girl, answer me."

She decided to respond to the last question first. "He's traveling with two children, a niece and nephew. I met the little boy first. Noah is about seven and such an endearing child—intelligent, curious, outgoing. The little girl, Pru, seems shy and quiet." Cassie Lynn searched her memory for all the little descriptive details, relating these tidbits as vividly as she could, knowing Mrs. Flanagan loved getting these glimpses of the outside world she was missing.

After a few minutes of that, however, her employer interrupted her. "Enough of the kids," she said with a grumpy frown. "Tell me about the uncle."

Cassie Lynn paused a moment to pull up Mr. Walker's image in her mind. "He has hair the color of coffee with a dash of cream stirred in, and his eyes are a piercing green." A glorious shamrock-green that she could still picture quite vividly. "He's lean but muscular, if you know what I mean, like he's used to doing hard work."

"And his age?"

"I didn't ask."

Mrs. Flanagan made a disapproving noise. "Don't be coy with me, Cassie Lynn. Take a guess."

She hid her grin. "I suppose I'd put him around twenty-four or twenty-five." Though there was something about the look in his eyes that spoke of experience beyond his years.

"How did you come to meet him?"

Cassie Lynn explained the circumstances as she crossed the room to retrieve an apron that hung on a peg near the stove.

"I can see the man has obviously impressed you."

Cassie Lynn stopped midstep and glanced over at her employer.

"Don't look so surprised, girl, I'm no simpleton. If he hadn't caught your eye, you wouldn't have put him on your list." Then she leaned back. "So what was it about him that made you decide after only ten minutes in his company that he might be the husband you're looking for?"

"I only said he might be worth considering." Then, under Mrs. Flanagan's steady gaze, she shrugged. "I suppose it was the fact that he had two young children in his care—it made me think he might be a man in need of a woman's help. And it was also the way he interacted with them. He obviously cares about them."

It made her think about her relationship with her own father. He'd never been very affectionate, but when she'd been Pru's age she felt he'd had a little more time for her.

"I agree with you there," Mrs. Flanagan said. "A single man in charge of two young'uns sounds like a gentleman in need of a wife if there ever was one." Dapple had wandered into the kitchen and, with a graceful motion, leaped into Mrs. Flanagan's lap. The woman stroked the cat's back, her eyes remaining fixed on Cassie Lynn. "So tell me about these newcomers. Who'd they come here to visit?"

"According to Noah, they don't know anyone in Turnabout."

"Humph. That's strange. Not many folks come to Turnabout unless they have some purpose."

"I'm sure they *have* a purpose, it's just not to visit someone they know." Cassie Lynn hadn't given the reason for their visit much thought until now. She hoped that, whatever it was that had brought them to Turnabout, it would keep them here for a while. Mr. Walker *had* taken a job, after all.

"If I am to advise you, then I think it's important that I meet this young man and his charges."

Cassie Lynn nodded in agreement, pleased that Mrs. Flanagan had given her the opening she wanted. "We could invite them to have supper with us tomorrow evening. Sort of as a neighborly gesture, welcoming them to town."

"Excellent idea." She stroked Dapple's head absently "In the meantime I'll think on what other men might also meet your requirements."

Cassie Lynn smiled as she pulled the cast-iron pot from its hook above the stove. Having the Walkers over for supper would do more than give her an opportunity to get to know them better.

It had surprised her that Mrs. Flanagan never had anyone, other than Dr. Pratt or Reverend Harper, drop in to see her since her accident. The woman apparently didn't have any close friends.

Cassie Lynn had been trying to come up with a way to remedy that. But how did she invite people to come by and visit a flinty widow who'd never made any effort to make friends with her neighbors?

And now she would be able to do just that. Having Mrs. Flanagan help her find a suitor wouldn't just benefit her, it would give the widow purpose, as well.

And wouldn't it be nice if Mr. Walker turned out to be *the one*.

From a purely expedient perspective, of course.

Chapter Four

Cassie Lynn exited the Blue Bottle Sweet Shop the next afternoon with a spring in her step. Eve Dawson had sold all four fruit tarts she'd delivered to her this morning, and was very happy with her customers' reactions to them. It had been the same story with Daisy Fulton over at the restaurant. Both of them had placed additional orders for her goods.

If the worst happened and Cassie Lynn ended up back at her father's farm—though she still wasn't ready to surrender to that possibility—she would have the pleasure of knowing that folks enjoyed her baked goods well enough to pay for them.

Of course, if she was being entirely honest with herself, part of the reason for the lightness of her mood was her current destination, the livery. She was looking forward to visiting Scarlett and Duchess again, of course. But she was hoping she might also run into Mr. Walker. He was working there, after all.

When Cassie Lynn arrived at the corral she saw Scarlett and Mr. Walker's horse, River, penned there. But Duchess wasn't anywhere in sight.

Scarlett trotted over to the fence, nickered and tossed her head.

"And hello to you, too," Cassie Lynn said as she reached into her basket for one of the carrots she'd brought for just that purpose.

To her delight, River wasn't far behind. "Well hello, boy. Ready to be friends." She held out a carrot and the horse took it as if it was nothing out of the ordinary.

"So where is our friend Duchess?" she asked as she rubbed the horse's neck. "Did she get the chance to leave the livery today?"

"She did indeed."

At the sound of the male voice, Cassie Lynn turned to see Mr. Walker leading the mare into the corral. Her pulse immediately kicked up a notch.

"She and the buckboard were rented out to a Mr. Hendricks to transport a load of lumber." Mr. Walker gave Duchess a final pat before removing the lead and closing the gate to the corral.

Cassie Lynn smiled. "I understand you're working here now?"

"I am. A few hours a day, just to pay for River's up-keep." He moved around to where the trough was situated, checked the water level and began working the pump. "So, do you stop by here every day?"

She nodded. "Most days, anyway. It's my favorite part of the day." She held out another carrot as Duchess pranced up to her. "These two ladies and I are good friends." Then she reached out to touch River's muzzle. "And I hope this handsome gent and I soon will be."

"River likes you." Mr. Walker sounded surprised. "He's pretty discerning when it comes to who he lets get close to him."

"I believe the carrot might have had something to do with it," she said drily. Then she turned to face him fully. "Actually, though, I was hoping I'd run into you."

He raised a brow. "Were you now?"

Her cheeks warmed as she realized how that had sounded, and she rushed to clarify. "I mean, I told Mrs. Flanagan, the lady I work for, about meeting you and the children. And she thought it might be good to have the three of you over for supper, just as a neighborly gesture, you being new to town and all. Anyway, she asked me to invite you to join us this evening. If you're free and you'd like to come, that is." Cassie Lynn mentally winced. She wasn't normally one to babble, but felt that's exactly what she'd just been doing.

He kept working the pump. "That's mighty nice of you ladies, but please don't feel obliged."

Was he going to refuse? "We're not inviting you because we feel obliged. It's something we want to do."

"Still, I wouldn't want to take advantage."

Why did he seem so reluctant? "Actually, you'd be doing me a favor," she said diffidently.

He looked up from his task. "How's that?"

"Mrs. Flanagan is currently confined to a wheelchair. That's why I'm working for her, to take care of her and do the things around the house that she can't do for herself from that chair."

He finished pumping the water and leaned against the fence, facing her. "Sorry to hear that, but I don't understand where the favor comes in."

"With her being confined to the house the way she is, I think it would really cheer her up to have some new folks to talk to."

He studied her face for a long moment, as if mentally

weighing some issue. Had she pressed too hard? Did he really *not* want to be their guest for some reason?

She was trying to steel herself to accept his refusal when he finally spoke up. "All right then. The kids and I would be pleased to accept your generous invitation. What time should we be there?"

Relieved, she gave him a bright smile. "We normally eat supper around six o'clock."

His lips twisted in a wry grin. "And I guess I should also ask just where *there* is."

Cassie Lynn gave him the directions, then looked around. "Where are Noah and Pru?"

His expression immediately closed off. "They're back at the hotel." He straightened and gave a short nod. "If you'll excuse me, I need to get back to work." And with that he turned and headed toward the stable.

Cassie Lynn stared at his back for a moment, wondering at his abrupt change in mood. Had he been put off by her question?

She turned and slowly headed back to Mrs. Flanagan's, replaying the conversation in her mind. He said he'd left the children at the hotel. Were they alone? She could see why that would embarrass him. But he was new to town, so it was understandable that he hadn't found a caretaker for them. If she wasn't already committed to Mrs. Flanagan, she would have been happy to take that position herself.

But she would make a point of giving him some recommendations this evening.

Not only was she happy to help, but she wanted to do anything she could to make it easy for him to settle in here.

If that's what he wanted to do.

* * *

Riley went about his tasks at the livery automatically. It was the kind of work he knew well and was comfortable with. He didn't mind working with and around horses, even when he was asked to muck out the stalls. It was good, honest labor.

But what he really itched to do right now was saddle up River and take him out for a long run. Riding across wide-open spaces was something he craved, the way a hawk craved skimming the air currents. It made him feel free and alive. It also cleared his mind and helped him see things more clearly.

And the ability to think clearly was something he definitely needed right now.

He wasn't sure why he'd just accepted Miss Vickers's invitation. Ever since he'd taken the kids from their home in Wyoming and set out on this never-ending journey, he'd made it a practice to keep the three of them to themselves as much as possible. All things considered, it was best if they not draw any attention to themselves. It also made it easier to slip away when the time came to move on.

And it always came.

He'd had every intention of following that same course of action here by politely refusing her invitation.

But somehow, when he'd opened his mouth, *yes* came out instead of *no*. He still wasn't certain how that had happened. Maybe it was because he was getting travel-weary, or that the constant worry over whether Guy would catch up with them was wearing on him.

Because it certainly couldn't have anything to do with Miss Vickers herself. After all, in other towns, there'd been other ladies, some equally as pretty, some equally as interesting, who'd tried to claim his attention, and he'd never faltered from his course.

Then again, none had been pretty and interesting in quite the same way as Miss Vickers. A way that tugged at something inside him.

Riley gave his head a mental shake, pushing aside that totally irrational thought. It was more likely that he'd slipped up because he was just tired.

Her question about the kids had brought him up short, though. Brought him back to his senses. It was probably innocent, but he'd been put in tough spots by nosy, well-meaning folks before, folks who wanted explanations about where they'd come from, where they were going, what had happened to the kids' parents. Trust had never come easy to Riley and nothing that had happened the last couple of years had changed that.

He toyed a moment with the idea of finding a plausible excuse to cancel on her. Then he discarded it. Doing that would call as much if not more attention to themselves than if he just followed through. Besides, reneging on a promise, even one as minor as this, didn't sit well with him.

It was just one meal, after all. And once he'd fulfilled his obligation to attend, he could insert some distance, put up some walls. Which shouldn't be difficult since he and the kids weren't going to be here more than a few days anyway.

Grabbing a pitchfork, Riley headed for the hay stall, but before he could get to work, he heard someone step inside the livery from the street.

A new customer? Riley quickly looked around for Mr. Humphries, but when he didn't spot the owner, moved forward himself. "Hello. Is there something I can do for you?"

The man gave him an easy smile. "Actually, I heard Fred had hired someone new and thought I'd come around and introduce myself. I'm Ward Gleason, the sheriff around these parts."

Riley hoped his expression didn't give anything away. "Good to meet you, Sheriff." He pulled off his work gloves and extended his hand. "I'm Riley Walker."

"Mr. Walker." The lawman shook his hand and gave a short nod. Then he released it and eyed Riley with a casual glance that didn't fool him one bit. "Mind if I ask what brings you to our little town?"

He's only doing his job, Riley told himself. Surely there wasn't anything more to it than that. "Not at all. I've got my niece and nephew with me and we're making our way to California. But since we're not in a hurry and they *are* kids, I'm making frequent stops along the way to give them a chance to get out and about and see other parts of the country." That was true, as far as it went.

"Any particular reason you chose to stop *here*?"

Riley shrugged, keeping his demeanor open and casual. "I make it a point of never traveling more than a few days at a time. My niece was getting restless and this just happened to be a good stopping off point."

"Just the luck of the draw, is that it?"

"I guess you could say that." How much longer would this thinly disguised interrogation last?

But the lawman didn't seem to be in a hurry to take his leave. He crossed his arms and leaned against a support post. "So this isn't a permanent stop for you?"

"Nope." Riley placed his hands on top of the pitchfork handle and leaned his weight against it, trying to emulate the sheriff's relaxed pose. "Don't plan to be here more than a few days." Maybe shorter if the sheriff took too keen an interest in them.

"And where are your niece and nephew right now?"

Keep it casual. "They're resting at your town's fine hotel."

"Hi there, Sheriff." Mr. Humphries's hail turned both men's heads toward the side office. "You looking to rent a buggy?"

Riley tried not to let his relief at the interruption show.

The sheriff straightened. "Hello, Fred. No, I'm just getting acquainted with Mr. Walker here."

Fred Humphries gave Riley a smile. "Well, he's a good worker, at least so far. And he seems to know his way around horses, too."

Uncomfortable with standing there while he was being talked about, Riley cleared his throat. "I think that's my cue to get back to work." He nodded to both men and headed toward the hay stall once more.

Riley jabbed the pitchfork into the hay with a little more force than was necessary. Did every newcomer to town come under such scrutiny or was there something about him and the kids that had brought them to Sheriff Gleason's notice?

Now that he *had* come to the sheriff's notice, though, he'd need to be more careful than ever. Not that he'd done anything illegal, but getting certain matters untangled if they came to light could prove tricky.

It seemed the sooner he and the kids left Turnabout, the better.

* * *

Later that afternoon, Riley exited the hotel with Noah and Pru, feeling unsettled. For one thing, he hadn't had the chance to saddle up River and go for a ride as he'd hoped. Mr. Humphries had asked for his help repairing one of the stall gates and he'd felt obliged to agree. By the time that was done he'd had to get back to the hotel and check on the kids. Riley didn't like to leave them alone for more than a couple hours at a time. But they'd be boarding the train again in a few days, and he had hoped to get a lot of riding in while they were here.

The other reason for his unsettled mood was that he found himself wondering for the hundredth time why he was going through with this. He'd let down his guard when Miss Vickers looked at him with such entreaty in her gaze, thinking that one meal with her and her employer couldn't hurt anything.

But it was better to remember that he couldn't afford to have someone look too deeply into their situation, than to keep pondering over the way he felt when he was with her.

It was probably just as well that this was only a temporary stop along their unending journey.

Noah all but skipped along the sidewalk, seeming hardly able to contain his excitement. "I like Miss Vickers. She's really nice."

Pru cut her uncle a quizzical look. "Uncle Riley must think so, too, if he's letting us go to her house."

Riley mentally winced that his distrust of everyone they met was rubbing off on the kids. "It's only for supper," he said, feeling strangely defensive. "Besides, she helped Noah at the livery yesterday, so it would have been impolite to turn down her invitation."

"It doesn't matter why we're going, Pru," Noah said. "This is gonna be a whole lot better than eating in our room or in the hotel restaurant."

"Just don't get used to it," Riley warned. "Like I said, this is a one-time thing." He felt a small pang of regret as he said that. Which was odd. How had the woman, after only two brief encounters, gotten under his skin this way?

As they approached the house Miss Vickers had directed him to, Riley studied it with an objective eye. It was a modest white, one-story structure with a high roof, a porch in front that stretched the entire width, and a large swing hanging on one end. Turning onto the front walk, he realized this would be the first time he and the kids would enter a family home since they'd left Pru and Noah's own home in Long Straw, Wyoming.

Riley ushered them up the porch steps, making certain to rein in some of Noah's exuberance. Knocking at the front door, he steeled himself. They would visit, share the meal and that would be that. In three or four days they'd board the train and resume their journey.

Miss Vickers opened the door almost immediately and smiled warmly. "Welcome. Please come in."

"Good evening." He nodded to her as they entered.

She returned his greeting, then smiled down at the children. "Hello, Noah, Pru. It's so nice to see you again."

Pru nodded shyly, while Noah looked around with eager curiosity. She led them into the parlor, where an older woman with faded blond hair sat waiting for them, commanding the room as if she sat on a throne rather than a wheelchair.

Miss Vickers quickly made the introductions. Then

she waved to the sofa. "Please, sit down. We have a few minutes before supper is ready."

Riley waited until she herself had taken a seat near her employer before ushering the kids to the sofa.

Mrs. Flanagan leaned back, with the air of a queen granting an audience. "Well now, Cassie Lynn tells me you all just arrived in town yesterday. What brings you to Turnabout?"

Riley repeated the answer he'd given the sheriff.

Their hostess frowned. "So you're not planning to be here very long."

"No, ma'am, not more than a few days." Was it his imagination or was there a shadow of disappointment in Miss Vickers's expression? If so, she covered it quickly.

Still, the thought that she might wish he would stay longer bolstered his spirits in a way that made no sense at all.

It was a good thing this would be a one-time visit and that they would be leaving town in a few days' time. It appeared the kids weren't the only ones who felt the pull of this taste of family home warmth.

Which was strange, because even before he'd had to go on the run with the kids, he'd led a less-than-settled life.

Well, there was no way he'd let one look from a young lady, no matter how winsome, further complicate his life.

Which meant he should do whatever he could, short of being impolite, to speed up this little outing.

He leaned forward looking for an opening to move things along.

Chapter Five

Cassie Lynn felt a stab of disappointment at Mr. Walker's announcement of his intent to leave Turnabout soon. Because he'd taken a job at the livery, she'd just assumed his move here was more or less permanent. Wishful thinking on her part, it seemed.

She hadn't realized until now just how much she'd been hoping Mr. Walker would be the man who would become her marriage partner. Then again, perhaps it was better this way. She'd already decided it would be best to marry someone she had no emotional ties to.

It was a setback, but not a major one. She'd just have to turn her attention to finding another candidate for her husband.

"Why are you in that wheelchair?"

Noah's artless question pulled Cassie Lynn back to the present.

"Noah!" Mr. Walker's sharply uttered reprimand was met with a confused look from the boy.

But Mrs. Flanagan flapped her hand at the boy's uncle. "Let him be." Then she turned to Noah. "Because I injured my leg, that's why."

He stood and moved closer. "Does it still hurt?"

The widow responded as if it had been a perfectly sensible question. "It aches a bit."

He tilted his head to study the wheels. "Can you get around in that thing yourself or does someone have to push you?"

She drew herself up. "I'll have you know, young man, that I manage quite well on my own."

Cassie Lynn hid a smile as she watched the exchange. Noah didn't seem at all put off by Mrs. Flanagan's manner. And for her part, the widow seemed to actually be enjoying the give-and-take.

A moment later Cassie Lynn noticed Pru, who was seated at her uncle's side, sit up straighter and stare at something across the room. Following the girl's gaze, she saw Dapple stretched out near the fireplace. The cat was watching them with half-closed eyes while his tail swished lazily back and forth.

While Noah and Mrs. Flanagan continued their spirited but unorthodox conversation, Cassie Lynn leaned toward the little girl. "I see you've spotted Dapple. Do you like cats?"

Pru nodded. "Yes, ma'am."

"I'm afraid Dapple's a little wary of strangers, but perhaps if I introduce you, you can make friends with him. Would you like that?"

Pru nodded more enthusiastically this time.

Cassie Lynn caught Mr. Walker's gaze for a moment. The approval in his expression caught her off guard and she felt warmth climb in her cheeks.

Quickly turning back to Pru, she stood and held out her hand. After only a moment's hesitation, the girl grasped it and let herself be led across the room.

As Cassie Lynn eased the way for Pru and Dapple to get acquainted, she imagined she could feel Mr. Walker's gaze on her. But that was foolish. He was no doubt just keeping an eye on his niece.

When she turned to escort Pru, who now held Dapple, back to her seat, Mr. Walker was once more focused on Noah and Mrs. Flanagan.

"If you'll excuse me," Cassie Lynn said to the room at large, "I'll go check on supper. We should be ready to eat in just a few minutes."

Mr. Walker stood as she made her way across the room. "Is there something I can help you with?"

He sounded almost eager, but she shook her head. "Thank you, but you're a guest here. I can manage."

"Nonsense. I hope you won't stand on ceremony with me. My ma taught me to help out in the kitchen rather than expect to be waited on. And helping is the least I can do to repay you ladies for your generous dinner invitation." He turned to Mrs. Flanagan. "That is, if you don't mind me leaving the kids here with you for a few minutes?"

The widow waved her hand. "Go on ahead, we'll be fine."

With a smile, Mr. Walker turned back to Cassie Lynn. "Lead the way."

She wasn't quite sure what to make of his offer. Her father and brothers had certainly never felt obliged to help her with what they considered women's work. She'd just assumed all men felt that way.

"Have you worked for Mrs. Flanagan very long?" he asked as they moved toward the kitchen.

His question brought her thoughts back to the present. "Just a little over two weeks. That's when she hurt her leg."

He nodded. "She seems like a feisty woman."

Cassie Lynn gave a smile at that understatement. "She is that. It's chafing at her not to be able to do for herself."

They'd arrived at the kitchen and Mr. Walker inhaled appreciatively, his expression blissful. "That sure does smell good."

"Thank you. It's a venison roast, one of Mrs. Flanagan's favorite dishes."

He rubbed his hands together. "All right now, what can I do to help?"

Cassie Lynn gave him a challenging look. "How are you at setting the table?"

He drew himself up with mock pride. "I'm an expert. It's a skill my mother insisted I master before I turned ten."

"Smart lady." She moved to the counter where the dishes were already stacked and waiting. "Mrs. Flanagan wants to eat in the dining room this evening rather than here in the kitchen, so I need to carry all the place settings down the hall. If you'll grab the plates and cutlery, I'll grab the glasses and napkins and you can follow me."

He gave a short bow. "I'm yours to command."

Taking him at his word, she led the way toward the dining room. Once there he helped her arrange the plates and flatware around the table, then returned with her to the kitchen and helped her transport all the food to the dining room, as well.

As they worked, they chatted about his horse, which she learned he'd raised from a colt and had a deep affection for. Just from some of the things he let fall in conversation, she could tell he thought of River as much more than a pack animal or means of transportation.

He seemed quite comfortable and at ease working beside her, as if he enjoyed her company. It was a novel feeling, interacting with a man this way. To be honest, she felt flattered and at the same time a little flustered by it all. The more she was around Mr. Walker, the more deeply Cassie Lynn regretted having to scratch his name off her husband-candidate list. She felt that they would have formed a very companionable partnership.

Were there other men who would as readily share her load, share their time and attention with her?

Is this what married life would be like? She was beginning to understand what Mrs. Flanagan had meant by not giving up on the thought of romance. Then she gave her head a mental shake. The man was leaving town in a few days. This was no time to be acting like a schoolgirl.

At last, the table was ready. Cassie Lynn returned to the parlor, with Mr. Walker ambling along at her side.

"Dinner is served," she announced.

Her companion crossed the room and stepped behind Mrs. Flanagan. "May I?" he asked gallantly as he put his hands on the back of her chair.

The widow sat up straighter, a delighted smile crossing her face before she schooled her expression into its normal disapproving lines. She gave a regal nod and waved a hand.

Cassie Lynn had already removed the chair that normally sat at the head of the table, so it was easy for Mr. Walker to wheel his hostess into position there. Once Mrs. Flanagan was properly situated, Cassie Lynn pointed him to the spot across from the widow, while she took a seat facing Noah and next to Pru.

Once they'd all taken their places, Mrs. Flanagan looked across at Mr. Walker. "Would you offer the blessing, sir?"

"Of course." He immediately bowed his head.

"Thank you, Jesus, for the meal we have before us and for the effort and skill of the one who prepared it. We newcomers are grateful that You have brought us to this place and for the generosity of the ladies who have welcomed us into their company. Bless this meal to the health and nourishment of we Your servants, and we ask especially that You provide a healing grace to Mrs. Flanagan. Amen."

Cassie Lynn echoed the amen, pleased to learn that Mr. Walker had what sounded like a familiar relationship with the Lord.

As the plates of food were passed around, Mrs. Flanagan took charge of the conversation. "So might I ask how you make your living, Mr. Walker?"

"I grew up on a ranch, and working with horses is about the only real skill I have."

"Uncle Riley is the best horse trainer around," Noah said proudly.

Mr. Walker leaned over and gave his nephew a mock punch in the shoulder. "At least the best you ever met," he said with a teasing grin.

"And is that where you all are headed, someplace where you can work with horses?"

Mr. Walker hesitated a moment as he shifted in his seat. It might have merely been irritation at the intrusive question, but Cassie Lynn got the distinct impression there was more to it than that.

"I do hope to one day have a horse ranch of my own, but that's something I've put on hold for the time being. In the meantime, I get work where I can."

She noticed he hadn't really answered Mrs. Flanagan's question. But before the widow could press further, he turned to Cassie Lynn. "This roast is mighty fine eating. My compliments to the cook."

She felt her cheeks warm as she smiled at his compliment. "Thank you."

"If you think this is good, just wait until we get to dessert," Mrs. Flanagan declared. "Baking is where Cassie Lynn really shines."

Cassie was surprised by the compliment. She didn't often get praise from her employer.

Mr. Walker pointed a fork at her. "I look forward to it."

The conversation moved on to safe, mundane topics for a few minutes, then Mrs. Flanagan circled back around to her probing questions. "Seems to me, if raising horses is something you aim to work at, that there's lots of good places around here just perfect for a horse ranch."

Cassie Lynn cringed at the woman's continued probing. Was this her fault? Was Mrs. Flanagan trying to convince the man to stay in town because she'd shown an interest in him?

She saw a small tic at the corner of Mr. Walker's jaw, but when he spoke his tone was controlled. "Thank you, but as I said, I've put those plans on hold for now."

Then he turned the tables on her. "Mind if I ask how you hurt your leg?"

Cassie Lynn paused midbite. Mrs. Flanagan hated

when anyone pointed out her infirmity. And Cassie Lynn had a feeling Mr. Walker knew that.

There was a tense moment of silence as the two at either end of the table stared each other down.

Then Mrs. Flanagan gave a nod, acknowledging Mr. Walker's point, and answered his question. "I fell off a ladder when I was trying to prune a tree out back." Then she turned to Noah. "Tell me, young man, are you as fond of horses as your uncle?"

Cassie saw the self-satisfied glint in Mr. Walker's eye. Apparently he'd figured out something she'd learned, as well. The best way to deal with Mrs. Flanagan's pushy manner was to meet it head-on.

When he turned her way, he seemed abashed to find her watching him. Her nod of approval a heartbeat later also seemed to momentarily startle him. Then he returned her smile with a conspiratorial one of his own, and her breath caught as she once more felt that connection with him, as if they were longtime friends. His smile deepened as he apparently noted her reaction and she felt the warmth rise in her cheeks. She quickly turned away, busying herself with passing another piece of bread to Noah.

As the conversation flowed around the table, Cassie Lynn suddenly realized Pru wasn't participating. Hoping to find a way to draw the girl in, she turned to her and only then noticed that Pru was picking at her food without really eating much of anything. Was there something more than shyness at work here?

Concerned, she leaned closer and asked quietly, "Are you all right, Pru?"

Pru gave her an embarrassed look and nodded. "I'm just not very hungry," she said softly.

Cassie Lynn patted the child's leg. "That's fine. You don't have to eat if you don't want to."

The girl nodded and broke off a small piece of bread to nibble on, as if to prove she was all right.

But apparently Mr. Walker had noticed. His expression concerned, he leaned toward his niece. "What's the matter, Pru?"

"I'm just not very hungry," she said again.

Cassie Lynn frowned. There seemed to be more than a lack of appetite going on with the girl. She was pale and her eyes had a slightly glazed look.

Placing her hand on Pru's forehead, Cassie Lynn shot Mr. Walker a worried glance. "She's running a fever."

He immediately pushed away from the table. "If you ladies will excuse our early departure, I should take her back to the hotel, where she can lay down."

Cassie Lynn moved her hand to the girl's shoulder and stood. "Perhaps it would be better to have Doc Pratt take a look at her first."

"Absolutely." Mrs. Flanagan's tone brooked no argument. "Let her rest on the bed in the spare room while Cassie Lynn fetches the doctor."

Mr. Walker's brows drew down. "I don't want to put Miss Vickers out—"

She gave him a smile. "Doc Pratt lives right next door, so it's no trouble at all. It won't take me but a few minutes to fetch him." She stood and pointed to the doorway. "The spare room is down that hall, third door on the left. Why don't you help Pru get comfortable and lie down, and I'll be back faster than a squirrel can climb a tree."

Mr. Walker hesitated and she saw the worry in his expression. The poor man likely had very little experience with childhood illnesses. She impulsively touched his arm. "Children seem to get these fevers with vexing regularity. I'm sure it's nothing to worry about, but it's always best to get a doctor to check it out if you can."

He nodded. "Very well. Thank you."

Riley picked Pru up and carried her down the hall to the room Miss Vickers had indicated. The little girl snuggled up against his chest with touching trust. Why hadn't he realized sooner that she was sick? Some guardian he was.

He gave her a squeeze that he hoped was comforting. Comforting the way Miss Vickers's touch on his arm had been.

Shaking off that stray thought, he looked down at his niece. "Don't worry, kitten, the doctor is going to come and fix you right up."

At least he sincerely hoped so.

Riley set Pru on one of the two narrow beds in the room and helped her remove her shoes.

His thoughts turned back to that fleeting touch Miss Vickers had given him. For just a moment there in the dining room, as she'd taken a moment to try to reassure him, he'd had a sense of what it would be like not to have to face all this on his own, to have someone at his side willing to support him in difficult times, willing to shoulder some of the responsibility.

It had felt good.

But it wasn't real. That kind of relationship didn't really exist, at least not for him.

As promised, Miss Vickers was ushering the doctor into the room in a matter of minutes. The introductions were made quickly, then the white-haired physician turned to Pru with an avuncular smile.

"Well now, young lady, I understand you're not feeling well."

"No, sir."

"Let me just have a look at you and see if we can do something to make you feel better." He turned to Riley. "Why don't you wait in the parlor? Miss Vickers here will assist me."

Riley started to protest, but Miss Vickers took his arm and gently led him to the door. "Don't worry, Doc Pratt knows what he's doing. He's been looking out for kids in this town since before I was born."

A moment later Riley found himself on the other side of a closed bedroom door. Shoving his hands in his pockets, he headed back down the hall.

He found Noah and Mrs. Flanagan in the parlor.

His nephew immediately popped up and rushed to him. "What did the doctor say? Is Pru gonna be okay?"

Realizing Noah was remembering his mother's illness and death, Riley placed a comforting hand on the boy's shoulder. "Of course she is. You heard Miss Vickers—kids get sick all the time."

Noah seemed only partially reassured.

Mrs. Flanagan spoke up then. "Your uncle is correct. I remember when my own two boys were little, they would get fevers and chills so often I near wore a path to Dr. Pratt's place. And my John has grown up to be a fine soldier in the army."

"Your son's a soldier?" Noah crossed back to Mrs. Flanagan.

She nodded. "A lieutenant, actually."

"I have some tin soldiers."

"Do you now. John had a set, as well."

As Mrs. Flanagan began to regale Noah with stories of some of her sons' exploits, Riley caught her eye and mouthed a heartfelt thank-you. The woman's expression softened for a moment as she nodded, then she resumed her conversation with his nephew.

While the two talked, Riley moved to the window and stared out into the shadowy dusk, trying to fight off panic. He should have been paying closer attention, should have noticed sooner that something was wrong. He'd promised the children's mother he'd look after them and keep them safe. What if there was something seriously wrong with Pru?

Father above, please keep Pru safe. She's just a little girl and she's already been through so much. I know dragging them from town to town is not good for them and it might even be what caused this illness she has. But I'm doing the best that I can to keep 'em safe. If there's another way, please show it to me. But please, don't take her from us.

It occurred to him it was providence that he'd been here tonight. He would have managed on his own, of course—got the hotel clerk to send for the doctor. But the way the two women had immediately taken charge—seeing that Pru was made comfortable, fetching the doctor, keeping Noah entertained and distracted—had been a true blessing.

Miss Vickers, especially, had a comforting presence, a way of calming the children and setting them at ease.

Dr. Pratt finally stepped into the room, with Miss Vickers at his side, and Riley immediately came to attention, moving toward them. "How is she?"

He spied Miss Vickers's sympathetic expression, but

something in her eyes communicated that it would all be okay.

A heartbeat later, the doctor gave him the diagnosis. "She has chicken pox."

Chapter Six

Riley grabbed the arm of the chair beside him and blindly sat down. Chicken pox! He vaguely remembered having that himself as a kid. He'd pulled through just fine. And neither Dr. Pratt nor Miss Vickers seemed unduly concerned, so that was a good sign.

A number of emotions washed over him—relief that it wasn't something worse, panic over the thought of nursing a sick child, worry over what this would do to his plans to move on quickly.

He looked up at the doctor, trying to pull his thoughts together. Then, mindful of Noah, he stood and crossed to the hall. To his relief, Mrs. Flanagan said something to his nephew, pulling the boy's attention from the doctor.

"How serious is it?" Riley asked.

"Most children get chicken pox at some point and come though unscathed, except for a few scars as souvenirs."

Relieved for at least this glimmer of good news, he let out a long breath. "And you're sure that's what it is?"

Dr. Pratt nodded. "I've seen this countless times before. Besides, there are a few spots already forming on her back and neck." He gave Riley a penetrating look. "You *will* need to make certain your niece is closely cared for until she recovers. And you should be prepared for your nephew to start exhibiting signs in a few days, as well. The disease is easily spread from child to child. Which also means you should keep the children isolated as much as possible."

Riley jammed his fists in his pockets, feeling as if he was in way over his head. He didn't know anything about caring for sick kids. So far he'd only had to contend with sniffles and cuts and scrapes.

The doctor continued. "Your niece is a very sick little girl right now, but don't worry. In a week or so, she'll be good as new."

"A week!"

"Actually, it'll probably be a little longer. It usually takes ten days to two weeks for chicken pox to run its course." He eyed Riley sympathetically. "And then there is your nephew."

Riley felt the panic tighten in his chest. Caring for two sick kids, for at least two weeks—how in the world was he going to manage that?

Dr. Pratt glanced Mrs. Flanagan's way and raised his voice to carry across the room. "How are you doing, Irene? Is that leg giving you any more trouble?"

The widow flapped a hand irritably. "I'm fine. If I need you fussing around me, Grover Pratt, I'll let you know."

The doctor gave her a long-suffering look, then turned back to Riley. "I've left instructions with Cassie Lynn on how to care for your niece, as well as a lotion to relieve some of the itching, and something for fever.

I'm afraid that's all we can do for now. If there's anything else you need me for, you know where to find me."

"Yes, sir. And thank you." Then Riley straightened. "How much do I owe you for the visit and the medicines?"

"We can discuss that later. Right now you have sick children to see to."

Miss Vickers gave the doctor a smile. "Thank you for coming so quickly, Dr. Pratt. Sorry I had to interrupt your supper. Please let me make it up to you by sending some pie home for you and Mrs. Pratt."

The doctor gave her an appreciative smile. "You certainly don't have to twist my arm."

Riley followed them down the hall, wanting to ask the doctor another question. "Is there any chance at all we'll be ready to travel in less than two weeks?"

The doctor gave him a pointed look. "I'm sorry if it messes up your plans, son, but I wouldn't recommend taking those kids out in public until the blisters are gone. You don't want to be spreading it to others, do you?"

"No, of course not." So that was that. But if he missed the meeting with Claypool and Dixon in Tyler on Wednesday, he might not get another chance. And Dixon could hold the key to getting Guy put away for good.

Riley waited while Miss Vickers served up a generous portion of pie for the physician and escorted him out the back door.

Then she turned back to Riley with a bracing smile. "I know this seems overwhelming right now, but I assure you, you'll get through it okay."

"I appreciate your faith in my abilities." He hadn't

been able to keep the sarcasm out of his voice, which wasn't fair to her. "And thank you, too, for all you've done." This time his tone was much more sincere.

Miss Vickers waved a hand dismissively. "All I did was fetch the doctor." She eyed him thoughtfully. "It seems you'll be spending more time here in Turnabout than you'd planned. I hope it's not too inconvenient."

It was, but that wasn't her fault. He shrugged. "No point in railing against what can't be changed."

"That's a very practical attitude."

If she only knew how badly he wanted to kick and scream over this setback right now. "I'm just thankful that, if it had to happen, it happened here where we'd already made such gracious friends. I don't like to think what might have happened if we'd still been aboard the train or had stopped in a town where we didn't know anyone."

By this time they'd made it back to the parlor, and he turned to Noah. "We'd better be heading to the hotel. You say your goodbyes while I fetch Pru."

He saw Miss Vickers open her mouth to protest, but Mrs. Flanagan beat her to the punch.

"Absolutely not," the woman said forcefully. "There is no sense in disturbing that child, especially when she needs her rest. She will spend the night right where she is."

That he couldn't allow. "But—"

"Mrs. Flanagan is correct," Miss Vickers said in a milder tone. "Dr. Pratt gave her a liquid for her fever that also made her drowsy. She was half-asleep by the time he finished his examination." She glanced toward his nephew. "In fact, since Noah's already been exposed, he could take the second bed in that room and sleep here tonight, as well." She gave Riley a be-reasonable look. "Dr. Pratt *did* say to keep them both isolated."

Riley rubbed his jaw while he thought over the offer. It was downright embarrassing just how tempted he was to let them take this responsibility from him, even if it was just for one night. But he had promises to keep. "I appreciate what you ladies are offering, but I think it's best I keep the kids with me."

Cassie Lynn admired the man's sense of responsibility, but one could carry that a little too far. "Have you ever nursed children through something like this?"

He grimaced, but his stubborn demeanor didn't soften. "No, but I reckon this won't be the last time I find myself in this situation. Best I go ahead and figure it out now while I have some folks I can count on to help me if I get in a bind."

"That's very admirable and responsible of you. But it will be a whole lot easier for us to help you if the kids are here. They'll be closer to Doc Pratt, too, if you should need his services." When Mr. Walker still didn't look convinced, she played her trump card. "Unless you don't trust us with the children?"

It wasn't a fair question, and she knew it. After all, what could he say?

"No, of course I trust you." He rubbed his jaw. "It's just—"

Mrs. Flanagan didn't let him finish that thought. "That's settled then." She shifted in her chair. "The children will stay here while you get some rest back at the hotel—believe me, you'll need it. We'll discuss long-term arrangements in the morning."

"Long-term—"

Cassie Lynn saw the concern on his face and intervened by changing the subject. "By the way, Pru mentioned something about a Bitsy. Does that mean something to you?"

He nodded. "It's her doll. She never goes to bed without her." He seemed to gather his thoughts as he turned to his nephew. "What do you say, buddy? Are you okay with staying here tonight and keeping Pru company?"

Cassie Lynn was pleased. As much as he seemed to be uncomfortable with being separated from the children, he was doing a good job of not letting that show to his nephew.

Noah nodded. "Don't worry, Uncle Riley, I'll look out for her tonight."

Mr. Walker gave his shoulder a light squeeze. "I know you will."

Then he turned back to her. "I'll go check in on Pru and then head back to the hotel to fetch Bitsy and a few other things they'll need tonight."

Once Mr. Walker made his exit, Cassie Lynn glanced back at the boy and saw a confused look on his face. "Is something the matter, Noah?"

He nodded, his nose wrinkling in puzzlement. "I was just wondering... The doctor said Pru has chicken pox, but we haven't been around any chickens lately."

Cassie Lynn gave him a grin. "You don't get chicken pox from being around chickens." Then she lifted her hands in an it-makes-no-sense gesture. "I don't know why it's called that. It *is* kind of a silly name for an illness, isn't it?"

She suddenly snapped her fingers. "You know what? I just realized that with all this excitement, we never had dessert. How about I fix you and Mrs. Flanagan each a piece of that cherry pie I baked earlier, and you can eat it while I'm cleaning up the supper dishes. Would you like that?"

"Yes, ma'am." Then Noah turned serious. "But if you need help with the dishes, I can do that first."

It appeared the boy had been taught his manners. "Thank you, Noah, that's very kind. But you're our guest, and it would hurt my feelings if you didn't try out that pie I baked just for you and your family."

With a nod, the boy happily moved to the table.

As Cassie Lynn carried a load of dishes to the kitchen, she pondered what impact this unexpected situation would have on her plans.

First she'd learned Mr. Walker was not going to settle in Turnabout, which took him out of the running for a potential husband. Then, in a twist, it turned out that he and his charges were not only going to remain in Turnabout for a couple weeks, but they were most likely going to be spending most of that time here at Mrs. Flanagan's place.

Of course, Mr. Walker still wasn't a candidate. Problem was, could Cassie Lynn effectively look for another man with the extra workload she now had? Not to mention the extra distraction, no matter how pleasant that distraction might be…

On the other hand, it seemed Mr. Walker's plans were rather loose. Could he perhaps develop a fondness for Turnabout during the time he was here?

Then she grimaced. Why did her wayward mind keep trying to add Mr. Walker to her husband list? She needed to accept he wasn't a candidate and move on.

Didn't she?

* * *

Riley stepped into his hotel room and began gathering up the few things the kids would need for an overnight stay. The first thing he grabbed was Bitsy. He studied the cloth doll and winced over how bedraggled it had become since his sister-in-law's death. Just one more sign that he was not as observant about the kids' everyday needs as he should be.

Then he found the few items of clothing they'd need and stuffed them all in a carpetbag.

He didn't like this arrangement, not one bit. The kids were his responsibility, not that of the ladies. And while they seemed nice enough, what did he really know about them? Other than that Miss Vickers was pretty and sweet and could cook better than his ma? And that Mrs. Flanagan had a sharp manner but seemed well-meaning at heart.

Of course, one could never count on outward appearances and first impressions. He just had to look to his stepfather and stepbrother to learn the truth of that.

Then there was the lady in Kansas City he'd hired to look after the kids while he worked. She'd seemed responsible enough, but she'd ended up not only neglecting her charges, but absconding with a necklace that had belonged to Pru's mother.

No, trust was something he didn't give lightly.

On the other hand, even he didn't think the kids would be in any real danger with the ladies for one night. Apparently, unlike him, they'd both dealt with sick kids before and knew how to take care of them. And it was unlikely Guy would show up in the middle of the night.

Riley had to admit he wasn't opposed to seeing more

of Miss Vickers. Not that it could go anywhere, but still, it was nice spending time in her company.

He shook his head, trying to clear it of such dangerous thoughts. He couldn't afford to make connections of that sort, not while he and the children were still on the run.

Perhaps a good night's sleep would help him see matters more clearly in the morning.

Chapter Seven

Cassie awoke earlier than normal the next morning. As she took extra care brushing and pinning her hair, she told herself it was definitely *not* because she'd see Mr. Walker soon. Last night, when he'd delivered the children's things, she'd told him that he was welcome to join them for breakfast this morning, and he'd told her to expect him bright and early.

Her room was right next to the one the children were in and she quietly peeked inside to check on them. To her relief they were both still asleep, though Pru rolled over restlessly as Cassie watched.

She left the door slightly ajar as she stepped out, then headed for the kitchen. Her first order of business would be to set a nice hearty vegetable and bone broth simmering on the stove for Pru, and then she'd get breakfast started for the rest of them.

Mrs. Flanagan's hens usually produced five to six eggs a day. With four people to feed she'd have to use every one of them for the meal. Any eggs she needed for her baking would have to be purchased from the mercantile. But she supposed that was only right—she shouldn't be counting on Mrs. Flanagan to provide her with ingredients, anyway. After all, her employer was providing the kitchen and the baking pans she needed.

As Cassie Lynn neared the kitchen, she wrinkled her nose in confusion. Was that coffee she smelled?

She hurried forward and saw Mr. Walker sitting at the kitchen table, a cup of coffee wrapped in his hands, a look of worry furrowing his brow.

He stood as soon as she entered the room. "Good morning. I hope you don't mind that I let myself in."

She gave him a sympathetic smile. "Couldn't sleep?"

He shook his head ruefully. "How did Pru and Noah do last night?"

"Pru was a bit restless, but for the most part they slept through the night. I imagine today is going to be rougher for Pru, though, as the blisters form and start itching. I remember what an ordeal it was to keep my brothers from scratching themselves raw when they had it."

He winced at that. "I vaguely remember having it myself, but not any of the particulars."

She raised a brow as she crossed the room to fetch an apron from the peg by the door. "You must have been mighty young." She tied the apron strings behind her back. "Taking care of Pru and Noah is going to require lots of patience, as well as a bit of creativity in finding ways to distract them."

He grimaced. "Right now two weeks sounds like an excessively long time."

"About that." Cassie Lynn crossed her arms. "Mrs. Flanagan and I spoke about your situation last night. We'd like to offer to help you care for the children for as long as they're sick. Both of us have dealt with this before—me with my brothers, she with her sons. But that means letting them stay here with us while they get through this."

As she'd expected, his jaw set in that stubborn line again. "That's a generous offer, but—"

She held up a hand. "I understand your hesitation at being separated from them for so long, but all the reasons we discussed for not moving them last night still apply today. Besides, we've come up with a solution that should make this easier on everyone—you can stay here, too."

He raised a brow at that, his lips twisting wryly. "You're inviting me to, what—camp out on the sofa in the parlor for two weeks?"

She fetched her large stockpot and started filling it with water. "Well, you could do that," she said, as she transferred the pot to the stove. "Or you could use the attic. I'm afraid there's no bed up there, but it's roomy and will provide you with some privacy. Mrs. Flanagan has lots of extra quilts you can use to make yourself a passably comfortable pallet, if you don't mind bedding down on the floor."

Mr. Walker shook his head. "Believe me, I've bunked down in far less comfortable accommodations." Then he rubbed his jaw, his expression indicating he still wasn't convinced.

Did he have that much trouble letting go of his notions of how things should go?

Cassie Lynn began cutting up carrots, holding her peace, giving him time to make up his mind.

"I'll admit," he said slowly, "I'm not sure how good a nursemaid I'd make to a pair of sick children." He gave her a speculative look. "If you're sure you and Mrs.

Flanagan are okay with me moving in, then I guess I have no real choice but to take you up on your generous offer."

It sounded as if he still wasn't convinced. Some folks just didn't like to admit they couldn't do it all. "Very sensible of you."

"But I do have one condition."

"And what's that?"

"That the kids are my responsibility and I'll help with their care."

"Good." Cassie Lynn couldn't stop the happy bubble rising inside her. It would be nice to have some new faces around here—for both her and Mrs. Flanagan. "Just give me a little time to get some things moved around in the attic, and do a bit of sweeping and dusting, and it'll be all ready for you to move in."

He shook his head. "You have enough to do around here, especially with all of us moving in on you. I can do any rearranging that's needed up there."

Again she was surprised by his willingness to jump in and help her with her chores. "Very well. But first I need to collect the eggs from the henhouse and get breakfast started. Then get Mrs. Flanagan up and ready to face the day. *Then* we can tackle the attic together."

He stood. "I can gather the eggs while you take care of breakfast and Mrs. Flanagan. But first I want to look in on the kids."

Cassie Lynn nodded, figuring he needed to reassure himself that they were okay. "Thank you. Just try not to wake them. The more sleep they get, the better." She moved toward the cupboard, then looked back at him. "And the newspaper should be on the front porch by the time you collect the eggs, if you don't mind bringing it in."

With a nod, he moved toward the hall.

She still couldn't get over how eager he was to do his part, no matter that most of this was women's work. Perhaps if her pa and brothers had had more of that attitude, she wouldn't be so dead set against moving back home.

Thirty minutes later Mrs. Flanagan was seated at one end of the kitchen table, while Cassie Lynn worked on breakfast at the stove. Riley sat at the other end of the table, sipping his second cup of coffee.

Mrs. Flanagan ignored the coffee in front of her as she rested her arms on the sides of her chair. "Cassie Lynn tells me you agreed to let the kids stay here and to move into the attic yourself."

"Yes, ma'am. And I'm very grateful for the offer. I can pay you the same rate the hotel charges, if that's agreeable."

The woman stiffened. "Young man, I invited you and those two young'uns to stay here out of the goodness of my heart. It is an insult for you to offer me money as if I were nothing more than an innkeeper."

Cassie Lynn did her best to hide a grin. No one could do righteous indignation better than Irene Flanagan.

"I meant no disrespect," Mr. Walker said quickly. "I just—"

"Apology accepted." Mrs. Flanagan appeared to unbend. "So we're agreed that you all will stay here as my guests and we'll hear no more about payments."

Apparently considering the matter closed, the widow turned to Cassie Lynn. "I suppose you're okay with cooking and cleaning for our guests."

Before she could answer, Mr. Walker spoke up. "That won't be necessary, at least not the cleaning part. I can take care of my own cleaning—don't want to make extra work for anyone." He gave her a boyish grin. "The cooking, on the other hand..."

Cassie Lynn returned his smile. "Don't worry. It's not any more work to cook for five than for four."

He lifted his coffee cup in salute.

Just then, Noah came padding into the kitchen, rubbing his eyes. "Is it time for breakfast yet?"

Mrs. Flanagan gave him a stern look. "And good morning to you, too, young man."

"Good morning." Noah didn't appear at all intimidated by her tone. He turned back to Cassie. "Pru's hungry, too. But she says she doesn't feel like eating." He shrugged. "That don't make no sense to me."

Cassie Lynn smiled. "I think she means her mouth hurts—Dr. Pratt warned me that might be the case. Don't worry, I have some broth simmering on the stove for her. And as for you, breakfast will be on the table in just a few minutes."

Mr. Walker stood. "I'll go check in on her."

"Good idea." Cassie Lynn moved to the pantry and retrieved a jar. "Why don't you bring her a bowl of applesauce. The broth is not quite ready and this shouldn't be too difficult for her to eat."

He nodded, then glanced at his nephew. "And you come along, as well. Time to get you out of that nightshirt and into your day clothes."

As Riley walked down the hall with Noah, he wondered if he was doing the right thing, moving in here. Not that he'd had much choice. Still, it was going to be difficult for the kids to not start forming relationships with these two women.

Because motherly influences were something they were sorely missing in their lives.

He was glad to find Pru awake now. She'd been asleep when he left last night. "Good morning, kitten. How are you feeling?"

The girl pushed herself into a sitting position, her doll clutched in her arms. "I'm sorry, Uncle Riley."

Pru's softly uttered apology tugged at something protective and guilt-laden inside Riley.

Had his own distraction and worry made her feel guilty about anything she perceived would cause him trouble? That wasn't a burden he wanted the little girl to feel, especially over something she couldn't help, like this.

He smiled down at her reassuringly. "No need to apologize, Pru. This isn't your fault. Everyone gets sick occasionally." He drew himself up with a deliberately solemn expression. "Why, one of these days I'll get sick myself and then you'll have to nurse me."

She gave him the smile he'd hoped for, and he used his free hand to pat her knee through the blanket. "The important thing right now is that we do what we can to get you well."

Pru nodded. "I'm sure I'll be better soon." She held up her doll. "Thanks for fetching Bitsy for me."

From her tone and appearance, Riley could tell she was still feeling down. "Bitsy was lonesome without you." He lifted the bowl he carried. "I brought you some applesauce. Want to try and eat some?"

Her face brightened somewhat. "Yes, sir."

Across the room, Noah had already shed his nightshirt and was slipping his arms into the sleeves of a faded blue shirt. "I like it here, Uncle Riley," he said. "Can we stay?"

The eagerness on the boy's face drove home to Riley again just how much they all hated living in hotel rooms and boardinghouses. Having grown up on a farm, these kids were used to having plenty of room to run around and play out in the open. They missed that freedom and he couldn't blame them. Before he could answer, though, the boy continued to make his case.

"Mrs. Flanagan said it was all right with her." Noah's voice took on a pleading quality. "They seem like nice ladies and this place is so much better than any ole hotel room. Besides, you said Pru needs some looking after."

"That's true."

Noah nodded, then gave Riley an earnest look. "And I promise I won't say anything about Pa or where we came from."

"I know you won't." Hopefully, the boy had learned his lesson last time. "Even if we do stay here, it'll only be for a little while, just until Pru gets better. Understand?"

Grinning widely, Noah nodded. "Yes, sir."

Knowing that Noah didn't truly understand how difficult it would be to go back to their previous life when they left here, Riley stood. "Very well. The ladies have offered to let me sleep upstairs, so I've agreed to stay here, but just until Pru is better." No point in letting the boy know he'd probably be sick for most of their stay, as well. Time enough when he actually started showing symptoms.

Riley patted his niece's shoulder. "Enjoy your applesauce. Miss Vickers has some broth cooking that you can have later. I'll be back to check on you in a bit."

He turned to his nephew. "Noah, you can join us in the kitchen as soon as you're dressed."

Riley paused in the doorway. "I'll leave this open so we can hear you call out if you need anything," he told Pru.

As he headed back to the kitchen it occurred to him that in less than twenty-four hours, this place had begun to feel like home.

Once they were finished with breakfast, Cassie Lynn opened the oven to check on the fruit tarts. Pleased with the golden color of the crust, she began carefully transferring them to the counter.

"Those look really good," Noah said, an appreciative gleam in his eye.

"Thank you." She set the last of them on the cooling rack. "But I'm afraid they aren't for us. I baked them to sell to the lady who runs the tea shop."

"Oh."

Cassie Lynn smiled at his crestfallen expression. "Don't worry, I plan to do some more baking this afternoon. We'll be having pie with our supper tonight."

She moved to the table and began clearing the dishes.

Mr. Walker immediately stood to help, instructing Noah to do likewise. When the last of the dishes had been transported to the sink, the man rolled up his sleeves. "Do you prefer to wash or dry?"

Cassie Lynn started to wave away his offer, then changed her mind. He likely wanted to contribute and she was becoming accustomed to his unexpected offers to help with the housework. "Wash."

"While she gets started on that," Mrs. Flanagan said to Mr. Walker, "you can push my chair into the parlor." She turned to Noah. "If you will come along, I have something to show you."

As Cassie Lynn watched Mr. Walker obediently push her wheelchair from the room, she smiled. She'd been right about how having company would be good for her employer. The woman was more alert and spirited than Cassie had seen her in all the time she'd been here. And she seemed to have taken a shine to Noah especially.

Riley accepted a clean plate from Miss Vickers and set about drying it. "Mind if I ask what all those pies and tarts are for?"

"I'm trying to start up a bakery business. Those have been ordered by the restaurant and the tea shop."

Impressive. "That's very enterprising of you."

She gave him a challenging look. "Women are capable of more than housework, you know."

He lifted a hand as if to ward off a blow. "You'll get no argument from me on that. I just meant with all you do around here that I'm surprised you have time to work on this, too."

That seemed to mollify her. "I baked the pies after everyone else went to bed last night. And while they were baking I made the filling for the tarts. This morning I just needed to make the crusts and stick them in the oven."

"So do you plan to go into baking full-time when your work here for Mrs. Flanagan is done?"

He saw some emotion flash in Miss Vickers's face. It was there and gone too quickly for him to read, but he got the distinct impression his question had touched on a sore spot for her.

"I hope to." Her tone gave nothing away. "But I'll have to wait and see how things go."

He wondered idly why such a pretty, clever, ambitious woman didn't have a husband or at least a beau. Was there a story there?

Not that it was any of his business.

"By the way," she said, handing him another plate, "do you mind if I ask what your work schedule is?"

"Mr. Humphries asked me to work for an hour or so in the mornings, and again in the afternoon during his busy times. I also told him I'd meet the trains when they pulled into the depot, to see if anyone needed to rent a horse or buggy." He shrugged. "But now that the kids are sick, I'm going to talk to him about cutting back—"

She raised a wet hand to stop him. "No need. In fact, it's probably good for you to get out some. I just wanted to know what to expect." She gave him an earnest look. "I'd like to make certain you and I aren't gone at the same time, so Mrs. Flanagan isn't left alone with the kids. I mean, she'd probably be able to handle whatever came up, but just in case—"

It was his turn to interrupt her. "No need to say more. I agree completely."

"Then, if you don't need to be at the livery right away, I'd like to deliver these baked goods as soon as we finish here. I promise it won't take me long."

After she'd gone, Riley went to check on the kids. Pru was sleeping again and Noah was in the parlor playing with the cat, while Mrs. Flanagan watched them.

Feeling at loose ends, Riley stepped out on the back porch and stared at nothing in particular. Already, this place was weaving a spell on him. It was a real honest-to-goodness home, and moreover it felt like one.

And it was such a seductive feeling, one that made it easy to forget the danger they were in.

Of course, if his meeting with Detective Claypool and the informant he'd tracked down actually resulted in the break they were hoping for, perhaps he and the kids would actually have a chance to lead a normal life again.

But that was a big if.

He bowed his head.

Please, Father Almighty, let this meeting on Wednesday lead to something solid. I'm not certain how much more of this me and the kids can take.

Chapter Eight

"I take it your deliveries went well."

Cassie Lynn nodded in response to Mrs. Flanagan as she set her hamper on the counter. Mr. Walker had headed out the door almost as soon as she'd walked in, stating that he needed to stop at the hotel to have their things sent over before he went to work at the livery. Apparently, Pru had a book among her things that she'd been asking after.

"Daisy put the pies on her menu," Cassie Lynn said in answer to the question, "and Mrs. Dawson told me the choir was meeting there for tea this afternoon and she was sure they'd want the tarts."

Mrs. Flanagan nodded in satisfaction. "This bakery business is going to do well, just you wait and see."

Cassie Lynn smiled, then looked around. "Where's Noah?"

"With his sister. I got out my sons' old checker game and suggested he play with her to keep her mind off of her chicken pox."

Cassie Lynn nodded. "That's good. I don't suppose he's showing symptoms yet?"

"Not yet. But I expect he will in the next day or so."
Then her employer turned serious. "You and I need to
talk."

Puzzled, Cassie Lynn walked to the table and took
a seat across from her. "Of course. Is there something
you need me to do?"

"What I need is to know whether or not you're still
interested in pursuing a marriage partner."

Cassie Lynn felt an unexpected twinge of guilt at the
question. But she tamped it down. "Of course I'm still
interested. Why wouldn't I be?"

"I've seen the way you look at Mr. Walker. It's going
to be difficult for you to find yourself a husband if
you're already smitten with another man."

"Smitten! That's absurd. I hardly know Mr. Walker."
But even as she protested, she felt a flush warm her
cheeks.

Mrs. Flanagan didn't say anything, just continued to
stare pointedly at her.

Cassie Lynn felt compelled to break the silence. "Besides, even if it were true, that doesn't change anything.
You heard Mr. Walker. He plans to leave town just as
soon as Pru and Noah are well and able to travel."

"But that doesn't change the fact that you *are* at-
tracted to him."

"I barely know the man," she protested. "And as I've
said all along, my selection of a man to marry will have
nothing to do with emotional entanglements."

"Easier said than done. And don't forget, you'll be
living under the same roof with Mr. Walker and sharing
your meals with him for the next two weeks."

"That won't make any difference." Cassie Lynn
stood. "But you're right about how busy my days are

going to be for a while. Perhaps I'll limit my search for the time being to developing a strong list of candidates and to figuring out my approach. Then, once Mr. Walker and his charges leave, I'll be prepared to act." Or as prepared as she could be. "After all, the goal wasn't necessarily to be married in five weeks, just to have a committed suitor by then."

Cassie Lynn tied her apron behind her back. "That being said, have you thought of any additional men I should consider?"

Mrs. Flanagan had apparently been ready for that question. "What do you think of Jarvis Edmondson?"

"Mr. Edmondson, the blacksmith?"

Her employer nodded. "He's a widower, going on five years now. He and Mary Ann had a happy marriage, as far as I could tell. He lives here in town, no one's ever complained about his honesty, and he attends church every Sunday. And Mary Ann made beautiful tatted lace that she sold to Hazel at the dress shop, so I don't think he'd have a problem with a wife who wanted to sell baked goods. Sounds to me as if he meets all the requirements you laid out."

"But he must be close to fifty years old."

"He's forty-eight." Mrs. Flanagan raised a brow. "And you never mentioned having an age requirement. I thought this was to be a businesslike arrangement."

"Yes, of course, but…" Cassie Lynn's voice trailed off, since she couldn't think of a good way to end that sentence.

But he's not Mr. Walker.

She moved to the pantry, feeling the need for action. "Mr. Edmondson sounds like a very good candidate.

I'll add him to the list along with Mr. Drummond and Mr. Morris."

"Have you given any thought to how you'll approach these gentlemen? After all, it's not very often a woman proposes to a man."

That, of course, was the most difficult part of her plan. "I believe the direct approach will be best. Explain my situation and how a marriage based on practicality rather than emotion could be a mutually beneficial arrangement."

"I see. Well, I suggest you practice exactly what you plan to say before you approach one of your candidates. And if you could practice with a trusted male friend, that would be best."

Cassie Lynn couldn't hold back a quick grimace. Problem was, she didn't have any male friends, trusted or otherwise. Mr. Chandler was the closest thing, but even though he'd been in a similar situation not too long ago, she couldn't picture herself confiding in him.

Then, she straightened. The stakes were too high for her to let pride stand in her way. When the time came, she would do what needed to be done.

But now was not that time. "I think I'll go check on the children and see if I can talk Pru into another bowl of broth. The more we can get her to eat, the better."

Cassie Lynn walked down the hall, her mood sober. She was afraid. There, she'd admitted it. As much as she talked about just being direct and matter-of-fact, she wasn't certain she could pull it off. She'd been praying about it, and as much as she knew she should leave this all in God's hands, a part of her kept pulling the problem back into her own lap to worry over. The idea of approaching a man she didn't know and laying her unorthodox plan out before him left her shaking.

But she really didn't have any other choice.

Or did she?

Before she reached the kids' room, there was a loud buzz that indicated someone was at the front door. Cassie Lynn changed course and discovered Calvin Hendricks standing on the porch.

The youth doffed his hat and gave her a smile. "Morning, Miss Vickers. A Mr. Walker asked me to bring these here." He waved to a handcart at the foot of the steps that contained a trunk and a large leather satchel. "Would you like me to carry them in?"

She nodded and stepped outside. "It looks like you might need a hand with that trunk." Calvin stacked the satchel on top of the well-used trunk and they each grabbed an end. Within minutes they had the luggage situated in the parlor. She'd leave it there until Mr. Walker returned and decided what he wanted to do with them.

After Calvin had gone, Cassie Lynn studied the two pieces. The trio was apparently traveling light. Was this everything they owned or had they shipped the rest of their things to their ultimate destination?

She wondered again at this strange sort of nomadic lifestyle Mr. Walker was living with the children. He seemed to care so much about them, she would've thought he would want to give them more of a settled home life.

He must have his reasons, and it really wasn't any of her business.

Except that she was beginning to care a great deal

about these three travelers, a lot more than seemed possible for folks she'd known for such a short time.

When Riley returned to Mrs. Flanagan's home at the end of his morning shift at the livery, he went around to the back without letting himself ponder why he wanted to enter through the kitchen. He paused before climbing the porch steps. Though he was anxious to check on the kids, he figured the ladies would probably appreciate it if he washed up from his work before entering the house.

He dipped some water from the rain barrel near the back porch and quickly washed. Feeling more presentable, he climbed the steps and knocked on the screen door before stepping inside without waiting for a response.

Miss Vickers looked up from her work at the stove and gave him a welcoming smile. "Hello. How was your morning at the livery?"

He leaned against the doorjamb. "It was busy, but I enjoy the work. How's Pru doing?"

"Itchy and uncomfortable, but she's resting right now."

"And Noah?"

"He hasn't shown signs of coming down with chicken pox yet, but it could be as long as a week or two. He and Mrs. Flanagan are in the parlor entertaining each other."

Riley cast a quick look in that direction, his brow furrowed. "I hope he's not bothering her."

"On the contrary, I think she's enjoying herself more than she has in quite some time." Cassie put down her cook spoon. "Lunch will be ready in about thirty minutes, but if you're hungry now I—"

He held up a hand. "I can wait. I don't expect you to go out of your way to accommodate me." Then he straightened. "I'll go say hello to Noah and Pru."

He returned a few minutes later. "Pru was sleeping when I looked in on her, so I didn't wake her."

"That's good. As long as she's sleeping, the itching can't bother her." Miss Vickers closed the cabinet door. "Did you see Noah?"

"Just for a moment. He and Mrs. Flanagan were in the middle of what appeared to be a tiebreaker game of checkers."

She grinned. "I told you Mrs. Flanagan would enjoy his company."

Riley inhaled appreciatively. "Whatever it is you're cooking smells mighty good."

"Thanks. It's lamb and vegetable stew."

"Sounds as good as it smells." Then he moved to the cupboard. "Why don't I get started on setting the table for you?"

"Thank you. I talked Mrs. Flanagan into having lunch here in the kitchen, so we won't need to carry the dishes very far. She's insisted that we will have our evening meal in the dining room, though, like civilized people."

He smiled at Miss Vickers's droll tone and began pulling out the dishes. "By the way, did our luggage arrive?"

She nodded, looking up at him. "It did. But I wasn't sure if you'd want it in the attic with you or in the room with the kids, so we set it in the parlor for now."

"I'll put it away before I head back to the livery this afternoon."

Miss Vickers waved her hand. "There's no rush. It's certainly not in anyone's way where it is."

She eyed him curiously. "Do you mind if I ask you a personal question?"

Riley paused, glad he had his back to her. What did she want to know? There was so much he couldn't say, so many secrets he had to keep. It was one reason he'd avoided making any kind of close friendships for the past year and a half.

But he could hardly refuse to let her ask her question, not with all she'd done for him in the past twenty-four hours. "What did you want to know?"

Please, God, don't let her ask me something I can't answer. I surely don't want to tell her a lie.

"I was just wondering, is that your only luggage?"

The relief that washed over him was almost a physical thing. That was a question he could answer freely. "It is. We travel light." He kept his tone carefully casual. There was no need to explain that they'd had to leave a large part of the kids' belongings behind three towns ago.

He began placing the dishes on the table.

After a few moments of silence, she asked another question. "Do you know if Pru likes to read?"

Her sudden change of subject surprised him, but he nodded. "She does. And she's trying to teach Noah to read, as well."

Miss Vickers straightened, a concerned frown on her face. "Did Noah have trouble with reading in school?"

Riley had said too much. How did she get under his guard that way? "Noah hasn't been able to spend much time in school this past year."

"Oh?"

He heard the question in her one-word response, but pretended not to. Her obvious concern over the children missing school chaffed at his conscience. But they'd moved around so much it just hadn't been practical.

After a moment, she seemed to get the message and gave him a bright, it's-none-of-my-business smile. "Well, school starts back up in about four weeks. If you all are still around at that time, perhaps you can enroll both Noah and Pru. Turnabout has some mighty fine teachers."

"I'm sure you do." Riley inserted a firmness in his tone. "But we won't be here that long. As I mentioned before, this was a temporary stop on our trip." Best to make sure she understood that was *not* going to change.

He needed to keep reminding himself of that, as well.

Cassie Lynn turned back to the stove. Wherever the three of them ended up, she hoped Noah would get the schooling he needed. Without the ability to read, a person missed out on so much.

Perhaps she'd mention something to Mrs. Flanagan about Noah needing reading lessons. The widow was a former schoolteacher and would probably relish having the opportunity to slip into that role again.

But Cassie Lynn still wondered why Noah hadn't spent much time in a classroom. Surely Mr. Walker hadn't pulled the kids out of school the way her father had done with her. Noah's uncle didn't seem the type to place such little value on education.

Mr. Walker had definitely looked uncomfortable with her question, though. There seemed to be something important he was leaving unsaid. Then again, she was a relative stranger to him—she shouldn't expect him to share confidences with her.

So why did she find herself wishing he would?

Chapter Nine

Once the kitchen was set back to rights after lunch, Riley turned to Miss Vickers. "I have a couple of hours before I go back to the livery. Why don't you show me to the attic, and I can tackle whatever needs doing to get it set up for tonight."

"Of course." She led him to the end of the hallway and opened a door to reveal a narrow set of stairs. Leading the way, she climbed with graceful movements.

When they reached the top, Riley paused to study the space. It was surprisingly roomy. The ceiling was tall in the center and sloped down near the eaves. There were two dormer windows on the front portion and large round ones on either end. The windows were a bit grimy, but provided enough light to make out the objects in the room.

There were a lot of odds and ends stored haphazardly about the place, but with some rearranging there should be more than enough open space to make a decent sleeping area.

"What do you think?" she asked.

He stepped farther into the attic. "This will work just fine."

She waved a hand toward the nearest window. "I thought we'd clear a space over there so you could take full advantage of the light. It'll mean moving quite a few things around, though." She pointed to the other dormer. "And if we move things away from that window and clean it up a bit, it will let in even more light."

He nodded. "I agree. I'll get started shifting items around. Does it matter where I place them?"

"As far as I can tell, there's no rhyme or reason to how objects are stored up here. Oh, and while you're working, if you see anything you can use as furniture or for storage, feel free to do so while you're here." She moved back toward the stairs. "I'll fetch the broom and some cleaning rags."

Riley went to work. Most of the pieces were light—someone had had to cart them up those stairs, after all. But there were a few heavier items that required muscle. He did find a few odd pieces of furniture he could make use of—a sturdy chair with a loose arm, a crate that would serve as a bedside table, a bench he could use as a shelf to set things on, and a trunk he could use for storage.

While he worked, Miss Vickers returned with her cleaning supplies and promptly started wiping down the window. Before long, the sun was shining through with unobstructed brightness.

Then she wended her way through the clutter to the other dormer and cleaned that window, as well.

Riley smiled as he caught the sound of her soft humming. Strange how comfortable this felt, as if they didn't need to fill the silences with words to feel connected.

She was still working on the windows when he finished moving things around, so he grabbed the broom and began sweeping.

A few minutes later she turned and met his gaze across the room. He saw surprise flicker across her expression before she bustled toward him.

"I'm sorry." She reached for the broom. "Here, let me do that."

What was the matter? Didn't she think he was capable of sweeping the floor? "No need. I'm just about finished."

She watched him uncertainly for a moment, then nodded. "In that case, I'll go fetch the quilts we can use to make your bed."

He watched her go, still wondering at her strange reaction. Did she really not expect him to do his own chores? What kind of people had she been raised around?

She made three trips, carrying two quilts the first two times. By the time she made it up with her third load, a pillow and sheets, he'd finished sweeping and had dragged his "furniture" pieces in place.

"I figured I would fold each quilt in half and stack them on top of each other to build your pallet."

"Easy enough." He grabbed two corners of the top quilt and waited for her to do the same.

When they were done, there was a pallet that was not only wide and long enough to accommodate him, but one that stood over a foot tall. She placed the pillow on top and covered the whole thing with one of the sheets.

Then, she stepped back. "I'll admit it's nothing fancy, but I hope you'll find it adequate."

He stroked his chin as he studied it. "Actually, considering the roominess of this place and the comfortable-looking furnishings, I could argue that I have the nicest room in the house."

She grinned. "I'll let Mrs. Flanagan know that you're pleased."

"All kidding aside, do you mind if I ask why you're doing all this for us—nursing the kids, inviting us to stay here? Don't get me wrong, I'm very grateful, but we're strangers to you. And this is no small service you've volunteered to perform." It was his experience that there were often ulterior motives behind offers of this sort. And even if that wasn't the case here, their current situation was precarious enough that a bit of good-intentioned interference could place them in a difficult situation.

"Not entirely strangers," she responded. "Even though I only met you two days ago, I think I know enough about you to know you're a good person."

He raised a brow. "Do you, now?"

She nodded, seeming absolutely confident. "I do. I can tell you really care about your niece and nephew, so you can't be all bad. And not only did you immediately find yourself a job your first day in town, but you've been helping out around here a good bit as well, so you're not a layabout. And you've taken all the right steps since you discovered your niece was sick, so you're a responsible person."

Then, Miss Vickers gave a curiously self-deprecating grin. "Besides, I've taken quite a liking to Noah and Pru. In fact, I sort of miss being around kids. I suppose it comes from growing up with four brothers."

It still didn't sound like reason enough to take in a sick child she barely knew, much less all three of them.

But perhaps he should stop looking for reasons to question his good fortune and just accept it.

Then she spoke up again, her expression diffident. "Besides, I do have another reason to be happy you all are here."

"And that is?"

"Mrs. Flanagan, for all her bluster, is a lonely woman. Her husband and youngest son died in an accident about six years ago. Her oldest son, John, joined the army the year before that, so he's rarely around."

Riley sympathized with the woman—he, too, had lost people close to him. "But you're here with her, so it's not as if she's alone."

"True, but I work for her, so that's really not the same. Even though I've grown quite fond of Mrs. Flanagan in the time I've been here, from her perspective, I'm here because she pays me to be."

Riley wasn't sure he agreed with that. From what he'd seen so far, it appeared Mrs. Flanagan treated her a lot like family.

But he let Miss Vickers do the talking.

Her expression softened. "You should have seen her face when she was speaking to Noah after you left this morning. She came alive in a way I haven't seen her do before. I think she would truly be saddened if you should leave and take the children with you."

"But our stay here is only temporary—just until the children get better."

"I know, but by then she'll be that much closer to having the use of her leg again, and in the meantime you will have filled her days with something besides her own thoughts."

Riley lifted his hands in surrender. "Well, whatever

your reasons, Miss Vickers, I hope you know how much I appreciate everything you're doing for me and the kids."

"I would consider it a favor if you would call me Cassie Lynn instead of Miss Vickers."

Her request startled him, but not unhappily so.

"After all," she continued, "it appears we'll be living under the same roof for a couple of weeks. It seems a bit silly to stand on ceremony."

"Of course, Cassie. And you should call me Riley."

He noticed a bit of pink staining her cheeks and that she wasn't quite meeting his gaze any longer.

"I think we've done all we can for now," she said, then finally turned to meet his gaze again. "If you don't have to return to the livery just yet, I do have a quick errand I'd like to run."

"Of course." Was she just trying to make her escape? He was fairly certain she'd made that request about names impulsively and that it had embarrassed her. But she wore the pink in her cheeks quite well.

Thinking back over all the reasons she'd given for helping him, a part of him wished there'd been something in there that indicated she'd wanted him close by, as well.

And the twinge of disappointment he'd just felt at that thought was yet another good reason to move on as soon as possible.

As Cassie Lynn headed down the sidewalk, she wondered if she'd been too bold in suggesting the use of first names. It wasn't something she'd planned, but it had seemed natural when she'd said it. It wasn't until she'd seen the surprise in his expression that she realized what she'd done.

Ah well, it was done now and she couldn't say she regretted it. Realizing she'd been moving slowly, Cassie Lynn picked up the pace. She'd considered canceling her normal afternoon walk today. The additional responsibilities she'd taken on with the children didn't leave her with much free time. But there was one errand she really wanted to run.

Resisting the temptation to head out in the direction of the livery as usual, Cassie Lynn resolutely turned her steps toward the restaurant, which just so happened to also house the town's library.

As soon as she walked in the door, Daisy came bustling over to her. "Hello again. I have to say, my customers are loving those pies of yours. I'd like to order three for tomorrow if that's okay."

"Absolutely!" Then Cassie Lynn gestured toward the bookshelves to her left. "I was hoping to be able to find some reading material for a sick little girl who's staying with Mrs. Flanagan."

Daisy waved her on. "Abigail isn't here right now, but pick out what you want and leave the information in her ledger."

Conscious of the hour, Cassie Lynn resisted the urge to take her time browsing and quickly selected two works she thought a ten-year-old might enjoy.

On her way back to Mrs. Flanagan's house, she saw Mr. Drummond, the undertaker, step out of the mercantile. She tried to study him objectively without outright staring. This man could be her husband soon. Finicky was how Mrs. Flanagan had described him, and Cassie Lynn supposed he was.

As usual, he was fastidiously dressed, his clothing trim and neatly pressed, his hat perfectly situated on his no-hair-out-of-place head. He was a tall, spindly, bespectacled man who reminded her a bit of a farsighted grasshopper.

Chiding herself for the unkind comparison, she continued on her way. What would he think of her? Though she kept herself neat, she didn't consider herself fastidiously so. And would he expect his home to be kept completely spotless and perfectly organized? Would such a wifely requirement give Cassie Lynn much time to run her bakery business?

Those were things they would need to discuss if she made it to the point of proposing to him.

For some reason, thinking of that made her mood turn gloomy.

She arrived back at Mrs. Flanagan's house just in time to see Riley carrying the trunk on his shoulder down the hall. The effort had drawn his shirt taut across his back. She paused a moment to admire the play of muscles in his arm and back. Nothing spindly or grasshoppery about this man.

She quickly placed the books on the hall table and bustled forward. "Just a moment," she said as she slipped past him. "Let me get the door for you."

She tried hard not to stare as he set the trunk down in the children's room, but she couldn't seem to help herself. There was just something about this man...

He straightened, then turned back to her. "Now that you're here, I need to head out to the livery."

Hoping he hadn't caught her staring, she nodded quickly. "Of course. I'm sorry if waiting for me made you late."

He led her back into the hall and toward the kitchen. "Not at all. In fact, I have a favor to ask." His expression held a self-deprecating grimace. "If you don't mind my leaving the kids in your care for a little longer than planned, I'd like to take River for a run after I finish at the livery. He hasn't had a chance to really stretch his legs since we got here."

"Of course."

"Thank you. To be honest, I can use the exercise, as well. I always think better when I'm out riding."

"In that case, take as long as you wish." The man probably needed to do quite a bit of thinking, given the circumstances of the past twenty-four hours.

When he had gone, she remembered the books she'd left in the entryway. Fetching them, she headed to the kids' room, where she smiled at Pru. "I have a surprise for you."

The little girl sat up straighter, her expression uncertain.

"I stopped at the library today and picked up some new books for you to read."

A wide grin split her face. "For me?"

Cassie Lynn nodded, not certain if the girl understood what a library was. "You can take as long as you like reading them, and when you're done, I'll bring them back to the library and trade them for new ones."

Pru's expression changed to one of wonder. "You mean as many times as I want?"

Cassie Lynn nodded. "For as long as you are here in Turnabout, anyway."

Cassie Lynn could understand Pru's delight. As far as she was concerned, there was nothing better to help you forget how miserable you were feeling than to lose yourself in a good book.

Riley finished hitching Scarlett to the livery's buggy and led the conveyance to a waiting customer. It had been a busy afternoon, but he was glad of it. Working kept his mind from fretting over circumstances he couldn't change.

Horses were so much less complicated than people. Just one of the many reasons he preferred them to most folks.

As soon as Mr. Olson rode off in the rented buggy, the buckboard that had gone out earlier was returned. Riley unhitched the horse, checked her to make sure she was okay, and then brushed her down and gave her a bit of feed. Once that was done, he led the mare out to the corral and turned her loose.

And then he was free to leave.

Riley quickly saddled River and mounted up. Before long he was heading out of town, looking for a nice open stretch of road where he could let River have his head and stretch out in a full gallop.

He'd wired Claypool this morning to tell him the situation with the kids and to let him know he wouldn't be at the meeting on Wednesday. He'd received Claypool's response today and the detective had strongly encouraged Riley to find a way to attend. That he wasn't sure their informant would be forthcoming with him alone.

So now Riley was pondering options.

And there really was only one: ask the ladies to watch over the children while he went to Tyler. Which would mean he'd have to be away from Pru and Noah overnight.

Could he do that—go off and leave the kids in someone else's care while he was so many miles away?

If he *did* ask the ladies to do this, how much of the children's story should he tell them? And if he did, would they still be as welcoming?

Growling in frustration, Riley saw the stretch of road he'd been looking for and nudged River into a full gallop.

Chapter Ten

After supper that evening, Cassie Lynn stood up from the table and fetched the pie that rested on the sideboard.

"So, what have you baked up for us tonight?" Mrs. Flanagan asked.

"A cinnamon-apple-pecan pie."

"Sounds delicious," Riley said.

"Baking is Cassie Lynn's specialty."

He nodded. "So I hear."

"She's always experimenting with new flavors."

"Experimenting, you say?" Riley raised a brow. "Should I be worried?"

"What, you're not adventurous?" Cassie Lynn teased as she set the pie tin on the table.

"Not when it comes to food."

Noah, however, leaned forward eagerly. "Well, I am, especially when it smells as good as this does."

"Why, thank you, Noah. Just for that, you get the first piece."

He sat up straighter, chest puffing out in selfimportance. Cassie Lynn dished up a piece and handed the saucer to the little boy. Then she cut another serving and passed it to Pru, who had joined them at the table for supper tonight. The third slice went to Mrs. Flanagan.

Finally, Cassie Lynn turned to Riley. "What do you think? Have I given you enough time to gather your courage to try a piece?"

"Since no one else seems to have suffered any ill effects, I suppose I'm willing." His voice was solemn, but she saw the laughter in his eyes.

"It's good, Uncle Riley, real good," Noah assured him.

Riley accepted his serving of pie from her and tasted it with exaggerated caution. Then his eyes widened in exaggerated surprise. "Well, what do you know? This really *is* good."

Cassie Lynn rolled her eyes at his playacting, but her heart was warmed by the way he was willing to act foolish for the benefit of the kids. Not many a grown man would do that.

After the meal, Riley offered to help her clean up, and had the children help carry the dishes back to the kitchen.

"That's the last of it, Uncle Riley," Noah said as he and Pru each placed a bowl on the counter. "Mrs. Flanagan said she had something to show us in the parlor. Can we go now?"

Riley nodded. "Go ahead. I'll help Miss Vickers with the dishes."

Cassie Lynn was starting to get used to having him help her with the housework. "Just give me a minute to take my pies out of the oven."

"Are those for your customers?"

Cassie Lynn nodded. "Daisy over at the restaurant has ordered three for tomorrow. I set them to bake while we were eating." She placed the second one on the table next to the first. "I'll make the six fruit tarts for the tea shop later."

"Sounds like you're going to have a late night."

She shrugged. It was true, but that was just how things were going to be for a while.

He studied her a moment, then nodded, as if coming to a decision. "I tell you what. Why don't you let me handle the dishes while you go ahead and start work on your tarts now?"

He'd managed to surprise her yet again. "That's very kind of you, but it's not necessary. It won't take much time—"

"Exactly. It won't take much time for me to handle this while you work on that."

Deciding she was tired of arguing, she nodded. "All right. And thank you."

She floured the end of the table that was clear and began mixing her dough. "How was your ride?" she asked as she worked.

"Both River and I enjoyed it," he answered, looking back over his shoulder. "It was almost like old times."

"Old times?"

His expression closed off and he angled his face away from her. "Back before the kids and I began this trip."

But she got the distinct impression there was something he was leaving unsaid.

He asked her a question about the tarts she was baking and the conversation veered off into other inconsequential topics. Riley finished with the dishes before she had her tarts ready for the oven.

Drying his hands on a rag, he met her gaze. "If you'll

excuse me, Cassie, I think I'll go ahead and get the kids ready for bed."

She nodded and went back to work.

She'd give a pretty penny to know just what had put that unexpected strain into the conversation earlier.

Later, after she'd helped Mrs. Flanagan settle down for the night, Cassie Lynn returned to the kitchen to roll out the dough for her last two fruit tarts. She had just four tart pans, so she not only had to bake them in two batches, but had to wait until the first batch cooled enough to get them out of the pans before she could deal with the second batch. If this bakery business went well, she'd definitely need to purchase additional pans.

Once the tarts were in the oven, she stepped out on the back porch. Fireflies flickered across the lawn. A dog barked somewhere in the distance, but the sound was muffled and there was no sense of urgency in it.

She loved this time of day, when the world seemed to be pulling a blanket over itself in preparation for sleep. Most people waited until they were ready to slip into bed to say their prayers. But she preferred to be out here, where she was surrounded by the starry beauty of God's creation, to speak with the Heavenly Father. She bowed her head and closed her eyes.

Dear Lord God, thank You for this beautiful day and for the many blessings You've gifted to me. By Your grace I have a place to live, and work to occupy my hands. Watch over Mrs. Flanagan as she deals with the trials brought on by her injury, and help me to be a blessing to her. Thank You, too, for sending the Walker family our way—I know that was an answer to my prayer to find a way to help Mrs. Flanagan feel needed and engaged again.

And please help me to figure out how to best plan for my own future.

Cassie Lynn opened her eyes again and sat on the top step. She hugged her knees, inhaling deeply of the warm summer air. A slight breeze stirred the leaves of a woodbine vine growing near the far end of the porch, wafting the floral scent around her like a fragrant caress. She found herself thinking of Riley and trying to figure out yet again why she found him so interesting.

The door opened behind her and she glanced over her shoulder. Riley stood on the threshold, hesitating.

"I hope I'm not intruding, Cassie," he said when she met his gaze. "If you'd prefer to be alone, I can—"

Feeling her languor suddenly slough away, she smiled. "Not at all. I'm just enjoying the evening breeze." She waved him forward. "Feel free to do the same." She'd noticed, since she'd invited him to use her given name, that he called her Cassie rather than Cassie Lynn. The first couple times she'd thought to correct him, but then changed her mind, deciding she rather liked it. It seemed more personal and grown-up than the other.

He stepped outside, then moved to lean a hip against the porch rail beside her.

"Are Noah and Pru settled in?" she asked.

He nodded. "They are."

Cassie clutched the edge of the step. "I figured you'd have turned in for the night after the day you had."

He gave her a direct look. "Actually, I wanted to talk to you alone, if you don't mind."

Her heart did a funny little flutter at that. "About what?"

"First, I want to thank you for all you did for Pru today. Not just watching over her, I mean. She showed me the books you got for her."

Cassie felt her cheeks warm. "I was glad to do it. Pru is a sweet child. And she's been a good patient. The itching is starting to bother her but she's doing her best not to complain and is apologetic every time she has to ask for something." In fact, Cassie was worried that the girl was a little *too* apologetic.

"Sweet is a good way to describe her. I've always thought she was a bit too fragile. Anyway, I appreciate you going out of your way for her."

"It was no trouble to stop at the library and pick out some books for her. In fact, I always enjoy perusing the new titles Abigail has brought in."

Then, uncomfortable with his gratitude, Cassie decided to redirect the conversation. "Was there something else you wanted to discuss?"

He folded his arms across his chest. "I know Mrs. Flanagan said she wouldn't take any payment for allowing us to stay here, but it doesn't sit well with me to not pay my way."

"If you want me to try to change her mind, I'm afraid—"

He held up a hand and Cassie stopped speaking.

"Not at all," he said. "I just figure, since she won't take my money, that maybe I can help out in other ways, at least while we're staying here. Are there any maintenance or other chores that need doing?"

That's why he wanted to talk to her? Ignoring the deflated feeling, she nodded. "I've noticed that the wire fence around the chicken coop is sagging in a few places. I'd meant to tend to it myself but hadn't gotten around to it yet."

"Easy enough for me to take care of. What else?"

"One of the windows in the parlor is stuck tight. I haven't been able to open it since I moved in here."

He nodded. "I can take a look at that, as well. Anything else?"

Cassie searched her mind for other household needs. "I don't know if this is the sort of thing you would want to take on, but there's a limb from that old pecan tree around on the east side of the house that's touching the roof. I'm afraid it might do some damage to the shingles come the next big storm."

"I'll just need a ladder and a saw to handle that. And I'll take a look at the gutters while I'm up there." Then he waved a hand. "So far the items you've mentioned would take me two, maybe three afternoons. Surely there's more work that needs doing."

"You could always ask Mrs. Flanagan if there's anything she'd like taken care of."

He grimaced. "I'd rather not. Asking her would only give her the opportunity to tell me not to do any of it. Much better if I can just do the work and not say a thing."

Cassie did think of something else, but it was probably not the kind of task he had in mind.

Apparently, something in her expression gave her away, though. "What is it you're holding back?" he asked.

"Just a passing thought. I don't really think it qualifies as a household chore."

He raised a brow. "Why don't you let me be the judge of that?"

"All right." She took a deep breath, wondering what he'd think of her unorthodox idea. "I think Mrs. Flanagan really chafes at not being able to come and go as she pleases. Right now, because of the steps, she can only go as far as the porch."

"Go on." His expression held a hint of puzzlement.

"I was thinking," Cassie said diffidently, "if you would offer to carry her down the porch steps while I roll her chair down, then I could push her wheelchair along the sidewalk and she could have a stroll of sorts. Of course, you'd also need to be available to carry her back up the steps at the end of her outing."

Riley rubbed his jaw. "You're right, it's not exactly what I had in mind." Then he grinned. "But I can sure sympathize with not wanting to be cooped up inside all day. If you can convince Mrs. Flanagan to let me carry her down the steps, then I'll be more than happy to perform the service."

"Excellent. However, as for convincing her, that might come better from you." Cassie gave him a knowing glance. "You are, after all, her guest, and as such your suggestions carry more weight than mine would. Just don't mention it was my idea."

"I'm not sure I agree with your thinking, but I'll see what I can do."

"Of course, once we convince her, it means you would need to keep an eye on the children while I am pushing her chair."

"I can do that." He lifted a hand. "In the meantime, if you can think of anything else, anything at all, that needs a handyman's attention around here, please let me know."

"I'll do that."

Now that they'd taken care of what he'd wanted to speak to her about, she expected him to go back inside. But to her surprise, he merely looked out toward the fireflies as if he didn't have anywhere else to be. "I also want to thank you one more time for inviting us into your home. Pru and Noah really like it here."

What about him? Did he like it here, too? "You've already thanked us, multiple times. But to be fair, it's actually Mrs. Flanagan's home and it was her invitation."

He raised a brow at that. "No need to be coy, Cassie. We both know who I owe our current accommodations to, and you must allow me to thank you."

"In that case, you're quite welcome." She studied him a moment, realizing it wasn't his gratitude she wanted. "Do you mind if I ask you a question?"

His expression took on a hint of wariness, but he nodded. "Ask away."

"How long have the children been in your care?"

"About a year and a half."

"It can't have been easy for you, a bachelor trying to make a living and having to care for two young children."

He shrugged. "They're good kids and they are family, so I don't regret any of it. Except that I can't make a better home for them."

"Perhaps someday you'll find a place you like enough to settle down in, and then you can provide a nice home for them. A place where they can put down roots and make friends and go to school."

"That would be nice."

There was a resignation, a sort of regret in his voice that made her think he didn't believe that would happen.

"And if you found that place," she continued, "you could find a kind, matronly housekeeper to help you give the children a feeling of home and permanency."

He didn't respond.

Cassie Lynn tilted her head to one side, studying him curiously. "That *is* what you want for them, isn't it?"

"Of course." He paused and she saw his jaw tighten. "We just don't always get what we want, when we want it."

"True. But that doesn't mean we shouldn't make the attempt."

He didn't say anything to that, just kept looking at the fireflies with an unreadable expression on his face.

Cassie realized she was trespassing on his privacy, just as Mrs. Flanagan had done earlier, and gave him an apologetic smile. "But they're your children, and I'm sure you're doing the best you can with them."

Then she stood and brushed at her skirt. "If you'll excuse me, I need to get my tarts out of the oven."

He nodded. "I think I'll stay out here a little longer, if you don't mind. I'll be sure to close the house up good and tight when I go in. And I'll check on the kids one last time before I turn in."

"Don't worry over much about the children. My room is right next to theirs, so I'll hear them if they should wake and need anything."

Cassie opened the oven a few moments later and was pleased to see the crust on the tarts was a nice golden brown. She pulled them out and set them on the table beside the pies.

She took care of the stove, then glanced out the back

door before heading to her room. All she could see was the shadowy silhouette of Riley, who now sat on the porch step. There was something achingly lonely about that sight, something that made her want to go back out there and let him know he had a friend.

Instead, she turned and headed toward the bedrooms. She walked quietly past her door and paused outside the room where the children were sleeping. She opened the door and peered into the shadowy interior. Both were turned on their sides, and neither stirred at her intrusion. All she heard was their rhythmic breathing.

She smiled softly at the sweetness of that sound. Children were such precious gifts. She supposed she couldn't blame Riley for being so protective of them.

But how could she help him understand that he and his charges were safe here, that no one intended them harm?

Chapter Eleven

After Cassie went inside, Riley settled down on the spot she'd vacated. It was surprising how difficult it had been not to confide in her. He'd detected a faint note of censure in her voice and he'd found himself longing to replace it with admiration.

Which was altogether vain and totally irrelevant to the situation at hand. Because he had more than himself to worry about—he had those two kids sleeping inside counting on him.

Still, what if he could trust her with their story, tell her why things were the way they were? Being able to share that burden with someone, someone he could truly trust, would be such a gift.

But such thoughts were getting him nowhere and he'd had a long day. Riley placed his hands on his knees and levered himself up. Time to turn in.

As he stepped inside, he thought about what an unexpected turn this day had taken. From his restless night, to the unexpected invitation to move in here, to this feeling of almost being part of a family. Not that these cozy new accommodations didn't come with their own set of issues.

His first day at the livery had gone well, and Fred Humphries was an easy man to work for. And even though Riley had been worried about how Pru was doing, and whether he'd made the right choice in trusting the ladies to not get too close to their secrets, knowing that the children were being well looked after when he had to be away had brought him a measure of peace.

Trains stopped at the depot here in town twice a day, regular as clockwork, at ten in the morning and at three in the afternoon. He'd negotiated with Mr. Humphries to meet both trains each day to see if anyone needed to rent a wagon or have freight delivered. So Riley would be able to keep an eye on incoming visitors to town.

This was one of the benefits of stopping off in a small town—it was much easier to keep an eye out for his stepbrother, Guy. The disadvantage was that it was much more difficult to melt into the background and not stand out.

Riley paused at the door to the kids' room, and something in his chest tightened as he watched them sleep. Such precious little lives, and they'd been entrusted to his care. He simply could not fail them, doing so was unthinkable.

He stepped away and moved quietly to his attic room. Looking around, he smiled at the little touches that Cassie had gone to the trouble of adding at some point this afternoon. She'd placed a cloth on the crate he was using as a bedside table, and topped it with an oil lamp. There was also a braided rug next to his make-shift bed. A part of him wondered if she was just a little too good to be true. Perhaps it was cynical of him, but he'd been fooled too many times in his life to be completely trustful.

Still, it was hard to imagine there was any falseness or treachery behind the innocence he sensed in her. In fact, if it was only his own well-being at stake, he'd trust her with the whole story.

When Riley stepped into the kitchen the next morning, he was surprised to see Cassie sitting at the table hunched over a cup of coffee.

She glanced up with a smile, but he saw the circles under her eyes and the weary lines at her mouth.

He grabbed a cup, moved toward the stove and lifted the coffeepot. "Rough night?" he asked as he sat down across from her.

"I'll be fine as soon as I finish my coffee."

"It was the kids, wasn't it?"

"It wasn't her fault—she's sick."

"Tell me." When it appeared Cassie would try to put him off, he gave her a stern look. "I'm not wanting to cast blame, but I *am* Pru's uncle. I need to know how she's doing so I can better help."

Cassie nodded. "Of course. Pru's symptoms have moved deep into the itchy phase, and she was miserable." Cassie took a small sip from her cup. "I finally sent Noah to my room and spent the night on his bed, so I could read to her and try to take her mind off her misery."

"I'm sorry. That should have been me watching over her."

Cassie lifted a hand in a lazy wave. "Don't worry," she said with a lopsided smile. "I have a feeling there'll be enough of these episodes to go around over the next few days."

He smiled at her attempt at humor. But when she went to get up, he captured her hand with his. "Wait."

She stilled as if frozen. Her gaze went to their joined hands and then shot to his own. Something passed between them, something warm that he definitely needed to explore more deeply.

He released her hand and leaned back, clearing his throat. "I think it's my turn to apologize. You go do whatever it is you need to do to get Mrs. Flanagan ready to face the day, then send Noah back to his own bed, and get some rest yourself. I can handle cooking breakfast this morning. And I'll slip down to the livery to let Mr. Humphries know I need the morning off."

"That's very thoughtful of you, but I—"

"I insist. I only agreed to this arrangement on the condition you allow me to pull my weight in taking care of them, remember? Besides, as you said, there's going to be a lot of these episodes to go around the next few days. You won't do Pru or anyone else any good if you wear yourself out."

Cassie was silent for a moment and he could almost see her mind processing what he'd just said. Then she nodded. "Very well. But I'm only going to take a short nap, so there's no need for you to tell Mr. Humphries anything."

Riley made a noncommittal sound as he stood and moved around the table to help her stand.

She smiled with a raised brow. "Thank you, but I'm merely tired, not infirm."

He waved his hands in a shooing motion. "Then get

on with you—take care of whatever you need to with Mrs. Flanagan and then be off to bed."

She gave a little curtsy. "Yes, sir." And with a saucy smile, she headed out the door.

Smiling at her playful exit, Riley stoked the stove, then grabbed the egg basket and stepped outside. He'd have to make certain they shared the overnight duties tonight. He might not be as good at tending to sick kids as she was, but if it was just a matter of trying to soothe Pru, and read or otherwise distract her from her discomfort, he could manage that well enough.

Cassie opened her eyes and was confused by the bright sunlight streaming into the room. Then she remembered—she'd agreed to take a nap.

How long had she been asleep? She glanced at the small porcelain clock on her bedside table and saw that she had indeed slept for nearly two hours. Oh dear, she was going to be late making her deliveries.

She'd lain down fully dressed, so had only to pull her shoes back on and put her hair up again. She took care of that quickly, then hurried to the kitchen.

She entered the room to find it empty, but almost immediately the back door opened and Riley stepped inside.

"Oh, hello," he said, sounding inordinately pleased with himself. "Up already?"

"Already? I should have gotten up an hour ago." Then she looked around. "Where are my baked goods?"

"Delivered. I just got back."

"Oh." Realizing that had sounded less than grateful, she conjured up a smile. "Thank you."

"You're welcome. Care for some breakfast?"

She reached for one of the two biscuits on a plate in the middle of the table. "I'll just have these and a cup of coffee."

Before either of them could say anything else, Mrs. Flanagan appeared in the doorway, with Noah proudly pushing the wheelchair.

"Well, hello there," the woman said. "Thought I heard you in here."

"Where's Pru?" Riley asked with a frown.

The widow waved a hand. "Back in bed."

"Good." Cassie set her biscuit down as she reached for the cup of coffee Riley had poured for her. "She didn't sleep well and needs to get all the rest she can."

"Speaking of sleep," Riley said, turning to Mrs. Flanagan. "I have a favor to ask you."

The widow sat up straighter, as if happy to be asked. "And just what might that be?"

"There's a tree right outside my window with a limb hanging over the house. When the wind blows, it scratches and bumps against the roof, and that makes it hard to sleep. I was wondering if you'd mind if I trimmed it off."

Mrs. Flanagan nodded. "I suppose that would be all right. In fact, I was planning to take care of that myself before I had my accident."

"Then if you'll just tell me where to find a ladder and a saw, I'll get it all taken care of before I turn in tonight."

While her employer gave Riley the directions he needed, and some he didn't, Cassie smiled. She was impressed with how smoothly he'd handled that, getting the widow's permission to do one of the maintenance chores by making it sound as if she was doing him a favor.

And Cassie had noticed he'd been doing other chores, too, all without fanfare. The pantry door no longer squeaked, the cabinet door that had been sagging on its hinges was now tight, the broken slat on the porch rail had been fixed. He'd even replaced the rotten board on the old swing in the backyard with a new one.

Yep, Riley was one handy man to have around.

He glanced up and met her gaze for just a moment, and she let her smile tell him how much she appreciated his approach.

Chapter Twelve

Pru wasn't a very demanding patient. The biggest problem Cassie encountered that morning was trying to keep her from scratching at her blisters. She applied the calamine lotion Dr. Pratt had prescribed, which did seem to provide some relief, but not enough to sooth her completely. Cassie also trimmed the girl's fingernails short enough to minimize any damage she might do if she gave in to the urge to scratch.

When delivering a bowl of broth midmorning, Cassie nodded toward Pru's doll. "What a pretty little lady. Is that Bitsy?"

The girl nodded as she clutched the doll protectively against her chest.

Cassie could see the cloth doll had been lovely at one time. But one of the button eyes was hanging by a mere thread and the other seemed loose, as well. The yarn hair was frayed and tangled. The gingham dress was soiled and worn, but it was obvious the doll was well-loved.

"Bitsy is a perfectly lovely name for a lovely little lady."

Pru stroked the doll's hair. "My momma made it for me."

"Then that means she's an extra special doll, because she was made with lots of love."

The little girl moved the doll to her lap, where she studied her forlornly. "Her eye is messed up."

"I see that. Would you like me to fix it for you?"

Pru's expression was wary but hopeful. "Can you really?"

"I certainly can. It'll take just a few minutes with a needle and thread and it'll be good as new."

"I have something Ma made for me, too," Noah interjected.

Giving Pru time to decide if she would entrust her precious doll's well-being to her, Cassie turned to the boy. "And what might that be?"

He scrambled off the bed and moved to the trunk. After a moment of rummaging around, he pulled out a soft leather pouch and held it up proudly for Cassie to see. "Ma made it from a deer hide. And she stitched my name on it in blue thread. See?"

"I do. It looks like a very well-made pouch, and the stitching is exquisite."

"She said it was a special bag to hold all my treasures in."

"And what sorts of treasures do you keep in it?"

Noah opened the bag and poured the contents out on the bed. "This rock comes from the creek where I used to go fishing with Uncle Riley. And this is the brass hook that used to hang on the front porch to hold a lantern. And this is a blue jay feather I found once when Ma took us blackberry picking."

"What splendid treasures." Cassie noticed he hadn't

mentioned his father. Was there a story there? She was tempted to ask, but decided not to. No point putting the boy on the spot if it was a sensitive topic.

She put a finger to her chin. "You know," she said slowly, "I imagine Mrs. Flanagan would enjoy getting a look at these fine treasures of yours."

Noah started tucking his things back into the pouch. "I'll go show her right now." And with that, he sprinted out of the room.

Cassie turned back to Pru. "So, shall I see about fixing Miss Bitsy's eyes for you?"

After another moment's hesitation, the little girl nodded. "Yes, please."

Cassie stood. "Then why don't I draw you a nice warm bath and add some baking soda to it? That ought to give you at least a small bit of relief from all that itching. Would you like that?"

Pru nodded, but her expression was uncertain.

Ignoring her reservations, Cassie smiled. "Very well. You stay here while I go draw your bath, and I'll fetch you once it's ready. Then, while you're soaking in the tub, I'll work on getting Bitsy fixed up."

Twenty minutes later, Cassie entered the parlor with the doll and her sewing box in hand.

Mrs. Flanagan sat near the sofa, an open book in her hands. Noah sat on the floor playing with a half-dozen tin soldiers, while Dapple watched him with lazily slitted eyes.

The widow glanced up and frowned. "What's that you've got there?"

Cassie explained the situation as she sat on the sofa. "Anyway, I could tell this doll means a lot to Pru and I thought it might cheer her up to have it fixed up."

She went to work immediately, reattaching Bitsy's left eye and securing the right one more firmly for good measure. Not satisfied leaving it at that, Cassie studied the doll critically. "Her dress could do with a good washing. I just wish I had something to fashion another garment from while this one dries."

Mrs. Flanagan straightened in her wheelchair. "I have just the thing." Turning adroitly, she exited the room and then returned a few moments later with a colorful scarf that she held out to Cassie. "Use this."

Cassie studied the bright yellow, flower-bedecked fabric and glanced up uncertainly. "Are you sure? I'll have to cut it."

The widow waved a hand dismissively. "Go right ahead. I never wear the thing—yellow is not a good color for me."

As Cassie washed the doll's original dress in the kitchen basin, she took note of the small, evenly spaced stitching. Pru's mother had taken a great deal of care when she'd stitched this for her daughter.

To fashion the new doll-sized garment, Cassie cut the scarf to a suitable length, then simply folded it in half and cut a hole at the fold large enough to fit the doll's head through. She quickly basted the sides together and then used one of her own ribbons to serve as a belt.

Then, for good measure, she worked on cleaning the doll's face and smoothing out her yarn hair.

She was quite pleased with the result and even Mrs. Flanagan called it a job well done.

Once Cassie was finished, she helped Pru dry off and dress, and then brought Bitsy to her. Pru was delighted with her changed appearance.

"Don't worry," Cassie assured her, "as soon as the

dress your mother made for Bitsy is dry, you can change her right back into it. And then you can keep this one as a spare so she doesn't have to wear the same clothes all the time."

"Thank you." Pru held up the doll. "And Bitsy says thank you, too. She likes having two dresses."

Cassie was touched by the girl's simple gratitude. Perhaps, if she had some spare time, she would make the doll another proper dress.

When Riley retuned to Mrs. Flanagan's home that afternoon, he found the widow and Noah in the kitchen with Cassie. Cassie was at the table pouring a custard-like substance into a dough-lined pie dish.

He set a small sack of apples he'd picked up at the mercantile on the counter. "I had a hankering for an apple this afternoon and figured it would be rude to eat one in front of you all, so I bought enough for everyone." He picked one up and polished it on his shirt. Then he held it out. "Any takers?"

Mrs. Flanagan and Noah each accepted one, but Cassie shook her head.

"Maybe later," she said with a smile.

"Working on another pie, I see. Will this one be an experiment, as well?"

Mrs. Flanagan replied for Cassie. "Every dessert she makes these days is an experiment of one sort or another."

"She said I could help if I wanted to," Noah declared, his chest puffing out in self-importance.

"Helping is good," Riley said mildly. Then he remarked, to no one in particular, "You folks sure do have some fine weather in these parts."

"Better than where you came from?" Cassie asked curiously.

"It was raining there the day we left." Then he turned back to Mrs. Flanagan. "I imagine a lady as independent as you obviously are has a hard time being confined to the house."

The widow nodded. "I sure do miss being able to come and go as I please."

"Then how would you like to go for a bit of a stroll this afternoon?"

She glared at him. "That is not amusing."

"I didn't intend for it to be. In fact, I was quite serious."

"Then you must be addled. As you can see, I'm not in any condition to be doing any strolling."

"Perhaps I should have said how would you like to accompany Miss Vickers on a stroll."

Mrs. Flanagan's lips pinched even tighter. "Again, given the steps, I'm confined to the house and porch."

"Ah, but that's not strictly true. You need to use your imagination to see the possibilities."

Her frown took on a tinge of curiosity. "What do you mean?"

"Come on, I'll show you." Riley pushed the wheeled chair out onto the porch, inviting Cassie and Noah to follow.

Once they were all gathered there, Riley bent down and lifted the startled woman from her chair, cradling her carefully in his arms. Holding her as if she weighed nothing at all, he turned to the younger woman. "Miss Vickers, if you don't mind."

She quickly maneuvered the chair down the stairs and settled it on the walkway.

Riley followed with his surprised-speechless burden and settled her in the chair once again. "How's that?"

Mrs. Flanagan finally found her tongue. "That, young man, was highly impertinent. I will thank you not to ever take such liberties with my person again, at least not without my permission."

Riley schooled his expression in some semblance of contrition. "Yes, ma'am. I surely will not."

She shifted in her chair, her back straight as a fence post and her chin tilted up imperiously. "But now that I'm down here, I might as well take advantage of it. Cassie Lynn, I have a hankering to take a turn down Main Street."

"Yes, ma'am." Cassie's tone was bland, but Riley noticed the amused glint in her eye as she moved behind her employer and grasped the chair's handles.

Riley caught her gaze and gave her a quick wink. Cassie had a sudden coughing fit, no doubt to cover the laugh he saw threatening to spill out of her.

Then he stepped back. "Enjoy your stroll, ladies. And don't worry, Mrs. Flanagan, I'll be here to carry you back up the steps when you return."

With that, he nonchalantly stuck his hands in his pockets and went back inside. The fact that he'd made Cassie smile at him more favorably again had brightened his day more than it should have.

Cassie couldn't hide her smile as she began pushing the chair down the sidewalk. Who would have guessed Riley would be so good at charming her employer?

"Slow down," Mrs. Flanagan said. "We're not running a race here."

"Of course." She slowed her pace. "Just let me know if there's somewhere you want to stop, or when you're ready to turn around and head back for home."

"Of course I will," Mrs. Flanagan said acerbically. "You know I'm not one to be afraid to speak up."

It was nearly forty minutes later before they returned to the house. Noah was sitting on the porch, and as soon as he spotted them he sprinted inside. A few minutes later Riley stepped out, ready to carry Mrs. Flanagan up the stairs. This time, before he lifted her from her chair, he asked permission with exaggerated formality.

He was rewarded for his efforts with a glare. "Don't think you're fooling me, young man. I know impertinence when I see it." Then she gave a regal nod. "But yes, you may carry me back up the stairs. "

Later that afternoon, after Riley had taken care of the wayward tree branch, he paused at the back door. Looking into the kitchen, he wasn't surprised to see Cassie at the stove.

He watched as she stirred a pot, and listened to her soft humming. The domesticity of the scene tugged at him, stirred a longing in him he hadn't realized was there.

A moment later she lifted her cook spoon and took a taste of whatever was in the pot. Her gaze met his just as she swallowed. Her eyes widened and her cheeks colored prettily, as if she were embarrassed to have been caught in the act.

Hiding a grin, he opened the door and stepped inside. "Hope I didn't startle you?"

She returned his smile self-consciously. "Just a little bit."

"Please let me make it up to you. What can I do to help?"

She shook her head. "You've been working all day. I'm sure you want to sit back and relax for a bit before supper."

But he was having none of that. "Surely there's something I can do."

Before she could answer, Mrs. Flanagan wheeled herself into the room, Noah at her side. "Good, you're both here. I wanted to speak to you."

Noting that Cassie once more looked like a schoolgirl who'd been caught at something, Riley turned with a smile to his hostess. "What can we do for you, ma'am?"

"I want to make certain you are both planning to go to church service tomorrow."

Cassie responded first. "Riley should go, by all means. But I'll stay. I can't leave you here to take care of Pru by yourself."

But the widow didn't agree. "I won't be by myself. Noah can help me keep Pru entertained."

Riley's nephew nodded. "Yes, ma'am. I'm real good at that."

Riley spoke up. "No, that's mighty generous of you to offer, but the kids are my responsibility. We'll be fine here while you ladies are at church."

Mrs. Flanagan drew herself up. "Young man, I'm not being generous, I'm being practical. As long as I'm stuck in this chair I won't be attending church service. My home's not the only building in town with porch steps that prevent me from entry on my own.

"And no," she continued before he could speak, "I will *not* allow you to carry me up and down the church steps. You will please allow an old woman her dignity."

She settled back in her chair. "Now, you two will go on to church, Noah and I will watch over Pru and that's that." She eyed Riley sternly. "And don't tell me again that you aren't going. I won't be housing any heathens in my home."

"Yes, ma'am. I mean, no, ma'am. I mean, of course I'll go. If you're sure you can handle watching the children on your own."

"Oh, for goodness sake, I'm quite capable of watching over a sick child for a few hours. If you don't believe me, remember that I raised two boys of my own and nursed them through any number of illnesses and injuries. Besides, if there's something I can't reach or do because of this confounded chair, then, since Pru is not entirely bedridden, she'll be able to get up and help me."

Riley stepped out on the porch that evening to find Cassie in the exact spot he'd seen her in last night. Only this time she wasn't hugging her knees. She was leaning back, with her hands grasping the edge of the step on either side of her.

"Mind if I join you?"

"Not at all."

He leaned against the support post and folded his arms. "So how did your walk with Mrs. Flanagan this afternoon *really* go?"

Cassie looked up at him, her eyes sparkling in the moonlight. "Actually, I think she enjoyed it quite a bit. We stopped in at the mercantile and she told everyone there the story about how her roguish houseguest just picked her up without so much as a by-your-leave and carried her down the steps. But even though her words were tart, I could hear the smile in her voice. "

"Good. Then we'll try it again tomorrow afternoon. And I won't let her give me no for an answer." Then he grimaced. "Did she really call me roguish?"

Cassie grinned. "Her exact words."

Riley decided it was time to change the subject. "What did you do before you came to work for Mrs. Flanagan?"

"I worked at the restaurant."

That made sense. "Baking those tasty pies of yours, no doubt."

"Sometimes. But Daisy, the owner, is a terrific cook and she loves preparing the dishes for her customers, so I was mostly there to help with the cleanup and the serving."

"That's a waste of a good talent." He studied her curiously. "Will you stay here with Mrs. Flanagan when she's on her feet again, or go back to the restaurant?"

"I'm not sure." Cassie hugged her knees, as if in need of comfort. "I mean, I won't be going back to the restaurant—Daisy only hired me because she needed help when her youngest was born. Little Danielle is nearly nine months old now and, with her family's help, Daisy seems to have things well in hand."

Her tone had been matter-of-fact, but he detected some emotion under the surface.

"And staying with Mrs. Flanagan?"

Cassie kept her face turned away. "She's offered to help me with my bakery business, to let me live here and have the use of her kitchen, for a twenty percent share of the business."

"Sounds like a fair offer."

"Oh yes, more than fair."

When she didn't continue right away, Riley gave her a conversational nudge. "But?"

"But I'm not certain there will be a bakery business."

That surprised him. Cassie seemed so animated when she spoke of the orders she received and the new recipes she was concocting. "Have you decided it's too much work?"

"Not at all. I enjoy baking, and the idea of earning my own way doing something I truly enjoy is like a wonderful dream." Her enthusiasm faded as quickly as it had appeared. "But not all dreams are meant to come true."

He hadn't figured her as one to back down from a challenge. "Most good ideas start with a dream."

She lifted her hand in an uncharacteristically fatalistic gesture. "Perhaps."

Then she cut him a challenging look. "And if owning a horse ranch is your ultimate dream, why are you putting it off?"

He recognized that she was trying to move the attention away from herself, but he let it go. "It's definitely my long-term goal. But for the time being, I need to focus on caring for the kids and keeping them safe."

"An admirable goal. But you say that as if you can't you do both. I'm sure the children would enjoy living on a horse ranch. And not just enjoy it, but thrive there. Noah especially, since he seems quite fond of animals. And having a permanent place to call home would do them both good."

That again. "The timing's just not right at the moment. Maybe someday." How had she got him talking about himself? Time to change the subject.

But before he could do so, she spoke up again.

"You know, Mrs. Flanagan was right when she said there was plenty of land around here that would be perfect for a horse ranch. And Turnabout is a very nice place for a kid to grow up in."

Riley needed to snuff out this topic of conversation with the finality of a candle flame doused in a downpour. "I don't doubt it, but I'm afraid this is not the area of the country I aim to settle down in."

Her brows drew down. "You have something against Turnabout?"

Was she deliberately trying to misunderstand him? He raised his hands, palms out. "Turnabout seems like a fine town, but I think I'd like something a little farther West."

"And what can you find farther West that you can't find right here?"

"The land of opportunity."

She wrinkled her nose. "And California is where you find that?"

"That's right. Do you have something against California?"

"I don't know enough about the area to have an opinion one way or the other. I'm just curious as to what exactly you think you'll find there."

"Exploring a new place and learning new ways of doing things is part of the draw. And I imagine we'll see all sorts of other new and interesting sights along the way." He hoped his tone and expression didn't betray just how tired he was of traveling—no, running—from place to place.

Riley hated seeing the disapproval in Cassie's eyes,

hated not being able to explain to her why it was best
for them to keep moving.

Part of him felt that she would understand, would
even help him if he explained things to her. And if it
was just his well-being at stake, he might have done so.
But he knew he couldn't take that chance with Pru and
Noah's future, no matter how tempted he was.

Cassie found Riley's words disturbing. That foot-
loose way of life might appeal to someone with an
adventurous nature and no real ties, but he had responsibilities, children who were depending on him. He appeared to care a great deal for Pru and Noah—did he
really not understand how constantly moving around
from town to town, without the opportunity to form
any permanent connections, would affect them? For one
thing, she suspected this was why Noah hadn't spent
much time in a classroom.

Perhaps she'd been too hasty in forming an opinion
of Riley's character. Was his concern for the children
secondary to his own thirst for travel and adventure?

Land of opportunity indeed. Surely he wasn't trying to chase some pot of gold at the end of a rainbow.
She hadn't figured him for the mercenary sort, but then
again, how well did she really know him? But she felt a
sharp stab of disappointment at the very idea that this
might be true.

Later, as Cassie lay in bed, she tried to reconcile what
she thought she knew about Riley with his seeming in-
difference to what his gallivanting about was doing to
the children. A part of her refused to believe that indif-
ference was real. Perhaps it was just her seeing what

she wanted to see, but she sensed a struggle in him, a travel-weariness, whenever the subject came up.

Who was the real Riley Walker and what was his story? And why was it so important to her to find the answer?

Chapter Thirteen

Riley was surprised when he stepped into the kitchen the next morning to find Cassie awake and up before him once again. Not only was she up, but she'd stoked the fire in the stove and gathered up the eggs. How much, or little, sleep did the woman get in a night?

When she spotted him, she offered a polite smile. "Good morning. How did it go with Pru last night?"

He shrugged. "She woke a few times whimpering about how much she itched. I did what you suggested— gave her the lotion to use, told her a few stories, tried to keep her mind off her discomfort." He took a long swallow from his cup. "She's asleep right now, so I figured I'd slip out to get some coffee."

Cassie nodded as she grabbed the flour. "Hopefully there will just be another day or two of this severe itching before she starts feeling better."

Remembering her disappointment in him last evening, he studied her without further comment as she prepared the dough to make biscuits, trying to gauge her feelings this morning. But he couldn't really tell.

"I see you repaired the fence around the chicken

coop," she finally said as she placed the sheet of biscuits in the oven. "I suppose you took care of that while I was out with Mrs. Flanagan yesterday."

He nodded, encouraged by the friendliness of her tone.

She shoved a stray hair off her forehead with one flour-dusted wrist. "Thank you."

Was that thank-you prompted merely by gratitude for a good deed? Or had that small act been enough to sway her into letting him back into her good graces? "You're quite welcome. But there's no need to say anything to Mrs. Flanagan about it."

"Of course not. Informing her is entirely up to you."

Good. He really didn't want to deal with the woman's prickly pride. "Speaking of maintenance work, which of the windows is it that's stuck?"

"The one in the dining room that faces Dr. Pratt's home."

Riley made a mental note. That would be the next chore he tackled.

Cassie placed a large bowl on the table and started cracking eggs and dumping them into it.

"After sitting up with Pru last night, I'm wondering if I should leave Mrs. Flanagan alone with her, after all," Riley murmured.

Cassie paused and gave him a probing look, as if trying to gauge his motives. "There isn't anything in Pru's care that requires the person watching over her to stand up and walk. And Noah will be here to help."

The same arguments Mrs. Flanagan had used last night. "Still—"

"And it isn't as if we'll be gone all day." Cassie grabbed a whisk and began whipping the eggs. "However, if you want to tell Mrs. Flanagan that you don't think she's up to it, either because she's old, or she's in that chair, or both, then that's your right." Her expression took on an exaggeratedly pious look. "Perhaps you won't hurt her feelings too terribly."

He frowned at her. "You, Miss Vickers, do not play fair."

Her only response was a saucy grin.

Cassie strolled down the sidewalk toward church feeling slightly self-conscious. She'd never had a gentleman at her side like this, at least not one who wasn't her father or a brother.

And they were drawing quite a bit of notice. Most of the looks, she was sure, were due to the fact that Riley was new to town. And since most of his time had been spent either at the livery or Mrs. Flanagan's house, not many of the townsfolk had met him yet.

The two of them stopped along the way several times to exchange greetings and for Cassie to introduce Riley.

And was it her imagination or was he getting more than one interested second glance from some of the single ladies in town?

They arrived at church just as the bells rang to indicate the service would soon begin. Riley escorted her inside and then let her choose the pew.

Cassie slipped into one near the back, not wanting to walk the gauntlet of eyes that sitting farther up would have cost her.

As they settled in their seats, she remembered Mrs. Flanagan's instructions. The widow had pulled her aside just before they left. "I know you've had your hands full since our houseguests moved in, and haven't had much time to yourself. This will be a good opportunity to look around at the bachelors in this town and see if there are any other names you want to add to your husband list."

To be honest, Cassie was becoming more disenchanted with the whole idea of this husband-candidate list by the day. Not that her situation had changed any. Just her enthusiasm.

She spotted Mr. Edmondson seated two rows ahead of her. He was a broadly built, well-muscled man, as was fitting for a blacksmith. She could see why Mrs. Flanagan had suggested him. Though his beard sported more than a hint of gray, he seemed quite vital.

As unobtrusively as she could, Cassie glanced around the rest of the congregation while the last few stragglers took their seats. Ignoring the married men and those she considered too old or too young, she tried to identify any additional candidates she should consider for her list.

Her gaze paused when she spotted her older brother, Verne, and his wife, Dinah, across the aisle and three rows up. They had her youngest brother, Bart, with them. She was glad Dinah had taken a stand about going to church on Sunday and that Verne had supported her. After Ma died, Pa had decided going to church service was a waste of time, and allowed them to go only at Christmas and Easter.

Moving on, Cassie spotted a few men who seemed to be unattached, but who she didn't know by name. Perhaps—

"Looking for someone?"

Riley's question brought her back to her surroundings with a snap.

She shook her head as she tried unsuccessfully to

hold back the warmth climbing in her cheeks. "No one in particular."

Then, thankfully, the organist began to play and the two of them faced forward to participate in the service.

Reverend Harper's sermon was based on Colossians 3:17 this morning. As Cassie listened to him speak on doing everything in the name of the Lord, she wondered if she was truly doing that. Had she prayed for guidance on this matter of whether to return home to her father or not? Was this marriage-for-convenience's-sake that she was contemplating really what the Lord wanted for her?

Many people married for reasons other than love, but were her own strong enough to do so? Cassie couldn't shake the feeling that perhaps she had set her feet on the wrong path.

As they exited the church following the service, Reverend Harper was there to greet the members of his congregation.

"Well, hello, Cassie Lynn. It's so nice to see you here this morning. I trust Mrs. Flanagan is doing well."

"Thank you, Reverend, and yes, she is." She indicated Riley with a wave of her hand. "Allow me to introduce Mr. Riley Walker. He and his niece and nephew are visiting in Turnabout."

"Mr. Walker, welcome to Turnabout. I've heard about your niece's unfortunate situation. I hope she recovers soon."

Riley took the proffered hand and gave it a quick shake. "Thank you, Reverend. Fortunately, Miss Vickers and Mrs. Flanagan took pity on us and are helping with the nursing duties."

"You couldn't find two finer ladies to take you in."

After that, he turned to the next in line and Cassie and Riley moved on.

They hadn't taken more than a few steps into the churchyard when she was hailed from behind.

Turning, she saw her brothers and sister-in-law bearing down on them. Hoping they weren't going to mention anything about her father's plans for her, Cassie smiled and exchanged greetings, then introduced Riley.

Fifteen-year-old Bart seemed to be taken with a petite blond-haired girl across the way, and as soon as the introductions were complete, excused himself to join her.

Verne, however, didn't seem quite so eager to move on. He extended his hand toward Riley. "Mr. Walker, you're new to town, aren't you?"

Riley shook it firmly. "Just got here Wednesday."

Cassie was confused. It appeared to her that the men's hands were clasped a bit too tightly and that Verne was studying Riley with an assessing, none too friendly look. What had gotten into him?

"You planning to stay long?"

"Just until my niece gets over the chicken pox."

While Verne's tone continued to sound confrontational, Riley's had a slightly amused hint to it.

Ignoring the menfolk, Dinah linked her arm with Cassie's. "Did you hear that Verne and I are getting our own place?"

Trying to keep one ear on the other conversation, Cassie nodded and smiled. "Pa told me." She gave Dinah's arm a squeeze. "I'm so happy for you both."

"I'm so excited. Our own place at last." She spent several minutes talking about the new house Verne was working on, and then she paused and gave Cassie an abashed look. "Not that I don't enjoy living at your pa's place, but—"

Cassie squeezed her arm again. "No need to explain. I moved out as quickly as I could, remember?"

Dinah's lips curved up in a shared grin, but her smile quickly faded. "I'm sorry if our good fortune means you'll have to move back."

This time Cassie cut her off for an entirely different reason as she cast a quick glance Riley's way. "Let's not talk of that now. And no matter what, I'm still happy for you."

She caught sight of Verne's expression just then and was alarmed by how belligerent he looked. What had they just been discussing—something about Riley's living arrangements? Mercy, was Verne playing the role of her protector?

She quickly stepped forward. "Verne, Dinah has just been telling me about the new place you are building. It sounds wonderful."

Verne's expression immediately shifted to one of pride. "Nothing but the best for my wife."

Time to bring this exchange to a close before anything was said that shouldn't be. "Well, it was nice seeing you all, but I need to get back to the house. I don't want to leave Mrs. Flanagan alone with the sick little girl for too long. Tell Pa and Norris and Dwayne hi for me."

With that Cassie gave Riley a let's-go look and turned toward the sidewalk. To her relief he said his goodbyes and fell into step beside her.

"I apologize if my brother made you uncomfortable. I don't know what he was thinking."

"He was thinking 'who is this stranger with my little sister?' And there's no need to apologize—I would probably have done the same thing if I'd been in his shoes."

She thought about that all the way back to Mrs. Flanagan's house.

The widow and the kids had indeed managed quite nicely on their own. When Cassie and Riley returned, they found the trio at the kitchen table, a child sitting on each side of the woman while they pored over a book with pictures of exotic animals. They seemed almost disappointed when Cassie and Riley walked in and Mrs. Flanagan said it was time to put the book away and get ready for lunch.

Riley struggled all through lunch with his decision over what to do about Wednesday's meeting. He'd held his own counsel, relied on his own resources, for so long that letting someone in at this point seemed both wrong and uncomfortable. But he couldn't let this opportunity to take care of Guy once and for all slip through his fingers out of misguided pride.

By the end of the meal he'd reached a decision. As soon as the table was cleared and the children had been sent off to take naps, he asked Cassie if they could talk out on the back porch.

She followed him out, took her customary seat on the steps, arranged her skirt and then looked up at him. "Now, what was it you wanted to speak to me about?"

Riley tugged one of his cuffs, gathering his resolve. This was it. He either trusted her enough to tell her the whole truth, or he didn't.

He looked into her concerned face and made his decision.

"I have a favor to ask of you."

Chapter Fourteen

Cassie could tell by the expression on Riley's face that there was something of great import on his mind. Was it just because he found it so difficult to ask for help, or was something else going on here?

"What can I do for you?"

"I need to be in Tyler early Wednesday morning for a very important business meeting. And of course, I can't take the kids with me in their current condition."

Was that all? "You want me to watch them while you're gone. I'll be glad—"

He lifted a hand to stop her. "Before you agree, there are some things I need to tell you that might change the way you feel about us."

She doubted that, but merely nodded. "Go on."

"It concerns the man who is the children's father and my stepbrother, Guy Simpson."

Now she was confused. "But, I mean, isn't the children's father deceased?"

"No, but their mother is." Riley tightened his lips for a moment, as if repressing some unpleasant thought. "Let me start at the beginning. My mother married

Guy's father when I was eight years old and Guy was fifteen. They came to live on the horse ranch my father had built and operated before he passed. At first I not only liked but admired Guy. He was charming, athletic, handsome and very articulate—everything an eight-year-old boy would like to grow up to be. He could charm the rattle from a rattlesnake. And, as it turns out, he was just about as treacherous."

Cassie heard the disgust in Riley's voice and wasn't certain she really wanted to hear the rest of this story.

"After a while," he continued, "I began to sense he wasn't the person he appeared to be on the surface. But even then, it took some time for me to understand the depths of his corruption. He didn't seem to be bothered by any of the treachery he took part in, as if he didn't have a conscience."

Cassie's stomach tightened as she absorbed his words. How awful it must have been to know such a person was a part of his own household.

"Then he met Nancy Greene. She came from a fairly well-to-do family and spent most of her adolescence back east in boarding and finishing schools. It was when she returned home for good that her and Guy's paths crossed. Guy brought all his charm to bear in wooing her and quickly won her favor. Her father wasn't as easily won over, however. I'm not sure if it was because he suspected what kind of man Guy was or because he wanted better for his daughter than some horse rancher's son."

Already Cassie felt her heart go out to Nancy. It sounded as if neither her father nor her suitor were really honorable men.

"Mr. Greene promised to disown his daughter if

she married Guy, but Guy vowed that it was Nancy he wanted, not her money. Of course, that was a lie. No one really believed Jerome Greene would disown his only child.

"But he did. On the day of their wedding, Greene made out a new will, leaving everything he owned to some distant cousin who lived hundreds of miles away." Riley's lips twisted in a crooked smile. "I think he would have eventually relented, but he never had the chance. Three days after the wedding he died of a heart attack."

Cassie could guess how the man Riley was describing would have reacted to that.

"My stepfather was more generous—he gave the newlyweds sixty acres of our ranch land, a piece that was suitable for farming, as a wedding gift. But Guy never thought he was cut out to be a rancher or farmer— he had much loftier ambitions. He blamed Nancy, and he was not above abusing her when he drank or his temper flared."

Cassie saw Riley's hands curl into fists and felt her own anger burn.

"Of course, not many people knew this darker side of Guy. He and Nancy put on a good front when they were in public. But I saw evidence of it with my own eyes."

There was a haunted look in his face and she refrained from asking exactly what it was he'd witnessed.

"Guy began hunting for other ways to make the kind of money he thought he deserved. He took long trips away from home, leaving Nancy to tend to the farm on her own, and would eventually return with large sums of money. At first I thought he'd taken to gambling, and that might have been part of it. But when Pru was barely four, he took her, against Nancy's will, on one of these trips, and when he returned I heard him brag about how easy it was to charm rich widows into just handing over their money, especially when there was a young child in the picture.

"Eventually, his crimes caught up with him. Four years ago Guy was arrested and put in prison for taking part in a bank robbery. He was given a three-year sentence."

Four years ago... Noah would have been little more than a toddler. But Pru would have been old enough to have a sense of what was happening.

"Nancy was left running the farm and raising the kids on her own, though that wasn't much different than it had been before Guy went to prison. She actually did well, until she got sick. That's when she contacted me for help.

"I stayed with her, keeping the farm running and doing what I could, until she passed two months later. Before she died, she made me promise not to let Guy get hold of the children again. She was afraid of how he would use them to further his own ends. And also what kind of treatment they'd receive at his hands."

There was a long pause and Cassie spoke up. "That's all so horrible. I can see why you're so protective of Noah and Pru. Where is their father now?" She'd done the math—the man had been out of prison for a year at this point.

"Unfortunately, I have reason to believe Guy's trying to track the kids down. That's why we move around so much. I'm trying to stay ahead of him."

"Do the children know that's the reason?"

"Yes. I thought it best to be honest with them so that if Guy does show up they won't be caught unawares."

"But I don't understand. If he's as bad as you say, surely you can make a case for not letting him have control of the children."

Riley's jaw tightened. "There's no 'if' to it. And the stakes are too high for me to take a chance. He's their father, after all. I'm just their uncle. By law, he has more right to them than I do, and I'm afraid I'd ultimately be forced to hand them over." Riley shook his head. "You don't know Guy. I've seen him talk his way out of situations where he's been caught dead to rights, more times than you could imagine. When I said he's charming I wasn't exaggerating. You sit down and talk to him, and look into those sincere blue eyes of his, and before long you find yourself believing every word coming out of his mouth. I can't risk the kids' futures on my ability to convince the law that he's a liar and a crook. Especially a lawman or judge who has no reason to take my word over his."

Cassie turned the topic back to its original focus. "And this meeting on Wednesday… It has something to do with keeping him away from Noah and Pru?"

Riley nodded. "Before she died, Nancy told me about another crime Guy committed—the Ploverton bank robbery. That crime was much worse than the one he got arrested and went to prison for. In the Ploverton robbery a great deal more money was involved and two people were killed, including a young man whose wife was expecting their first child."

The black marks against the children's father just kept growing.

"Guy bragged to Nancy about his involvement, but

there was no proof she could offer the law besides what they called hearsay."

"But now you've found some kind of proof?"

"One of the first things I did when Nancy died was hire a Pinkerton detective to try to find some evidence that would prove Guy was indeed involved in that robbery. If I can find that proof, then Guy will be sent back to prison, this time for much, much longer than three years. That detective, Mr. Claypool, thinks he's finally close to finding that proof."

Cassie placed a hand on Riley's arm. "Then of course you must go. And don't worry about the children, I'll keep a close eye on them."

He stared at her hand a minute and she started to pull it away. But then he covered it with his own and met her gaze. "I need to make certain you understand that Guy is actively looking for them. I think it's unlikely he'll show up here the one day I'm gone, but if he does, things could get ugly."

"I'll be ready. Besides, with the children having chicken pox, he won't be able to go anywhere with them." She drew herself up. "I can fetch Sheriff Gleason if Guy so much as thinks about doing so."

Riley grinned at that. "Feisty. Like a bear protecting her cubs."

Cassie's cheeks warmed, but so did her heart.

She reluctantly drew her hand away, missing the warmth of his touch almost immediately.

No wonder the children never spoke of their father. Noah, of course, would have been only two or three when the man went to prison, so he likely didn't remember much of him.

But Pru, poor Pru, who had been used in some of

his schemes and who had likely witnessed how the man treated her mother... The memories she had were no doubt of the nightmare variety.

If there was anything she could do to help Riley keep those children safe, Cassie would do it.

Even if it meant watching them walk out of her life.

Chapter Fifteen

"Cassie, I need you to do me a favor when you go out to deliver your baked goods."

Cassie paused from packing the hamper and glanced up at her employer. Breakfast was over and she and Mrs. Flanagan had the kitchen to themselves for the moment. Riley was in the backyard with Noah, and Pru was settled in her room with a book.

"Of course," she replied. "Do you need me to pick something up from one of the merchants?"

Mrs. Flanagan held out a slip of paper. "I'd like you to deliver this to Betty Pratt on your way back. And wait for an answer."

Cassie took the missive and slipped it into her pocket. "Pru passed a much easier night last night. I know she has a way to go yet, but hopefully she's been through the worst of it now."

"That's good news," the widow said with a nod. "Especially since Noah's likely to show symptoms soon."

Cassie lifted her basket, feeling the weight of it. If she received many more orders she'd need to make her deliveries in two trips. All in all, not a terrible problem to have.

As she went about delivering her baked goods, she found her mind playing back the conversation with Riley yesterday evening. It was hard to believe that anyone could be as truly reprehensible as Riley had described his stepbrother. But she knew, even though she'd never experienced it herself, that there really was evil in the world.

It warmed her heart that he'd trusted her, not only with such a personal, painful story, but with the care of the children. She only hoped she could be strong enough to protect them should the need arise.

Cassie stopped at the Pratt home on her way back, as Mrs. Flanagan had asked, and gave Mrs. Pratt the note.

After reading it, the doctor's wife looked up and smiled at her. "Tell Irene that, yes, I'd be delighted." The twinkle in her eye made Cassie wonder just exactly what the two older women were cooking up.

When she reported back to Mrs. Flanagan, the widow gave a satisfied nod. "Excellent." Then she turned to Riley, stopping him as he headed out for the livery. "By the way, Mr. Walker, I would appreciate it if you could be back by ten thirty this morning. I have something I'd like you to do for me."

"That shouldn't be a problem." He raised an eyebrow. "Mind if I ask what it is you need me to do? Just in case I should pick up some tools or supplies."

She waved a hand. "No tools required. Now, there's no time to get into everything right now. I'll explain when you get back."

Riley exchanged a look with Cassie, and she

shrugged to indicate she was as much in the dark as he was.

Not that she wasn't curious. But the widow was apparently enjoying this little touch of mystery, and Cassie wouldn't begrudge her that.

Riley had a smile on his face as he headed back to Mrs. Flanagan's home after his morning shift at the livery was complete. Had the widow put off the explanation because she was afraid he'd turn her down? Or was she planning some sort of surprise? Whatever it was she had for him to do, he'd do it. The woman had been too generous to him and the kids for him to refuse her anything.

He jammed his hands in his pockets, thinking about that. Mrs. Flanagan and Cassie had been more than generous. They'd treated him and the kids like family. And that was something he no longer took for granted.

He stepped into the kitchen to find Cassie, Mrs. Flanagan and a woman he'd never met already there.

Mrs. Flanagan was the first to greet him. "Oh, good, you're right on time."

"On time for what?"

"To meet Doc Pratt's wife. Riley Walker, this is Betty Pratt. Betty, this is Riley Walker."

"Pleased to meet you, ma'am." Was Mrs. Flanagan going to ask him to do something at the house next door?

"I've been watching you two young people work yourselves ragged trying to do everything—take care of the kids, the house, the upkeep, the cooking, your job." She waved a hand. "Like I said, everything."

Cassie's brow furrowed. "But that's what—"

Mrs. Flanagan didn't let her finish. "You two are not going to be any good to me or the children or anyone else if you wear yourself down to nubs."

Riley crossed his arms and waited, intrigued to see where she was going with this.

"Now, Betty has agreed to stay with the kids and me for the next several hours, and Riley here doesn't need to get back to the livery until later this afternoon, so that leaves about four hours for you two to get out of this house and do something relaxing. Take a walk, or better yet, go on a picnic. Cassie, you can show Riley here some of the nice spots in the area—Mercer's Pond, Gibson's meadow, the old lookout point on the bluff."

"Oh, and there's that pretty spot out near the Keeter farm," Mrs. Pratt added. "And see—" she pointed to a hamper on the kitchen table "—at Irene's request, I packed a cold meal for two, so there's no need to worry about your lunch."

"Of course, it's entirely up to you where you go and what you do," Mrs. Flanagan stated. "I just want you two away from this house for the next several hours. We'll all benefit if you come back refreshed."

Cassie crossed her arms over her chest, her raised brow and stiff posture making it obvious something had got her back up. "Are you saying you're not happy with the way I've been doing my job lately?" she asked.

"Goodness, girl, don't get prickly. All I'm saying is you deserve a bit of time off before you wear yourself out. And if you don't believe you do, then what about Riley here? Don't think I haven't noticed all the little things that are suddenly working again around here. Don't you think he deserves a bit of relaxation?"

Riley wasn't sure how he felt about Mrs. Flanagan

using him as leverage to get Cassie to agree to her plan. Then again, he found he liked the idea of a guilt-free outing with Cassie, so he decided to hold his peace.

She glanced his way. "What do you think?"

He spread his hands in a gesture of surrender. "I'm thinking we don't have much choice."

A few minutes later Cassie found herself on the front porch, with Riley holding the food basket provided by Mrs. Pratt. She gave her companion a wry smile. "So what do we do now?"

He lifted the basket slightly. "I think we go on a picnic. I'll provide the transportation if you'll direct us to somewhere appropriate." He swept a hand out. "Shall we?"

Fifteen minutes later, when Riley handed her up into the wagon they'd procured at the livery, she noticed River was tied to the back. So he planned to get some riding done while they were out. She supposed she couldn't blame him—he'd had little chance to ride since he'd been here. Duchess was pulling the wagon so she could visit with her old friend while he was getting in his ride.

Riley took his seat and lifted the reins, then turned to her. "So, where shall we go?"

"Since you're bringing River along, I think we should head out to Mercer's Pond. It's a pretty spot and there's a meadow that's fairly open and level that'll be good for riding."

"Sounds perfect. Point the way."

"You know," Cassie said as they headed out of town, "if we'd already told Mrs. Flanagan about your plan to leave for Tyler tomorrow, she might not have thought this outing necessary."

"I don't know about that. It appeared to me that she was just as worried about you getting some time to yourself as she was me."

"For all her brusque ways, she really is a dear lady."

They rode in a comfortable silence for a while.

It was Cassie who broke that silence first. "Do you mind if I ask you a question about your stepbrother?"

He inwardly groaned. It wouldn't be much of an outing if they focused on Guy. But he could hardly tell her no. "Ask away."

"Why would he be so interested in the children? I mean, it sounds as if he didn't pay them much mind before he went to prison. And now that he's free once more, it doesn't seem as if a man like that would want to encumber himself with the care of young children."

That was a fair question. And an intelligent one. "You need to understand the kind of person Guy is. He viewed Nancy and the kids as possessions. They were his, and though he might not pay much attention to them, he never shares anything he considers his with anyone else."

Riley chose his next words carefully. "As I said last night, he's also used Pru to further some of his shady schemes in the past. I'm certain he has plans to do more of the same sort of thing."

Riley saw Cassie's jaw tense. "We can't let him get his hands on them," she declared.

He was warmed by her use of *we.* "We won't." Then he gave her a smile. "Let's not let Guy spoil our outing today. Tell me how your bakery business is going and what plans you have for it moving forward."

To his relief, she took her cue and the conversation moved on to more pleasant topics.

Cassie was almost sorry when they arrived at the pond. She'd enjoyed the ride, sitting close to Riley on the seat of the buckboard, having him listen so attentively to her dreams about the bakery, and not only listen but provide his own thoughts and opinions when she'd asked for them.

When he came around to help her down from the wagon, his hands seemed to stay at her waist a little longer than necessary, not that she found it at all unpleasant.

Once he released her, he let his gaze roam the open meadow and pond. "You were right—this is perfect for a nice ride."

Was he going to abandon her for River so soon?

He studied the pond for a moment. "That looks like a good fishing spot."

"From what I've heard, it is."

He glanced her way. "Don't you fish?"

"I tagged along with my brothers when I was younger, but haven't in a very long time."

"We should have brought some fishing poles today. It's been a while since I baited a hook."

Cassie started to say they could do that next time, but then he remembered there wouldn't be a next time. Instead she gave him an overly innocent look. "How are you at skipping stones?"

"Fair to middlin'." Then he raised a brow. "That wouldn't by any chance be your way of issuing me a challenge?"

"Maybe."

He rolled up his sleeves. "Then you're on."

She was inordinately pleased that he wasn't ready to abandon her for his ride just yet.

They spent the next fifteen minutes or so trying to best each other at the art of skipping stones, while haggling over whether the objective was to get the stone to skip the farthest or the most times.

In the end, they agreed to call it a draw.

Riley took her arm and began moving back to the wagon. "Now it's my turn to issue you a challenge."

"And what challenge would that be?"

He released her and moved toward Duchess. "I think it's high time a person as fond of horses as you are learns to ride."

She frowned, not sure what she thought about that. "Today?"

"No time like the present," he said cheerfully.

"But I'm not dressed for riding."

He studied her garment. "Your skirt is sufficiently full to protect your modesty and you can mount from the bed of the wagon to make it less awkward."

Once he had Duchess unhitched, he led the mare to the back of the wagon, where he lifted out a saddle that had been stowed under a sheet of canvas.

It didn't seem to take him much time at all to get the mare saddled. Then he turned to her. "Ready?"

With a nod she allowed him to assist her into the wagon bed, suddenly feeling quite daring.

Once Cassie was settled in the saddle, he smiled. "Don't worry. Duchess is a steady mount. And you two are already old friends. Now, I'm going to lead her around for a bit and let you get used to the feel of her, okay?"

Cassie nodded and he set Duchess in motion. Riley kept an eye on them, advising Cassie on how to adjust her position, and describing how to give instructions to the horse. He was a patient and articulate teacher and his love of horses really came through. Finally, he gave her an approving look. "I think you're ready to try this on your own."

Cassie wasn't certain she quite agreed with his assessment, but he was already turning to River.

Riley untied the horse from the back of the wagon and mounted him in one quick, graceful movement that earned her admiration. A moment later he had pulled his horse up alongside hers. "We'll ride side by side. Just relax and enjoy."

Easier said than done. By his own admission, he'd been riding since before he could walk. This was her first time riding a horse solo.

But Riley kept his word to stay beside her, mixing words of encouragement with casual conversation, and gradually Cassie felt her apprehension ease. And before long she was actually enjoying herself. So much so that when Riley asked her if she was up for increasing the pace she allowed Duchess to break into a trot without a moment's hesitation.

They ended their ride by letting the horses drink their fill at the pond, then rode them back to the wagon.

Riley dismounted first, then came around to assist Cassie. He had enjoyed watching her gain confidence as a rider. She'd taken to it as easily as he'd figured she would.

Cassie smiled down at him, her face flushed with triumph and exhilaration from her ride. In that moment, she was so achingly beautiful that she took his breath away.

As she slid down trustingly into his arms, his hands tightened around her. Their gazes met and locked, and he could not for the life of him release her. She felt nice in his arms like this—soft, warm, feminine. It was as if they were in a little bubble—isolated, protected, uplifted. Her lips looked so sweet and kissable. What would she do if he put that thought into action?

Then Duchess nickered and the spell was broken.

Chapter Sixteen

Riley abruptly released her and stepped back.

Clearing his throat, he reached for Duchess's reins. "Why don't you get our picnic set up while I tend to the horses?"

"All right."

He heard the confusion in her voice. Was it because of what had almost happened? Or because he'd broken it off before anything could happen?

Best not to ponder that question. Instead he focused on tending to the animals while she retrieved the picnic basket and blanket.

By the time he had the horses taken care of she had the blanket spread under a tree and was unloading the food and dishes.

When he neared, she looked up and offered an easy smile of greeting, as if that little moment of awkwardness between them had never happened. Relieved, he sat down on the blanket across from her.

He wasn't going to push his luck by getting too close to her right now.

"So what did our friends pack us for lunch?" he asked.

"They did very well by us. There's some cold fried chicken, bread, cheese and a couple slices of pound cake."

"A feast, indeed."

Cassie filled their plates, and then Riley asked the blessing.

As they began eating, she gave him a smile. "I can see why you enjoy riding so much. It makes one feel on top of the world."

"So you don't think that'll be your last ride?"

"Not if I can help it."

If only he could stick around here to go on some of those rides with her.

Once they'd finished the main portion of the meal, Cassie placed a piece of cake on two plates and handed one to him. As he took his first bite, though, he realized she was just picking at hers with her fork. Was something worrying her?

"Not hungry?" he asked lightly. "Or do you just prefer pie?"

She glanced up guiltily and then smiled sheepishly. "Last night, you asked me for a favor and shared something very personal with me in order to explain exactly what it was you were asking."

He nodded. "And I truly appreciate your ready agreement to help."

"I was wondering if perhaps I could turn the tables on you now."

"How so?"

"I have a favor to ask, but it involves something a bit personal."

Now this sounded interesting. "Ask away." Whatever this favor was, it must be something big. She seemed unduly nervous and slightly embarrassed.

"The thing is, I don't have much experience speaking to men besides my pa and brothers." She pushed a stray tendril behind her ear, not quite meeting Riley's gaze. "I mean, of course there are shopkeepers and such, but I'm talking about speaking to men on a more personal basis. In fact, there's only you and maybe Mr. Chandler."

Who was this Mr. Chandler? And why had she been speaking to him on a personal basis? But Riley supposed that was none of his business. "Go on."

She fidgeted a moment, then seemed to gather up her courage. "I need to propose marriage to someone, and I don't quite know how to go about it."

That completely unexpected confession set him back, hard. Propose marriage? Had he really heard her right?

She grimaced. "I suppose I should explain."

"That might be best."

"You heard me talking to my brother yesterday about how he and Dinah are going to be moving into their own place soon."

Riley nodded.

"Well, when they do, my pa wants me to move back home so I can take care of him and my other three brothers—cook their meals, do their laundry, keep the house clean, that sort of thing."

In other words, be an unpaid housekeeper. "And you don't want to go." Riley could certainly understand that.

She shook her head, looking miserable. "You must think me a wretchedly ungrateful daughter."

He reached over and clasped her hand. "Not at all.

You're a grown woman, with a life of your own to live. And you deserve to have the opportunity to live it."

"I wish my pa felt that way." Then she sobered again. "The thing is, it's what I did for most of the last ten years. My ma died when I was thirteen, and my pa pulled me out of school so I could do all those chores she always managed." Cassie gave him a weak grin. "I'd never appreciated how much my ma really did until her chores became mine."

Pulled her out of school? Seeing as she set such a great score by schooling, that must have been hard on Cassie.

"The farm is several miles from town, and not on the main road, and after Ma passed, Pa didn't have much use for church. So without school or church services, I didn't get to see many folks besides the family."

"That must have been difficult." And lonely.

She shrugged off his sympathy and continued with her story. "All that changed eight months ago when Verne married Dinah. They moved into the house and I was able to turn it all over to her. I came to town and haven't been back since."

"I can't say I blame you for that. And now your father wants you to return home when your brother and his wife move out."

Cassie nodded. "But don't get me wrong, my pa has a good heart and is a very hard worker. He gets up when the sun rises and works until it sets. He just doesn't think he should be expected to do all the woman's work around the place, too."

Before Riley could respond to that, she hurried on. "That's why I need to find a husband. I've tried reasoning with my pa, and then I tried standing up to him, but he just waves aside everything I say. But I figure if I was married, he couldn't very well expect me to leave my husband to go take care of him."

That seemed a rather drastic solution. "Surely there are other options."

Her lips set in a stubborn line. "You don't know my father." Then she waved a hand impatiently. "Besides, I don't have much time. Pa expects me to return home as soon as Mrs. Flanagan is back on her feet."

"That's still no reason to get married."

"It may not be the *best* reason to get married, but it's better than some. At least I'll make certain we both know what we're getting into, unlike some lovesick pair who feel cheated later when the reality doesn't match their dream."

That was a mighty cynical outlook for a young woman. What sort of marriage had her parents had? "What about your bakery business?"

She nodded as if he'd just agreed with her. "That's yet another reason for me to go through with this. If I don't convince my father that I won't be returning home, then there won't *be* a bakery business."

Was Cassie so afraid of her father? Or was this some exaggerated form of daughterly obedience?

"Besides, it's my fault my ma is not around to do for him," she stated.

That brought Riley up short. "What do you mean?"

"I mean it's my fault she passed when she did."

Surely it hadn't been as dire as Cassie made it sound?

"Ma always made sure Pa didn't interfere with my schooling and that I had time to do my studies," she began. "She said she wanted me to have a chance to be a schoolteacher if I wanted." Cassie's expression turned bittersweet. "I think that had been her own dream before she gave it up to marry Pa."

"It sounds like she was a mighty fine woman."

"She was. Anyway, on this particular day, I was supposed to hoe the weeds in the garden. But I didn't want to. So I told Ma about a spelling bee we would be having in class the next day."

Wherever this was headed, Riley knew it wasn't going to end well. "You were a child. Sometimes children act childishly."

The look Cassie shot him said clearly just what she thought of *that* statement. "She insisted I stay in and study while she took care of the garden, just as I'd known she would." Cassie's gaze dropped to her hands. "I already knew most of the words, but I told myself I could use some more practice."

"I take it something happened."

She nodded. "While Ma was out in the garden, doing work I should have been doing, she got bit by a coral snake."

Riley saw the grief on Cassie's face, heard the self-blame in her tone. "That wasn't your fault," he said firmly.

She glared at him. "Wasn't it? I didn't really need to study. In fact, I was doing more daydreaming than studying. And while I was thinking about Asa Redding, who'd smiled at me in class that morning, my ma was dying in the garden. She never even made it back to the house."

"Your mother did what she did because she loved you and wanted you to have a better life. If she hadn't taken your place, and it had been you who died of a snakebite, how do you think she would have felt?"

Cassie waved her hand again, dismissing his argument. "I told you all of that so you would know why I need to take this step. Because unless I find a husband, something that allows me to turn down Pa's request with a reason he'll accept, then I will have no choice but to return home as he asks. And I need to do this before my work for Mrs. Flanagan is complete."

Riley raked a hand through his hair, not at all comfortable with where this conversation was headed.

"Well, will you help me or not?"

"Help you how?"

"Figure out how to go about this."

He couldn't believe he was in this situation. "Let me make sure I understand. What you're asking is if I can tell you the best way for you to propose to a man?"

She beamed at him. "Exactly."

"Any man in particular?" he asked, trying desperately to stall in giving her an answer.

"Actually, I have a list of men who meet the qualities I'm looking for."

She'd come up with a list of both requirements and men who fit them? That seemed to be a very…practical approach to finding a husband. "And what might those qualities be?"

She listed her three criteria, then leaned back. "So you see, I've given this quite a bit of thought."

"How well do you know these men?"

She picked at a piece of lint on her skirt. "Not well at all."

"Mind if I ask how many are on your list?"

"Three."

She said that proudly, as if it were a major accomplishment.

"And I've prioritized them. That way, if the first one turns me down, I have some backups."

"Very practical."

The look she shot him let him know she'd caught the hint of sarcasm in his tone. But she apparently decided to let it pass. "The first name on the list is Mr. Edmondson, the blacksmith, if that makes a difference."

Riley immediately pulled up a mental image of the man. Edmondson had to be more than twice her age. He was a big, burly fellow with hands the size of dinner plates, and who seemed to wear a perpetual scowl. The idea of him being married to young, sunny-tempered, idealistic Cassie was totally appalling.

But she hadn't asked for Riley's opinion on her choice. She'd asked for his help in executing her plan. And he owed it to her to give it his best shot. "However you approach Edmondson, he's going to be taken by surprise. Has he always been a bachelor or is he a widower?"

"Widower."

"How long ago did his wife pass?"

"About five years ago, I believe."

"Then his loss isn't so recent that your proposition would be unseemly."

"At least not on that account." Her wry tone told him she hadn't lost her sense of humor.

"Right. If this were me you were proposing to, I guess your best approach would be to explain, without any histrionics, what the situation is and what you are proposing. And if you could come up with any benefits to me in the arrangement, you should stress those, as well."

She hugged her knees with clasped hands. "That's

the same thing I thought." Her lips curled in a crooked smile. "And don't worry, I never was one for histrionics." She cut him a sideways glance. "Mrs. Flanagan suggested I practice before I actually approach anyone."

"That makes sense."

"So, do you mind if I practice with you?"

He was afraid she'd ask that. But he saw the pink climbing up her neck and into her face. It hadn't been easy for her to ask this, so how could he refuse? "All right." Then he stood and reached down a hand to her. "But this will probably be a more effective practice if we stand face-to-face."

With a nod, Cassie took his hand and allowed him to help her up. She brushed her skirt for a few moments, not meeting his gaze.

Then she squared her shoulders and looked Riley in the eye. "Mr. Edmondson, may I have a moment of your time?"

Okay, so she was ready to move right into this. Riley crossed his arms over his chest and pasted on the kind of puzzled frown he expected the blacksmith to give her. "Is there something I can do for you—Miss Vickers, is it?"

"Yes, sir, Cassie Lynn Vickers, Alvin Vickers's daughter. I have a proposal for you, one I hope you will see as mutually beneficial."

He held on to his serious, slightly disapproving demeanor. "And what might that be?"

"I want to build a bakery business here in town, but my father wants me to move back home to be his housekeeper. The only thing that would please him more than that is for me to get married. So I'm looking for a husband."

Well, that was direct. "Now wait a minute, if you're suggesting—"

"Please hear me out, sir."

He was surprised by her tone. Somehow she managed to be both firm and polite.

"I'm not looking for romantic entanglements," she continued, managing to keep her voice mostly steady, "so you don't have to worry about that. And I'm a good cook and housekeeper. I would make sure you had hot, tasty meals every day and that your house was clean and neat and your laundry got done."

She moistened her lips as if they'd gone dry. "I would also provide as much or as little companionship as you wish. All I ask is that you give me your name and your word that I will be free to operate my bakery business."

Her gaze resolutely held Riley's as she stood there waiting for his answer. There was an earnestness about her, along with a touch of vulnerability in her eyes, that gave her an endearing, hard-to-say-no-to air. For a moment he was tempted to tell her yes, not as her stand-in practice partner, but as himself.

What would it be like to have a woman like Cassie at his side? A sweet, caring, giving companion to share his worries and burdens, joys and triumphs? The thought of that kind of life filled him with an aching yearning that was almost too strong to resist.

He almost reached out to her, but at the last minute regained control.

Still, the target of her proposal would have to be hard-hearted indeed to tell her no.

Riley cleared his throat. "You did well. I think if you approach Mr. Edmondson in just that manner, then you will be giving yourself your best shot. It'll come down to how interested he is in acquiring a wife." The man would be a fool to turn her down.

Her relieved smile was Riley's payment.

"When do you plan to tender this proposal?" he asked, trying to come to terms with the idea that she would soon belong to another.

"I haven't quite decided, but soon."

"And what if Edmondson says no?" Not that Riley believed that would happen.

"There are those two other names on the list. And if all three turn me down—" she lifted her shoulders in a fatalistic shrug "—then perhaps that's my sign that I should just give in to my father's demand."

Riley had a feeling she didn't need to worry about that. There was no way three separate men would turn her down.

Determined to ignore the stab of jealousy that realization brought with it, he quickly changed the subject. "I think it's time to start packing up to head back. Much as I've enjoyed our outing, I do have to get back to the livery this afternoon, and then figure out when and what I'll tell Noah and Pru about being gone overnight tomorrow."

"Of course." Cassie immediately turned and began putting everything back in the basket.

Why wouldn't she look at him? Had he handled this wrong, not given her the kind of help she was looking for?

Or had she sensed something of his mood, his longing to be *that* man, the one who would stand by her side and care for her as she deserved?

Because, much as he hated to admit it, he really did.

Chapter Seventeen

Cassie wasn't sure what Riley was feeling right now. Strange how it had been both very easy and very difficult to practice that proposal with him.

He'd been so good about listening to her story without judging her, and then allowing her to practice with him. Much as she'd tried to picture herself speaking to the blacksmith while she talked, it was Riley's face she focused on, his answer she waited anxiously for.

Deep down—so deep that she hadn't acknowledged it even to herself before this very moment—she'd hoped he might step up when she explained her situation and told him she needed a husband. And for just a moment, when she'd spoken those potentially life-changing words, she'd seen his eyes darken and his jaw clench, as if he'd been taken by some strong emotion. Or had it only been her imagination, a fantasy conjured by a wishful heart?

A small part of her had hoped that he might…

Might what? Declare himself in love with her?

Which was totally ninny-witted of her. How many

ways did he need to tell her he wasn't interested in settling down, before she accepted it as the absolute truth?

As she lifted the picnic basket, Riley took it from her
and moved toward the wagon with it. She shook out the
blanket and followed.

It was probably just as well he was leaving tomorrow for that meeting.

A day apart would allow her to get her bearings again,
to figure out where she *really* wanted to go from here.

"Noah woke with a fever this morning. I'm afraid
he's taking his turn with the illness." Cassie bustled
around the kitchen, trying to get her biscuit dough ready
to go in the oven.

Riley groaned. "I know Dr. Pratt said to expect this,
but I was hoping Noah would somehow miss it this
time."

She gave him a sympathetic smile. "I know it's wor-
risome, but try not to let it make you overly anxious.
You see how Pru is getting better now, and Noah will,
too. At least they didn't both go through the worst of it
at the same time."

"It's not me I'm worried about. It doesn't feel right,
me leaving you to bear the brunt of his care alone.
Maybe I should—"

She quickly cut Riley off. "Don't even say it. It won't
get really bad for a day or two, and by then you'll be
back. If you look at it right, if it had to happen this is
really the best time for it."

He leaned back. "How do you do that?"

"What?"

"No matter how much is thrown at you, you always
seem to find a silver lining."

She smiled self-consciously. "I've found that looking only at the dark cloud serves no purpose but to make you feel sad, angry or helpless." She absently tucked a tendril behind her ear. "There is a Bible verse I took to heart many years ago. It states 'whatsoever things are true, whatsoever things are honest, whatsoever things are just, whatsoever things are pure, whatsoever things are lovely, whatsoever things are of good report; if there be any virtue, and if there be any praise, think on these things.'"

He smiled. "I can see the influence it's had on your life."

She returned his smile, then grew serious. "With your permission, I'd like to give Mrs. Flanagan at least part of the story you told me about your stepbrother."

Riley seemed to consider that for a moment, then nodded. "If you think that's best and that it won't rattle her too much."

"She's a lot stronger than you think. And you told me the story because you wanted me to be prepared if Guy came around and tried to get to the children. I think it only fair that we do the same for her. You can trust her to keep your secret, and to protect Noah and Pru with all that's in her."

Riley rubbed the back of his neck. "Speaking of secrets, it's probably time I tell the kids I'll be heading out of town today and won't be back until tomorrow."

"Do you want help?"

"Thank you, but I can do this on my own. They're good kids and they've gotten comfortable being here with you ladies. All things considered, I think they'll be fine."

* * *

Later that afternoon, as Cassie watched Riley head for the train station, she felt strangely bereft, as if it was a longtime friend walking away. Funny how quickly Riley had become familiar and comfortable.

How would it be when he and the children left for good?

She turned back to her work, not wanting to dwell on that very unhappy thought.

Instead she kept busy, experimenting with new pie recipes and doing her best to keep the children entertained and unconcerned about Riley's absence. And she sent up more than one prayer for the success of his quest.

When she finally heard the afternoon train whistle on Wednesday, it was all she could do not to hurry out to the depot to meet him.

Had he and the detective gotten the information they needed from the informant?

Would he stop at the livery before he came to the house, maybe take River out for a run? Or was he anxious about the children's safety, so would rush back to check on them first?

Ten minutes later her question was answered when Riley walked into the house. Funny how her first instinct was to run into his arms and give him a welcome-home hug.

"How did your meeting go?" she asked instead.

"It went quite well. Mr. Claypool now has some significant leads, and if things pan out the way we think they will, we may finally be able to put Guy away for quite some time."

"That *is* good news. Is it something that you think will happen soon?"

"Perhaps. Claypool is very hopeful." Riley moved toward the hall. "How are the kids?"

"Pru is getting stronger every day, but Noah is getting worse, as was to be expected." Cassie smiled. "They'll be glad to have you back."

With a nod he disappeared in the direction of their room.

Cassie went back to work in the kitchen. While supper simmered on the stove, she planned her baked goods for the next day and checked that she had all the necessary ingredients on hand. But she found herself listening for the sound of Riley's footsteps.

He returned about ten minutes later, a smile on his face. "It appears they are doing well under your care. I hope they didn't cause you too much extra work."

"We managed quite well."

Riley watched her a moment, liking the efficiency of her movements and the gentle smile she seemed to always wear when busy. "And how is your husband hunting going? Did you approach Mr. Edmondson yet?" Almost as soon as the words were out of his mouth he wished them back. He'd promised himself he'd stay out of her business, would not torture himself asking about the progress of her scheme.

But it was too late to undo it now.

For her part, she didn't quite meet his gaze. "Not yet," she admitted. Then she changed the subject, asking him abut his trip and whether or not he'd stopped in to see River.

Riley got the message—she didn't want to discuss

her husband hunt. Was it just that she didn't want to discuss it with him? Or was she having second thoughts?

He hated himself for wishing it was the latter, especially since he didn't have anything to offer her in its place.

That evening, as had become routine with them, Riley joined Cassie in the kitchen once the kids were put to bed. "Noah is finally asleep," he said, helping himself to one of her pecans.

She swatted at his hand. "Good. Let's hope he sleeps straight through the night."

Feeling not one whit remorseful for the theft, Riley crossed his arms. "So what delicacies are you preparing tonight?"

"Two pecan pies and a buttermilk pie for Daisy, four cherry tarts and two peach tarts for Eve, and two apple pies for Mrs. Ortolon over at the boardinghouse."

"Ah, so you have a new customer."

"I do." Cassie's smile had a satisfied edge. "And she sought me out rather than the other way around."

"Good for you." He glanced about. "What can I do to help?"

She cut him a skeptical look. "You know anything about pie making?"

"I know how to follow directions."

Cassie studied him a moment, then tilted her head toward the door. "There's an extra apron you can use, on that peg over there."

He hesitated, not at all interested in wearing one of those ruffled aprons. But she raised a brow as if to say *I thought as much* and he couldn't leave the challenge unmet. With a shrug, he grabbed the apron and tied it around his waist.

"Now what?"

"I've already taken care of the apple pies, and am going to work on the fruit tarts next. While I'm doing that, you can shell those pecans in that bowl on the table for me."

He reached for the bowl. "And for this you thought I needed to wear an apron?"

She grinned. "Kitchen work is kitchen work." Then she touched her chin. "You do know how to shell pecans, don't you?"

"I've shelled my share."

"Good. If you can clean 'em up and try to give me large pieces, that would be appreciated."

Nodding, he reached for a pecan. They worked in silence for a while until she had the tarts in the oven. When she'd shut the stove door, she returned to the table and peered into the bowl where he was putting the shelled nuts. "Nice job."

For some reason, those simple words gave him a feeling of pride.

A feeling she deflated with her next words. "How did you manage to get flour on your shirtsleeve?"

The amused light dancing in her eyes drew an answering grin from him. "You didn't come through this unscathed, either," he said with mock severity. "There's a large smudge of flour on your cheek."

She reached up guiltily to swipe at it, but missed.

"No, here, let me do it." He stood and reached over and brushed the hair from her face, then used his thumb to rub away the powdery substance. The sound of her soft, breathy inhalation made him pause as his gaze shot to hers. Had she felt it, too, that warm, tingly spark when his hand touched her face?

From the way her eyes darkened and her breathing quickened, he'd guess she had.

There was such a sweetness about her, such an enticing mix of courage and vulnerability, innocence and awareness.

Did she have any idea how she affected him?

He lowered his face, keeping his gaze locked with hers, looking for any sign that she didn't want this kiss he was aching to give her. But all he saw was invitation. When she tilted her face up in anticipation, he eagerly closed the distance and allowed himself to deliver the kiss he'd been longing to give her almost from the moment he'd met her.

And she seemed just as eager as he. It was sweet and tender and wonderfully electric. He'd never experienced anything quite like this before.

Then reality returned and he broke it off, pulling her into a hug, tucking her cheek against his chest, trying to get his breathing back under control.

What was he doing? He couldn't offer Cassie any kind of future that included him, and she was not a woman to be trifled with. She was a lady—sweet, generous, tenderhearted, and she deserved to be treated as such. Oh, but he couldn't find it in himself to be sorry for what he'd done. Holding her in his arms, tasting the sweetness of her lips, feeling her heart beat against his—the memory of this perfect moment would stay with him for some time to come.

But how could he undo what he'd just done?

* * *

Her first kiss. As she leaned her head against the warmth of Riley's chest, felt his hand rub small circles on her back, Cassie let all the wonderful, head-spinning sensations roll over her. She'd never imagined it could be this way. The emotions she felt from him—gentleness and possessiveness, tenderness and strength—made her feel cherished and needed. She'd never felt as if she mattered to someone in quite this way before.

Did he sense it, too, this connection, this feeling of meant-to-be?

Oh, he had to. He wouldn't still be holding her otherwise.

When they finally separated, Riley smiled down at her with such tenderness that it took her breath away. Could there be a future for them, after all?

Then his expression shifted and some distance crept in. Was he regretting having kissed her? If he apologized she would be absolutely mortified.

"Cassie, I—"

To stave off whatever was coming, she turned to the stove as if she hadn't heard him. "Time to check on my tarts—don't want them to burn."

But he didn't accept her not-so-subtle attempt to change the subject. He closed the distance between them and captured her hands with his. "The pies will be fine for another few minutes. We need to talk."

He gently drew her back to the table. Once she'd taken a seat, he pulled up a chair beside her and sat, as well.

She didn't meet his gaze, didn't want to see what might be reflected there.

After a few moments of silence, he grasped her hand again. "Cassie, look at me."

Reluctantly, she finally glanced up. His serious, what-do-I-say-to-her expression confirmed her worse fears.

"I want to apologize to you."

There they were, the words she'd dreaded hearing. He was sorry he'd kissed her.

He squeezed her fingers. "I can see what you're thinking and you're wrong. The apology is not because I regret that kiss. Kissing you was something I've wanted to do almost from the moment I saw you, and it was every bit as wonderful as I imagined it would be."

Still confused, she searched his eyes, looking for some insight.

"What I do need to apologize for is any expectations it might have given you. Nothing has changed as far as my situation. I still can't let Guy catch up with us and try to take the kids. So when Noah is able to travel, we will be leaving Turnabout and continuing our never-ending journey."

"I see." He wasn't asking her to go with him. Was he waiting for her to hint that she was willing to go? She gathered her courage in her hands. "Did you ever consider that you don't have to do this alone?"

Surprise flickered in his expression, along with some other emotion she couldn't quite identify.

He gave her hand another gentle squeeze. "No matter how much I might want that, I could never allow it. Not only because of how unfair it would be to that other person, but because of what a distraction it could be from my mission." He stood and paced across the room, as if unable to stay still. "Having someone else to be responsible for, to worry over, is not something I can add to my plate right now."

Was that how he saw her, as another burden to bear? Everything in Cassie screamed to tell him that she was perfectly able to care for herself, that she would be more than willing to help him keep the children safe.

But she knew that wasn't something he'd ever agree to. No, the best she could do right now, if she truly cared for him and wanted to help, was to relieve him of any guilt he might be feeling. "You should know I don't regret that kiss, either. You didn't force it on me, and I held no illusions as to your willingness to settle down here permanently."

She stood in turn, moving back to the oven. "At least now, when I do eventually marry, I will have an idea of what a kiss from a man should be like."

The silence stretched out, vibrating with an emotion she couldn't quite name, but which was anything but comfortable.

Finally, she heard him straighten the chairs at the table. "I'm glad I could be of service." His voice was strained, controlled.

She didn't respond—after all, what could she say to that? Instead, she kept her back to him as she removed the tarts from the oven. When she finally turned around, he had made his exit.

She set the kitchen to rights, trying not to think of anything but the task at hand. Then she padded down the hallway and checked on the children. Both were asleep.

Leaving just a sliver of space between the door and the frame, she moved to her own room.

She managed to keep her emotions under control

until she slipped under the covers. How in the world had the evening gone from such a high note to that disaster? That kiss had been so wonderful—everything a first kiss should be. And she had wanted it with all her heart. Like Riley, she didn't regret that it had happened.

But would she be able to face him in the morning?

And how in the world had she managed to fall in love with the man in such a short space of time? Because she was in love with him. And now she knew why her mother had warned her about falling in love—because it hurt. It hurt a great deal.

But even so, it was so achingly sweet...

Cassie rolled on her side and peered into the darkness. Despite what she'd said, she couldn't go through with her marriage plan, not feeling as she did about Riley.

But she couldn't go back to her father's farm, either.

Which left her with what?

She closed her eyes and poured out her fears, questions, dreams and desires in a prayer.

And sometime around midnight, she finally fell asleep.

Riley lay in his attic room, calling himself all kinds of a fool. What had he been thinking, kissing her that way? Cassie deserved so much better than that. So much better than him.

Still, that kiss, and her innocent, trusting response to it, had been every bit as sweet as he'd imagined it would be. If only his life was his own...

He placed an arm behind his neck as he stared up at the night-shrouded rafters. Despite what he'd said about marriage, he knew they weren't all bad. His parents had seemed very happy together. He remembered lots of playful teasing and laughter in their home. And even when the barn had caught fire, something very scary to a six-year-old boy, his parents had pulled together and drawn strength from each other, and from prayer.

It was so tempting to ask Cassie to come with them, or at least wait for him, especially after the meeting in Tyler. Since his and Claypool's talk with Dixon, Riley was much more confident that this whole running nightmare would come to an end soon. But there was no guarantee, and he'd probably need to move on from Turnabout before that happened. Was it fair to Cassie for him to speak of all that now? Especially knowing she had to face her father with an answer soon.

But the thought of her proposing to the blacksmith set Riley's teeth on edge, made his stomach twist. To think of her bargaining her way into a loveless marriage turned him inside out. And it was so unnecessary. She had so much strength and courage when it came to other aspects of her life. Why couldn't she use those same qualities in standing up to her father?

Should he try to reason with her on that one more time? Perhaps he could enlist Mrs. Flanagan's help on that score. Or was the woman on Cassie's side? She had mentioned the widow was helping her with this husband-hunting scheme.

The way Cassie had turned from him so quickly after that kiss concerned him. Had she been upset or merely embarrassed? Or had it been something else altogether?

Which brought his thoughts full circle—what should he do now?

Chapter Eighteen

"About last night…"

Cassie didn't look up from her work at the stove. She had to keep an eye on the eggs in the skillet, after all. "Yes?"

"You have to know that I've grown to care about you a great deal," Riley went on.

"And I you." She really didn't want to rehash this again. "But you have responsibilities to the children and can't deal with any other distractions right now. You made that perfectly clear last night, and I understand your reasons. The children come first with you, and that's how it should be." She glanced over her shoulder at him. "In fact, I admire you for it. I just wish you would let me share that responsibility with you."

She heard the rattle of dishes as Riley retrieved a cup from the cupboard, and then forced herself not to tense as he reached past her to lift the coffeepot from the stove. Her effort met with mixed success. She was so attuned to him now, so affected by his nearness, that she couldn't completely tamp down her reaction.

He didn't say anything else, but she could feel his

stare on her as she worked. There was a tension between them now—did he feel it?

She put his plate of eggs and biscuits on the table in front of him. The butter and jam were already there.

"I hope you don't mind eating alone," she said as she wiped her hands on her apron. "I'm running a little behind this morning and I need to go tend to Mrs. Flanagan."

Something flickered in his expression, but he merely nodded.

She moved toward the hallway, then paused and turned back to him. "By the way, I have something I need to take care of today, and it'll probably take me most of the morning. Do you think you can stay around here to help out Mrs. Flanagan and the children until I return?"

"Of course. Just give me time to run by the livery and let Mr. Humphries know I won't be available this morning."

Riley pushed his chair back and made as if to stand, but she waved him back down.

"There's no need. I'll be going by the livery and I can let him know for you."

He studied her as he settled back in his seat, as if wanting to ask a question. But he just nodded once more and retrieved his fork.

Which was just as well, because she didn't want to discuss her errand with him.

Two hours later, Cassie stopped the buggy in front of her father's home. She sat there a moment, letting the familiar smells and sights wash over her. Life here hadn't been all bad. In fact, she had very fond memories of her childhood. Her father had always been more interested in the farm than in people, but her mother had had a way of softening him, of making him stop occasionally and take time to enjoy himself.

It was only after her mother's passing that he'd hardened, grown stricter, had retreated into the world of his farm with a focus that shut just about everything—and everyone—else out. Cassie would suffocate if she allowed herself to be sucked back into that world.

The door opened and Dinah stepped outside. A wide smile split her face. "Hi, Cassie Lynn." She wiped her hands on her apron. "It's so good to see you. We never get visitors out here."

Cassie climbed down from the buggy and returned Dinah's smile. She should have made more of an effort to come for an occasional visit. Dinah must have been lonely as the only female in this household of men.

"Hi. I come bearing pie."

"Well, bless your heart, your pa and the boys are going to love this. They're always telling me how much better your pies are than mine."

Cassie mentally winced as she approached the house. Yet another reason she should have befriended her sister-in-law sooner. Her father and brothers were anything but tactful. "Don't pay them any mind—they just don't take well to change. I'm sure your pies are wonderful."

Dinah held the door open and allowed her to enter the house first. Cassie looked around, noting the changes that had been made since she'd moved out. There were new curtains on the parlor windows and a pretty glass vase on the mantel that had replaced the canning jar she'd used to hold wildflowers in the past. And the cabinets had been painted a bright yellow. She was impressed that Dinah had been able to convince her pa to do even that much. Had Verne stepped in and backed her up? Or had Dinah up and done it herself without asking? Whatever had happened, Cassie's respect for her sister-in-law bumped up a notch.

"The place looks nice."

"Thanks." Dinah seemed inordinately pleased by the faint praise. "I have some ideas of the things I want to do with our own place once we move in."

"I'm sure it'll look lovely. You seem to have a real knack for decorating."

"Thank you." She touched her hair nervously. "It's nice to hear that. Menfolk don't really appreciate what little touches can do for a home." Then she waved a hand. "But here I go, nattering on. Was there a specific reason you came all this way?"

"I'm here to talk to Pa. Do you know where he is right now?"

Dinah studied her face a moment, then nodded, as if satisfied. "You're not moving back here, are you?"

Cassie shook her head. "No, I'm not."

"Good for you." Then she gave her a speculative look. "Is it because of that Mr. Walker?"

If only she could say yes. "No, he plans to move on after his niece and nephew get better."

"Too bad."

Cassie couldn't agree more.

"Your pa's over in the barn, I think. He said something earlier about the milking stall needing some work."

Cassie thanked Dinah, then headed for the barn. When she reached it, she stood in the doorway for a few moments, letting her eyes grow accustomed to the dim interior. She saw her father at his worktable, hunched over something he was applying a file to.

She loved him, she truly did—he was her father, after all. And she was very afraid he was going to be hurt by what she had to say to him. But it had to be said.

She stepped forward, leaving the bright sunshine behind her as she crossed into the half-light of the barn. "Hello, Pa," she said softly.

His head came up, a confused frown on his face. As soon as he recognized her, though, he smiled and pushed back his stool. "Well, hi there, Cassie Lynn. Is Irene Flanagan finally back on her feet?"

"No, sir."

He frowned, his confusion returning.

"I came to tell you I've reached a decision. I won't be moving back here once Mrs. Flanagan is able to get by on her own again."

The frown turned stern, authoritarian. "Now see here—"

She held up a hand. "Please, Pa, let me finish. I won't be abandoning you completely. Once Dinah and Verne move out, I'll come by here every Tuesday and Friday to cook and clean and do whatever else you need me to do." Those were the days the *Turnabout Gazette* came out. She figured she'd bring a copy when she came and deliver a little of the outside world to this isolated farmstead. If Pa didn't want to read it, perhaps her brothers would.

She pulled her thoughts back to the here and now. "But I won't be living here," she said firmly.

"Where will you stay?"

"Mrs. Flanagan is going to be my business partner in the bakery and she's offered me a room." Cassie swallowed, trying to hold on to her calm demeanor. "I'm sorry if this grieves you, Pa, but I'm a grown woman now and I need to make my own life."

"A woman needs a man to look out for her. If she doesn't have a husband, it falls to her family to fill that role."

"That may be true for some women, but not all. Not for me."

Her father's disapproving expression didn't relax.

On impulse she stepped forward and embraced him in a hug. After a moment she felt his arms go around her. "I worry about you, baby girl. The world isn't kind to women without a man's protection."

Her heart melted at those words, this proof that he was still her loving, albeit stern, pa.

She stepped back and smiled at him. "You can come to town and check on me whenever you like," she said, a gentle teasing tone in her voice. "And I just promised to return here twice a week."

"You've got your ma's stubborn streak, that's plain as day." Then he nodded, as if finally accepting her decision. "That will stand you in good stead, I suppose."

Cassie bit her lip, the old feelings of guilt ambushing her with unexpected force at his words. "I'm so sorry, Pa. About Ma, I mean." Her voice cracked on the last word, but she managed to hold the tears back.

Her father appeared startled by her sudden shift in mood. "What's the matter, Cassie girl? What about your ma?"

"It was my fault she was out in that garden, my fault she's gone. If I'd been doing my own chores—"

His arms went around her again. "Gracious, girl, you been carrying that around with you all this time?"

He set her back and stared solemnly into her eyes. "You got it wrong, Cassie Lynn. Your ma asked me to take her to town that day. She wanted to buy some fabric to make new curtains for the parlor. If I'd said yes instead of telling her what a wasteful notion that was, she might still be alive today."

"Oh, Pa, no." His confession touched Cassie, helped her relate to him in a way she hadn't in a very long time. "You can't go blaming yourself."

He brushed her hair with his gnarled, work-roughened hand. "I can and I did, for a long time. But I finally realized that thinking on such things does no one any good. You've got to trust in the Lord, forgive yourself and move on."

Easier said than done.

He must have seen something of her thoughts in her face because he squeezed her hands. "Now that you know the part I played, you can't take the blame on your shoulders without shifting some of that burden on mine, as well." He folded his arms across his chest. "We're tied together in this. You think about this anytime you go thinking the Lord ain't big enough to forgive us."

His words were a balm to the ache that had been gnawing inside Cassie for a very long time.

A few minutes later, as she turned the buggy back toward town, she felt as if a tremendous weight had been lifted from her shoulders.

She decided that, for the time being, she wouldn't mention this visit and its purpose to Riley. He might misunderstand her motives, might feel an added layer of guilt for something that had been no one's decision but her own.

She also didn't want him to feel that she'd read anything into last night's kiss that he hadn't intended.

If he inquired about her husband hunt, she would merely respond that it was progressing just as it should.

He'd be gone in a week and that would be that.

And if she was lucky, she'd wait until then to fall apart.

Riley had spent the morning wondering just what sort of business it was that had taken Cassie away from the house. She'd said she was going by the livery, and the blacksmith's place was just down from there. Was she proposing to Edmondson? It was all Riley could do not to march out there and stop her.

But he knew he had no rights where she was concerned.

Still, as one hour turned into two and then three, he found himself growing concerned on her behalf. Had she had to go down to the second or even the third choice on her list? Or was she merely spending time with her new fiancé?"

It was nearly eleven o'clock when Cassie returned to the house.

"How are the kids?" she asked promptly.

There was a new look about her, as if she'd accomplished some major feat, as if a burden had been lifted from her. So had she gone through with her proposal, after all? If so, why didn't she just announce that she had a fiancé?

Pulling his thoughts back to her question, Riley answered as coherently as possible. "Noah is complaining about the itching. Mrs. Flanagan's been trying to entertain him with stories and games, but she's been meeting with mixed results. "

"Oh dear, I don't know whether to feel more sympathy for Noah or Mrs. Flanagan. I'll go check on them in just a moment."

Riley decided to do a bit of subtle probing to see if she'd reveal anything. "Did you get your business taken care of?"

"I did."

That still didn't give him the answers he wanted, so he tried again. "It all went well, I hope."

Cassie nodded, a satisfied expression on her face. "It wasn't an easy step to take, but yes, it ended even better than expected."

She didn't elaborate, and other than out and out asking her what she'd been up to, he had to be satisfied with that.

Later, as Riley brushed Duchess with long even strokes, his mind was still on that cryptic conversation. He'd just unhitched the animal from the freight wagon and the horse was now contentedly munching some oats while Riley groomed her.

Cassie had remained closemouthed as to the nature of her errand all through lunch and the cleanup after. Perhaps he'd misread her intent.

If she had proposed marriage this morning and one of her three candidates had accepted, surely she would have announced it? And if the man had refused her, she wouldn't appear nearly so serene. There was a third option, of course—the man may have asked for time to think it over.

No, that couldn't be it. She had the look of a woman

who had settled matters. Perhaps she had been dealing with another matter altogether.

This was ridiculous. The only way he was going to get peace of mind was to come right out and ask her. Maybe tonight, when they were doing the supper dishes—

"Hello, Riley."

Riley froze. He knew that voice, would know it anywhere, anytime.

Guy had found them.

Chapter Nineteen

Riley turned and faced his stepbrother, trying to keep hold of his emotions.

"You're quite predictable," Guy said with a selfsatisfied sneer. "When I arrive in a new town, I always check at the livery first."

"What do you want?"

"What do you think I want? I want my kids."

"Nancy entrusted them to me."

"But Nancy's not here anymore. I'm their father and by rights they belong to me, not you."

"You talk about them like they're animals or furniture. They're not possessions, they're children."

"And they're *my* children. And I aim to have them come with me."

"That's not going to happen."

"Shall we let the law decide?"

"Your record with the law is far from stellar."

"But I've done my time, and now I'm a changed man, ready to walk the straight and narrow."

Riley very much doubted that. "I've heard that all before."

"But this time, it's true. And you can't prove otherwise. So, take me to my kids."

"You might want to wait on that. They have chicken pox." The surprise on Guy's face was quite satisfying to see.

"You're lying."

"Not at all."

"Do you mean to tell me that you went off and left them on their own with them being sick?"

"Who said they were by themselves?"

"I want to see for myself." Guy straightened. "I can just ask around town if I want to know where they're staying. A little backwater like this, everyone here likely knows everyone else's business."

It appeared there was no putting this off. "Let me finish up here and then I'll take you to them."

Guy tugged his sleeve in that irritatingly superior way he had. "I'll wait."

"Riley, why'd you knock? You know you can bring a visitor right on in," Cassie said as she opened the door.

Before Riley could respond, his stepbrother doffed his hat and stepped forward. "Good day to you, ma'am. I'm Guy Simpson, Pru and Noah's father."

"Oh." Cassie's gaze flew to Riley's and he saw the surprise and uncertainty there. She recovered quickly and gave his stepbrother a nod of greeting. "Good afternoon." But she stepped out on the porch, casually pulling the door shut behind her.

If Guy noticed anything awkward in her greeting, he gave no sign of it. "Riley tells me the kids are a bit under the weather right now, but didn't mention the cause. I hope it's not anything serious?"

So Guy was trying to confirm his story.

"It's chicken pox." She tilted her head slightly, her nose wrinkled in apparent concern. "May I ask if you've had this illness yourself?"

An uncertain look crossed Guy's otherwise smooth expression. "I'm not really sure."

She lifted a hand in a gesture of dismay. "Oh, dear. Chicken pox is highly contagious, so we have the children under quarantine. And according to Dr. Pratt, it's much worse for an adult to catch it than a child."

Guy rubbed his jaw. "I don't care so much for myself, but I don't suppose it would do the kids any good for me to finally show up just to become too sick to care for them." Then he met her gaze, his expression troubled. "Are they suffering much from it?"

Riley wanted to roll his eyes. Guy was a consummate actor.

But Cassie was continuing to speak to him as she would to any genuinely concerned parent. "They're definitely uncomfortable and a bit cranky when they go through the worst of it. But thankfully, they're not suffering any real pain."

"Well, thank the Good Lord for that." Guy gave her one of those charming, self-deprecating smiles of his that could make women swoon. "It's very kind of you to be caring for them. I hope you'll allow me to repay you for all your trouble. I'm afraid I don't have much in the way of funds, but I'm willing to help out in other ways."

"Thank you, but there's no need. Mr. Walker here has been doing some fix-up work around here and he's really been doing a lot of the looking after Noah and Pru."

"I'm glad my little brother here has been doing

his part, but I'm their father and I like to pay my own debts."

"There's no debt here." Her tone was firmer this time. "I've grown quite fond of the children and I am happy to do what I can to help."

"Miss Vickers is very forthright," Riley said.

Guy ignored his comment and kept his smile focused on her. "I can see why Riley was so comfortable leaving them in your care. Tell me, how much longer do you reckon they'll be contagious? I certainly don't want to impose on your kindness any longer than necessary."

"Another week, at least. And as I said, it's no imposition."

"Well then, since I can't see the children just yet, I guess I'd best find myself a place to stay for the next week." He turned to Riley. "Where are you staying— the hotel? A boardinghouse?"

"Actually, I'm staying right here, where I can help take care of the kids when I'm not working at the livery." He rather enjoyed the flash of irritation he saw in his stepbrother's face.

Guy frowned. "I'm surprised that you would impose on the kindness of this lady, not to mention put her in such a socially precarious position."

Before Riley could respond, Cassie spoke up. If anything, her spine got straighter and her chin higher. "I believe you are under some misapprehensions, sir. Mr. Walker was invited to stay here by Mrs. Flanagan, my employer and the owner of this house. She issued the invitation so he could be close to Pru and Noah. He's a welcome guest, there is nothing socially precarious about his presence here and he has been nothing but a gentleman his entire stay."

Riley felt a little prickling of guilt at that statement. That kiss last night didn't exactly qualify as a gentlemanly act.

But Guy was already bowing to her in his courtliest fashion. "My apologies, ma'am. I meant no offense." Then he turned to Riley. "Perhaps you will be so good as to show me the way to the hotel and we can catch up on the latest news while we walk."

Riley was tempted to refuse, but decided it was best to hear what Guy had to say.

As Cassie watched the men walk away, her hands began to tremble. The only thing that had kept her from panicking earlier was Riley's reassuring presence. It had been obvious, to her at least, that he wasn't happy with the circumstances—undoubtedly a major understatement—but he had remained calm and businesslike.

She hugged herself with arms crossed tightly over her chest. Riley's fears had come to pass. The children's father had caught up with them.

What would happen now? Surely there was something they could do to prevent Guy from gaining control of the children. She understood now why Riley was so protective of them. The thought of those precious little ones falling into the hands of a man who would use them in the manner Riley had described was absolutely unthinkable.

Would Sheriff Gleason help them? Or would his hands be tied by the law?

Cassie stepped back inside and closed the door, leaning against it while she tried to pull her thoughts together. She should tell Mrs. Flanagan as soon as possible, but she would leave it to Riley to tell Noah and Pru, when he thought the time was right.

How would the kids feel if they knew their father was here? Would they want to see him? Would they fear him?

It was hard to believe the man she'd just met had done all those things Riley had described. Even though he'd told her his stepbrother was charming, she'd pictured a brute of a man with a boorish demeanor, not this very pleasant-looking, well-mannered gentleman. Not that she doubted Riley's story.

Which made his stepbrother all the more dangerous.

She looked into the dining room, to find Mrs. Flanagan reading a book, flanked by the children. Cassie took a moment to savor that sweet picture, then reluctantly cleared her throat.

The trio glanced her way and she flashed them all a calm smile. "What story are you reading?"

Noah gave a wide grin. "Mrs. Flanagan is reading us a story about a prince who was turned into a frog."

"Oh my, that poor prince."

Noah puffed out his chest. "I think it would be fun to be a frog. You could hop around and get as dirty and wet as you want and never have to do chores."

Pru wrinkled her nose. "But you would be green and squishy and have to eat flies."

Noah merely shrugged, as if he didn't consider that a hardship.

Cassie smiled and then turned to Mrs. Flanagan. "Can I speak to you for just a minute?" She tried to communicate the importance with her eyes.

"Of course." Her employer handed the book to Pru as Cassie moved to the back of the wheelchair. "Why don't you continue reading while I see what Cassie Lynn needs?"

"Yes, ma'am."

Cassie pushed the chair into the kitchen and then quickly updated Mrs. Flanagan on the situation.

"That man is going to have to climb over me to get to those little darlings." The widow's grim expression made it clear she meant every word.

After she returned Mrs. Flanagan to the children, Cassie went back to the kitchen and finished chopping the carrots that would be a side dish for this evening's supper.

What was Riley doing right now? Was he still with his stepbrother? Had he taken River out for a gallop so he could think?

Waiting for him to come back was excruciating. She needed to know what he was thinking, what he might be planning to keep the children safe.

Because there had to be a way.

As she'd hoped, Riley soon reappeared, entering through the back door. She immediately turned to him and her heart nearly broke at the drawn, worried look on his face.

"Where are Noah and Pru?" he asked.

"Mrs. Flanagan is reading to them in the dining room."

He nodded and crossed the room.

"Oh, Riley, what are we going to do?"

He dropped down on one of the chairs. "Whatever I have to do to keep Guy away from those kids."

She grabbed the coffeepot and poured a cup, figuring he needed something to grab on to. While she was still at the counter, he shot her a suspicious look. "You didn't say anything to them, did you?"

"Of course not." How could he think she would scare them that way? She set the cup in front of him and crossed her arms.

"I'm sorry, I should have known better. It's just…"

"It's just that your stepbrother's arrival has rattled you."

He grimaced. "That's an understatement."

She sat at the table across from him. "I did tell Mrs. Flanagan, though. I thought she needed to know."

Riley nodded, but didn't respond.

"Are you going to tell the children that their father is here?"

He absently turned the cup of coffee in his hands. "I don't want to put that burden, and that fear, on them."

"But he may find a way to make his presence known."

Riley nodded. "I know." He stared at the cup as if just now realizing it was there, then took a sip. "I'll tell them. But I think I'll wait until morning. Let them have one more night of peace."

"Perhaps, in the next day or two, this detective of yours will find what he needs to put your stepbrother away."

"Doubtful. He only left Tyler today."

"What did the two of you discuss just now, when you left here? Did Guy tell you what his plans are?"

"He did all the talking. He tried to convince me that he was truly reformed, that he had learned his lesson and paid for his transgressions, and that he was ready to be a proper father to the children."

"But you don't believe him."

Riley grimaced. "I've been fooled by that kind of talk from him too many times. He comes to you with eyes filled with sorrow, and confides how deeply he regrets the wrong he's done. You hear the emotion in his voice, see it in his expression and bearing, and you just know that this time it's genuine." Riley waved a hand in disgust. "But as time passes, you watch as he slips back into his old ways, begin to doubt that he ever truly abandoned them, and you come to realize that the only thing he truly regrets is having been found out."

Cassie reached across the table and touched his arm. "Oh Riley, I am so sorry."

He took her hand and gave it a gentle squeeze—a silent thank-you—then released it. "This is my fault. I let down my guard."

"It is *not* your fault. Pru and Noah catching chicken pox was not your doing, and that's the only reason he was able to catch up with you."

"Still, I should have found a way."

"You just stop that right now. Wallowing in selfre-crimination will not do you or the children any good."

Cassie suddenly realized this was what her father had said to her, what he'd wanted her to understand.

But this discussion was about Riley, not her. "Those two kids need you to be sharp and alert right now."

His tense expression relaxed into a crooked grin. "Yes, ma'am."

"That's better."

"It appears I only have one choice. I need to find a way to slip away with the kids before Guy realizes they are able to travel."

"You don't think he'll be keeping an eye on the train station?"

"The train isn't the only way to leave. I'll camp out in the woods with them if I have to, until Guy gives up searching for us."

"Surely it won't come to that."

Riley gave her a meaningful look, but didn't say anything.

He didn't have to.

She knew that Riley was prepared to do whatever it took to keep Noah and Pru safe. And while she admired him for that inherent love and courage, a part of her was frightened of what that could lead to.

Especially if there was an actual face off between the two men.

And regardless of what else happened, he'd just told her that he and the children were leaving. Without her.

Chapter Twenty

The next morning Riley took Cassie up on her offer to help him break the news to Noah and Pru. He figured she might be better able to soothe their fears than he was.

And he was correct.

She knew all the right things to say to calm Pru's worst fears, to explain matters to Noah in a way that made sense to him.

Later, when he and Cassie were alone in the kitchen, Riley took a deep breath, feeling as if a major chasm had been crossed. "Thank you for that. I appreciate how you were able to find the right words to ease the majority of their fears."

"You're welcome, but I'm sure you would have done just as well without me. Those children look up to you, trust you."

If only he felt he deserved that trust. Time to change the subject. "I think it'll be best if I stay close to home now that Guy is here. I'm going to head for the livery and tell Mr. Humphries I can't work there anymore."

"You must do what you feel best, but what about

River's stabling fees, if I may be so bold as to ask? Because I'd be glad to give you some of my pie money if you need it. For the children's sake, of course."

"That's mighty generous of you, but it won't be necessary. I have some funds put by."

Cassie continued to amaze him with her unselfish generosity. And it hurt more than he cared to admit that he had nothing to give her in return except his gratitude. He couldn't even promise her he would return anytime soon.

But oh, how he wished he could.

Cassie stepped out of the restaurant, her mind troubled. She'd delivered three pies, and Daisy had requested that she begin delivering four. At this rate she would soon have enough saved up to order the extra baking tins she wanted. And then she could begin saving her way to true independence.

That thought should have brought her joy, but her mind was too troubled about the uncertain future of the children to let that be so.

Please, Lord Jesus, keep those little lambs safe, give Riley the strength and discernment to know what to do, and show me how best to help them all.

"Miss Vickers."

Hearing her name called brought Cassie back to her surroundings. She was passing the Rose Palace Hotel, and Guy Simpson was standing in the doorway.

She offered a smile that carried a politeness she didn't feel. "Mr. Simpson, good morning. I trust you slept well."

He stepped forward to join her. "Unfortunately, no.

But it wasn't the fault of the hotel. I was just too worried about my children to relax."

"Quite understandable." If it were true. "But please try not to worry overmuch. It's quite common for children to get chicken pox and the vast majority come out unscathed."

"Thank you for those reassurances to a concerned father. And I must say, I do feel better knowing they are in such good hands."

She nodded her acknowledgment of the implied compliment, then straightened. "If you'll excuse me, I have some errands to run and I don't want to be away from the house for too long."

"Of course. But if you don't mind, I'd like to walk along with you for a while so we can chat."

What could she say to that? "By all means."

Cassie started forward again and he fell into step beside her. "I suppose Riley has warned you about me."

Startled by his directness, she faltered slightly, then resumed her pace.

"That's all right," Guy said with a rueful shake of his head. "You don't need to answer. And I really can't say as I blame him. Riley was always the responsible one, so serious, so loyal."

"You say that as if those were bad things."

"No, of course not. It's just that, well, there is such a thing as self-righteous as opposed to righteous. Riley doesn't seem to have it in him to forgive those of us who are weaker than he is, who stumble and fall at times."

Guy waved a hand. "I'll be the first to admit that I did some terrible things, things that hurt my family, things that broke the law. But I served my time for those crimes and I've deeply repented of the hurt I caused my family."

"I understand you've repented before."

"So Riley *has* been talking. He's right, of course. But there's one big difference this time. While I was in prison there was a preacher who came by to visit us. At first I didn't want anything to do with him. But that man of God was nothing if not persistent. And he eventually got through to me, and after that, the Good Lord got through to me, too."

Could he be telling the truth? Cassie wanted to give him the benefit of the doubt, but Riley had warned her how convincing he could be.

His smile took on a self-mocking edge. "Of course you don't believe me—that's to be expected. Perhaps this forced layover here in your town is a good thing. It will give you and Riley a chance to see the truth of what I'm saying."

"Mr. Simpson, it's not my place to judge you or what you are saying. My only concern in this matter is making sure the best interests of the children are focused on."

"For which I'm grateful, because that is what I want, as well."

He looked and sounded so sincere, but Cassie refused to be taken in. As Riley had said, the stakes were too high. "Then I suggest you go very slowly with this so that you don't upset them. Give the children a chance to get used to the idea of having you back in their lives. And, as you yourself said, give everyone else a chance to see that you have indeed changed your ways." *And give Riley time to figure out what to do.*

Guy executed a short bow. "Those are very wise words."

She didn't believe for a minute she'd changed his mind about anything at all.

"It saddens me to think what my brother might have told my children about me these past months."

"Mr. Walker would never lie to them."

"No, of course not. My brother is too sanctimonious for that. But his own feelings about me, no matter how well deserved they might be, no doubt colored everything he said."

"Knowing your stepbrother as I do, I'm certain he did his best to be fair."

"But is he really looking out for their best interests? To know that he's been dragging them across the country, from town to town, never staying in one place very long—well, as their father, it just breaks my heart. That way of life may suit Riley—even as a kid he was restless. In fact, he left home as soon as he was able. I doubt he'll ever be happy settling down anywhere."

That seemed a deliberate jab aimed her way.

"But subjecting my children to that sort of life," he continued, "not allowing them to set down roots anywhere, make friends or even go to school, saddens and angers me. My kids deserve so much more. They deserve stability and a real home and a chance to just be children. And that is what I aim to give them."

"Mr. Simpson, your stepbrother is a good man. Regardless of any inclinations he may have about how he wants to live his life, he is now entirely focused on doing what he thinks is best for Noah and Pru, what he believes he must do to keep them safe." No matter who he has to leave behind.

"Safe from me, you mean."

The only bitterness Cassie detected seemed self-directed. If the man was acting, he was doing a very good job of it. "Safe from anything, or anyone, that could do them harm."

She stopped in front of the Blue Bottle. "Now, if you will excuse me, I have some business to conduct inside."

"Then I shall leave you to it. But I am certain we will be seeing each other again very soon."

Had Guy Simpson been deliberately trying to drive a wedge between her and Riley, with all his talk of how his stepbrother would never settle down and what a disservice he'd done to the kids by keeping them on the move?

Well, it hadn't worked.

She'd take Riley's side over Guy's no matter what the issue.

True to his word, Guy showed up at the front door around eleven o'clock, holding a bunch of flowers.

"These are for the other lady of the house—I believe you said her name was Mrs. Flanagan. I would like to meet her, and thank her as well for the kindness she's extended to my children."

"But do you think that wise? I mean, with the quarantine—"

"It was my hope, if it isn't too much of an imposition, that she would join me here on the porch for a few moments." He smiled apologetically. "I heard about her injury, which makes it even more remarkable that she would go out of her way on my children's behalf."

Cassie noticed that he never called Noah and Pru by their given names. It was always "my children" in that possessive way that set her teeth on edge. She also realized that he must have been checking up on them if he now knew about Mrs. Flanagan's condition.

Cassie hesitated a heartbeat, then nodded. This wasn't her decision to make. "I'll check to see if Mrs. Flanagan is available to come out here." She waved to a pair of wooden chairs located by the swing. "Please, have a seat while you wait."

She found her employer where she'd left her, in the dining room with Riley. "That was Mr. Simpson at the door. He'd like to meet you."

Riley immediately stood, his expression darkening. "You don't have to see him if you don't want to. I'll deal with—"

"Sit down, Mr. Walker." Mrs. Flanagan had drawn herself up to her full sitting height. "It's me he asked to see, not you." She set down her book and folded her hands in her lap. "I believe I would like to meet him, as well. Take me to him, Cassie."

"Perhaps I should be the one to push your chair—"

"No, I want to see him without interference from you, Mr. Walker. The children are in their room, but I think it would be best if you joined them just in case they get a notion to get up and go wandering around."

Without waiting for his response, she looked up at Cassie. "What are you waiting for? Let's go."

Cassie, seeing the frustrated expression on Riley's face, almost felt sorry for him. She'd been on that side of Mrs. Flanagan's high-handedness before and it had left her feeling the same.

As soon as she rolled the wheelchair out onto the porch, Mr. Simpson was on his feet, holding out the flowers and smiling down at the older woman.

"What beautiful flowers," Mrs. Flanagan exclaimed. "It's been such a long time since anyone has brought me such a lovely gift."

"Why, I find that hard to believe—a lady as charming and generous as yourself."

"Oh, pish-posh, go on with you."

"It's just a small token to thank you for all you've done for my children."

"Your children are easy to do for. I can see where Noah gets his charm and Pru gets her lovely looks from."

"You flatter me, ma'am."

Cassie could scarcely believe it. Was Mrs. Flanagan actually *flirting* with the man?

"Cassie Lynn, dear, would you take these flowers inside and put them in some water?"

Leave that man alone with her? "But—"

Mrs. Flanagan waved her hand to halt the protest. "Run along now, we don't want these lovely flowers to wilt. Mr. Simpson and I will be just fine out here, getting to know each other better."

"Please, call me Guy."

"Then you must call me Irene."

Cassie couldn't figure out what had brought on the change in Mrs. Flanagan. Surely the woman was just putting on an act. She couldn't be that taken with the man.

Uncomfortable leaving them alone for any length of time, Cassie quickly poured two glasses of lemonade and carried them out to the porch. "I thought you and your guest might enjoy a little refreshment," she said by way of explanation as she stepped outside once more.

"Thank you, dear." Mrs. Flanagan accepted the glass,

then turned to Guy, continuing their conversation. "It does my heart good to know that you have turned to God and away from wickedness. The Good Book says that there is more joy in heaven over a sinner that repents than over ninety and nine just persons. You must attend service at our local church on Sunday. Reverend Harper is a fine preacher and I know you will find joy in being part of the congregation."

Cassie thought she spied just a hint of smugness in Mr. Simpson's expression, but he covered quickly.

He took Mrs. Flanagan's hand in both of his. "Dear lady, you are most kind—your words both humble me and bring me joy. And of course I will attend the church service here—it was already my intent to do so. May I have the honor of escorting you?"

"Oh no. I'm afraid our church isn't set up in such a way as to make it easy for a person in a wheelchair to attend. Besides, someone needs to stay here with the children, since they aren't able to leave the house yet."

Then she frowned. "But you shouldn't have to walk in alone—not that a charming man such as yourself wouldn't be immediately welcomed. But it is always nice to have someone at your side." Mrs. Flanagan's expression suddenly cleared. "I know, you can accompany Cassie Lynn and your stepbrother. I'm sure they'd be happy for you to join them." She turned to Cassie expectantly.

Cassie took her cue. "Of course. We'll be passing right by the hotel on our way."

Guy smiled in acknowledgment, then turned back to the widow. "But it's a shame you're trapped here in this house."

"Your brother is kind enough to help me down these

stairs occasionally so that Cassie Lynn can push me about town and give me a bit of air. Though I do hate to add to her already heavy burdens here."

"I don't mind at all," Cassie said.

Guy jumped on Mrs. Flanagan's statement as if Cassie hadn't spoken up. "Oh, but please, you must allow me to take over this most delightful task. I am sadly without employment while I'm here, and since the quarantine makes it impossible for me to go inside and help with the children, at least I can do this."

"Oh, but surely you have something better to do than to be pushing an old widow woman about town." Her tone was almost embarrassingly coy.

"There is nothing I would enjoy more. I'll hear no further arguments. This is but a small way to repay your kindness."

"Then I accept. Cassie usually takes me for my stroll around four o'clock, but I would much prefer two o'clock, if that is all right with you?" Mrs. Flanagan smiled sweetly. "That way, at the end of my outing, I could stop in at the Blue Bottle and have some tea and visit with that nice Eve Dawson. If you don't mind such frivolous indulgences, that is."

"I have always thought afternoon tea to be a very civilized practice. Two o'clock it is." He stood. "Now, I will bid you goodbye until then."

Mrs. Flanagan waited until Guy had turned from her front walk onto the sidewalk before she allowed Cassie to push her back into the house.

"I take it from your disapproving frown that my performance was convincing."

"Performance?" So it had been an act.

"Of course. I've met men like him before. Trying to

win you over with gifts, pretty words and grand gestures. Smooth and pleasant as rose petals on the outside, but dark and nasty as rotted fruit on the inside."

"But why did you fawn over him?"

"Cassie Lynn, I know you don't have a deceptive bone in your body, and that's a good thing. However, I've learned that if you allow people like Guy to think they have you under their spell, there are all kinds of things you can find out about them."

"And is that why you're allowing him to push your chair through town?"

"That, and the fact that if he's with me, he can't be causing mischief here or elsewhere. It also leaves you and Riley time to take a breather from keeping such close guard over the children."

"I just realized, you actually manipulated him into offering to take over that task, didn't you?"

The woman shrugged. "It's always best if they think the idea was theirs."

"But why two o'clock?"

"Because the three o'clock train is never late and I intend to keep him out until we hear the whistle. That way you'll have a bit of warning before we return home."

Cassie shook her head. "I never imagined you could be so outright devious."

"I'll take that as a compliment."

Riley joined them, seeming a bit agitated. "Noah's awake and complaining about the itching. And we're all out of calamine lotion."

Cassie grimaced. "I meant to get more while I was out earlier. I'll run down to the pharmacy right now. In the meantime, if you would fill the kettles with water and put them on the stove to heat, we'll let him take a nice warm soak with some baking soda."

Riley nodded, then looked from one to the other of them. "How did it go with my stepbrother?"

Cassie gave a quick recap of Mrs. Flanagan's performance and Guy's reaction to it.

When she was done, Riley had a worried frown on his face. "I appreciate what you're trying to do," he told the widow, "but please be careful. Guy is very good at reading people."

"Well, he's never encountered me before. I think that stepbrother of yours wouldn't ever dream that an old woman like myself, especially one who's stuck in a wheelchair, wouldn't be taken in by his charm and flattery."

"Still, please promise me that you will be careful."

"You have my word."

Seeing the smugly confident look on the widow's face, however, Cassie found herself as worried as Riley.

Chapter Twenty-One

Later that afternoon, Cassie watched Guy carry Mrs. Flanagan down the steps and settle her in her chair before wheeling her down the sidewalk. There was nothing improper about his manner, but she still had an uneasy feeling about the whole business.

Stepping inside, she sought out Riley. "Now that we know your stepbrother will be occupied elsewhere, I was thinking perhaps we could let the children go outside in the backyard for a little while."

"Do you think that wise?"

"As long as we don't let them overdo it, and keep a close eye on them, then I think the fresh air and sunshine would actually be good for them."

The children were excited by the idea and eagerly followed the grown-ups out the back door.

Riley turned to Pru. "I think what you need, young lady, is a ride on a swing. What do you say? Would you like me to push you?

"I want to swing, too." Noah's expression threatened to turn to a pout.

"Maybe in another day or two," Cassie responded.

Would they still be here then? "But don't worry," she continued, "we're not going to let them have all the fun. I've got something for the two of us."

"What's that?"

She reached into her skirt pocket and pulled out the two long pieces of chalk she'd purchased at the mercantile. "I thought we could draw some pictures right here on the porch floor."

"Pictures of what?" Most of the enthusiasm had gone out of his voice.

"Remember those fairy tales Mrs. Flanagan has been reading to you and Pru?"

He nodded.

"Well, I was thinking we could draw some of our favorite things from the stories. Like a castle, or a dragon, or a knight with a sword."

"Or the frog prince?"

"Absolutely. You could even draw him as a giant frog, bigger than Dapple here."

"Yeah, with a crown on his head and everything." Noah's enthusiasm had definitely increased. "And I could draw a castle next to him?"

"Whatever you like."

The boy reached for the piece of chalk, then met her gaze. "What are you going to draw?"

"I think I'll draw a princess to go with your frog."

Noah shrugged. "I guess that'll be okay."

Cassie supposed princesses were not particularly exciting to little boys. "Would you rather I drew something else?"

Noah started work on his frog. "I didn't like that princess very much. She tried to go back on her word to the poor Frog Prince after he dived down really deep and got her golden ball back for her."

"I see. But she did finally keep her word, didn't she?"

He grimaced, obviously unimpressed. "Only because her pa made her. I just think the Frog Prince should've had a nicer princess, like Cinderella, maybe."

"So you liked Cinderella."

"Uh-huh. She worked really hard and even when her stepmother and stepsisters were mean to her she was always really nice. Kinda like you." Noah looked up and met Cassie's gaze. "Not that you have a mean stepmother and stepsister, but you always seem to be working and you're really nice to everyone."

"Why, thank you, Noah. I believe that is the nicest thing anyone has ever said to me." Oh, how she was going to miss them when they were gone. "Why don't I draw Cinderella and we can pretend that she and the Frog Prince are really good friends?"

The boy nodded enthusiastically.

As they drew their pictures, Cassie made up a story of how Cinderella and the Frog Prince met and became friends. Noah contributed bits and pieces about some of the adventures they had together.

Occasionally little-girl giggles drifted their way and Cassie would glance over to Riley and Pru at the swing. They made such a poignantly beautiful father-and-daughter picture, even if Riley wasn't truly the girl's parent.

How dear these three people had become to her. A lump formed in her throat and she had to fight to swallow it. The thought of them leaving in a few days and disappearing from her life entirely was nearly more than she could bear.

"Are you okay, Miss Vickers?"

Cassie glanced up to find Noah watching her with a concerned look. "I'm fine." She waved to her drawing, which so far consisted of a head and face. "I'm just trying to decide if I should draw Cinderella dressed in her ball gown or in her rags."

Noah seemed to give that some thought. "Not in her rags, because that was the unhappy time for her. But ball gowns aren't very good for adventures." He looked up again. "Do you reckon, after she became a princess, that she had any regular clothes?"

Cassie hid her grin. "I imagine she did."

He gave a satisfied nod. "Then that's what you should draw. And she could still wear her crown, just so everyone knows she's a princess."

"Perfect!" Cassie went back to work with a smile at the child's unique but very valid insights.

Yes, she was definitely going to miss these precious children.

And their uncle.

Riley was waiting on the porch when Guy escorted Mrs. Flanagan back to her house. "And how did you enjoy your outing?"

Guy lifted her from the chair before Riley could perform that service, so instead he carried the chair up the steps.

Mrs. Flanagan smiled up at him. "I had a grand time. You never told me you had such a charming stepbrother. Why, I declare, he was turning heads everywhere we went."

Guy laughed good-naturedly. "I don't know about that, Irene. I only had eyes for you."

Mrs. Flanagan actually tittered. "Go on with you. I only hope all my silly errands didn't overtax your patience."

"Not at all. It gave me a chance to get better acquainted with the town."

She sighed as he lowered her into the chair. "Like I said, simply charming."

Guy gave her a short bow. "I will leave you now, gracious lady, but will return tomorrow so that we can do this again."

"I shall be looking forward to it." She turned to Riley. "Will you be so good as to roll me inside?"

"Of course."

As soon as they were safely in, Mrs. Flanagan laughed. "I haven't had so much fun in quite a while. I had Guy taking me to the dress shop to check out the new fabrics, the restaurant to look through the new romance books in Abigail's library and the Blue Bottle for afternoon tea." She gave them a waggish smile. "We happened on Eunice Ortolon on the way to the Blue Bottle and I invited her to join us and catch me up on all the news about town."

Riley raised a brow. "Should I know who this Eunice Ortolon is?"

"Eunice runs the boardinghouse," Cassie said. "She is also quite fond of talking."

"I see."

Mrs. Flanagan gave a very unladylike snort. "Cassie is just being polite. Eunice is actually the town's most notorious busybody. And I do believe she was quite taken with your brother."

"Of course she was."

"An interesting thing, though. We left the Blue Bottle about the same time as the train whistle sounded. Your stepbrother then asked me if I'd mind making a stop at the depot. He professed to enjoy watching people come and go on the train and imagining where they were coming from or going to."

"He's watching the trains to make certain I don't try to slip away."

The widow nodded. "That was my guess, as well." She straightened, and tapped her cheek with her forefinger. "I think tomorrow I shall need to visit the apothecary to pick up some more of my liniment. And now that Constance Harper is back from her schooling and is working there again, I'll have all kinds of questions for her. I also may have to stop at several merchants to pay my bills." She nodded confidently. "Between that and having tea at the Blue Bottle, I should be able to keep Guy busy until the train comes in."

Riley bent down and planted a kiss on her cheek. "You, my dear, are a true treasure."

Mrs. Flanagan turned to Cassie. "In case you were wondering, this is what genuine charm looks like."

Cassie couldn't agree more.

Chapter Twenty-Two

The first part of Saturday passed pretty much the same way Friday had. Riley stayed close to the house, Cassie delivered her baked goods to her three customers and took orders for Monday, and Mrs. Flanagan had her outing with Guy.

The only difference was, when Mrs. Flanagan and Guy had their outing, Cassie insisted Riley take River for a ride.

"As good as that sounds," he answered, "I wouldn't feel right going off and leaving you alone with the kids."

"Nonsense. Pru's almost completely recovered and Noah is getting better—we'll be fine. And Mrs. Flanagan is keeping Guy occupied, so there's no worries on that front."

When Riley still hesitated, Cassie pressed harder. "It's been a few days since you've taken River out for a run and the poor animal is probably pining for it. And you said yourself that a good ride clears your head and helps you think through your problems better." She put a hand on her hip. "And goodness knows we need some good problem-fixin' thinking right now."

"You're right." He grabbed her hand and gave it a squeeze. "Thank you."

She waved off his gratitude. "Get on with you. If you're going to be back before the train whistle sounds, you'd best not tarry."

Cassie watched him go, a worried frown on her face. Riley seemed outwardly calm, but she could feel the tension thrumming from him. This had to be difficult for a man who was used to taking action. She wanted to help, but didn't know how. She didn't think Riley had figured out a solution yet, either.

What were they going to do?

She thought about trying to hide them all at her father's farm—it was certainly remote enough. But Guy would find out about it sooner or later and then they'd be right back where they started, and maybe worse. Then again, it could buy them a little time, and if Riley's detective was really close to proving the case against Guy, it might be enough.

She would mention her idea to Riley as soon as he returned. Of course, if they decided to actually follow through with it, she'd have to convince her father to let them stay. And that could be a difficult task.

Riley found a long stretch of open road and gave River his head. The horse immediately surged into a gallop. For a few moments Riley just savored the movement, the sensation of almost flying, of the powerful animal beneath him and the open sky above.

But his mind wouldn't empty of his worries for long.

Sheriff Gleason had come to him after having that same welcome-to-town meeting with Guy that he'd had with him.

"I understand Guy Simpson is your brother," he'd said.

"Stepbrother."

"Anything you care to tell me about him?"

The sheriff's expression had been impassive, but Riley got the distinct impression the lawman was troubled by something he'd seen in or heard from Guy. His respect for the man went up several notches.

He'd given Sheriff Gleason the information about Guy's crimes and time in prison, but he'd left off anything to do with Nancy or the kids. He didn't see any point in airing that particular dirty laundry.

The sheriff had accepted the information with a nod and moved on. He was prepared now, if Guy should attempt to break the law. Not that that was particularly comforting, because Riley knew Guy well enough to know he wouldn't make any attempts to break the law until he had everything he'd come here for, namely Noah and Pru.

Riley felt the walls closing in on him. Noah would be better soon and then there'd be no excuse to keep Guy from seeing the boy and his sister. Pru was already terrified her father would snatch her away again, as he had when she was younger. Riley didn't like to think what his stepbrother had put her through back then.

He had to protect those two innocent children from Guy, no matter what.

But how?

Cassie and Riley didn't have a chance to speak when he returned. Noah was having a hard time with his illness and that kept everyone hopping most of the afternoon.

After Noah and Pru had been settled in bed for the

night, Mrs. Flanagan called Riley and Cassie into the parlor. "We should discuss who goes to church tomorrow," she announced without preamble.

Riley spoke up first. "I should stay here." He held up a hand to forestall any protest his hostess might make. "Not because I think you can't handle the children, but because there's no telling what Guy might do if he knows I won't be around the entire duration of the church service. It gives him too large a window of opportunity to act. And forgive me, but you are not equipped to stop him if he sets his mind to take the kids."

Mrs. Flanagan made an inelegant noise. "If worse came to worse, I have my husband's shotgun. But that won't be necessary. I've already considered all that, which is why I made sure you and Cassie Lynn would be escorting him to church. If you get to the hotel and he's not there, or makes an excuse not to accompany you, then you can come right back here and guard us to your heart's content."

Riley raised a brow. "You arranged for us to escort him?"

Cassie nodded. "Yes, as a matter of fact, she did. I was there. And it was masterfully done, I might add."

"And I reminded him of it on our outing today, so he will have no excuse to forget." The woman sounded understandably smug.

Then she waved a hand. "I know Pru is no longer contagious, but she does have a few lingering spots. I think it best we keep her here, since contact with her father in such a public venue could upset her and cause a scene. Besides, she can help me tend to Noah if I should need a hand."

"It seems you've given this quite a bit of consideration," Riley said, eyeing her thoughtfully.

She nodded. "The children and I will have our own prayer and Bible study service here while you two are gone."

"Is Guy planning to take you on your afternoon outing tomorrow?" Cassie asked.

Mrs. Flanagan nodded. "Oh yes. I specifically told him I wished to visit the graves of my dear Ernest and Willy. That I hadn't been able to do so since I'd been confined to this chair." She grinned impishly. "He should have fun pushing it over that rough ground."

Cassie spoke up in dismay. "Do you really want him to take you on such a personal visitation?"

"Land sakes, girl, Ernest wouldn't mind. In fact, he'd probably enjoy the joke as much as I do. As for my boy Willy, ah well, a grave is just a grave. Both those menfolk of mine are up in heaven with the Lord."

Riley shook his head. "As I said, a true treasure."

Mrs. Flanagan's eyes twinkled. "And don't you forget it."

Later, after the widow retired for the night, Riley and Cassie headed for the kitchen.

"I'll just be making pies tonight," she told him. "The Blue Bottle will be closed tomorrow, since it's Sunday."

He professed himself ready to lend a hand regardless.

He'd gotten quite good with handling the dough these past few nights. He would have made a good partner if her business expanded.

As they worked, Cassie gathered her courage and cleared her throat. "I hope you won't think me too forward, but I've been trying to think of some way to get you and the kids out of your stepbrother's reach, and I have an idea."

Riley smiled, obviously intrigued. "I don't think that's too forward at all. In fact I'd love to hear what you came up with."

Cassie explained her idea. "What do you think?" she asked when she had finished. "I mean, I know it's not ideal, and we would have to convince my father, who can be quite stubborn, I'm afraid. But I thought it worth a try."

Riley nodded and she could see him mulling over what she'd just said. "The idea does have merit. It would be a quick, easy move from here, and we'd be helped by someone familiar with the place. The problem is that it *is* close. If Guy should discover our location, and then bring the sheriff in on it, he'd have the law on his side. I'd be forced to turn the children over to him."

"I just thought—"

Riley touched Cassie's hand, his smile tender. "It's a good plan. I'll keep it in mind as a backup, in case I can't come up with something else."

So he hadn't decided on a course of action yet.

And time was running out.

Chapter Twenty-Three

Sunday morning, Cassie and Riley left a little early for church so that Cassie could drop off her baked goods at the boardinghouse and the restaurant. Then they headed for the Rose Palace Hotel, where Guy was already waiting for them in the lobby.

As they headed for the churchyard, Guy turned to Cassie. "Once the children are better and your duties are not so onerous, I would like to take you out for a meal at your fine restaurant. As a thank-you for all you've done for my children."

"That is most kind," she said noncommittally. "Does this mean you plan to stick around for a while once the children are well?"

"I do. As we discussed, it'll take a bit of time for this skeptical brother of mine to see that I'm truly a changed man. And I'm also coming to appreciate Turnabout and all it has to offer." He smiled at her meaningfully. "It might be the perfect place to raise my children."

"We do take pride in being an open, welcoming town." Could they take him at his word? If he planned to stay here, at least for the time being, that would give

Riley some breathing room, might get them through until the detective was able to close his case.

They made small talk for the rest of the walk, though Cassie found the effort to continue to be pleasant trying.

She sat in the pew between Riley and Guy. When it came time to sing the opening hymn, she was surprised by the richness of Guy's voice. It was deep, full and absolutely on key. She noticed that he had quite a number of heads turning his way with smiles of appreciation.

How could a man be gifted with so many blessings and still turn to wrongdoing?

Once the church service was over Cassie and Riley were put in the position of introducing Guy to Reverend Harper and others of the community.

Guy, with his gallant smile and boyish looks, seemed to be making a good impression. Which made Cassie feel like a bit of a fraud.

As they walked away from the churchyard, Guy invited them to have lunch with him at the hotel, but they refused, referring to the need to check in on the children. It was a relief when they left him at the hotel and continued on to Mrs. Flanagan's place.

When they stepped inside the house, it was to discover that Pru, with Mrs. Flanagan's help, had prepared their lunch. It was a simple meal consisting of sliced ham, boiled potatoes, some pickled squash and green beans that had been put up from last year's garden, and the second batch of biscuits Cassie had baked before heading out this morning.

Cassie clasped her hands together. "What a pleasant surprise! I can't believe you did all this."

"Pru has the makings of a fine cook," Mrs. Flanagan said proudly. "All she needs is a good teacher and a little bit of experience."

Both of which Cassie would love to provide for her.

When Guy arrived at Mrs. Flanagan's that afternoon, he was carrying a large brown paper bag with something inside.

"What have you got there?" Mrs. Flanagan asked archly.

"It's a surprise, but it will have to wait until after our outing."

"Oh, I do like surprises."

"As do I."

Riley didn't care much for the smug look on Guy's face as he made that last statement. The man was up to something.

Guy set the bag on the porch near the swing, then glanced at Riley. "Can I have your word that you won't look inside? That would spoil the surprise."

Yep, he was definitely up to something. But Guy had him—he knew if Riley gave his word he wouldn't break it. He nodded assent.

After Guy had taken Mrs. Flanagan away, Riley turned to Cassie. "I need to go down to the livery for a little while. I want to check on River." He'd finally come up with plan.

Riley was once more waiting on the porch when Guy returned with Mrs. Flanagan. Once they had the widow settled in her chair at the top of the steps, Guy straightened and gave him a direct look. "I would like to see my daughter now."

Riley was taken aback by the unexpected request. Though in hindsight he should have seen it coming.

Mrs. Flanagan spoke up before he could marshal his thoughts. "I know the doctors say patients aren't contagious anymore after new blisters stop forming, but she still has a few spots left and we thought it best to be safe."

"I'll take my chances. I haven't seen my children in over four years now, and I think it's high time I remedy that."

"She's napping right now," Riley protested.

"Then I'll wait." Guy moved to the porch swing and sat.

After a long moment during which the stepbrothers stared at each other without blinking, Mrs. Flanagan spoke up again. "Bless your heart, of course you want to see your baby girl—what father wouldn't? It does my heart good to know that you care about her so much that you'd risk exposure to the chicken pox at your age. If Riley will be so kind as to roll me inside, I'll go check on the little lamb myself."

Riley gritted his teeth. Mrs. Flanagan was taking this act of hers a bit too far. But he obediently pushed her chair inside the house and straight to the kitchen, where he knew Guy couldn't overhear their conversation.

"I am not letting Guy anywhere near Pru."

"You don't have any choice."

"What's this all about?" Cassie asked, looking from one to the other.

"Guy is sitting out on the porch, demanding to see Pru now that she's no longer contagious."

"Oh no."

"Listen, you two, I know this is not ideal, but she's going to have to face her father sooner or later—"

"Not if I can help it."

"You can't. Do you want to test the legalities of your guardianship right here and now? Because all Guy has to do is go talk to Sheriff Gleason, and then you'd have to face that showdown you've been dreading."

Riley raked his hand through his hair. "But Pru doesn't want to see him."

"I'm well aware of that. But she'll have us close by."

"Absolutely. I'm going to be right by her side, and if Guy so much as—"

"You will do no such thing. You'll be in the children's room, making sure Noah is not upset by what's going on around him. Cassie Lynn, pull out your sewing box. You're going to sit on the other end of the porch, doing your mending, while Pru and her daddy get reacquainted."

Riley didn't move. "I don't like this."

"Neither do I. But the sooner we get to it, the sooner it will be over. Now, who should tell Pru?" The widow held up a hand. "I don't mean who wants to do it. I mean who can best explain this without frightening the girl or unduly upsetting her."

Riley looked to Cassie and saw her staring back at him. Finally he turned to Mrs. Flanagan. "I think perhaps Cassie and I should do it together."

The woman nodded. "Now you're thinking and not just reacting."

Five minutes later, when Cassie led a pale and frightened-looking Pru from her room, Mrs. Flanagan stopped them. "I just wanted you to know that I told Pru's daddy that she shouldn't stay out very long because she's still weak from her illness. I also told him you would be on the bench nearby in case Pru shows signs of needing to retreat."

The widow patted Pru's arm. "Don't be frightened. We're all right here and we won't let anything happen to you."

Pru nodded, then looked up at Cassie.

Cassie had one hand on Pru's shoulder and her sewing basket handle in the other. "It'll be all right." She tried to infuse as much assurance in her tone as she could. "I'll be sitting a few feet away the whole time. I promise I won't leave you alone."

As soon as they stepped out on the porch, Guy stood. "Prudence, what a beautiful young lady you've become. You look so much like your mother."

"Thank you." The little girl's words were barely above a whisper and she moved closer to Cassie's side, practically gluing herself to her leg.

Guy retook his seat on the swing and patted the spot next to him. "Come here and sit beside me. I have something I want to show you."

Pru glanced up at Cassie as if asking what she should do. The girl's terrified eyes tore into Cassie's heart and fueled her anger against the man. What had the child's father done to her all those years ago that she should still fear him so much?

She gave Pru's shoulder a little squeeze. "Go on, sweetie, sit with your pa. And just remember, I'm right here."

Pru nodded resignedly, then turned and slowly plodded across the porch. The poor girl had the air of a prisoner going to meet her executioner. It would be a blessing if this little family reunion didn't last too long.

Cassie moved to the bench on the other end of the porch, though she turned it to face the swing before sitting down. As she opened her sewing basket, she saw Guy reach for the brown paper bag that had been placed nearby. Did he refrain from hugging his daughter out of deference for her feelings or because he himself had no real interest?

He drew a large box out of the bag, one tied with a wide pink satin ribbon that formed a bow on top.

"This is for you," he said, laying it in Pru's lap. "A present to make up for all those birthdays and Christmases I missed."

For a moment Pru just sat staring at the package, as if uncertain what to do with it.

"Aren't you going to open it?" her father finally asked.

With a nod, she began delicately tackling the ribbon. After several minutes, when she'd made very little progress, Guy reached down. "Here, let me help you with that."

He quickly removed the ribbon, then sat back, allowing her to open the lid on her own.

Curious, Cassie ignored her mending to see just what it was he'd brought Pru.

Setting the lid aside, the little girl reached in and drew out a doll. From what Cassie could see, it was breathtaking. The doll had a porcelain face and hands. The head was covered in springy golden curls and the dress was a frothy cascade of ivory lace and pink fabric.

For a long time Pru just stared at the doll, not saying anything, and then she gently laid it back in its box. "Thank you," she said politely. Then she reached for the lid.

This restrained politeness was obviously not the re-action Guy had been hoping for. "Don't you like the doll? The shopkeeper assured me this was the best one on the market."

"She's very pretty." Pru's toned remained unenthu-siastically polite.

"It's okay to play with it, you know. That's why I bought it for you."

"I already have a doll to play with—Bitsy. Momma made her for me."

This drew a frown from him. "A rag doll? You'd pre-fer a rag doll to this beautiful little lady?"

Pru's chin went up stubbornly. "Bitsy's my friend, even if she doesn't have fancy hair or fancy clothes. And *Momma* made her for me." She repeated that last as if he hadn't heard it the first time and it should ex-plain everything.

And to Cassie, it did.

But apparently not to Guy. It was obvious he didn't like the way his grand gesture had been received. But then he cut a quick glance her way, as if just remem-bering her presence, and his whole demeanor changed.

He smiled down at his daughter, and when he spoke, his tone had softened once more. "I can see as how you are very loyal to your old friend Bitsy, and loyalty is a very fine quality." He tapped the box, which still sat in her lap. "But this little lady needs a home and someone to love her, as well. Do you think you and Bitsy can find it in your hearts to take care of her?"

It was exactly the right thing to say to get Pru to ac-cept the doll. She glanced down at the box, her expres-sion changing from rejection to uncertainty to tentative acceptance. Then she nodded. "We can do that."

"That's my girl."

A look of panic crossed Pru's face and she cast a quick glance toward Cassie.

The look wasn't lost on Guy. But instead of showing irritation, he smiled fondly at the little girl. "I imagine you want to show your new friend to Bitsy and your brother, so I won't keep you sitting here much longer. But I do have one more thing." He drew another, much smaller box from the bag. "This one is for your brother. Since I can't visit him just yet, would you give it to him for me?"

Pru nodded and accepted the second box.

"Before you go," he added, touching a finger to his cheek, "it would please me to no end if you would give me a goodbye kiss right here." And he leaned closer to her.

Pru hesitated a heartbeat, then gave him a quick peck and scrambled off the swing and moved toward the door, as if afraid he would try to pull her back.

Cassie hastily put her mending away and stood.

Guy stood, as well, and gave her a chagrined smile. "It appears my first attempt to make friends met with mixed success."

"She'll need some time to adjust to the idea."

He nodded. "I know. I guess it was unrealistic of me to expect her to love me right away, the way I do her."

He was the picture of a forlorn but hopeful parent. "But as you say, time will mend those broken fences. And I aim to give her and Noah all the time they need." He twisted his hat in his hands. "I just hope Riley doesn't try to keep poisoning them against me."

"He wouldn't do that."

Gut's look said he believed differently. But he set his

bowler hat back on his head and then moved to open the door for her. "I will bid you good day and hope to see you when I return again tomorrow."

Cassie nodded and then walked past him to enter the house. He stood in such a way that it forced her into closer proximity than she liked. It gave her an unpleasant, queasy kind of feeling that lasted for a moment even after she closed the door. How could it be that so many women apparently found him charming?

Then Riley appeared in front of her. "I take it he's gone?"

Cassie nodded and pulled herself together. "Your stepbrother behaved with decorum." Mostly. "How is Pru?"

"A little quieter than usual, but otherwise okay. She and Noah are playing with their gifts—Guy's way of trying to win their affection."

"What did he give Noah?"

"A whole bag of marbles, including a few aggies and a shooter." Riley grimaced. "Noah's thrilled with his present."

"Any boy would be." She remembered how much her brothers prized their marbles, all the more because they didn't have many.

"And Pru is busy introducing her new doll to Bitsy. Seeing how delighted they are made me realize I haven't been much for gift giving since they've been in my care. I'm not even sure when their birthdays are." Riley gave Cassie a troubled look. "Little kids should get to celebrate their birthdays—especially kids who don't have much else to celebrate."

She placed her hand on his arm. "You've given them so much more than mere things. You've given them your love, and have put them first over your own needs, and have done everything in your power to keep them safe. Believe me, those things are much more important than a doll and a bag of marbles."

He placed his hand over hers and gave it a squeeze. "Thanks."

With a nod, she turned and headed down the hall to check on the children, wanting to reassure herself that Pru was okay.

She smiled when she saw them playing with their gifts, just as Riley had said. Cassie sat on the edge of Pru's bed. "Have you given your new doll a name yet?"

Pru nodded. "Cindy."

"That's a pretty name."

"I named her after Cinderella, because she was mostly alone and looking for someone to love her. And now she's a princess."

"I see. That is quite fitting." Apparently both children had been taken with the Cinderella story. Mrs. Flanagan must have done an extraordinary job reading it to them.

Pru looked at her other doll. "I'm worried about Bitsy. She doesn't have beautiful clothes like Cindy and she's not a princess. Do you think that will make her sad?"

"Not if you continue to love her. That's the greatest thing for any doll, to be loved by the little girl who owns her."

Pru hugged the rag doll tightly against her chest. "I do love her a whole bunch."

Cassie had an idea. "Wait here just a minute. I'll be right back."

She went to her room, opened the top drawer of the

dresser and lifted out a small, somewhat battered card-board box nestled there. Opening it, she stared at the contents. Inside was a bracelet, a delicate gold chain barely long enough to fit around her wrist, with a single red stone. Her mother had given it to her on her thirteenth birthday and it was the only piece of jewelry she owned.

Cassie stared at it a moment, then closed her fist around it and headed out of the room.

She sat down next to Pru. "I believe that even though Cindy is a princess, Bitsy is secretly a queen. She just doesn't make a lot of fuss about it because she's a very practical queen who likes to wear sensible clothes that she can play in and not have to worry about getting dirty."

Pru cocked her head, studying her doll thoughtfully. "She is?"

"Yes indeed. One can always tell a queen by her good character and her generous spirit." Cassie opened her hand to show the bracelet. "But occasionally she still wants to feel like a queen, so when she does, she puts on her crown, like so." Cassie placed the bracelet on Bitsy's head, carefully displaying the stone in the center of the doll's forehead. Just as she'd hoped, it fit nicely.

Pru's eyes widened. "She *does* look like a queen now." Then the girl turned to Cassie. "And being a queen is better than being a princess, isn't it?"

"Well, a queen is usually older and wiser than a princess."

Pru nodded, obviously satisfied with that answer.

"Of course, we both know Bitsy won't want to wear her crown all the time. She's much too practical for that. So you must keep it safe for her when she's not wearing it." Cassie lifted the bracelet and undid the clasp. "And perhaps Bitsy will allow you to wear it on your arm sometimes, as a bracelet." She placed it on the girl's wrist and fastened it there. "And when you wear it you must promise to think of me and how very much I love you." She pulled Noah over and embraced them both in a tight hug. "How much I love both of you."

How would she bear watching these precious children walk out of her life when the time came for them to go?

Chapter Twenty-Four

Riley stood quietly in the doorway to the children's room. He'd arrived in time to observe that entire exchange with the bracelet. He didn't know anything about the gold chain, but would be willing to put River on the line to bet it had a very special meaning to Cassie.

And she'd just handed it over to his niece and her doll as if it wasn't difficult at all to part with.

He'd never met another woman—another person— who was as selfless and courageous as Cassie Lynn Vickers, someone who could touch his heart with a word or gesture, someone he could love for the rest of his days.

Riley abruptly turned and walked away. He headed for the backyard, feeling the need to get out in the fresh air, to do something physical. He retrieved an ax from the tool shed and proceeded to make kindling from one of the chunks of firewood stacked near the house.

Love her—how could he? He cared for her, of course. Who wouldn't—she was sweet, generous, practical, and she'd been exceptionally kind to him and his charges.

But true love, the man-and-wife kind, that wasn't

for him. Besides, he'd known her for only a little over a week and most of that time had been under extraordinary circumstances.

He wasn't the settling down kind of man, and that's what she needed, what she deserved. Riley reached for another piece of wood and began attacking it with the same fervor.

And even if he *was* in love, he'd made his plans with Mr. Humphries earlier. The wheels were in motion and soon he and the kids would be leaving here. And there was a chance they wouldn't be back. Then again, even if they did come back, Cassie would likely be married to one of the names on that confounded list of hers. In fact, she could be engaged to one of them already.

He swung the ax with a force that jarred his arm all the way to the shoulder when it hit.

"What are you doing?"

He looked up to see Cassie standing on the porch, staring at him with a frown on her face.

He wiped his brow with his sleeve. "Just chopping a bit of wood. Sorry if the noise bothered you."

"It's not the noise. Members of this household don't do that sort of unnecessary labor on the Sabbath."

Riley winced. "I'm sorry. I guess I forgot it was Sunday. I just felt the need for some fresh air and physical activity."

Her expression turned sympathetic. "I know having your stepbrother around is trying, but don't let it get to you this way."

Riley was guiltily relieved that she had misread the situation. "Hard not to."

"I know. But you'll figure out something, I have confidence in you."

Riley slammed the ax into the chopping block, then joined her on the porch. "Have a seat," he said, waving to the steps. "I want to talk to you."

Her expression grew apprehensive, but she nodded and did as he asked. Once she'd seated herself and arranged her skirts, Riley joined her, careful to leave what space he could between them on the narrow stairs.

"What did you want to talk to me about?"

"That something you were confident I'd figure out, I think I have." At least he sincerely hoped so.

"You're planning to leave, aren't you?"

He hated to see the sadness in her expression, the brave resignation. But she deserved to hear this, to know what was coming. "I am. Noah is not completely well, I know, but he's no longer contagious and he's getting better every day. Before long Guy will demand to see him, too, and then there will be nothing to stop him from laying claim to them."

"He said he would take it slow, would give them time to get used to him. If your detective is close to—"

"I've learned to never trust Guy's promises. And even so, there is no guarantee Claypool will get the answers this week or next week or the week after. And I can't afford to take the chance that things will just magically all work out. The stakes are much too high."

"I understand." Cassie's tone said she wished she didn't. "But how are you going to get out of town? We already know he's keeping an eye on the depot when trains pull in and out. It'll be hard to slip by him."

"We're not leaving by train. I took Mr. Humphries into my confidence and he's agreed to help."

"So you're leaving by wagon."

"Yes. Mr. Humphries is going to meet me at the edge

of town with a horse and buggy just before dawn on Tuesday morning."

"So soon!" She grimaced. "Sorry, of course you must get away as quickly as you can."

"I'd actually hoped to leave tomorrow, but he'd already promised the buggy to someone else and he didn't have another wagon to spare." Riley just hoped the delay didn't cost him. There was an itch in him, an instinct, that said they should leave as soon as possible.

"What do you need me to do?"

She uttered no more protests, just looked for ways to help. Always practical, even if it hurt her to the quick.

"I need you to go about your day as usual, as if nothing has changed," he answered. "The longer we can keep Guy thinking me and the kids are still here, the better." He raked his fingers through his hair. "I'm not asking you to lie to anyone, mind you, just don't make it obvious we're gone."

"Of course. The three of you haven't been out in public much, so your absence shouldn't be noted by anyone. But won't you need help getting the children to where the carriage will be parked?"

He shook his head. "We don't have far to go—he's meeting me on the western edge of town. I can carry Noah if need be and Pru's got most of her strength back, so she can walk." He rubbed the back of his neck. "But that means we won't be able to take many of our things with us."

Cassie waved a hand dismissively. "We'll keep your luggage for you, of course. When you think it safe, you can let us know where you are and we'll send it to you."

"There's more than luggage." Riley clenched his jaw. "I won't be able to take River with me, either."

She placed a hand on his arm. "Oh, Riley, no."

Her dismay, and the touch of her hand, were oddly soothing. "It can't be helped. The town Mr. Humphries is directing us to, Burnt Pine, is off the railroad line, which is what I wanted. It'll make it that much harder for Guy to track us."

"But doesn't that mean you'll be more or less trapped there without a quick exit?"

"No, because we won't be staying. About two miles outside of Burnt Pine is a stagecoach relay station. Mr. Humphries knows the man who runs it. It's where I'll leave the buggy for someone to pick up and return to him, and it's where the kids and I will begin the next leg of our journey. We'll head out on the first stage that passes through and then look for a crossroads and take a roundabout path to just about anywhere. That should make it harder for Guy to locate us. Until we're ready to be found."

"Which is why you can't take River."

She was quick. "There's no way to take him with me if we're traveling by stage. I have no guarantee I'd be allowed to tie him behind the vehicle, and even if I could, such travel would be very difficult for him."

"I give you my word I'll take real good care of him. I'll treat him as if he were my very own. And he'll be waiting right here for you when you return."

But would *she* be waiting, as well?

Cassie felt a stab of pride. Riley was putting his beloved horse into her keeping—not just for a day or a week, but for however long it took him to work this all out and return. He must really trust her.

But his next words took some of the starch out of her sheets.

"I already spoke to Mr. Humphries about this and gave him some money I'd put aside. It's enough to pay for River's stabling and feed for about two months."

So she'd misunderstood—he wasn't putting River into her keeping. "Oh, I see. You don't need—"

"I told him that in my absence he is to consider you River's owner. If any issues at all come up concerning River, he is to come to you about them." Riley took her hand. "Mr. Humphries will have the responsibility of the day to day boarding and feeding of my horse, but I am entrusting you with his ultimate care. But only if you are willing to accept such a burden."

She nodded. "Gladly." This meant he would have to come back. He would never abandon River altogether.

"Any word from your Pinkerton detective yet?"

"No."

Cassie heard the world of frustration Riley managed to infuse into that one word. It was easy to recognize, because it mirrored exactly what she herself was feeling.

She decided to change the subject. "When will you tell the children?"

"Not until the last minute. I don't want them fretting about this any sooner than need be."

She nodded, hoping she didn't give it all away with her longing looks.

"As for Mrs. Flanagan," he continued, "I thought we'd wait until after her outing with Guy tomorrow afternoon. There's no need to burden her with keeping this secret if we don't need to."

Cassie nodded, pleased by the way he'd said *we*, as if they were in this together.

Which they absolutely were.

Until they left her behind.

Chapter Twenty-Five

Monday morning Cassie woke with a sick feeling in her heart. It was her last day with Riley and the children—at least the last day for some time to come.

Mrs. Flanagan received a note from Guy midmorning apologizing for the fact that he would have to cancel their afternoon outing—he was feeling under the weather.

The widow cackled as she read it. "Under the weather—hah! More likely I plum wore him out with our trek through the graveyard yesterday. I'll have to think of something extra special for tomorrow, if he dares show up."

With that distraction out of the way, Riley and Cassie sat down with Mrs. Flanagan and told her of the getaway plans.

She nodded when he mentioned Mr. Humphries would be helping them. "Fred Humphries is a good man."

She turned to Cassie. "You need to bake a pie to deliver to Fred Humphries this afternoon. You'll carry it to him in that extra large hamper we have. Along with it

I want you to pull together whatever food you can find that Riley and the kids can eat on the road. Bread, fruit, cheese, pickles—you know what to look for. Riley, you can also gather up any of the smaller items you want to take with you that will fit in the hamper, too."

Before Cassie could ask, the widow explained. "Fred can put all of this in the buggy tonight, so it'll be there for you tomorrow. That'll be less you have to carry when you leave here on foot."

Cassie stood and gave the woman a hug. "You are amazing. I don't know why I didn't think of all that myself."

Later that afternoon, Cassie had the kitchen all to herself.

Mrs. Flanagan was in the parlor reading her Bible. She'd mumbled something about needing some extra fortifying this afternoon.

Pru was on the back porch with Dapple and her dolls, drawing chalk pictures of castles and rainbows. She was also wearing the bracelet. She said it made her feel like a princess, too.

Riley was with Noah in the kids' room. Last time she'd checked on them, Noah was asking him questions about how kites were able to fly.

Oh, but she was going to miss this so much. The people and the feeling of family and having these children who looked up to her. But Cassie couldn't let herself think about that. Not today, when they were all still here. Tomorrow would be soon enough for the mourning.

She'd decided to go all out for supper tonight, to make it really memorable. She would prepare sweet corn pudding, which seemed to be Pru's favorite, and thick slices of ham, which Noah had told her he liked best. And to add to that, she had smothered turnip greens with bacon and cornbread. For dessert she'd decided to bake an apple, cinnamon and raisin cobbler.

The pie Mrs. Flanagan had instructed her to bake for Mr. Humphries was on the counter, waiting for her to deliver it. Beside it was an extra one she'd made, and on impulse she decided to slice it and offer everyone an afternoon treat.

She served the first piece to Pru, carrying it out to the porch to let her eat it picnic style. After taking a moment to praise the child's drawings, she stepped back and sliced two more pieces. Loading them on a tray to deliver to Riley and Noah, she smiled as she heard Pru explain to Dapple and the two dolls just why she had drawn four towers on her castle.

As Cassie headed down the hall, she reflected on how Pru was really starting to come out of her shell, becoming more an active ten-year-old girl than a subdued shadow.

When she got to the kids' room, she eased the door open with her hip. "Hello, you two. Anyone interested in a slice of cherry pie?"

Noah's head shot up and he gave her a wide, gaptoothed grin. "I sure am."

Riley's smile was warmer, more intimate. "Me, too." He stood to take the tray from her.

"What are you two up to in here?"

"Uncle Riley is teaching me how to tie different kinds of knots. Want to see?"

"Well, of course I do." She sat on Pru's bed across from them. "Show me."

For the next ten minutes or so, Noah tried, and mostly succeeded, in showing her his newly acquired skill, carefully explaining the various uses for each type of knot.

Finally, Cassie stood. "That's quite impressive, but I need to get back to the kitchen and check on supper." She turned to Riley. "I thought I'd deliver that pie to Mr. Humphries in about an hour, if you'd like to accompany me."

He nodded and she made her exit to the sound of Noah begging his uncle to please show him just one more.

She hadn't quite made it to the kitchen when she heard a knock at the front door.

Who could that be? The only visitors they ever received were Reverend Harper and Doc Pratt, and both of those gentlemen normally made their visits in the mornings.

Had Guy decided to take Mrs. Flanagan on an outing, after all? She glanced at the hall clock. It was nearly three o'clock—a bit late for that.

She bustled forward and to her surprise saw Betty Pratt from next door.

Cassie opened the door wider and smiled as she waved her in. "Mrs. Pratt, what a pleasant surprise. If you'll come on in you'll find Mrs. Flanagan in the parlor."

But the woman didn't move and Cassie realized she looked a bit agitated and uncomfortable. "I'm sorry, is something the matter?"

"I'm not sure. At least I hope not. Oh dear, I hope you won't think I'm poking my nose in where it doesn't belong."

"I would never think that. Now tell me, what's the matter?" What was bothering the woman? Cassie had never seen her so agitated before.

"It's just that I was coming home from the mercantile a little while ago and I saw him with her, and the little girl looked so uncomfortable." Mrs. Pratt was wringing her hands now. "I mean, I know Mr. Simpson is her father and he seems like a nice man, and all children can be a bit fractious with their parents at times, but something just seemed a bit odd about the way they were acting that I just thought I'd stop by and make sure everything was all right."

Cassie had felt the blood drain from her face about halfway through the woman's convoluted explanation. "Are you telling me Guy Simpson has Pru?"

The woman had barely gotten the word *yes* out of her mouth before Cassie was flying through the house, yelling for Riley. She found herself on the back porch without remembering how she got there, and leaned heavily against the doorjamb as she took in the scene— a half-eaten piece of pie being examined by the cat, two abandoned dolls and a smudged drawing of a once pristine castle.

A great shuddering sob tore from her throat and then she felt strong arms go around her, pulling her to him.

"What is it?" he asked gently. "What's happened to upset you?"

"It's Pru," Cassie choked out. "Guy has her."

At that moment, as she watched the horror spread across Riley's features, they heard the sound of a whistle, signaling the train's departure from the Turnabout depot.

Chapter Twenty-Six

"You've got to do something, Sheriff! We can't leave that child in that horrible man's clutches!" Cassie was wringing her hands, mostly to keep them from trembling.

As soon as Riley verified that Guy and Pru had indeed been on the train when it departed, he'd raced to the livery to saddle up River. Mr. Humphries had told him about a shortcut to the next stop on the train line, but even so it was going to be close. If Riley didn't catch up with that train before it departed its next stop, he might never find Pru.

Once he'd galloped off, right after answering Cassie's "what will you do if you catch up to them" question with a grim-faced "whatever it takes," she had headed directly to the sheriff's office. It hadn't escaped her notice that Riley had had a gun with him when he rode off.

"Miss Vickers, I want to help—you can't imagine just how *much* I want to help—but there's nothing I can do. The man served his time and he is her father, so he is well within his rights to take her wherever he cares to."

Cassie fisted her hands in frustration. She was

equally as concerned over what would happen if Riley did find them as she was over what would happen if he didn't.

"Unless…" the sheriff murmured.

She glance up hopefully. "Unless what?"

"Unless he was guilty of some kind of crime that we could arrest him for, or at least hold him on." The lawman gave her a speculative look. "For instance, has anything gone missing at your place, anything at all that one could reasonably suspect him of having taken?"

Cassie was sorely tempted to lie. Then she had a sudden thought. "My bracelet!"

Sheriff Gleason straightened. "Tell me."

"There is this gold chain bracelet my mother gave me when I was younger. Pru was playing with it this afternoon and I assume she still had it when Guy took her. Will that work?" Cassie had left out the part about her having given the bracelet to Pru, but maybe she could be forgiven for that.

"Absolutely. The charges may not stick, but it is definitely enough to get him hauled off that train and held in custody until you can get there and clear the matter up." He moved to the door. "I'll send a telegram to Sheriff Calhoun over in Needle Creek to be on the lookout for him."

"And Pru?"

"Sheriff Calhoun is a good man. He'll make sure she's looked after until Riley gets there."

A great wave of relief washed over Cassie as her knees threatened to buckle. She felt for the chair behind her and plopped down.

The sheriff moved toward her. "Are you all right? Do you need me to get you some water? Or the doctor?"

She waved him away. "I'm fine, just a little overexcited. Go, take care of that telegram. I'll be right here when you get back."

Cassie twisted the fabric of her skirt in her hands, feeling the guilt trying to beat down her defenses. Why had she left Pru outside unattended? She should have know better, should have been more alert.

But why hadn't the girl struggled, made more noise? What had Guy threatened her with?

Cassie was worried about what Pru was going through, worried about what Riley was thinking and feeling, and what he was prepared to do to get Pru back. And Cassie was scared, more scared than she'd ever been in her life, of how this all might turn out.

She bowed her head and prayed, pouring out her fear and desires, her heart and soul into those prayers, focusing on every Bible verse she could remember that promised solace, mercy and love.

She wasn't certain how much time passed, but the door suddenly opened, bringing her back to the present. A curious little man, one Cassie had never seen before, walked in. He was short, not much taller than her in fact, and rather rotund, with a bespectacled face and mutton chop whiskers, and carried a derby hat and a sheaf of papers in his hands.

He glanced around, obviously looking for the sheriff, and then his gaze rested on her. He gave a short bow. "Forgive me, miss, but might I inquire as to whether the sheriff is about?"

Cassie was immediately taken with his formal, slightly accented speech and his gentlemanly manner. "He's stepped away to send a telegram, but he should be back shortly." She waved to the chair a short distance from hers. "You can wait if you like."

"Thank you." He moved to the chair, but before he sat, executed another short bow. "Allow me to introduce myself. I am Alexander Claypool."

Cassie immediately straightened. This was Riley's Pinkerton detective? He wasn't at all as she'd pictured him. "Mr. Claypool, I am so very glad to meet you. I'm Cassie Lynn Vickers, a friend of Riley Walker's, and I sincerely hope you have good news for him."

His face split in a smile of genuine pleasure. "Ah, Miss Vickers, of course. Mr. Walker has spoken of you in the most glowing of terms." Then he sobered. "But I'm sorry, I can only divulge the information I've brought to Mr. Walker himself."

"I understand, but that may be difficult to do right now."

The man must have heard the tightness in her voice because he frowned. "What is it? Has something happened to Mr. Walker?"

"Not Mr. Walker, at least not yet. His stepbrother, Mr. Simpson, grabbed Pru this afternoon and left with her on the train before we had time to react. Riley's ridden off after them on his horse, but he may be too late."

"How could this have happened?"

"It's my fault." Cassie's voice threatened to crack. "I should have been watching her more closely, should have—" She couldn't go on.

Mr. Claypool reached out and touched her arm briefly. "Dear lady, please do not do this to yourself. The only person at fault here is that criminal Guy Simpson."

"Thank you. But that doesn't make me feel any better."

"But I don't understand. I told Mr. Walker in my telegram that I would be here today with the proof we've been searching for. He only had to hold out for one more day."

"What telegram?"

"Why, the telegram he should have received yesterday."

"I assure you he didn't receive a telegram from you yesterday." She was absolutely certain Riley would have told her had something this significant occurred.

She stood. "Come on, we're going down to the telegraph office at the train depot to find out just what happened."

With a nod, Mr. Claypool crossed the room and opened the door, allowing her to sweep past him before joining her in her rapid march down the sidewalk.

Cassie's mind was churning. Had Guy somehow gotten hold of that telegram? It would explain so much— why he'd canceled the outing with Mrs. Flanagan, why he'd picked today of all days to leave town.

About two blocks from the train station they met Sheriff Gleason heading back to his office. Cassie made quick introductions and then told the sheriff he needed to follow them to the depot. "I think I know why Pru's dad took her and left town." And without another word, she headed off again, leaving the two men no choice but to follow her.

Not waiting for either man to open the door for her, Cassie pushed into the depot and made a beeline for the counter. "Zeke Tarn, I need to have a word with you."

The young man looked up guiltily, his Adam's apple

bobbing convulsively. "Miss Vickers. What can I do for you?"

"This gentleman here is Mr. Alexander Claypool, a Pinkerton detective. He tells me he sent Mr. Walker an official telegram yesterday, a telegram I know for a fact Mr. Walker never received. Would you care to explain that?"

Zeke glanced from one to the other of them, looking like a mouse caught in a trap. "I'm so sorry," he finally blurted. "I thought it would be okay."

"Slow down, Zeke," Sheriff Gleason said. "You thought what would be okay?"

"Lionel's been sick for two days now and I've been running this place all by myself. We were sure enough busy yesterday when the morning train came in, what with that big order for the mercantile and Mr. Johnston's crate getting busted and all. And Mr. Johnston was sure 'nuff angry."

"Yes, you were busy," Cassie said impatiently. "Get to the part about the telegram."

Sheriff Gleason shot her a quelling look, then turned back to Zeke. "Then what happened?"

"That telegram came right in the middle of all that ruckus and I had to set it aside while I tried to calm Mr. Johnston down. But then Mr. Simpson, he heard me say who it was for, and offered to deliver it for me. I thought it would be okay, him being Mr. Walker's brother and all."

The sheriff stared the man down. "Zeke, I'm afraid you've caused quite a bit of trouble. We're going to need to talk about the proper handling of telegrams, but not right now. You go on about your business and we'll discuss this after Lionel gets back on his feet."

"Yes, sir, Sheriff. And I promise it won't ever happen again."

The sheriff turned to Mr. Claypool. "What exactly did that telegram say?"

"It advised Mr. Walker that I had finally found the evidence he'd been looking for in regards to the Ploverton robbery, and that I would be here today with the information in hand."

The sheriff nodded to the sheaf of papers in the detective's grasp. "And is that the evidence?"

"Yes, sir. And this is your copy."

Sheriff Gleason perused the papers while Cassie fidgeted impatiently. Why were they all just standing here? They should be doing something, anything, to help Pru and keep Riley from doing something he'd have to live with the rest of his life.

Finally the sheriff looked up, his expression grim. "This changes everything." He turned back to the depot worker. "Zeke, I need to send another telegram to Sheriff Calhoun over in Needle Creek."

Gleason turned to Cassie. "Rest assured, the sheriff is going to yank him off that train as soon as it arrives, and Guy Simpson is going to be put away for quite a long time."

That relieved Cassie a bit, but there was still a worry nagging at her, a feeling that the nightmare wasn't completely over yet. "I'm going to Needle Creek myself," she blurted out.

"Now, Miss Vickers—"

But Cassie wasn't going to let herself be deterred. "I'm going and that's the end of it. No matter what comes of this, I need to be there for Pru." And for Riley.

"The next train to Needle Creek won't come through

until tomorrow afternoon. By then, God willing, Mr. Walker and his niece will likely be headed back this way."

"That's not quick enough. I'll rent a buggy and horse from the livery."

"Now, you know I can't let you go gallivanting around the countryside on your own, especially somewhere you've never been before."

She lifted her chin and headed for the door. "I don't believe you have the right to stop me." Then she changed her tone as she stepped outside. "I'm sorry, Sheriff, I know you mean well, but this is just something I have to do."

"I'll go with her."

Startled by this sudden support from the Pinkerton detective, Cassie gave him an uncertain smile, but didn't pause. Her sense of urgency was growing. "That's very kind of you, Mr. Claypool, but you don't have to—"

"Oh, but I think I do. Mr. Walker hired me to take care of his interests in this matter, and something tells me you have become one of his interests. In fact, I do believe he would be very angry with me if I didn't do my utmost to assure that you reached your destination safely."

Riley hated to drive River this hard, but he had to get to Needle Creek before the train pulled out. The alternative was too nightmarish to contemplate.

How had Guy anticipated his plans this way? Or was it mere coincidence that his viper of a stepbrother had made his move on this particular day?

Whatever the reason, it was all Riley's fault. He'd let down his guard, relaxed his vigilance just when he should have been shoring it up. He'd been so intent on making sure they enjoyed this last day with Cassie and Mrs. Flanagan that he'd let the weasel traipse right into the henhouse.

He wanted to howl in anger at the thought of what Pru must be going through right now. Would she ever forgive him, ever trust him again?

Riley leaned forward and rubbed River's neck, trying to coax a little more speed out of the already over-exerted horse. No time to think about forgiveness right now. He had to focus all his efforts on getting her back.

He would deal with the aftermath later.

Ten minutes had passed when the first outbuildings of what had to be Needle Creek came into view. He was close now, just a little bit farther.

In the distance, he heard the sound of a train whistle.

Chapter Twenty-Seven

Cassie and Mr. Claypool accomplished most of the one-hour trip from Turnabout to Needle Creek in silence, for which Cassie was grateful. Her tangled thoughts weren't conducive to conversation and small talk.

When they'd left the train depot, Mr. Claypool had gone to the livery to make arrangements for the buggy, while Cassie returned to Mrs. Flanagan's to update her on the situation. Noah was understandably upset and Cassie wished she could stay longer to help soothe his fears, but she couldn't shake the feeling that every minute counted and that she needed to get on the road. She quickly made arrangements for Mrs. Pratt to spend the night at Mrs. Flanagan's home, to tend to those things a wheelchair-bound woman could not. Dr. Pratt insisted on accompanying his wife, so Cassie felt relieved to know she was leaving the widow and Noah in such good hands.

When the first homes on the outskirts of Needle Creek came into sight, Cassie leaned forward, as if she could see through them into town and search out Riley and Pru.

"I know it's futile to tell you to relax, Miss Vickers, so instead I will say take heart. We will soon be able to appraise the situation for ourselves."

She cast a glance at the detective, whose kind eyes mirrored some of her own worry. She liked this man, and understood now why Riley had put such trust in him. It wasn't just the prestige and reputation of the agency he worked for, it was the man himself.

Five minutes later, they had made it into the town proper. Mr. Claypool stopped the first person he saw and asked for directions to the sheriff's office.

"You turn left there on Pine Street and go three blocks and you'll see it on the right." The helpful stranger frowned. "But you won't find Sheriff Calhoun there right now, if that's who you're looking for."

"Why not?" Mr. Claypool asked.

"'Cause he's got a big ole ruckus to take care of. Some stranger got off the train dragging a little girl with him and tried to steal a horse. He's holed up in the livery stable right now, threatening to shoot anyone who steps inside."

Pru! She must be frightened beyond bearing. And where was Riley?

Cassie looked down from her seat on the wagon. "There was a man headed this way who was trying to get back the little girl. He was riding a silver-gray horse. Have you seen him?"

The helpful stranger nodded. "He's down at the livery, too, and the sheriff is having a hard time keeping him out of things." Their informant narrowed his eyes. "You folks mixed up in this, too?"

Mr. Claypool stepped in again, ignoring the man's question to ask one of his own. "Where is this livery?"

"One block over on Second Street, down toward the train tracks. You'll see the crowd of gawkers before you get there. Fools all of 'em. Likely to get themselves hit by a stray bullet."

Cassie's heart lurched. "There's been shooting?"

"Not yet. But it's coming, you just wait and see. I don't plan to be there when it does."

Cassie turned to her companion. "Let's go."

To her surprise, he didn't argue, merely flicked the reins to set the horse in motion again.

When they were within a block of the livery, Mr. Claypool pulled the buggy to a halt, unable to continue due to the crowd.

Not waiting for him to so much as set the brake, Cassie jumped down and began searching the crowd for Riley. She spotted him almost immediately, arguing with someone, who from the looks of the badge on his shirt, was the sheriff.

Hands tried to hold her back, but she kept elbowing her way through, until she was close enough for him to hear her call.

Riley halted midargument and turned. He had to be hearing things. He'd know that voice anywhere, but Cassie couldn't be…

Then he saw her, struggling with a deputy who was trying to hold her back. Riley abandoned his argument with the sheriff without a backward glance and crossed the distance to her in quick, ground-eating strides. Without a word he pulled her into his arms, buried his head in her hair and hugged her for all he was worth.

She felt so good, so right. He could draw strength from her, wanted to hold on to her as if she were a lifeline.

Then sanity returned and he pulled back. "What in the world are you doing here?"

"I came to help." She said the words matter-of-factly, as if they provided the most reasonable answer in the world.

"Help? The best thing you can do right now is get yourself out of harm's way."

"I intend to stand with you."

He had no answer for that, so tried a different approach. "How did you get here?"

"Mr. Claypool and I came by buggy."

"Clayp—" He looked around and spotted the detective standing a few feet away, his signature sardonic smile on his lips.

"Hello, Riley," the detective said in greeting. "I assure you I had no choice in the matter. If I hadn't come with her, I have no doubt Miss Vickers would have attempted to make the journey on her own."

Riley had no doubt of that, either. "So you've noticed how stubborn she is, have you?"

Cassie gave an inelegant sniff. "I believe the word you're looking for is *determined*." Then she waved her hand. "But we can discuss all of this later. Tell us what's happening."

Riley relayed basically the same story they'd heard from the man on the street earlier. He rubbed the back of his neck as he finished. "He's demanding we give him a horse and let him ride away, or he's going to come out shooting, using Pru as a shield."

Cassie's hand flew to her mouth. "Oh, how awful."

Then her brow crinkled. "But I don't understand. All he wants is a horse, and he's in a livery…"

Riley shook his head. "It just so happened that at the time Guy ran in, the owner had all the horses that weren't leased penned in the corral behind the stable. As soon as he realized what was happening, he opened the gate and ran 'em out."

She shook her head over that, then moved on. "Have you been able to see or talk to Pru?"

Riley shook his head in turn. "He was already holed up inside when I arrived and he hasn't allowed Pru to say anything." Which could mean any number of things, some of them worse than others.

"What does the sheriff want to do?"

"That's what we were just discussing when you arrived." Arguing about, actually. "Sheriff Calhoun thinks the best way to keep Pru safe is to let Guy have what he wants for now, in the hopes that he can be recaptured and dealt with later under better circumstances."

"And what do you think?"

Without answering her question, he turned to the detective. "I take it your presence means you have the evidence we've been searching for?"

"I do, and it's about as ironclad as it can be."

Cassie spoke up again. "And Guy knows all about it."

Again, Riley felt the urge to howl in frustration. But he had to keep his wits about him. "That's it, then. If we let Guy drive out of town with Pru, we will likely never see her again. She's become a liability to him. He knows he needs to travel light, travel fast and change his entire identity if he's going to escape capture. Pru just won't fit into those plans once she helps him get out of town."

"You can't mean—"

"He will either abandon her somewhere, or worse. We have to end this here." Riley gave Cassie's hands a squeeze, trying to draw strength from her. Then he reluctantly let them go. "Stay here, out of the line of fire, in case he makes good with his threats. I need to speak to the sheriff again."

Riley headed toward the lawman, rock-solid determination in his steps. His argument was no longer based on a hunch. Sheriff Calhoun had to listen to him now. Pru's life depended on it.

But he'd hardly launched into his argument when Cassie stepped up beside them.

"Let me talk to him." Her voice was steady, as if she'd just commented on the fine weather they were having.

"Absolutely not!" Riley felt his voice thunder from him, but Cassie didn't look the least bit fazed.

"I wasn't speaking to you," she answered calmly. "I was speaking to the sheriff."

"And just who might you be?" Sheriff Calhoun asked.

"I'm Cassie Lynn Vickers from over in Turnabout. And I'm also someone who cares very much about that terrified little girl in there."

"Cassie…" Riley's voice was a growl now. This was ridiculous. It was bad enough he had Pru's safety to worry about. He would not allow Cassie to put herself in Guy's hands, as well.

But the sheriff raised his hands to halt Riley's protest. "I want to hear what the lady has to say."

"Thank you, Sheriff. I think we're all agreed that the

primary concern is getting Pru to safety. What happens to or with Guy Simpson is secondary."

"I'm with you so far."

"Mr. Walker tells me that no one has seen or heard Pru since Guy dragged her in there. I want to try to make certain she's all right, to see if she needs any medical help."

Cassie was voicing thoughts Riley had been trying to avoid since his arrival.

"I want to try to talk to him, to get him to let me in."

Riley opened his mouth to issue another strong protest, but the sheriff's glower held him off. He clamped his teeth tight enough to tense his jaw. He'd let the sheriff hear her out, but he'd be hanged if he'd let her go through with any of it.

The lawman crossed his arms. "And what makes you think he'll listen to you?"

"Because I'm a woman, he won't see me as a threat. In fact, he'll likely see me as another potential hostage, doubling his chances of negotiating his way out."

"And you don't think that's what you'll be handing him?"

She shook her head. "I'm pretty nimble and more clever than I look. If he lets me get close to Pru, and if she's not seriously injured, I'm pretty sure I can get her out. I have to try, at least."

"I heard a lot of ifs and pretty sures in that statement."

At least the sheriff wasn't letting himself be bowled over by Cassie's harebrained logic.

"But none of them were very long shots. Besides, I don't believe either you or Mr. Walker here has come up with a better plan, have you?"

Riley fumed as the silence drew out. Finally, he bit out the only response he had. "Any plan would be better than that one." He could not bear to have her fall into Guy's clutches, too.

She raised a brow. "I'm listening."

This time it was the sheriff who spoke up. "I know you want to save that little girl, but I don't see how giving this Simpson fellow another helpless hostage—no offense, Miss Vickers—is going to do that."

"And what makes you think I plan to be a helpless hostage?" Cassie reached into her pocket and drew out a derringer. "Mrs. Flanagan gave me this before I left Turnabout. And don't worry, I know exactly how to use it."

Riley had had enough. "So now you're planning to shoot your way out, with Pru in tow, no less? This is utterly ridiculous. I won't have it."

Claypool cleared his throat, making his presence known. "Actually, I think the lady's plan makes a great deal of sense, given the dire circumstances. And I think that for her to even suggest it, much less do so in the calm, logical manner she has, makes her one of the bravest women I have ever known."

Didn't Claypool think he knew that? "Miss Vickers's courage is not in doubt here, it's the soundness of her plan." Riley just couldn't risk losing both her and Pru. It would kill him.

Cassie patted his hand as if he were a child, and then turned to the sheriff. "What do you think of my plan?"

"It could work. Or it could get you killed."

Cassie offered him a crooked smile. "Let's focus on the *could work* part."

A great deal more discussion ensued, but in the end, the sheriff was convinced to let her do it.

Riley, however, was *not* happy.

She looked at him, her eyes liquid wells of emotion. "Before I do this, there's one thing I need from you."

There was nothing on this earth he could refuse her when she gazed at him that way. "Name it."

"Kiss me. Kiss me like you want me to come back out of there. Like you wish you could go in with me. Like I truly matter to you."

He stepped forward and took her gently into his arms. "Yes, to all of the above," he whispered. Then he bent down and gave her the kiss she'd asked for, a kiss that came pouring from him with all the force of his pent-up emotions, a kiss that didn't care who was watching or what they might think.

When he finally pulled away, he gently pushed a few tendrils of hair from her forehead, not surprised to see his hand trembling slightly. How could he let her do this? "Now I need you to do something for me."

"Anything," she whispered.

"Promise me you won't do anything stupid in there, that you will do all in your power to come back to me."

"I promise." Then she stepped away from him and faced the livery. She didn't see him reach for her again and then drop his hands in defeat.

Cassie took a deep breath. Now that the moment was upon her, doubts were creeping in.

But she had the memory of that amazing, soul-searing kiss to give her courage.

"Guy!" She was surprised that her voice came out steady and strong. "It's me, Cassie Lynn Vickers."

It took a moment for him to respond, and when he did, she could tell he was close to the door. "Well, well, so it is. It appears my do-gooder brother has got his woman to do the talking for him."

She heard a snarl from somewhere behind her, but ignored it. "No one has gotten me to do anything. It's Pru I'm worried about and it's her I'm here for."

"I've already told the sheriff what needs to happen if he wants to keep Pru safe."

"I just want to see her, to talk to her and make sure she's all right."

"You think I would hurt my own flesh and blood?"

That's exactly what she thought. "You've both been through a lot these past several hours. Lots of bad things could have happened to a little girl in that time."

"I told you all, she's fine. But she won't be if I don't get my horse."

"Come on, Guy, I just want to see her, assure myself she's okay, maybe cosset her a little bit and let her know it's all going to turn out okay." Cassie infused a touch of incredulousness in her voice. "Surely you're not afraid of what I'll do if I get inside?"

He made an inelegant noise. "That's a laugh."

"Then let me see her. I'll just come in, check her over and come right back out. Then I can reassure all these gents that you're a man of your word and maybe they'll give you that horse." Not that she really thought he'd willingly let her back outside once he had her in there.

There were a few moments of tense silence, and then Guy finally answered. "All right, have it your way. Come on in, but only you, and you'd better not try any tricks."

Resisting the urge to look back and draw support

from Riley, Cassie squared her shoulders and started forward. If she turned around and saw that passion in his eyes, she might not be able to go through with this.

She finally reached the livery door. It was a large, two-panel affair, with the panels sliding in opposite directions. She grasped one with both hands and began opening it.

"Only far enough for you to step inside," Guy called out. She realized he'd move farther back into the interior.

She followed his instructions and slipped through the narrow opening.

"Now close it."

She did so and the space was immediately shrouded in shadows. It took a moment for her eyes to adjust, but she moved forward, toward the sound of his voice. Then she spotted them, man and child standing in the middle of the spacious building. Guy held a gun in one hand and the collar of Pru's dress in his other.

"Pru, sweetheart, are you okay?"

The little girl nodded. Her sniffles, though, told a different story.

Cassie was within a few feet of them now. And as expected, Guy put a halt to her progress.

"That's far enough. You wanted to see her? Well, here she is, fit as a fiddle, just like I said."

Cassie smiled, trying to disguise the bile rising in her throat. "I told them you wouldn't hurt your own little girl. You're not that kind of man. Why, anyone can tell how truly deep your love for her is by looking at how you risked getting caught by taking her with you, rather than leaving her behind and running off on your own." It was the one thing she couldn't figure out. If he'd slipped away as soon as he intercepted that telegram, he'd probably have been able to disappear cleanly.

"You think I'd leave my daughter, *my* daughter, in the hands of my do-gooder, self-righteous stepbrother? No, and if I could have, I would have grabbed the boy, too. And I will someday, mark my words. Riley will *never* have anything that's rightfully mine, no matter how jealous he is of me."

The man was truly mad. Cassie knew now that he would never willingly let Pru go.

But right now she had a part to play. She frowned petulantly. "Must you wave that gun around?" She gave a delicate shiver. "I have a strong distaste for such instruments of violence. Surely a grown man such as yourself can control one little girl without it."

"The gun's not for little girls or women." His sneer made it clear he was speaking of her. "It's to protect myself against those men out there."

She nodded, as if in agreement. "Before I go and tell the others that Pru is okay, can I at least give her a hug?"

He rolled his eyes and then nodded. "Make it quick."

Was he really planning to let her leave, after all? Cassie knelt before Pru, heartbroken by the fear and despair she saw in the little girl's eyes. "You are so, so brave," she said, as she brushed hair back from the child's face. "Your uncle Riley and Noah and Mrs. Flanagan all send their love to you."

"I want to be back with them," Pru said in a voice that trembled.

"I know, sweetheart. And you will be. You need to just hold on a little longer."

Guy laughed at that—an ugly, hateful sound.

Cassie embraced the girl in a gentle hug, and pitched

her voice so that only the child could hear. "When I say the word," she whispered, "run to the door, just as fast as you can. Your uncle Riley is waiting on the other side."

"That's enough," Guy growled. "And I've changed my mind. I don't think you'll be heading back outside, after all. I like the idea of having two things Riley wants. He might even trade the boy for you, if he's properly motivated."

Cassie gave Pru a tight squeeze, then released her. She yanked Guy's hand, surprising him enough to have him release the child's collar.

"Now!" Cassie yelled, and still in a stooped position, rolled into Guy, catching him at the knees and causing him to fall backward.

She scrambled to her feet, pleased to note Pru was already halfway to the door. This was going to work! And she hadn't had to use the gun. But before Cassie could get way, Guy grabbed a fistful of her hem and yanked hard, pulling himself up into a sitting position. Calling her a vile name, he raised his gun and, to her horror, pointed it toward Pru rather than her.

Desperate to stop him, Cassie reached in her pocket for the derringer.

A moment later, a shot rang out through the stable.

Chapter Twenty-Eight

Riley shoved the door to the livery open with an almost superhuman force. Where were Pru and Cassie? Who had fired that shot? More importantly, who had it hit?

The first thing he saw was Pru, just inside the door, lying facedown. His knees nearly buckled. *No. Please, God, no.*

Then she moved and looked up. When she saw Riley, her face split into the most beautiful smile he'd ever seen, and she scrambled to her feet and ran to him. "Uncle Riley, Uncle Riley." He stooped down to catch her and she latched on to his neck. "I ran and ran, just like Miss Cassie told me to, but then I heard the gun and I tripped."

"It's okay, kitten, you did just fine."

He stood, his eyes scanning the interior over Pru's shoulder. Where was Cassie? Now that he knew his niece was safe, he frantically searched for some sign that she was okay, too. But other men had swarmed the stable—the sheriff, his deputy and a half dozen other deputized men. Riley couldn't see past them.

Then he felt a touch on his shoulder and looked

around to see Claypool standing there, hands out to take Pru.

Riley gently disengaged his niece's arms from around his neck. "Pru, honey, this nice man here is Mr. Claypool, a friend of mine. Would you go with him for a moment while I look for Cassie and make sure she's okay?"

Pru nodded and allowed herself to be transferred to the other man's hold. Then she pointed behind Riley. "She's okay, Uncle Riley. Look!"

He spun around and there Cassie was, apparently unharmed, making a beeline for him. He saved her some steps and met her halfway.

He caught her up in an embrace and without preamble kissed her soundly. This time the emotions that poured from him were relief and victory and exultation. Somehow, against all odds, both his girls were safe.

When they finally parted, he took Cassie's face in his hands. "You did it. You saved Pru and came out of it whole."

"Which is more than I can say for Guy." There was more than a hint of amusement in the sheriff's voice.

"What do you mean?" Riley glanced from the sheriff back to Cassie and saw her face turning beet red in embarrassment.

The lawman laughed. "That shot we heard that got you charging inside like a bull after an interloper? That wasn't Guy's gun we heard, it was Miss Vickers's derringer."

Riley stared at her incredulously. "You shot Guy?"

"He'd pointed his gun at Pru. I had to do something to stop him."

"She stopped him, all right. Shot his big toe right off."

"I just aimed for his foot. It seemed the least gruesome of my possible targets." She lifted her chin. "And it worked."

Riley grinned, deciding she was quite beautiful when she was embarrassed.

She frowned at him and the sheriff both. "This is not funny, gentlemen. I don't take what I did lightly."

"No, ma'am," the sheriff said meekly.

But Riley heard the man chuckle again as he walked off.

He linked his arm with Cassie's, not wanting to let her go so soon after he'd discovered her again, and turned to Claypool. "What do you say we take these two lovely ladies out of this stable and find them somewhere more comfortable to relax?"

The sheriff told them that they would have a couple hotel rooms free of charge for the night, compliments of the town council. Cassie asked Riley to order some food to be sent upstairs for Pru, and took the girl upstairs to settle her in. She carried with her the small carpetbag Mr. Claypool had retrieved from the buggy, and set it on the bed. She opened it and pulled out two things—a hairbrush so that she could brush the tangles from Pru's locks, and a surprise she'd packed as an act of faith that they would get Pru safely home.

"Look who came along to keep you company tonight."

"Bitsy!" The girl's delighted smile warmed Cassie's heart.

"Cindy will be waiting for you when you get back

to Mrs. Flanagan's," Cassie said. "I'm sorry I couldn't fit both of them in my bag."

Pru's gaze shifted and her gaze didn't meet Cassie's. "That's okay."

Guessing what the little girl was feeling, Cassie took one of her hands. "It's okay if you don't want to play with Cindy anymore. But I want you to think about this. It's not Cindy's fault she came from your father, any more than it's your fault that he's your pa."

Cassie stood up. "Now, let's get you cleaned up and get your hair brushed. What do you say?"

With a nod, Pru followed her to the vanity.

An hour later the child was freshened up, fed and tucked into bed, sound asleep.

Cassie headed downstairs, knowing she would find Riley waiting for her there.

And she did.

Her heart gave a little pitter-patter as she saw the way he looked at her. Could he possibly return her feelings? Those kisses today had certainly said yes. Or was she fooling herself, and was this all merely gratitude for what she'd done for Pru?

He stepped forward to greet her as she reached the bottom step, and tucked her arm in his.

"How's Pru doing?"

"She's still a bit clingy, but that's to be expected after all she's been through. But right now she's sound asleep. One of the hotel maids is sitting with her, in case she wakes up before I return, but I honestly think she'll sleep through the night."

Riley nodded as he led her to a secluded corner of the lobby. "I sent a telegram earlier to Sheriff Gleason to inform him that it all ended well and we would be back in Turnabout tomorrow. I asked him to share the information with Mrs. Flanagan and Mr. Humphries.

"Thank you. I know Mrs. Flanagan and Noah will sleep better tonight."

Riley seated her on a padded bench, then settled beside her. Taking her hands, he held her gaze with a steady one of his own. "We need to talk."

Her heart fluttered again, but she ignored it. This could be about anything. "I'm listening."

He shifted, as if uncertain what he was about to say. "I know you're probably already spoken for, but—"

"What?"

"Perhaps 'spoken for' is not the right term here. Should I have said you've already made your marriage bargain?"

"Whatever are you talking about?"

"That day you were gone all morning, weren't you visiting the men on your husband list?"

"Absolutely not." She held his gaze. "I was actually visiting with my father that day. To tell him I would not be returning home on a permanent basis, that I had my own life to live and would be opening a bakery business."

Riley's whole demeanor brightened, as if a weight had been lifted. "Good for you."

"I did agree to a compromise, however." She explained to him the bargain she'd struck with her father, then frowned. "How could you think I would kiss you like I did today if I'd promised to marry another man?"

He had the grace to look sheepish. "To be honest, I didn't know what to think. Why didn't you tell me about the visit to your father?"

Now it was her turn to squirm. "I didn't want you to think… I mean, it was…"

He grinned. "You didn't want me to think it had been on my account."

"And it wasn't." At least not entirely. "It was something I had to do for myself."

"I'm proud of you."

That should have sounded condescending, but somehow it didn't. She sat up straighter. "Was that all you wanted to speak to me about, or was there something else?"

He grinned. "Oh yes, there's definitely something else. And now that I know you've given up that husband hunt of yours, it is even more pressing. Cassie, you have to know, especially after all that happened today, that I am absolutely, totally, incredibly in love with you."

"You are?"

He laughed. "Yes. How could I not be? You make me laugh—at myself and at my problems. You make me think—of possible futures and of different ways of seeing the world. You make me a better man.

"And you make me want to have you at my side, today and always."

"Oh Riley, I love you, too. I don't know how it's possible to love someone so much after knowing him only two weeks, but I think I fell in love with you the moment you stooped down beside me to help me up in the livery yard. It's like I've known you forever."

He squeezed her hands. "Then you'll marry me?"

She slipped her hands from his and threw her arms around his neck. "Yes!"

The kiss that they sealed their agreement with was the best one yet.

Epilogue

Riley gave the nail one final thwack, then stood back to study his work. It was coming along nicely. Within the next two days, he should have half the roomy attic walled off into two bedchambers, one for Pru and one for Noah.

It had been nearly a month since Guy had been arrested and just yesterday they'd learned that he'd been sentenced to life in prison. At last the children were safe and they could begin to set down roots again. Even Pru's nightmares had faded and she and Noah were thriving the way children were intended to.

The two were looking forward to having their own rooms. In fact, if they hadn't been in school right now they would probably be up here helping him. That the rooms were up in the attic was seen by them as an added bonus. Apparently the kids were looking at this as the tower from one of those fairy-tale stories Mrs. Flanagan liked to read to them.

The woman had become a surrogate grandmother to the two kids, and the affection ran both ways. As soon as Mrs. Flanagan had heard he and Cassie were getting married, she had insisted that they move in permanently with her. Riley had tried to protest, then tried to insist on paying rent, but the feisty widow was having none of it.

"I've realized over these past few weeks how empty this house has been since all my menfolk left me," she'd said. "And I've gotten used to having young people around me again. Not only used to it, but fond of it. In fact, I'd consider it just plain cruelty if you were to take those two children away from me."

The only thing she would allow was that they help with the groceries and the chores, which was fine by him.

"You look like you could use a glass of lemonade, Mr. Walker."

He turned to see that his lovely bride of two weeks had joined him. She was carrying a glass in one hand and what looked like a document of some sort in the other. "Why, thank you, Mrs. Walker, I don't mind if I do."

She smiled. "I don't think I'll ever grow tired of being called Mrs. Walker. "

"I sincerely hope not." Riley took the glass from her, then pulled her close, giving her a quick but oh-so-sweet kiss before releasing her.

She looked up at him with shining eyes. "That's something else I'll never tire of."

He tapped her nose affectionately, then indicated the paper she held. "What's that you have?"

"I stopped by Reggie's studio while I was out. Our wedding picture is ready."

He'd learned that Regina Barr was the town photographer, and he'd hired her to memorialize their special day.

Cassie handed the photograph to him and then nestled against him as he studied it.

Riley gazed at the photograph, a feeling of contentment settling in his chest. They were all pictured there—he and Cassie in the center, Noah and Pru on the left and Mrs. Flanagan and Cassie's father on the right.

Riley had found a place to belong, and settling down had been no sacrifice at all.

In fact, with Cassie at his side, he was right where he wanted to be.

Cassie looked at the picture Riley held and couldn't believe what a beautiful life the Good Lord had planned for her. Two beautiful children, a wonderful, loving, God-fearing husband, a father she was now reconciled with and a woman who was as precious as a mother to her.

There was no richer life she could imagine. Like the Cinderella in the children's favorite story, she'd found her prince and her treasure, and she planned to live her very own happily ever after.

* * * * *

Regina Scott has always wanted to be a writer. Since her first book was published in 1998, her stories have traveled the globe, with translations in many languages. Fascinated by history, she learned to fence and sail a tall ship. She and her husband reside in Washington State with an overactive Irish terrier. You can find her online, blogging at nineteenteen.com. Learn more about her at reginascott.com or connect with her on Facebook at Facebook.com/authorreginascott.

Books by Regina Scott

Love Inspired Historical

Frontier Bachelors

The Bride Ship
Would-Be Wilderness Wife
Frontier Engagement
Instant Frontier Family
A Convenient Christmas Wedding
Mail-Order Marriage Promise
His Frontier Christmas Family
Frontier Matchmaker Bride

Lone Star Cowboy League: Multiple Blessings

The Bride's Matchmaking Triplets

Lone Star Cowboy League: The Founding Years

A Rancher of Convenience

Visit the Author Profile page
at LoveInspired.com for more titles.

WOULD-BE
WILDERNESS WIFE

Regina Scott

For this reason a man will leave his father and mother
and be united with his wife,
and they will become one flesh.
—*Genesis* 2:24

To Joe Mullins and Angela Rush,
real estate agents extraordinaire, who helped us
find a house on the new frontier, and to the Lord,
who makes a house a home

Chapter One

Seattle, Washington Territory
May 1866

"I need a doctor."

The commanding male voice echoed through the dispensary of Doc Maynard's hospital like a trumpet call. Catherine Stanway straightened from where she'd been bending over a patient, fully prepared to offer assistance. But one look at the man in the doorway, lit from behind by the rare Seattle sun, and words failed her.

He carried himself as proudly as a knight from the tales of King Arthur her father had read to her as a child. His rough-cut light brown hair brushed the top of the doorjamb; his shoulders in the wrinkled blue cotton shirt reached either side. He took a step into the room, and she was certain she felt the floor tremble.

Finding her voice, she raised her chin. "I can help you."

He walked down the narrow room toward her, the thud of his worn leather boots like the sound of a hammer on the planks of the floor. The blue apothecary bottles lined up on the shelves behind the counter chimed against one another as he passed. He was like a warrior approaching his leader, a soldier his commanding officer. Mrs. Witherspoon, waiting on a chair for the doctor to reset her shoulder, clutched her arm close, wide-eyed. Others stared at him or quickly looked away.

He stopped beside Catherine and laid his fingers on the curved back of the chair where the elderly Mr. Jenkins snoozed while he waited for his monthly dose of medicine. Scars crossed the skin of the massive hand, white against the bronze.

Up close, Catherine could see that his face was more heart-shaped than oval, his unkempt hair drawing down in a peak over his forehead. His liberally lashed eyes were a mixture of clear green and blue, like the waves that lapped the Puget Sound shores. The gold of his skin said he worked outdoors; the wear on this clothes said he made little income from it.

He was easily the most healthy male she'd ever seen, so why did he need medical assistance?

"Are you a doctor?" he asked. Everything from the way he cocked his head to the slow cadence of the question spoke of his doubt.

Her spine stiffened, lifting her blue skirts off the floor and bringing her head level with his breastbone. She was used to the surprise, the doubts about her vocation here in Seattle. Even where she'd been raised, a few had questioned that the prominent physician George Stanway had trained his daughter to be a nurse. More had wondered why their beloved doctor and his promising son had felt it necessary to get themselves killed serving in the Union Army. At times, Catherine wondered the same thing.

"I'm a nurse," she told their visitor, keeping her voice calm, professional. "I was trained by my father, a practicing physician, and served for a year at the New England Hospital for Women and Children. I came West with the Mercer expedition. Doctor Maynard was sufficiently pleased with my credentials to hire me to assist him and his wife."

"So you're a Mercer belle." He straightened, towering over her. "I didn't come looking for a bride. I need a doctor."

A Mercer belle. That, she knew from the newspapers back East, was synonymous with *husband hunter*. Obviously her credentials as a medical practitioner meant nothing to him.

Well, he might not have come to the hospital seeking a bride, but she hadn't come to Seattle after a husband, either. She'd already refused three offers of marriage since arriving two weeks ago. Her friend Madeleine O'Rourke had turned away six. Even her friend Allegra had had to argue with two would-be suitors before she'd wed her childhood sweetheart, Clay Howard, a successful local businessman, only two days after landing.

None of them had left the East Coast expecting such attentions. When Seattle's self-proclaimed emigration agent, Asa Mercer, had recruited her and nearly seventy other women to settle in Washington Territory, he'd talked of the jobs that needed filling, the culture they could bring to the fledging community. Already some of her traveling companions were teaching schools in far-flung settlements. Others had taken jobs they had never dreamed of back home, including tending a lighthouse. They were innovative and industrious, just as Catherine had hoped she'd be when she'd jour-neyed West.

"I'm not interested in marriage either, sir," she told him. "And I assure you, I am perfectly suited to deal with medical emergencies. Now, what's the trouble?"

He glanced around as if determined to locate her employer. Doctor Maynard had converted the bottom floor of his house for his patients. This room was his dispensary, the medicines and curatives lined up in tall bottles on the triple row of shelves along one wall, with a dozen chairs, frequently all filled, opposite them. The other room held beds along either wall, with an area at the end curtained off and outfitted for surgeries. That room was used primarily as a laying-in ward for women about to give birth.

After conversations aboard ship about the dismal state of Seattle's medical establishment, Catherine hadn't been sure what to expect of Doctor Maynard and his hospital. She'd been greatly relieved to find the wood floors sanded clean, beds nicely made and light streaming through tall windows. The doctor shared her father's view that fresh water, healthy food and natural light went a long way to curing any ill.

"I appreciate your offer," the man said, returning his gaze to hers. "But I would prefer a doctor."

She could see herself reflected in his eyes, her pale blond hair neat and tidy, her face set. She refused to be the first one to look away. In the silence, she heard Mr. Jenkins mumble as he dozed.

"Well, greetings, Drew!" The call from her employer caused their visitor to raise his head, breaking his gaze from Catherine's. She suddenly found it easier to breathe.

Doctor Maynard didn't appear the least concerned to find a mountain of a man in his dispensary. He strolled toward them with his usual grin. A tall man, he had a broad face and dark hair that persisted in curling in the middle of his forehead as if it laughed at the world like he did. After helping her organized father, Catherine had found Seattle's famous founding father undisciplined, impractical and irrepressible. He was also endlessly cheerful and generous. In the two weeks she'd been working at his side, he'd never turned anyone down, regardless of gender, race or ability to pay.

"And what can we do for you today?" he asked their visitor as he approached. "Are all the Wallins healthy? No more bumps, bruises or broken bones among your logging crew, I trust?"

The man hesitated a moment, then nodded. "My brothers are well enough. I'm here about another matter."

"I told Mr. Wallin I could assist him," Catherine assured her employer.

"O-ho!" Maynard elbowed the man's side and didn't so much as cause their visitor to raise an eyebrow. "Are you after my nurse, Drew? Can't say I blame you. Allow me to introduce Miss Catherine Stanway. She's as pretty as a picture and twice as talented."

Catherine didn't blush at the praise. She'd heard it and far more in her hometown of Sudbury, while she'd worked as a nurse in Boston and while aboard the ship to Seattle. Much of the time it came from no sincere motive, she'd learned. She was more interested to see how this Drew fellow would answer. Would he continue to argue with her in the face of her employer's endorsement?

He did not look at her as he transferred his grip to the doctor's arm. "May I speak to you a moment in private?"

Maynard nodded, and the two withdrew to the end of the dispensary nearest the door. Fine. Lord knew she had plenty of work to do. She had only determined the needs of about half those currently filling the chairs, and two women were expected any day in the laying-in ward. If Mr. Wallin couldn't be bothered to make use of her services, the fault lay with him, not her. She was fully prepared to do her duty.

Yet Catherine could hear the low rumble of his voice as she spoke to the woman next to Mr. Jenkins to determine her complaint, then went to reposition the pillow that had slipped out from where it had been cushioning Mrs. Witherspoon's shoulder. But though she tried to focus on the needs around her, she couldn't help glancing up at Drew Wallin again.

Whatever he and Doctor Maynard had discussed seemed to have touched his heart at last. His mouth dipped; his broad shoulders sagged. She could almost see the weight he carried, bowing him lower. What worries forced a knight to bend his knee? Her hand lifted of its own accord, as if some part of her longed to help him shoulder his burden.

She dropped her hand. How silly. She had work to do, a purpose in coming to Seattle that didn't involve any emotional entanglements. She was a trained nurse in an area that badly needed medical assistance. And that was a great blessing.

Every time she eased the pain of another, she forgot the pain inside her. Every time she helped fight off death, she felt as if she'd somehow made up for the deaths of her brother and father on those bloody battle-fields. Surely God did not intend her to leave her profession to serve as any man's bride.

Besides, she liked nursing. Medicine was clinical, precise, measured. It kept her from remembering all she had lost. And each time someone passed beyond her help, she watched their grieving loved ones and knew she could not allow herself to hurt like that again.

No, whatever way she looked at it, she had no business mooning over a wild mountain logger like Drew Wallin. He was a knight with no shining armor, no crusade worthier than her own. The sooner she forgot him, the better.

Andrew Wallin stepped out onto the stone steps of Doc Maynard's hospital and pulled in a deep breath of the late-afternoon air. It never ceased to amaze him how Seattle changed between his visits to town. Another new building was going up across the street, and wagons slogged by in the mud, carrying supplies to camps farther out. The sun beamed down on the planed-wood buildings, the boardwalks stretching between them, anointing the treetops in the distance.

Yet he could not enjoy the sight, thinking about what lay waiting for him back at the Landing. If only he'd been able to counter Maynard's logic. But how could he argue one life against many?

He glanced back at the hospital. Something blue flashed past the tall windows, and he couldn't help thinking about Catherine Stanway. For a moment there, when he'd first spied her in the dispensary, he'd wondered whether his mother had been right to encourage him to find a bride among the ladies Asa Mercer had brought to the territory.

He hadn't been interested. The last thing he needed was a wife to look after when he already had the lives of six people to consider. Besides, he doubted that a lady brought from the big cities back East would know how to handle herself on a backwoods farm without more tutoring than he had time to give.

Catherine Stanway seemed a perfect example of a lady more suited to civilization. She was obviously well educated, her skills suited to a city. Her manners had been polished, her voice cultured and calm. Of course, he much preferred that attitude to the coy smiles and giggles that had marked his interaction with the few unmarried ladies of the Territory.

Then there was the fact that she was so pretty. Her hair was like sunlight shafting through the forest, her eyes resembled a pale winter's sky and the outline of her curves looked lovely behind the apron covering her crisp cotton gown. He knew exactly what would happen if his brothers ever laid eyes on her. Either he'd be standing up as best man in a wedding, or his brothers would hog-tie him and wrestle him to the altar. They seemed determined to see him settled with a wife. They couldn't understand that he already had enough on his hands taking care of them, Ma and Beth. There was nothing left of him to give to a wife.

With a sigh, he started down the steps toward where his team stood waiting farther along the block. The two youths arguing at the side of the wagon gave him as much concern as what was happening at home. As he approached, his youngest brother shoved his friend back. Scout Rankin, scrawnier than Levi despite being the same age, took one look at Drew and loped away. Drew grabbed his brother's shoulders and spun him around.

"What?" Levi snapped, fists raised protectively in front of his lean frame. "I was watching the wagon, just like you asked."

"You'd do better to watch the horses than fight," Drew told him with a shake of his head. He went to check that the sturdy brown farm horses were munching from their feed sacks. "What was Scout doing here?"

"Seeing some people for his father," Levi said, lowering his fists as Drew patted their horses down. "And I thought you were more worried about Ma than the horses. Isn't that why we came to town?"

It was, but he didn't like admitting his fears to Levi any more than he liked having to remind his brother why they didn't associate much with their nearest neighbor. The Wallin family had chosen homesteads at the northern end of Lake Union for the timber. Benjamin Rankin had other reasons entirely to avoid town. He'd turned his cabin into a high-stakes gambling den, and the smells issuing from the place told Drew he was likely making his own liquor, as well. Ma had tried befriending Scout, teaching him to read and write beside Levi, but the son's sullen behavior said he was turning out no better than the father. Drew didn't want any of Scout's bad habits rubbing off on Levi.

He removed the feed sacks and tossed them up to his brother. "Stow these."

"Why? Are we leaving?" his brother asked, clutching the dusty burlap close. "Where's Doc?"

"He's not coming," Drew reported. "Too many patients in town right now."

Levi frowned, dropping the sacks into the wagon. He glanced in the windows of the hospital as he tugged at the hem of his plaid cotton shirt. "I saw you jawin' at that gal. She's pretty enough. Maybe she could convince him to come."

Drew leaned against the rough wood of the wagon. "In the first place, it would take more than a pretty face to get Doc to abandon his patients. In the second place, the less we have to do with Nurse Stanway, the better."

Levi threw up his hands. "She's a nurse? That tears it, Drew. You know how bad Ma needs help. You get back in there and tell that gal she has to come with us!"

Frustration pushed him back from the wagon. "I asked Doc, Levi. He says he needs her here right now. Some women are expected in to give birth."

Levi shook his head, curly blond hair creating a halo he didn't deserve. "Women give birth all the time without someone standing over them. Leastways, that's how Ma did it."

"Ma didn't have a choice," Drew pointed out. "And if you recall, that's how we lost Mary, her giving birth without a doctor there to help. Now simmer down. I still need to check for mail and load the supplies we ordered before heading back."

Levi narrowed his dark blue eyes, a sure sign rebellion was brewing. Drew couldn't blame him. His brother had just turned eighteen and was feeling his oats. Drew had been the same way at that age. Then his father had died and left the responsibility for their mother and five siblings on Drew's shoulders. He'd settled down fast. He was glad Levi didn't have to face the same fate.

Drew slipped a two-bit coin from the pocket of his work trousers and flipped it to his brother, who caught it with one hand. "Tell you what. Take the wagon down to the mercantile and get yourself a sarsaparilla. Ask Mr. Quentin to load up the supplies we bought. I'll meet you there."

Levi was still boy enough that he grinned over the treat as he climbed over the backboard for the bench.

Drew continued on to the post office, but he found nothing waiting for him. He wasn't surprised. Most of his mother's and father's relatives didn't write often. They couldn't understand why his father had left Wisconsin for the far West. They thought themselves pioneers already. But his father had wanted more than the lakes and hills.

He'd wanted a town of his own.

So instead of settling in the hamlet that had been early Seattle, he'd claimed a parcel along Lake Union's shores for himself and his wife. As each Wallin son had come of age, he, too, had laid claim to an adjoining parcel. Drew and his next brother, Simon, had put in the five years of hard work necessary to prove up their own claims, building cabins, tapping springs and clearing land for crops they had yet to plant. John and James were a few years from doing the same. Someday, they all might even have the town his father had dreamed of building.

If Drew could see them all safely raised first.

He headed back toward the mercantile his mother favored. Several wagons were crowded in front, but none of them were his. Where had Levi gotten to now? With a rattle of tack and the rumble of hooves, the wagon pulled up beside him in the street, his brother at the reins, eyes wild. "Come on! Jump in!"

Drew slung himself up on the bench, but he hadn't

even settled in the seat before Levi whipped the reins and whistled to the team. Drew grabbed the sideboard to steady himself as the wagon careened out of town.

"At least tell me you loaded the supplies," he called over the thunder as the two horses galloped up the track that lead north.

"All squared away," Levi shouted back. "Yee-haw! Go!"

Drew was afraid to ask, but he had to know. "You tick off the sheriff again?"

"Naw," Levi yelled. "Just in a hurry to get back to Ma."

Drew felt a twinge of guilt that he wasn't as eager. In truth, he dreaded what he'd find at Wallin Landing, about a two-hour ride from Seattle.

He'd watched, helpless, the past two weeks as his mother had sunk beneath a virulent fever. At first he'd kept his brothers and sister away to prevent the disease from spreading and neglected his work to tend her. The past few days, Levi and Beth had served beside him. Only the combined insistence of his family that they needed help had driven him from Ma's side today.

He hated having to relay the news that Doc Maynard wasn't coming. But he hated more the thought that his mother might not be alive to find out.

So Drew let Levi drive the team more than four miles, until the road petered out to a narrow track near the south of the lake, before he insisted on stopping and giving them a rest. Only when the horses had quieted did he hear the muffled cries from the back of the wagon.

"Now, don't get angry, Drew," Levi said, edging

away from him on the bench as Drew frowned toward the sound. "You know we have to have help."

Drew felt as if one of the firs he felled had toppled into his stomach. He stared at his brother. "What have you done?"

"Ma needs a nurse, and you need a bride," Levi insisted. "So I got you one."

Drew jerked around and yanked the canvas tarp off what he'd thought were only supplies in the bed of the wagon.

Rag stuffed in her mouth, hands trussed before her, Catherine Stanway lay on her back, her bun askew and hair framing her face. She had every right to be terrified, to cry, to swoon.

But the blue eyes glaring back at him were hot as lightning, and her look was nothing short of furious.

He'd have to do a lot of talking if he hoped to calm her down and keep Levi from ending up in jail for his behavior. But he feared no amount of talking was going to keep his brothers from interfering in his life, especially when Levi had just gone and kidnapped Drew a bride.

Chapter Two

"What do you think you're doing?" Catherine demanded the moment Drew Wallin set her on her feet and pulled the rag away. Her mouth felt as dry as dust, every inch of her body bruised by bouncing around on the wagon bed. "I am a citizen of the United States. I have rights! Untie me and return me to Seattle immediately, or I shall report you to the sheriff!"

"Bit on the spiteful side, ain't she?" the young man who had grabbed her said, sitting on the wagon's tongue, safely out of reach of both her and Mr. Wallin.

"Release her, Levi," Mr. Wallin said to him, jaw tight. "And apologize. Now."

The youth jumped down and hurried to Catherine's side. He didn't look the least bit contrite about snatching her out of the hospital, treating her as if she were no more than a bag of threshed wheat. She held out her hands toward him, and his fingers worked the knot he'd made in the rope that bound her wrists.

He'd looked so innocent when he'd appeared in the dispensary—a mop of curly blond hair, eyes turned down like a sad puppy's, cotton shirt and trousers worn but clean. He'd bounded up to her and seized her hands.

"Please," he'd said, lips trembling. "My ma's real sick. You have to come and help her."

She'd thought he'd had an ill woman in a wagon outside. He wouldn't have been the first to pull up to the hospital begging for help. It seemed Doctor Maynard tended to at least one logger a day with a broken arm or leg or a crushed skull. As soon as Mr. Wallin had left, her employer had gone into surgery with his wife, Susanna, assisting him. Catherine had known she couldn't call him away from that until she knew the severity of this young man's mother's illness.

"Show me," she'd said to the youth, taking only a moment to dry her hands before following him out the back of the hospital.

But instead of an older woman huddled on a bench, she'd found a long-bed wagon partially filled with supplies and tools and no other person in sight.

"Where's your mother?" she'd asked.

"About eight miles north," he'd said, wrapping one arm around her and pinioning her arms against her. "But don't you worry none. I'll get you there safe and sound."

She'd opened her mouth to call for help, and he'd shoved in that hideous rag. Though she'd twisted and lashed out with her arms and feet, his whip-cord-thin body was surprisingly strong. He'd tied her up, tossed her in the wagon and covered her with a tarp.

She supposed she should have been afraid, being abducted from her place of work with neither her employer nor any of her new friends to know what had become of her. In truth, she'd been furious that anyone would treat her like this. What, did he think her friendless, an easy victim? When Doctor Maynard realized she was gone, he would likely ask after her at the boardinghouse where she and some of the women who had come West with her were living.

That would concern her friend Madeleine. The feisty redhead would have no trouble enlisting the aid of the sheriff and his young deputy to find Catherine. A posse could be on its way even now.

If the men had any idea which way to go.

That thought gave her pause. As her young kidnapper worked on the rope and Mr. Wallin stood sentinel, arms crossed over his broad chest, she glanced around. The wagon was pulled over among the brush at the edge of the road, two horses waiting. A muddy track stretched in either direction, firs crowding close on both sides. In places she could still see the low stumps of trees that had been cut to carve out the road. She could make out blue sky above, but the forest blocked the view of any landmark that might tell her where she was.

Levi stepped back with a frustrated puff. "She went and pulled the rope too tight. We've going to have to cut it." His voice was nearly a whine at the loss of the cord.

"If you value your material so highly," Catherine said, "next time think before using it to kidnap someone."

"No one is kidnapping anyone," Mr. Wallin said, his firm voice brooking no argument.

She argued anyway. "I believe that is the correct term when one has been abducted and held against her will, sir."

He grimaced. "It may be the right term, but I refuse to allow it to be the right circumstance. We'll return you home as soon as possible."

He pulled out a long knife from the sheath at his waist, the blade honed to a point that gleamed in the sunlight. Though he towered over her as he reached for her, she felt no fear as he sawed through the rope and freed her.

"I haven't heard that apology, Levi," he reminded the boy with a look that would have blistered paint.

Levi shrugged. "Sorry to inconvenience you, but my mother is sick. Now, will you just get back in the wagon so we can go home?"

Catherine took a step away from them both. "I am going no farther. Return me to Seattle."

"Can't," Levi said, hopping back up onto the wagon's tongue. "Too far."

"He's right," Drew Wallin said before Catherine could argue with his brother, as well. He nodded to what must be the west, for she could see the light slanting low through the trees from that direction. "The horses are spent. We'll never make it back to Seattle before dark, and it isn't safe for the horses or us to be out here at night."

She could believe that. Since coming to the town, she'd rarely ventured beyond it. Those forests were dark, the underbrush dense in places. Allegra's husband, Clay Howard, who had accompanied them on their journey from New York, had explained all about the dangers of getting lost—bears, wolves and cougars; unfriendly natives; crumbling cliffs and rushing rivers. She certainly didn't want to blunder about in the dark.

She crossed her arms over her chest. "So where do you propose to take shelter tonight?"

"We'll make for the Landing," he assured her, "but I promise you I'll return you to Seattle tomorrow."

"But tomorrow we're supposed to fell that fir for Captain Collings," Levi protested before Catherine could answer. "We can't do that without you!"

Mr. Wallin turned away from them both. "As Miss Stanway said, there are consequences for your decision," he tossed back over his shoulder as he walked along the wagon to the team. "You should have thought before acting. Now get in the back. Miss Stanway will be riding with me."

Grumbling, the youth clambered deeper into the bed of the wagon and set his back to the sideboard, long legs stretching out over the supplies.

Catherine couldn't make herself follow the elder Mr. Wallin. She still wasn't sure where they were taking her.

"This landing," she said, "how far is it?"

"Another few miles," he replied, running his hands over the nearest horse as if checking for signs of strain. "On Lake Union."

Lake Union was north of Seattle's platted streets, she knew. The *Seattle Gazette*, the weekly newspaper, had been full of stories recently about how the lake could serve as Seattle's chief water source as the town grew. There'd been talk of building a navigable canal between Lake Washington to the east and Lake Union, perhaps even to Puget Sound for transporting logs.

But right now, all those were nothing but dreams. The only people she knew about who lived on Lake Union were Indians.

And, apparently, Drew Wallin.

"Are there any women at this landing?" she asked.

He had been frowning at her. Now his brow cleared as if he understood her concerns at last.

"My mother and my sister," he said. "Beth is only

fourteen, but I think most of the gossips in Seattle would count her as a chaperone. Your reputation is safe, ma'am."

Still she couldn't make herself move. Was he telling the truth? Was Seattle really so far behind them? She glanced back the way they had come and saw only the mud of the track stretching into the distance—no sign of smoke from a campfire or cabin, no other travelers. A gull swooped low with a mournful call. They were close to water, then, but she could say that of any location near Seattle.

She was tempted to simply walk away, but if a wagon and team couldn't reach Seattle by dark, what chance did she have on foot?

She nodded. "Very well, Mr. Wallin."

She followed him back to the box of the wagon, passing Levi's narrowed look. He acted as if she should feel guilty for inconveniencing *him*! A shame she was entirely too mature to stick out her tongue at him, however highly satisfactory that would have been. A shame Maddie wasn't here with her. Her friend would have given him an earful.

They reached the front of the wagon, and she put out her hand to climb in. Before she knew what he was about, Drew Wallin put both hands on her waist and lifted her onto the bench as if she weighed nothing. For the first time since this adventure had started, her heart stuttered. She took a deep breath to steady herself and busied herself arranging her skirts as he jumped up beside her and took the reins.

"Give her your hat," he ordered Levi without so much as looking back.

The youth, who had been lounging against the side of

the wagon, jerked upright. "Give her your own. You're the oldest."

"I don't require a hat," Catherine assured them both, but Mr. Wallin reached one arm over the back of the box and rapped his brother on the head. In answer, Levi tossed up a brown wool hat with a battered brim, which Mr. Wallin caught with one hand. He offered it to Catherine as if it were a jeweled ring on a velvet pillow.

"We still have a ways to go," he explained when she hesitated. "And I need to walk the horses, so it may take us a bit. I know my sister is always talking about how a lady needs to protect her complexion from the sun."

He was trying to be considerate, and though the hat had clearly seen better days, she knew it for a peace offering.

"Thank you," she said, accepting it and setting it on her hair. But one touch to her head, and she realized how disheveled she must appear. The bun she normally wore had come partially undone while she'd struggled. Strands clung to one ear; others hung down her back. As Drew clucked to the horses, setting them plodding up the track, she pulled out the last of her pins and let the tresses fall.

She had piled up the pins in the lap of her apron when something brushed the back of her hair. She jerked around to find Levi on his knees behind her, staring at her as he pulled back his hand.

"It's like moonlight on the lake," he said, voice hushed and eyes wide.

"Sit down," his brother grit out. He whipped the reins, and the horses darted forward. Levi fell with a thud onto the wagon bed.

Catherine faced front, mouth compressed to keep from laughing.

"I apologize for my brother," Drew said, slowing the horses once more. Catherine could see that his ruddy cheeks were darkening. "He's spent too much time in the woods."

"So have you," Levi grumbled, but Catherine could hear him settling himself against the wood.

Better not to encourage him. She twisted up her hair and pinned it carefully in place at the back of her head as the horses continued north. The track dwindled until the trees crowded on either side and the ruts evened out to ground covered by low bushes and broad-leafed vines. She sighted something long and dark hanging from a blackberry bramble, as if it had reached out to snag the last horse or human who had ventured this way.

Both Wallin men fell silent. The clatter of the wagon wasn't so loud that she could miss the scree of the hawk that crossed the opening between the trees. The breeze was coming in off the Sound, bringing the scent of brine like fingers combing through the bushes.

He leadeth me beside still waters. He restoreth my soul.

That chance for peace was what had brought her here so very far from what she'd planned for her life. She should not let the misguided actions of an impetuous boy change that.

Nor the fluttering of a heart she had sworn to keep safely cocooned from further pain.

How could his brother have been so boneheaded? Drew glanced over his shoulder at the youth. Levi had curled himself around the supplies on the wagon bed

like a hound before the fire, and it wouldn't surprise
Drew if his brother started snoring. The boy had absolutely no remorse for what he'd done. Where had Drew
gone wrong?

"I'm really very sorry," he apologized again to Catherine as he faced front. "I don't know what got into him.
He was raised better."

"Out in the woods, you said," she replied, gaze toward the front, as well. Her hair was once more confined behind her head, and he knew a moment of regret
at its disappearance. Levi might have been the one to
cry out at the sight of it, but the satiny tresses had held
him nearly as captive.

"On the lake," he told her. "My father brought us
to Seattle about fifteen years ago from Wisconsin and
chose a spot far out. He said a man needed something
to gaze out on in the morning besides his livestock or
his neighbors."

She smiled as if the idea pleased her. "And your
mother?" she asked, shifting on the wooden bench, her
wide blue skirts filling the space at her feet. "Is she
truly ill?"

It was difficult to even acknowledge the fact. He nodded, turning his gaze out over the horses. "She came
down with a fever nearly a fortnight ago."

He could feel her watching him. "A fever that lasts
that long is never good," she informed him in a pleasant voice he was sure must calm many a patient. "Do
you open the windows daily to air her room?"

He'd fetched gallons of water from the spring, even
trudged down to the lakeshore to draw it cold from the
depths. He'd stoked up the fire, wrapped Ma tight in
covers. But he hadn't considered opening the windows.

"No," he answered. "Doesn't cold air just make you sicker?"

She shook her head, Levi's hat sliding on the silk of her hair. "No, indeed. The fear of it is a common belief I have had to fight repeatedly. Fresh air, clean water, healthy food—those are what cure a body, sir. That is what my father taught. That is what I practice."

She was so sure of the facts that he couldn't argue. He knew from conversations with Doc Maynard that Seattle was woefully behind on recent medical advancements. As one of the few physicians, Doc was overwhelmed with the number of people ill or injured. He must have been overjoyed to have Catherine join his staff.

"I hope you'll be able to help her, then, ma'am," he told her. "Before we return you to Seattle tomorrow."

He glanced her way in time to see her gaze drift out over the horses. "You did not seem so sure of my skills earlier, sir."

With Levi right behind him, he wasn't about to admit that his initial concern had been for his brother's matchmaking, not the lack of her skills. "We've known Doc for years," he hedged.

He thought her shoulders relaxed a little. She sat so prim and proper it was hard to tell. "My father's patients felt the same way. There is nothing like the trusted relationship of your family doctor. But I will do whatever I can to help your mother."

Levi's smug voice floated up from behind. "I knew she'd come around."

Though Drew was relieved at the thought of Catherine's help, he wanted nothing more than to turn and thump Levi again.

"As you can see," he said instead to Catherine, "my brother has a bad habit of acting or talking without thinking." He glanced back into the wagon in time to see Levi making a face at him.

"My brother was the same way," she assured him as he turned to the front again with a shake of his head. "He borrowed my father's carriage more than once, drove it all over the county. He joined the Union Army on his eighteenth birthday before he'd even received a draft notice."

"Sounds like my kind of fellow," Levi said, kneeling so that his head came between them. "Did he journey West with you?"

Though her smile didn't waver, her voice came out flat. "No. He was killed at the Battle of Five Forks in Virginia."

Levi looked stricken as he glanced between her and Drew. "I'm sorry, ma'am. I didn't know."

"Of course you didn't," she replied, but Drew saw that her hands were clasped tightly in her lap as if she were fighting with herself not to say more.

"I'm sorry for your loss," Drew said. "That must have been hard on you and your parents."

"My mother died when I was nine," she said, as if commenting on the weather. "My father served as a doctor in the army. He died within days of Nathan. It was a very bloody war."

How could she sit so calmly? If he'd lost so much he would have been railing at the sky.

Levi was obviously of a similar mind. "That's awful!" He threw himself back into the bed. "Pa died when I was eight, but I think I would have gone plumb crazy if I'd lost Drew and Simon and James and John, too."

Her brows went up as she glanced at Drew. "You have four brothers?"

He chuckled. "Yes, and most days I'm glad of it."

"We had another sister, too, besides Beth," Levi said, popping up again. "She died when she was a baby. Simon says it about broke Ma's heart."

It had almost broken Drew's heart, as well. His parents had been grieving so hard that he'd had to be the one to fashion the tiny coffin and dig the little grave at the edge of the family land. He'd never dreamed his father would be dead just five years later.

Please, Lord, don't make me bury another member of my family!

The prayer came quickly, and just as quickly he regretted it. It was selfish. If a man prayed, he should ask the Almighty for wisdom to lead, strength to safeguard those he loved. The Lord had blessed him with strength. Some days he wasn't too sure about the wisdom.

Beside him, Miss Stanway's face softened, as if his pain had touched her.

"I'm sorry for your loss, as well," she said. They were the expected words; he'd just used them on her. He'd heard them countless times at his father's passing and his sister's. Yet the look she cast him, the tears pooling in her blue eyes, told him she understood more than most.

He wanted to reach out, clasp her hand, promise her the future would be brighter. But that was nonsense! He couldn't control the future, and she was his to protect only until he returned her to Seattle. He had enough on his hands without taking on a woman new to the frontier.

Besides, every settlement within a hundred miles needed her help. Catherine Stanway might not have realized it yet, but a nurse was a valuable commodity, even if she wasn't so pretty or one of a few unmarried women in the Territory.

Which made him wonder how far his brothers might go to keep her at Wallin Landing.

Chapter Three

Twilight wrapped around the forest by the time Catherine's host guided the team into a grassy clearing crossed by moss-crusted split-rail fences. A large cabin and a barn made from logs and planed timber hugged the edges, with trees standing guard behind them as if honoring their fallen brothers and sisters. Another light through the trees told her at least one more cabin was nearby. The glow through the windows of the closest cabin beckoned to her.

"Where's the lake?" she asked as Drew hopped down and came around the wagon.

He nodded toward the cabin, a two-story affair with a pitched roof and a porch at one end. It was encircled by a walk of planed boards.

"Through the trees there," he said. "We're on a bench fifty feet or so above the waterline. Keeps us out of any flooding in the spring."

His father had obviously planned ahead. She wouldn't have thought about spring flooding when choosing a plot for a house. Of course, she'd never had to choose a homesite in the wilderness!

She turned to climb down, and once again Drew reached out and lifted her from the wagon to set her on her feet. For a moment it was as if she stood in his embrace. His eyes were a smoky blue in the dim light. She couldn't seem to remember why she was here, what she was supposed to do next.

The sound of Levi scrambling out of the wagon bed woke her, and she pulled away. As the youth started past, his brother put out an arm to stop him.

"See to the horses and bring in the supplies. I'll take our guest inside."

Levi's face tightened, but then he glanced at Catherine. As if he finally realized it was his fault she was here, he shrugged and went to do as he had been bid.

"This way," Drew said with another nod toward the cabin.

The Wallin home might have been made from peeled logs, but it appeared the family had taken pains to make the place attractive as well as functional. Stained glass panels decorated the top of each window on the two floors. Boxes filled with plants underpinned the two larger downstairs windows; she recognized several kinds of flowering herbs. Someone had plaited a wreath from fir branches and hung it from the thick front door. The resinous smell greeted Catherine as she approached.

Drew reached for the latch, but the panel swung open without his aid. Catherine only had time to register blond hair darker and a good foot lower than hers before a young lady launched herself into her arms.

"Thank you, oh, thank you!" The girl drew back to grin at Catherine. "I know this was a terrible long way to come, but we need a nurse badly. Simon and James and John will be so glad to see you! They'll be by later, my brothers, all of them. They thought you or Doc or whoever was coming should have some time to yourself before they came stampeding in, but I couldn't wait to get to know you better."

"Beth," Drew rumbled beside Catherine.

The girl didn't even pause for breath as she seized Catherine's hand and pulled her across the colorful braided rag rug into the wide, warm room, which was lit by a glowing fire. "I'll make an apron for you to wear. *Godey's Lady's Book* says they're all the rage for the fashionable lady of industry."

"Beth," Drew said a little more firmly as he followed them.

"I have stew ready for dinner," his sister continued, and Catherine could smell the tangy scent drifting through the cabin as Beth tugged her past a long table with ladder-back chairs at each end and benches along the sides. Similar chairs rested against the walls, cane seats partially covered by small quilts, and a bentwood rocker stood near the rounded stone fireplace. Through the openings on either side of the hearth she caught sight of a step stove with kettles simmering. A massive iron tub leaned against the outside wall.

"I know it's not much," Beth said, "but I wasn't sure when you'd get here and I was afraid I'd dry out the venison if I kept it on the stove too long. Do you like stew?"

"Yes," Catherine assured her, pulling herself to a stop in the middle of the room, "but..."

Beth didn't wait for more. "Oh, good! This time of year we only have early carrots, of course, but I still had potatoes and turnips left from the fall. We have our own garden behind the house. Drew cleared the land. In a few weeks, we'll have peas and beans and cabbage and…"

"Beth!"

Drew's thundering voice made Catherine cringe, but it finally stopped his sister, in word and in action. She turned to frown at him, firelight rippling across her straight golden hair. "What?"

"Doc Maynard couldn't come," he said without a hint of apology in his voice. "This is Miss Stanway. She's a nurse, but she'll only be staying the night with us. I'll return her to Seattle tomorrow."

"Oh." The single word seemed to echo in the room. She dropped her gaze and tucked a strand of hair behind her ear. Now that she was still, Catherine could see that she had a heart-shaped face like her brother, wide-spaced eyes and the beginnings of a figure. Her cheeks were turning as pink as the narrow-skirted gingham gown she wore.

"It was a natural mistake," Catherine assured her with a smile. "And I'll be happy to help your mother while I'm here."

Beth glanced up and brightened. Her eyes were darker than her older brother's, closer to the midnight blue of Levi's. Catherine had a feeling that one day a large number of suitors would be calling.

"Thank you," Beth said, good humor apparently restored. "And I truly am happy to make your acquaintance. Would you like to see Ma now?"

Before Catherine could answer, Drew stepped forward, gaze all for his sister, his brows drawn down heavily over his deep-set eyes. "How is she?"

Beth's light dimmed, and she seemed to shrink in on herself. "Still the same. I'm not sure she knows me."

Catherine felt as if her spine had lengthened, her shoulders strengthened. Her father had always said it was a powerful thing to have a purpose. She felt it now, wiping away her weariness and soothing her frustrations. *Thank You, Lord. Help me do what You fitted me to do.*

"Take me to her," she ordered them.

Beth clasped her hands in obvious relief. Drew merely motioned Catherine to where a set of open stairs, half logs driven into the wall, rose to the second story.

Upstairs were two more rooms, divided by the fireplace and the walls that supported it. One room held several straw ticks on the floor, but only one seemed to be in use; the others were piled with rumpled clothing, tools and chunks of wood. The other room contained two wooden beds—a smaller one in the corner with a carved chest beside it and a larger bedstead in the center with a side table holding a brass lamp. Both beds were covered with multicolored quilts that brightened the room.

A woman lay on the wider bed. She had hair that was more red than gold, plastered to her oval face. She'd been handsome once, but now pain had drawn lines about her eyes, nose and mouth. By the way the collar of her flannel nightgown bagged, Catherine guessed she'd lost some weight, as well. Her skin looked like parchment in the candlelight.

Catherine sat in the high-backed chair that had been placed next to the bed and reached for Mrs. Wallin's hand. Setting her fingers to the woman's wrist, she counted the heartbeats as her father had taught her. She could feel Drew and his sister watching her. She'd been watched by family members before, some doubt-

ing her, some worried. This time felt different somehow. Her shoulders tensed, and she forced them to relax.

"Her pulse is good," she reported, keeping her voice
calm and her face composed. She had to remain objective. It was so much easier to do her job when she
viewed the person before her as a patient in need of
healing rather than someone's mother or wife. She
leaned closer, listening to the shallow, panting breaths.

"Mrs. Wallin," she said, "can you hear me?"

The woman's eyelids fluttered. Drew and Beth
leaned closer as well, crowding around Catherine. Their
mother's eyes opened, as clear as her eldest son's but
greener. She blinked as if surprised to find herself in
bed, then focused on Catherine.

"Mary?" she asked.

Beth sucked in a breath, drawing back and hugging
herself. Drew didn't move, but Catherine felt as if he
also had distanced himself. Who was this Mary his
mother had been expecting? Did Drew Wallin have a
wife he'd neglected to mention?

Drew watched as Catherine tended to his mother.
Ma had changed so much in the past two weeks that he
hardly knew her. As Beth had said, he wasn't sure she
knew them, either. It was as if the fire that had warmed
them all their lives was growing dim.

He had feared Catherine might confirm the fact, tell
them in her cool manner to prepare for the worst. Instead, she was all confidence. She opened the window
beside the bed and ordered the one opposite it opened
as well, drawing in the cool evening air and the scent of
the Sound. She directed Drew to smother the fire and
helped Beth pull off some of the covers they had piled

on their mother in an attempt to sweat the fever from her. She even removed Ma's favorite feather pillow and requested a straw one. It was testimony to how ill their mother was that she protested none of this.

"Do you have a milk cow?" Catherine asked Drew as Beth dug through the chest their father had carved for Ma to find the clean nightgown Catherine had suggested.

Drew shook his head. "Four goats. But they produce enough milk for our purposes."

Catherine accepted the flannel gown from Beth with a nod of thanks. "What about lemons?"

"Simon brought some back from town last week," Beth said, tucking her hair behind her ear and hugging herself with her free hand. "I used some for lemonade."

"Fetch the lemonade," Catherine advised. "We'll start with that and see if she can tolerate it. Later, I'll show you how to make lemon whey. Mrs. Child recommends it for high fevers."

"Mrs. Child?" Drew asked, but his sister nodded eagerly.

"I know Mrs. Child! Ma has her book on being a good housewife. She's very clever."

Beth might have gone on as she often did, but Catherine directed her toward the stairs, then turned to Drew. "I'll need warm water, as well."

Drew frowned. "To drink?"

Pink crept across her cheekbones, as delicate as the porcelain cups his mother had safeguarded over the Rockies on their way West. "No," she said, gaze darting away from his. "To bathe your mother. Can you see that it's warmed properly? Not too hot."

"Coming right up," Drew promised, and left to find some help.

He managed to locate the rest of his family at Simon's cabin, which was a little ways into the woods. His brothers were cleaning up before dinner, but they all stopped what they were doing to listen to his explanation of what had happened in town. He thought at least one of them might agree with him that Levi's actions were rash. But to a man they were too concerned about Ma to consider how Catherine Stanway must feel.

"So this nurse," Simon said, draping the cloth he'd been using to dry his freshly shaven face over the porcelain basin in a corner of his cabin. "What do we know about her? What are her credentials?"

Figure on Simon, his next closest brother in age at about two years behind Drew's twenty-nine, to ask. He was the only one tall enough to look him in the eye, for all they rarely saw eye to eye. With his pale blond hair and angled features, Simon was too cool. Even looked different from Drew. Every movement of his lean body, word from his lips and look from his light green eyes seemed calculated.

The middle brother, James, leaned back where he sat near the fire, effortlessly balancing the stool on one of its three legs. "Does it really matter, Simon? She's here, and she's helping. Be grateful." He turned to Drew. His long face was a close match for Simon's in its seriousness, his short blond hair a shade darker, but there was a twinkle in his dark blue eyes. "Now, I have a more pressing question. Is she pretty?"

"That's not important," Drew started, but his second-youngest brother, John, slapped his hands down on his knees where he sat at a bench by the table.

"She must be! He's blushing!" He shook his head, red-gold hair straighter than his mother's like a flame in the light.

Drew took a deep breath to hold back a retort. Of all his brothers, John was the most sensible, the most studious. If he'd seen a change in Drew, it must be there.

But he wasn't about to admit it.

He started for the door. "Pretty or not, she has work for us to do. She wants lots of water warmed. You bring it in. I'll heat it up." He glanced back over his shoulder. "And John, find Levi. He should have finished in the barn by now. I don't want him wandering off."

"Where would he go?" James teased, letting the stool clatter back to the floor as he climbed to his feet. "It's not as if he has tickets to the theatre."

"Or one to attend within a hundred miles," John agreed, but he headed for the barn as Drew had requested.

For the next couple of hours everyone was too busy to joke. His brothers took turns bringing in the water to Drew, who heated it in his mother's largest pot on the step stove. Then they formed a line up the stairs and passed the warm water in buckets up to Beth and Miss Stanway.

"She washed Ma with a soft cloth, then rubbed her down with another," Beth marveled to Drew at the head of the stairs when he ventured up to check on them after he and his brothers had eaten. "And she changed the sheets on the bed without even making Ma get up. She's amazing!"

Drew had to agree, for when Catherine beckoned him closer, he found his mother much improved. No longer did she look like a wax figure on the bed, and she smiled at each of her sons as they clustered around to speak with her.

"I think it's time to rest," Catherine said to them all after a while. "I'll come talk to you after I've settled her."

Drew herded everyone down the stairs. They all found seats in the front room, Simon and James on opposite ends of the table, John on a bench alongside, Beth in Ma's rocking chair and Levi sprawled on the braided rug with Drew standing behind him leaning against the stairs. He caught himself counting heads, even though he knew everyone was present. Habit. He'd been watching over them for the past ten years, ever since the day his father had died.

It had been a widow-maker that had claimed their father. Drew had been eighteen then, and only Simon at sixteen and James at fourteen had been old enough and strong enough to help clear the timber for their family's original claim. None of them had seen the broken limb high on the massive fir before it came crashing down.

"Take care of them," his father had said when his brothers had pulled the limb off him and Drew had cradled him in his arms. Already his father's voice had started wheezing from punctured lungs, and blood had tinged his lips. "Take care of them all, Andrew. This family is your responsibility."

He had never forgotten. He hadn't lost another member of the family, though his brothers had made the job challenging. They'd broken arms and legs, cut themselves on saws and knives, fought off diseases he was afraid to name. Even sweet Beth had given him a scare a few months ago when she'd nearly succumbed to a fever much like their mother's.

He'd kept them safe, nursed them through any illness or injury. His had been the shoulders they'd cried on, the arms that had held them through the night. He'd been the one to ride for medicine, to cut cloths into bandages. He'd been the one to sit up with them night after night. Having someone help felt odd, as if he'd put on the wrong pair of boots.

That odd feeling didn't ease as Catherine came down the stairs to join them. As if she were a schoolmarm prepared to instruct, she took up her place by the fire. The crackling flames set her figure in silhouette.

"I thought you would all want to hear what I believe about your mother's condition," she said, and Drew knew he wasn't the only Wallin leaning forward to catch every word.

"Two culprits cause this type of fever," she continued, gaze moving from one brother to another until it met Drew's. "Typhus and typhoid fever."

Neither sounded good, and his stomach knotted.

"Aren't they the same thing?" John asked.

She shook her head. "Many people think so, and some doctors treat them the same, but they are very different beasts. With typhus, the fever never leaves, and the patient simply burns up."

Beth shivered and rubbed a hand up her arm.

"Typhoid fever, on the other hand," Catherine said as if she hadn't noticed, "is generally worse for the first two or three weeks and then starts to subside. Given how long you said she's suffered, I'm leaning toward typhoid fever, but we should know for sure within the week."

Simon seized on the word. "A week. Then, you'll stay with us for that long." It was a statement, not a question.

"I promised to return Miss Stanway to Seattle to-morrow," Drew said.

Simon scowled at him.

"We need her more than Seattle does," Levi complained.

His other brothers murmured their agreement.

"That isn't our decision to make," Drew argued.

"No," Catherine put in. "It's mine."

That silenced them. She clasped her hands in front of her blue gown. "Doctors take an oath to care for their patients. My father believed that nurses should take one, as well. It is my duty to care for your mother and for you, should you sicken."

A duty she took seriously, he could see. Her color was high, her face set with determination as she glanced around at them all. "I will stay until your mother is out of danger."

Simon stood. "It's settled, then. Drew, clear out your cabin and let her have it. You can bunk with me. I snore less than Levi or James."

John rolled his eyes. "That's what you think."

"Oh, I couldn't take anyone's cabin," Catherine started.

Drew held up his hand. "No, Simon's right. Not about his snoring. He's louder than Yesler's sawmill." As his other brothers laughed and Simon shook his head, Drew continued, "You need a place of your own. I'll clear out my cabin tonight so you can sleep when you finish with Ma."

"I intend to stay up with her tonight," Catherine warned him.

"Then the cabin will be waiting for you in the morning," Drew assured her.

She smiled at them. "Well, then, gentlemen, I will leave you for the night. I understand the youngest Mr. Wallin sleeps upstairs. I'll send him if we need anything."

Again Levi looked as if he were going to protest, but one glance at Drew and he shrugged and settled back on the rug. Drew watched her climb the stairs, Beth right behind her.

"That's quite a woman," Simon mused, stretching his feet over Levi's prone form toward the fire.

"Never met one so determined," James mused.

"You never met one with that kind of education, either," John reminded him. "I like the fact that she isn't afraid to speak her mind."

"Bit on the bossy side," Levi said with a yawn. "But she'll do."

"That she will," Simon agreed. "The only question is, which one of us is going to marry her?"

Just what he'd feared. Drew stiffened. "No one said anything about marriage."

Simon glanced around at his brothers. "I believe I just did."

John nodded, brightening. "Inspired. She's smart, and she has a skill we sorely need."

"And she's not bad to look at," James added.

"You could do a lot worse, Drew," Levi agreed.

Drew shook his head. "You're mad, the lot of you. I'm not getting married."

"Suit yourself." Simon rose and went to the fireplace to scoop up a handful of kindling. "We'll draw straws. Short straw proposes."

Drew stared as his other brothers, except Levi, rose

to their feet. "Don't be ridiculous. She wouldn't have any of you."

James shrugged. "Doesn't hurt to try."

Simon squared up the sticks and hid all but the tops in his hand, then held them out to his brothers. "Who wants to go first?"

Drew strode into their group. "Enough, I said. No one is proposing to Miss Stanway, and that's final."

His brothers exchanged glances. Simon lowered the sticks. "Very well, Drew. For now. But you have to marry someday if you want kin to inherit your land. You'll never build that town for Pa unless you do. I think you better ask yourself why you're so dead set against her."

"And why you're even more set against us courting her," John added.

Chapter Four

So one of the Wallin brothers was going to marry her. Catherine shook her head as she crossed the floor to the big bed. Either they didn't know voices carried in the log cabin or they didn't care that she realized their intentions. It truly didn't matter which was the truth. She wasn't getting married.

"Do you think bonnets or hats are more fetching on a lady?" Beth asked, following her. "I'm of a mind for bonnets. They cover more of your face from the sun, and they have extra room for decorations. Feathers are ever so flattering."

She was chattering again, voice quick and forceful, but it seemed a bit more strained than usual, and Catherine couldn't help noticing that Beth's color was high as she joined Catherine. Was she trying to pretend she wasn't aware of her brothers' intentions?

Her patient was awake, green eyes watchful. "You mustn't mind Simon," Mrs. Wallin murmured, proving that she, too, had heard at least part of the conversation downstairs. The ribbon ties on her nightcap brushed the skin of her cheek. "Being the second son after Drew has never been easy. He tends to assert himself even when there's no need."

As Beth tidied up the room, Catherine raised her patient's wrist to check her pulse. It seemed just a little stronger, but perhaps that was because Mrs. Wallin was embarrassed by her sons' behavior.

"And there is no need to assert himself in this situation," Catherine told her as she lowered Mrs. Wallin's hand. "I'm here to help you. Nothing more."

Mrs. Wallin shivered, and Catherine touched the woman's forehead. Still too hot, but did she perhaps feel a little cooler than earlier? Was Catherine so desperate to see hope that she had lost her ability to be objective?

"Am I going to die?" Mrs. Wallin whispered.

Beth gasped. Catherine pulled back her hand. "Not if I can help it."

As Beth hurried closer, Mrs. Wallin reached out and took Catherine's hand, for all the world as if Catherine was the one needing comfort. "I'm not afraid." Her eyes were bright, and Catherine told herself it was the fever. "I know in Whom I've put my trust. But my boys and Beth, oh, I hate the idea of leaving them!"

Beth threw herself onto the bed, wrapping her mother in a fierce hug. "You're not leaving us, Ma. I won't let you!"

The room seemed to be growing smaller, the air thinner. Catherine pulled out of the woman's grip.

"Now, then," she made herself say with brisk efficiency. "I see nothing to indicate your mother must leave you anytime soon. The best thing now would be for her to rest. I'll be right here if she needs me."

Beth straightened and wiped a tear from her face.

"Yes, of course. I'll just go help Drew." She hurried from the loft.

"She's a dear child," her mother murmured, settling in the bed. "She'll need someone besides me, another lady, to help guide her."

Someone besides Catherine. "Rest now," she urged, and Mrs. Wallin nodded and dutifully closed her eyes, head sinking deeper into the pillow, face at peace.

A shame Catherine couldn't find such peace. She perched on the chair beside the bed and tried to steady her breathing. Still, the woman's fears and Beth's re-action clung to her like cobwebs. Who was Catherine to promise Mrs. Wallin's return to health? Only the Lord knew what the future held. Her earthly father had drummed that into her.

We may be His hands for healing, he'd say as he washed his hands after surgery. *But He will determine the outcome of our work.*

And the outcome of a life.

Did he have to go, Lord? Did You need another phy-sician in heaven? But why take Nathan, too? Did You have to leave me alone?

The tears were starting again, and she blinked them fiercely away. She'd had her fill of them months ago. She couldn't look at the sunny yellow rooms of their home in Sudbury without seeing the book her father had left before going to war, the galoshes her brother had forgotten to pack. The polished wood pew in their community church had felt empty even though another family had joined her in it. Every time she'd walked down the street, she'd seem nothing but stares of pity from her neighbors.

Still, her father had taught her well.

You cannot let sorrow touch you, Catherine, he'd admonished. *You are here to tend to their bodies. Let the Lord heal other hurts. Remember your calling.*

That was what she'd done in those dark days after her father and brother had died. None of the other physicians in the area had wanted to attach themselves professionally to an unmarried nurse. Even the big cities like Boston and New York had been loath to let an unmarried woman practice. Widowed men who had known her father well offered marriage, the opportunity to mother their motherless children. Even her minister had counseled her to find a good man to wed.

When she'd seen the notice advertising Asa Mercer's expedition to help settle Washington Territory, she'd known what to do. She'd put the house up for sale and donated their things to those in need. Then she'd packed her bags and sailed to the opposite side of the country.

All her experiences had taught her how to wall off her emotions. It did no good to question her past. She must look to her future, to the health of the community she could improve, the lives she could save. She had no intention of entering into marriage, with anyone.

For once she opened the door to feeling, she was very much afraid she'd never be able to close it again.

At the far edge of the clearing in his own cabin, Drew yanked a pair of suspenders off the ladder to the loft. As he tidied the place so Catherine could sleep there that night, all he could think about was Simon's ridiculous demand that one of them must marry the pretty nurse.

He ought to be immune to such antics by now. But after years of proximity, his brothers knew just how to get under his skin like a tick digging for blood.

Oh, he'd heard ministers preach on the subject. A man had a duty to marry, to raise children that would help him subdue the wilderness, make a home in this far land. Children were one way a man left a legacy. To him, the fact that his brothers had reached their manhood alive and ready to take on the world was enough of a legacy.

He knew the general course of things was for a man to find his own land, build a house, start a profession and marry. He had this house and was top in his profession, but he couldn't simply leave his mother, Beth or his brothers to fend for themselves. They were his responsibility, his to protect. That was what any man did who was worthy of the name. That was what his father had done.

How could he call himself a man and leave his family to tend to a wife? In his mind, a wife took time, attention. She'd have requirements, needs and expectations. He already felt stretched to the breaking point. How could he add more?

Oh, he had no doubt Simon and James were looking to marry one day, and John and Levi would eventually follow. But to stake a claim on a lady after a few hours of acquaintance? That was the stuff of madness.

Or legend.

He snorted as he gathered up the dishes he hadn't bothered to return to the main house. Their father had claimed he'd fallen in love with their mother at first sight when he'd met her at a barn raising. *Her hair was like a fire on a winter's night, calling me home*, he'd told his sons more than once.

Before his father had died, Drew had dreamed it would happen that way for him. Though there were

few unmarried ladies in Seattle, he'd thought someday he might turn a corner, walk into church and there
she'd be. But at twenty-nine, he knew better. Love was
a choice built from prolonged presence. And with six
lives already depending on him, he had chosen not to
participate in adding more.

"Hello, brother Drew!" Beth sang out as she opened
the door of his cabin, basket under one arm. She stepped
inside, glanced around and wrinkled her nose. "Oh, you
haven't gotten far, have you?"

Drew looked around as well, trying to see the place
through Beth's eyes. He'd built the cabin himself, his
brothers lending a hand with planing and notching the
logs and chinking them with dried moss and rock. He'd
crafted the fireplace in the center of one wall from
rounded stones gathered along the lake. As his father
had taught him from what he'd learned in his home-
land of Sweden, Drew had built a cabinet for his bed
tick, setting it next to the hearth for warmth. A table
and chairs of lumber cut from trees he'd felled rested
on the rag rug his mother had woven for him. A plain
wood chest sat against the far wall, waiting for him to
start carving. All in all, his cabin was a solid, practical place to sleep between long hours of working. Very
likely, Beth considered it far too plain.

But it didn't matter what his sister thought. It mattered what Catherine Stanway thought, and he had no
doubt she'd find it lacking.

He pointed his sister to the corn-tassel broom leaning against one wall. "If you think the cabin needs more
work, feel free to lend a hand."

He busied himself with shaking out the quilt his
mother had made for him.

Beth hummed to herself as she set down the basket and began sweeping dried mud off the floor. "I like her," she announced, and Drew knew she had to be talking about Catherine. "She knows a lot. And did you see that dress? There was one just like it in *Godey's*."

His sister devoured the ladies' magazine, which generally arrived in Seattle months after its publication back East. The editor of *Godey's*, Drew was convinced, had never laid eyes on a frontier settlement, or she'd never have suggested some of the outlandish fashions. What woman needed skirts so wide they couldn't fit through the door of a cabin or allow her to climb to the loft of her bed?

"I'm sure Miss Stanway was all the rage back home," Drew said, hauling the table back into place in the center of the room from where James and John had shoved it during a friendly wrestling match a few days ago.

"Here, too." Beth giggled as she paused. "I think Simon is smitten."

"Simon can go soak his head in the lake." The vehemence of his words surprised him, and so did the emotions riding on them. The first thought that had popped into his head at his sister's teasing was the word *mine*.

Beth must have noticed the change in his tone as well, for she turned to regard him wide-eyed. "You like her!"

Drew shoved the chairs into place with enough force to set the table to rocking on its wooden legs. "I like the fact that she can help Ma. That's what's important—not the rest of this tomfoolery."

"I suppose you're right." She resumed her sweeping, angling the pile of dust toward the doorway. "Still, I hope she'll let me talk to her about how they're wearing their hair back East. Every time I try the curling iron, I get it so hot I can hardly touch it. I bet she'll know how to do it right."

Hand on the wooden bucket to fill it with fresh water from the pump outside, Drew paused. "You think she curls her hair?"

"And irons her dresses." Beth nodded with great confidence. "She might even use rouge to get that glow in her cheeks."

What was he doing? This wasn't the sort of thing a man discussed, even with his little sister. He hefted the bucket and headed for the door. "You're too young to rouge your cheeks or curl your hair, Beth. And Miss Stanway is here to help Ma, not teach you things you don't need to know."

Beth made a face at him as he opened the door. "You don't get to decide what I need to know. You couldn't possibly understand. You're a man." When he turned to argue, she swept the dirt up into the air in a cloud of dust that nearly choked him.

Drew waved his hand, backing away. "I'm your brother, and the last time I checked, I'm responsible for your upbringing. If you can't leave Miss Stanway be on such matters, I'll make sure you have other things to do elsewhere."

"You would, too," Beth declared, lowering the broom. "But you're right. We should be thinking about Ma." Her face crumpled. "Oh, I sure hope Miss Stanway knows what's she's doing. I just can't lose Ma!"

Cold pierced him. Drew went to enfold his sister in his arms, getting a broom handle on the chin for his trouble. "We won't lose her, Beth. We won't let her go."

Beth nodded against his chest, and he heard her sniff.

When she pushed back, she wiped her face with her fingers, leaving two tracks of mud across her cheeks. This from the girl who admired rouge, of all things.

As Drew smiled, she turned to glance back into the cabin. "The place is looking better already. You go check on Ma, and I'll add a few finishing touches."

Drew cocked his head. "Like what? I'll have none of those doilies you're so fond of."

Beth turned to him, eyes wide. "Who could hate an innocent doily? They're so dainty and cultured."

Everything he was not, he realized, and trying to pretend otherwise served no one. "Just remember, this is a man's house," he told his sister as he stepped out onto the porch. "Miss Stanway may be staying awhile, but I'm the one who lives here."

With a feeling he was talking to the air, he left Beth humming to herself.

Rouge. He shook his head again. His mother had complained about the stuff from time to time.

A lady makes the most of what the good Lord gave her, she'd said after they'd visited Seattle a few weeks ago. *She doesn't need to paint herself or squeeze herself into a shape she wasn't born with.*

He had never considered the matter, but the thought of his sister prettying herself up made his stomach churn.

A few strides across the clearing brought him to their parents' house. Once, they had all lived there, his brothers curled up on beds on one side of the upstairs room, and Beth with their parents on the other. When he'd laid claim to the land next to his father's, he'd built his own house. Simon had done the same on the opposite side, clearing the land there. Now James was in the process of outfitting his cabin on the next set of acreage he had claimed. Tracts were already platted for John and Levi, as well. When they managed a town site, their father's name would go on even if he hadn't.

Simon, James and John had retired for the night, and Levi was still spread in front of the fire, rereading one of the adventure novels their father had brought with him across the plains. Drew could barely make out the words *The Last of the Mohicans* on the worn leather spine. Why his father and brothers wanted to read about the frontier when they lived on it Drew had never understood. He climbed the stairs to his mother's room.

At the top, he paused, almost afraid of what he might find. His mother lay asleep on the bed, her chest rising and falling under the quilt. He had not seen her so peaceful in days, and something inside him thawed at the sight. Beside her on the chair, Catherine Stanway put a finger to her lips before rising to join him at the stairwell.

His first thought on seeing her up close was that she was tired. A few tendrils of her pale hair had come undone and hung in soft curls about her face. Her blue eyes seemed to sag at the corners. But the smile she gave him was encouraging.

"Her fever appears to be coming down," she whispered. "But it's still higher than I'd like. The next two days will be very important in determining her recovery. Someone must be with her every moment."

Drew nodded. "We can take turns."

She gazed up at him, and he wondered what she was thinking. "I was under the impression you and your brothers had an important task to undertake tomorrow."

"Captain Collings's spar," Drew confirmed. "His

ship, the *Merry Maid*, was damaged in a storm crossing the mouth of the Columbia River. She managed to limp into Puget Sound, but she can't continue her journey to China without a new mast."

She stuck out her lower lip as if impressed, but the movement made his gaze stop at the soft pink of her mouth. Drew swallowed and looked away.

"I thought all trees felled around Seattle were destined for Mr. Yesler's mill," he heard her say.

"Most," Drew agreed, mentally counting the number of logs that made up the top story of the house. "My brothers and I specialize in filling orders for masts and yard arms for sailing ships. Simon's located the perfect tree not too far from the water, so it will be easy to transport, but it will take all of us to bring it down safely and haul it to the bay."

"If you should be working, sir, your sister and I can take care of things here."

He could hear the frown in her voice. She was probably used to being self-sufficient. Yet Drew had a hard time imagining her standing by to protect a frontier farm. She'd come on the bride ship, which meant she'd lived in Seattle for less than a month. By her own admission, she'd lived in larger towns back East. What could she know about surviving in the wilderness?

"Can you shoot?" he asked, gaze coming back to her.

She was indeed frowning, golden brows drawn over her nose. He had a strange urge to feather his fingers across her brow. "No," she said. "Do you expect me to need to shoot?"

"Very likely," Drew assured her, trying to master his feelings. "Pa made sure all of us knew how to protect each other and the farm. Ma can pick a heart from an ace at thirty paces, and Beth can hold her own. But if Beth is helping Ma, there will be no one left to protect you."

Her lips quirked as if she found it annoying that she needed such protection. And of course, his gaze latched on to the movement. He forced his eyes up.

"Is it truly so dangerous?" she asked. "You aren't living among the natives. You have homes, a garden, stock."

She needed to understand that the veneer of civilization was only as thick as the walls of the house. "James spotted a cougar while he was working on his cabin last week. We surprised a bear at the spring only yesterday."

She raised her head. "Well, then, we'll simply stay in the house until you return."

The silk of her hair tickled his chin, and he caught the scent of lemon and lavender, tart and clean. He needed to end this conversation and leave before he did or said something they'd both regret.

"You can't promise to remain indoors," he told her. "Even if we lay in a stock of wood and water, it might run out. Like it or not, Miss Stanway, you need me."

And she didn't like it. He could tell by the way her blue eyes narrowed, her chin firmed. This was a woman used to getting her own way.

And that could be trouble. He could only wonder: Over the next two days, which would prevail, her will or his determination?

Chapter Five

Two days. Surely she could survive two days. She'd sat longer vigils in the wards in Boston, taking breaks only for short naps, determined to cheat death. Two days was child's play.

Of course, normally, when she sat with a patient, she was either alone in the ward or a doctor or other nurse was nearby. This was the first time she'd served as a nurse in someone's home.

She found it decidedly unnerving.

For one thing, the Wallin house was anything but quiet. Levi had pounded up the stairs and thrown himself in bed on the other side of the loft. The buzz a short while later confirmed that Simon wasn't the only brother who snored. Beth crept up the stairs more quietly before slipping into a darker corner and emerging in her nightgown, then climbing into her own bed. The logs popped as the house cooled with the night. Wood settled in the small fire she'd had Drew rekindle. Something with tiny claws scampered across the roof over Catherine's head. Mournful calls echoed from the woods, as if all nature worried with the Wallins.

But worse was her awareness of Drew. He had agreed to take turns with her during the night, then left to finish some chores. She felt as if the entire house breathed a sigh of relief when he entered it again. His boots were soft on the stairs, and the boards whispered a welcome as he crossed to her side. He laid a hand on her shoulder, the pressure assuring, supportive. Then he turned and disappeared downstairs again.

Her pulse was too fast. She took a breath and leaned forward to adjust the covers over her patient again.

She had barely managed to restore her calm when he returned carrying a wooden platter and a large steaming pink-and-white china bowl with a spoon sticking from it.

"You've had nothing to eat," he reminded her. "You'll need your strength." He set the platter across her lap. On it rested a bowl of stew, a crusty loaf of bread, a bone-handled knife and a pat of creamy butter.

Catherine's stomach growled its answer. "Thank you," she said. She bowed her head and asked a blessing, then scooped up a spoonful of Beth's stew. The thick sauce warmed her almost as much as his gesture.

As she ate, he reached down, sliced off a hunk of the bread and set about eating it. Crumbs sprinkled the front of his cotton shirt, and he brushed them away, fingers long and quick. She wondered how they'd feel cradling her hand.

A hunk of venison must have gone down wrong, for she found herself coughing. He hurried to pour water from the jug by the bed into a tin cup, but she waved him back.

"I'm fine," she managed. Swallowing the last of the

stew, she set the bowl on the platter. "Thank you. That was very good. Beth is a talented cook."

"Ma taught her." He went to lean against the fireplace, the only spot in the room where he could stand completely upright. His gaze rested on the woman on the bed, who seemed to be sleeping blissfully through their quiet conversation. "She taught us all, saying a man should know how to care for himself."

Catherine couldn't argue with that. "My father had a similar philosophy. He said a woman should be able to fend for herself if needed."

"Yet he never taught you to shoot?"

He seemed generally puzzled by that. Catherine smiled. "There's not much call for hunting near Boston, at least not for food. I suppose parents try to teach their children what they need to survive in their own environment. I wouldn't expect your mother to teach you how to dance."

"There you would be wrong." Even in the dim light she could see his smile. "Pa used to play the fiddle, and Ma said if she didn't teach us boys to dance, she'd never have a partner." His smile faded. "Not that she needs one now."

Catherine had never been one to offer false hope, yet she couldn't help rushing to assure him. "We'll make sure she gets well."

Her words must have sounded as baseless to him as they did to her, for he said nothing as he pushed off from the hearth. He gathered up the dishes and disappeared down the stairs once more.

Catherine sighed. That exchange was simply a reminder of why it was better to stay focused on her task of nursing the patient, not on the emotional needs of the patient's family. She had found ways to comfort grieving loved ones before her father and brother had been killed. Now she felt hurts too keenly.

She tried to listen to Mrs. Wallin's breathing, which seemed far more regular than her own, but from downstairs came the sounds of dishes clanking, the chink of wood on metal, the splash of water. It seemed Mrs. Wallin had taught her sons to wash up, as well. Their future wives would be pleasantly surprised.

She expected him to return when he was finished, but the house fell quiet again. She added another log to the fire, then checked her patient once more. All was as it should be. The wooden chair didn't seem so hard; her body sank into it. The warmth of the room wrapped about her like a blanket. She closed her weary eyes.

Only to snap them open as someone picked her up and held her close.

"What are you doing?" she demanded as Drew's face came into focus.

He was already starting for the stairs, head ducked so that it was only a few inches from hers. "You fell asleep."

Catherine shifted in his arms. "I'm fine. Put me down. I have work to do."

Beth had sat up in bed and was regarding them wide-eyed as he started down the stairs. "Let Beth watch Ma for a while. I'll spell her shortly. We'll send for you if anything changes."

He reached the bottom of the stairs and started across the room as if she were no more than a basket of laundry destined for the line. "I can walk, sir," she informed him.

He twisted to open the door. "That you can. I've seen

you do it." He paused on the porch to nod out into the darkness, where the only light was the glow from a few stars peeking through the clouds. "But our clearing isn't a city street. There are tree roots and rocks that can trip you up in broad daylight. I know the hazards. Best you let me do the walking."

She hadn't noticed that the space was so bumpy when they'd arrived. Indeed, it had seemed surprisingly level; the grass neat and trim. Very likely the goats cropped it. Still, she didn't relish tripping over a rock and twisting her ankle. She hardly wanted to stay at Wallin Landing a moment more than necessary, and certainly not long enough to heal a sprain.

So she remained where she was, warm against his chest, cradled in his arms, as Drew ferried her across the clearing to another cabin hidden among the trees. Her legs were decidedly unsteady as he set her down on the wide front porch and swung open the door to enter ahead of her. She heard the scrape of flint as he lit a lantern.

The golden light chased the darkness to the far corners of the room, and she could see a round planked table in the center, set over a braided rug and flanked by two tall solid-backed chairs. A little small for a knight of the round table, but cozy. As if he thought so, too, Drew's cheeks were darkening again, and he seemed to be stuffing something white and lacy into the pocket of his trousers.

"There's a washstand and water jug in the corner," he said, voice gruff. "The necessity's between the two cabins."

In a moment, he'd leave her. Perhaps it was the strange surroundings or the lateness of the day, but she found herself unwilling to see him go. Catherine moved into the room, glanced at the fire simmering in the grate of the stone hearth. As if he was watching her, expecting her to find things wanting, he hurried to lay on another piece of wood.

"Should be enough to see you through the night," he said, straightening. "But I can fetch more from the woodpile if you'd like."

Was he so eager to leave her? "No need," Catherine said. "I'm sure I'll be fine. You could answer one question, though."

She thought he stiffened. "Oh? What would that be?"

"Who's Mary?"

Now she waited, some part of her fearing to hear the answer. His face sagged. "My little sister. The one who died. Ever since Ma took ill, she's been asking after her. We think maybe she's forgotten Mary's gone."

His pain cut into her. She wanted to gather him close, caress the sadness from his face.

What was she thinking?

"She's delirious," Catherine told him. "It's not uncommon with high fevers.

He nodded as if he understood, but she could see the explanation hadn't eased his mind. She should think of something else to say, something else for him to consider, if only for a moment. She glanced around the room again. Her gaze lit on the ladder rising into the loft. Oh, dear. Her hand gripped her wide blue skirts.

"Is that how you reach the sleeping area?" she asked, hoping for another answer.

"There's a loft upstairs," he said, "but the main bed's there." He pointed toward the fire.

What she'd taken for a large cupboard turned out to

be a box bed set deep in one wall. The weathered wood encircled it like the rings of a tree. Catherine wandered over and fingered the thick flannel quilt that covered the tick. Blues and reds and greens were sprinkled in different-size blocks, fitted together like a child's puzzle and stitched with yellow embroidery as carefully as her father's sutures.

"Ma made that when I turned eighteen," he explained, a solid presence behind her. "Those are pieces of every shirt she ever sewed for me. Waste not, want not."

How could she possibly sleep under something so personal? Catherine pulled back her hand and turned. "Perhaps I should stay with my patient."

He took a step away from her as if to block the door. "Beth and I can handle things. You deserve your rest." He nodded toward the bed. "She left you one of Ma's clean nightgowns, I see. If you need anything else, just holler."

Yell, and have nearly a half dozen men appear to help her? Some women would have been delighted by the prospect. She could imagine her friend Maddie crying out and then sitting back with a grin to watch the fireworks. But Catherine felt as if fine threads were weaving about her like her father's surgery silk, binding her to this place, these people.

Was she really ready to be that close to anyone again?

Drew left Catherine and returned to the main cabin so he could help Beth, bringing with him the lacy doily his sister had left on his table and depositing it on her bed. He dozed for a while on one of the beds he used to share with his brothers, rousing twice to poke Levi into silence. Beth woke him before dawn and stumbled off to bed herself. Drew leaned against the hard rocks of the hearth and watched his mother.

She was a proud woman, sure of her skills and her faith. Unlike Catherine, she'd never followed any calling but the keeping of hearth and home and the running of the family farm while his father was logging. She'd been the steadying presence behind Drew the past ten years, always ready to provide advice and comfort, a loaf of bread and a warm quilt. Sometimes he felt as if each stitch formed the word *love*.

More than one man over the years had attempted to court her. But his mother had refused to leave her claim, even after most of her sons had land of their own. He remembered the day not long after his father had died when men had come from town to try to persuade her to move in closer.

"A widowed woman with five boys and a girl?" one of them had scoffed. "You can't manage this property alone."

"I'm not alone," his mother had said, putting one arm around Drew and the other around Simon as their siblings gathered close. "If this is what the Lord wants for us, He'll make a way."

The Lord must have wanted them at Wallin Landing, for they'd been here ever since.

His mother was still sleeping when his brothers left for their work and Beth started about her chores of feeding the chickens, checking for eggs and letting the goats, horses and pigs out to pasture. Simon came upstairs long enough to assure Drew that everything else had been taken care of.

"We'll have the oxen," he murmured, glancing

around Drew as if to make sure their mother was sleeping peacefully. "And I wanted to let you know that John figured the costs for the plow. We should have enough from that spar for Captain Collings to make a good down payment. Then we can put James's field in corn and make better use of those horses he was so set on."

Drew nodded. James had convinced them to invest in the strong horses when another local farmer had given up his claim and needed to sell out. Drew had hoped to put the beasts to good use expanding the fields. Their family had run perilously short of corn and wheat the past two winters, and any profit they might have made logging had been eaten up by purchasing cornmeal and flour from town. He and his brothers were determined to lay in a greater store this year.

"Do what you can today," he told Simon. "If Ma feels better, I can come finish the job tomorrow."

Simon's face tightened, and he took another look at their mother before heading down the stairs. Though he hadn't spoken the words aloud, Drew could feel his doubts.

If Ma ever felt better.

Please, Lord, make her well!

Sometimes it seemed as if he'd been fighting off illness and injury his whole life. What he hated most was the feeling that there was nothing he could do but wait.

The house settled back into quiet. The sun rose over the lake, golden rays spearing through the windows and leaving a patchwork of color as bright as his mother's quilts across the worn wood floor. Still Drew waited. When his mother finally stirred, he straightened and strode to her side. Her gaze was more alert than he'd seen it in weeks.

"What did you do with my pretty nurse?" she asked.

Drew took her hand and clasped it in his. The skin felt warm from the covers but not as dry and hot as it had been.

"We wore her out," he said, giving his mother's hand a squeeze. "But I'll fetch her back for you shortly. In the meantime, are you hungry? Thirsty?"

She cocked her head as if considering the matter, and Drew noticed that her hair was stuck to her forehead like a row of ginger-colored lace. He put his hand to her cheek and found it cool and moist. Was it possible? Had the fever broke during the night?

"Now, why are you staring at me like that?" she asked, pulling back her hand and touching her hair. "Oh, but I must look a fright!"

Drew smiled, relief making the air sweet. "You never looked more beautiful to me, Ma. Shall I make you biscuits?"

She started to yawn and hurriedly covered her mouth with her hand. "Ask Levi. That boy makes better biscuits than the rest of you combined—light as a feather."

"He's out working," Drew told her. "You'll have to settle for my cooking instead."

She was regarding him out of the corners of her eyes, as if she knew she was about to ask something she suspected he wouldn't like. "You might ask Miss Stanway to join us for breakfast."

Not her, too! "Don't you go getting any ideas about Miss Stanway, Ma," Drew said. "She's here to nurse you."

She coughed into her hand, but the noise still sounded healthy to Drew. "Yes, of course she is. And I expect I'll need a great deal of nursing yet, probably for days." She lowered her hand and heaved a great sigh.

"I have a feeling you'll be up and about in no time," Drew said. On impulse, he bent and pressed a kiss against her cheek. Her face was a rosy pink as he started for the stairs.

Thank You, Lord! The thanksgiving was instant and nearly overwhelming. Catherine had been right. His mother was going to live. Their family was whole awhile longer.

Oh, he would have to watch Ma and his brothers while Catherine was at the Landing if he wanted to remain single, but Catherine probably wouldn't be in their lives much longer if his mother's recovery was as rapid as he hoped.

His spirits didn't rise as high as they should have at the thought.

He was halfway to his cabin when he heard the noise—the drum of horses' hooves rapidly approaching. As he pulled up, the sheriff's deputy, Hart McCormick, and several other men from Seattle galloped into the clearing, faces set and bodies tensed.

"Deputy," Drew said with a nod as they reined in around him. "Something wrong?"

McCormick tipped back his broad-brimmed black hat and narrowed his sharp gray eyes at Drew. "Could be. One of Mercer's belles went missing yesterday, and Scout Rankin tells me you might have had something to do with it."

Drew held up his hands. "There's no need for concern. Miss Stanway is here and perfectly safe."

Still Deputy McCormick glared at him, as if sizing up Drew's strength, taking note that he was unarmed.

McCormick was tall and lean, with close-cropped black hair and eyes the color of a worn gun barrel. He'd earned the reputation of being one tough character, having thrown off a rough beginning before riding down a number of outlaws in the two years he'd served as deputy. Drew didn't like his chances if the lawman decided to take him on.

Just then, one of the horses pushed forward, and Drew realized the rider was a redheaded woman. Though she wore a divided skirt so she could sit astride, the way she clutched the reins told Drew she didn't have much experience with horses.

"Then you won't mind bringing her out, now, will you?" she challenged, sharp words softened by an Irish accent.

Deputy McCormick relaxed in his seat. "Miss O'Rourke is particularly concerned about her friend."

Drew lowered his hands. "She's staying in that cabin over there. If you'll give me a moment…"

"Hold these," the redhead commanded, tossing the reins at Drew. As he caught them, she threw one leg over the horse and slid to the ground. "I'll just be fetching her myself." She stalked across the clearing, gait stiff.

"Bit of a spitfire," McCormick commented, watching her. His mouth hitched up as if he liked what he saw. "Still, there's something to be said for a woman who speaks her mind."

"Yeah," one of his posse members threw out. "Spinster."

The others laughed.

"Being uppity seems to be a pretty common failing among those Mercer gals," another commented, scratching his grizzled chin. "Doc Maynard said this Miss Stanway gave him an earful for some of his practices."

"She gave us an earful, too," Drew said, watching as Miss O'Rourke hopped up on the porch and rapped at the door. "And Ma is alive because of it."

That sobered them. McCormick touched his brim again in obvious respect. "I'm sorry to hear your mother was ailing, Wallin, but I'm glad to know she's on the mend."

The door to the cabin opened. Catherine stood in the shadows, hair tumbled about her shoulders, his quilt bundled around her. Stocking feet peeped out from below. The sight hit him square in the chest, and breathing seemed impossible. One look at her friend, and she gave a glad cry and a quick hug before pulling Miss O'Rourke inside and shutting the door.

Air found its way into Drew's lungs. What was it about Catherine that made him react this way? He'd seen pretty girls before—not many and not often it was true, but still.

"I thought you said she was stuck-up," one of the men commented with a frown to his friend. "She looks mighty nice to me."

"I heard they started calling her the Ice Queen," another agreed. "Looks as though the Wallins managed to thaw her out."

"Maybe that's why she needs a quilt," the deputy said with a warning look to his posse. "Either that or she's trying to shield herself from the criticism of people who came West themselves to escape it."

His men had the good sense to look abashed.

McCormick returned his gaze to Drew, shifting on the horse so that his gun belt brushed the saddle horn.

"The way I figure it, what you do with the gal is between you and her, so long as she's in agreement. If she has no complaints, we'll be on our way."

Drew nodded, though he still didn't like his chances, for Catherine had every right to complain. She'd been trussed like a calf on the way to market, thrown in the back of a wagon, jostled for miles, threatened with marriage to his brothers and exposed to a virulent fever. Though the last was probably common in her line of work, she hadn't even been given the opportunity to prepare. If she voiced those concerns to the sheriff's deputy, Drew didn't like thinking what would happen to Levi or to him.

McCormick was watching Drew as if expecting something more, so Drew offered, "It's good to know Seattle rallies when one of its own might be in danger."

The posse nodded. Deputy McCormick leaned closer to Drew.

"The sheriff wouldn't have it any other way. He'd have been here himself except he had to investigate a report of harassment to the south of you."

"Harassment?" Drew frowned. "What kind of harassment?"

Deputy McCormick straightened. "Stock let loose in the woods, a shed burned, reports of strangers riding past. Your brother Levi wouldn't know about any of that, would he?"

Drew stiffened. "Levi's been helping with Ma. And he knows better than to start a fire out here."

McCormick glanced around the clearing. "Where is your brother this morning?"

"With Simon and the others, out working." And he wasn't about to point the direction.

The deputy scratched his chin. "I suppose that's witness enough. Besides, the sheriff thought it might be Indian trouble."

Drew shook his head. "We've never had any trouble with the Duwamish, even during the Indian Wars. They were always helpful, until these new rules ended up pushing them from their land and trying to force them to settle across the Sound."

Two of the men bristled, and Drew heard someone mutter about being an Indian lover. He ignored them. His family had always dealt fairly with the natives they'd encountered, and in turn they lived in peace along the lake. But he knew not everyone agreed with that philosophy.

Knowing it might take Catherine a bit to change—at least, it always took Ma and Beth more time to dress in the morning than it did him and his brothers—Drew invited their unexpected visitors to see to their horses. He was surprised his sister didn't come hurrying out of the barn to greet them, but she must have taken the goats to the pasture by Simon's cabin, for he caught no sign of her or the animals.

"You having any trouble with your neighbors, the Rankins?" McCormick asked as Drew watered Miss O'Rourke's horse.

"They leave us alone, we leave them alone," Drew replied.

"Funny," the deputy mused. "I heard tell young Levi had words with Scout in town the other day. I thought they were friends."

It seemed there was little the deputy failed to hear about. But before Drew could answer, McCormick tipped his hat in the direction of Drew's cabin.

Drew turned to see Catherine and her friend coming toward them. Catherine's hair was once more pinned precisely in place, her blue gown surprisingly crisp after her activities yesterday. Never had he seen such purposeful strides. Dirt kicked up behind her with each step. She hadn't confessed to his family how she'd arrived at the Landing. Was she about to tell the law in no uncertain terms the full story of her kidnapping?

Chapter Six

Catherine tried not to shiver in the early-morning chill as she approached the group. She'd thought surely the events of the day or the strange surroundings would have kept her awake last night. But the moment she'd snuggled under Drew's quilt, which hinted of the scent of fir that seemed to cling to him, she'd fallen asleep, and only Maddie's knock on the door had roused her.

"So off you go running away to live in a palace of cedar like David in the Bible," Maddie had said, twinkle in her brown eyes. "Leaving your friends a-wondering."

Catherine had hugged her tight before pulling her inside. "It's fir, not cedar. And what are you doing here? How did you find me?"

Maddie had bustled into the room, picking up Catherine's gown and undergarments where they lay over one of the tall, stiff chairs. "Didn't you think I would raise the hue and cry the moment you went missing? It took a bit of persuading to get Deputy McCormick to move himself, and then I had to beg this skirt from one of the other travelers, but we started out before dawn and followed the hint from a lad and your Doc Maynard."

She'd held out Catherine's corset, the cream-colored quilted cotton looking warm in her grip. "Come along, now, Catie, me love. There are at least three worthwhile men out there. We want you looking your best. You can tell me what happened while you dress."

Catherine didn't much care whether the men outside were stellar candidates for marriage, but she couldn't have very well gone out in Mrs. Wallin's nightgown. So Catherine had explained the situation while her friend had helped her out of the soft flannel and into her corset and gown. The dressing had taken longer than she'd expected, even with Maddie's assistance, for Catherine's body was stiff from bouncing in the wagon the day before.

"You see why I must stay," Catherine had concluded after she'd put up her hair.

At the door, Maddie had glanced out to where Drew stood in conversation with Deputy McCormick. They'd made quite a contrast, the lawman all hard angles and trim lines, the frontiersman all brawn and power.

"Oh, I see exactly why you must be staying," Maddie had assured her. "He's a bit hard to miss, standing tall as a tree as he does."

Catherine had felt her cheeks warming as she'd joined Maddie in the doorway. "This has nothing to do with Drew Wallin."

"Drew, is it now? Sure'n if you've no use for him, you won't mind me batting my eyes in his direction."

Catherine had known Maddie was just teasing. Aboard ship and since arriving in Seattle, several fellows had sidled up to the redhead, but she'd never allowed them to be more than friends. Catherine didn't know whether Maddie was waiting for the right man or whether she simply had no interest in settling down. Certainly she was one of the most industrious women Catherine had met—doing laundry for men in the boardinghouses and hotels and saving money to open her own bakery. Perhaps that was enough for her. Given Catherine's own views on marriage, it had seemed presumptive to ask.

Now they stood beside the group, and Catherine recognized several of the fellows who served as storekeepers or businessmen in the fledgling city.

"Mr. McCormick," she greeted the deputy. "Gentlemen. Please tell me you didn't come all this way on my account."

Deputy McCormick nodded to her, hands gripping his horse's reins. "Just doing our duty, ma'am. Everything all right here?"

Catherine smiled at them all as Maddie went to retrieve the reins of her horse from Drew. She saw no need to tell them about Levi's hand in her transportation. With his mother ill and work waiting to be done, Drew hardly needed more trouble. "Everything is fine. Mr. Wallin and his youngest brother came to town yesterday seeking medical assistance. I was available to help."

Deputy McCormick frowned. He had the oddest colored eyes, dark and hard, like rocks at the bottom of a stream. She fought another shiver and knew this time it had nothing to do with the cool morning air.

"You left mighty quick," he pointed out, "without a word to anyone."

Catherine caught Drew's gaze. From the way he shoved his hands in his pockets, she could tell he was struggling not to join the conversation. She shook her head slightly, trying to warn him. She appreciated his help with the deputy, but she didn't want to see him run afoul of the law.

"I'm afraid I did dash off," she confessed to Deputy McCormick. "When I hear someone is ill, I tend to act. I'm sure you wouldn't want me to delay if it was your wife or mother lying at death's door."

"No, ma'am, of course not," the deputy agreed while some of the men shifted on their feet as if Catherine's words had made them uncomfortable. "But when our womenfolk disappear like that, we tend to worry."

"Especially when there's so few of us, I'm thinking," Maddie put in, patting her horse's neck.

"I'm very sorry to have worried you," Catherine said, keeping her smile in place from long practice. If she could remain calm while delivering the news to a family of death's final decision, she certainly wasn't going to faint under the deputy's hard gaze. "I promise to let someone know if I set out on my own again."

The deputy nodded. "All right, then. We'll be off. Look out for yourself, Wallin. Ma'am." He tipped his hat to Catherine.

As the men mounted, Maddie turned to Drew. "Would you be a darling, Mr. Wallin, and help me back on this horse? Sure'n it's a wily beast just waiting to trample me."

Catherine thought Drew might cup his hands to give Maddie a leg up, but he swept her up in his arms and deposited her on the saddle.

"Well, now," Maddie said with a grin as she adjusted her seat. "That's more like it. I hope to be seeing more of you, Mr. Wallin, when you come to bring my Catie-girl back."

Drew inclined his head, but Deputy McCormick's

face darkened. "Let's ride," he barked, and his men wheeled their horses and set off, Maddie with an airy wave over her head to Catherine.

"Thank you," Drew said as the noise faded among the trees. "Levi's already received two warnings from the sheriff for reckless behavior in town. If you had told them the truth, he might have ended up in jail this time."

"I did tell the truth," Catherine informed him, taking a deep breath. Her palms were damp, and she wiped them on her skirt. "I came here to treat your mother. I thought you were going to wake me last night to tend to her."

She nearly winced as her statement came out closer to a scold. Here she'd thought herself in control of her emotions, yet the entire incident with the deputy sheriff seemed to have thrown her off balance. Or maybe it was Maddie's outrageous flirting. Was her friend actually interested in Drew Wallin? Certainly, he was a handsome figure of a man, heroic even. Perhaps he was just the sort of fellow Maddie had been waiting for. She should be delighted for Maddie, but the thought made her feel as if someone had hollowed out her stomach.

To her surprise, his smile grew, peeling away the years from his face, brightening his eyes. "There was no need to call you. You did it. Ma's well."

Her heart leaped, but immediately she chided herself. She couldn't give in to such optimism, not until she had seen the lady herself and could verify Mrs. Wallin's recovery.

A humming from the woods heralded Beth's arrival. Today she wore a dress of blue gingham the color of her eyes. Seeing Catherine and Drew, she hurried up to them.

"Why are you out here? Who's with Ma? I thought we had to keep watch over her."

"Your brother says she's much better," Catherine explained. "I was just about to confirm that." She turned for the house, with Beth and Drew close behind. She could feel their excitement, but she refused to let it influence her judgment. Her own eagerness was danger enough for that.

Once in the loft, Catherine sat beside her patient and checked Mrs. Wallin's pulse, her eyes, her breathing and her temperature. Then she sat back with a smile.

"Much better," she proclaimed. "I'd say another few days and you'll be back on your feet."

Mrs. Wallin beamed at her. "Because of you, Miss Stanway. Thank you!"

"Yes, Miss Stanway, thank you!" Beth threw herself into Catherine's arms and hugged her tight. "You gave me back my mother!"

Catherine felt tears pricking her eyes. *This is why I practice medicine, Lord—to help people. Thank You for this healing!*

Disengaging from Beth, she glanced up to meet Drew's gaze. His eyes were overly bright, and he hurriedly looked away as if determined to keep her from seeing the emotions brimming in them.

"I suppose you'll be leaving us, then," he said.

Beth leaned back, and she and her mother exchanged glances. Mrs. Wallin drew in a shaky breath. "Oh, I'm sure I won't be myself again if Miss Stanway leaves us now."

Beth took Catherine's hand. "And I was so hoping we might have time to chat, Miss Stanway."

Drew glanced back, eyes narrowing. Did he see the

manipulation as clearly as Catherine did? They needn't have bothered. She knew she had work to do before she left.

"I'll stay a while longer," she told them all, and Beth and Mrs. Wallin grinned at each other. "I want to make sure there are no complications."

Mrs. Wallin leaned back against the pillows with a satisfied nod. "Very sensible."

"And I also want to track this fever to its source," Catherine continued.

Drew frowned. "Its source?"

"I thought chills brought on sickness," Beth said, glancing between them. "You know, you stand outside in wet clothes or you bathe in cold water like the lake."

Mrs. Wallin stiffened. "I have never bathed in the lake in my life, young lady, and you know it!"

"Typhoid fever is often caused by food or water that came in contact with something it shouldn't," Catherine informed Beth. "Until we discover what made your mother sick, all of you could be in danger. I'm not leaving until I know we aren't spreading the disease any further."

She meant the comment for a warning, but the smiles on Beth and Mrs. Wallin's faces were as deep as the frown on Drew's. Just what were the ladies planning that they were so determined for Catherine to stay?

Chapter Seven

Drew didn't like the way his mother and sister were looking at each other. He didn't think they knew about Simon's idea that one of the Wallin men must marry Miss Stanway. But if the Wallin women had hit on the same notion, he was doomed.

Best to focus them on something else. "So you think our food or water is contaminated," he challenged Catherine.

For a woman who didn't wear her heart on her sleeve, she could look remarkably determined. Her chin came up, and her blue eyes flashed like lightning.

His mother was nearly as indignant. "Contaminated food?" she sputtered, ribbons on her nightcap dancing about her pale face in her agitation. "What have you all been doing on my stove?"

"Nothing, Ma!" Beth cried. "I promise! It can't be the food. We all eat the same things. You were the only one to get sick."

Catherine nodded. "Very well, but I imagine you all drink the same water, too."

"Not entirely," Drew said. "The hillside above us is

littered with springs. Simon has a pipe from one coming in to his cabin. I tapped another for the pump on the side of my cabin. Ma is the only one still drawing from the spring Pa favored. It's closest to the house."

"But it's closest to the barn, too," Beth reminded him. "That's how we water the animals. None of them got sick."

"They wouldn't," Catherine said. "Some diseases are unique to humans."

"Well, Levi and I still live here," Beth pointed out. "Why didn't we get sick?"

"Half the time Levi is out with us," Drew said. "And you did get sick a while ago."

Beth sobered.

"It seems we must examine your spring," Catherine said.

"After you eat," his mother insisted, leaning back against the head of the bed as if satisfied her cooking had been exonerated. "You can bring water from Drew's spring if you're concerned about mine, but I won't have a guest in my house or any of my children starving."

"I'll cook them something, Ma," Beth said, hopping up out of her seat. "Drew can help."

Although he didn't mind helping, he didn't like the smile that crossed his mother's face or the way she glanced at Catherine. Who knew what the two would get up to if he left them alone for too long?

"We need more wood for the fire," he said. "I'll be right back."

His mother's smile widened.

"You're in trouble," Beth said as he followed her down the stairs. "I know that look on Ma's face. She wants something, and I think it's Miss Stanway as a daughter-in-law."

"Miss Stanway might have something to say about that," Drew replied, heading for the door. He glanced back in time to see his sister shake her head.

"It doesn't matter what Miss Stanway says. It doesn't matter what you say. And Simon has the least say of all."

So she had heard his brother's outrageous demands last night. "Don't start, Beth," Drew warned.

"Oh, it's far too late," his sister predicted. "You know that when Ma makes up her mind about something, it's going to happen. If I were you, I'd talk to the Reverend Bagley about a church date." Humming to herself, she disappeared into the back room.

First his brothers and now his mother. Were they all mad? Drew stepped onto the front porch and glanced around the yard in the cool morning air. A dozen projects called for his attention, from a loose shingle on the barn roof to the field waiting for the plow. Did his family really think he had time for a wife?

Well, they could scheme all they liked. He knew what must be done. Another day to make sure Ma had recovered and to track down this sickness, and Catherine Stanway would be out of his life. All he had to do was hold firm to his convictions.

And try to forget the warmth of her cradled against his chest.

"He's a good man, you know," Mrs. Wallin said after Drew and Beth had left the room. "Proved up a hundred and sixty acres all on his own, and raised his brothers and Beth when their father died."

Catherine kept herself busy tucking the covers

around her patient's waist. "Your family is certainly to be commended, making a home in the wilderness."

Mrs. Wallin caught her hand. "But he doesn't have a home."

Catherine frowned. "He most certainly does. I slept in it last night."

Mrs. Wallin shook her head. "He has a house. That's not a home. The Bible says a man is to grow up and start his own family. How can Drew do that when he won't let go of this one?"

From somewhere deep inside her, anger pushed its way out of Catherine's mouth. "Why would you want him to let go? He's trying to protect you all. I wish my father and brother had had that much sense. Maybe I wouldn't be alone now."

She turned away from the bed and went to stand by the fire. Her breath shuddered, and she forced herself to draw in the air, then let it out slowly. What was wrong with her? Mrs. Wallin had every right to be concerned for her son's future. That was what families did—care for each other.

But why didn't my father think about me, Lord? Was it really so important that he and Nathan had to go and fight? Or was I such a termagant of a daughter and sister they couldn't wait to escape me?

She heard the bedclothes rustle, and then the creak of the floor as feet padded toward her. Turning, she found Mrs. Wallin beside her. A tall woman, she gazed down at Catherine, face twisted as if she were in pain or feeling Catherine's.

"Oh, my dear, I'm so sorry," she said. She drew Catherine close and held her gently. "It's terrible to lose a loved one. Why, it cuts the heart right out of you."

Tears burned Catherine's eyes. As if of their own volition, her arms came up and she hugged the woman closer. "It's all right," she said. "I'll be fine."

Mrs. Wallin held her out and met her gaze, her face now stern. "Of course you will. Things will never be quite the same, though. Tragedy changes a body. How long has your family been gone?"

Catherine counted the months and was surprised by the answer. "Just over a year." That seemed like such a short time when it felt as if she'd been grieving forever.

"Well, then." Mrs. Wallin squeezed her shoulders. "Give yourself more time to accustom yourself to the changes. You left everything you knew to come to a strange place, with no friends or family waiting for you. That takes some adjusting, I know. And there will always be a part of you that misses them, no matter what else happens."

She glanced up at the mantel, and Catherine saw a daguerreotype there of a sturdy-looking man. He had Drew's eyes, Simon's rock of a chin and Levi's cocky grin. Mrs. Wallin rubbed a hand down the worn silver frame, and Catherine felt her sigh.

That was entirely enough of this sentimentality. She had to remember her purpose for being here, and it wasn't to wallow in the pain of her past. She turned her patient toward the bed with a smile.

"Thank you. I needed that reminder. Now, let's get you back under the covers. Despite what I told Beth, sudden changes in temperature aren't good for someone recovering from an illness. I want you cozy again."

Mrs. Wallin allowed herself to be tucked back into bed, but the smile on her face told Catherine that the older woman was humoring her. Catherine suspected

Drew's mother was feeling far better than she let on. But for all the lady wanted to be up and back to her usual routine, Catherine didn't want her to do too much and suffer a relapse. Nor did she want the illness to affect anyone else. And that meant she had work to do.

So after a breakfast of eggs, biscuits with honey and apple cider, she directed Beth on the types of food that would help her mother convalesce—beef tea, calf's foot jelly and honeysuckle conserve. Then she convinced Drew to accompany her on a survey of the Landing.

Between the dim light last night when she'd arrived and the need to appease the deputy sheriff this morning, she hadn't taken a good look at the Wallin property until now. The main house sat facing west, with its back to the lake. Now she could see the water, sparkling through the trees in the spring sunlight. It was the same deep shade of blue as Beth's and Levi's eyes. Hills rose sharply on the three sides, thick with dense stands of deep green fir and the reddish bark of cedar.

"There's a good-size stream north of us," Drew said as if he'd noticed the direction of her gaze as they stood between his cabin and his parents'. "That's where Pa got the name for the property. The ground slopes, making it a good place to land canoes or start logs on their way to the Sound."

"But you don't drink from that stream," Catherine surmised, turning for the barn.

"Only when we're working out that way," Drew admitted, long legs moving him past her. "It's too far to carry the water for the house or the stock." The shadows of the barn swallowed up his tall frame.

Catherine followed him inside. The barn was of weathered wood, with a pitched roof of silvered cedar shingles turning green with moss. The upper part was open at each end, and as she looked, swallows darted past the triangle of sky.

Stalls and pens lined up along the packed-earth aisle, many with hinged doors allowing access to fenced pasture.

"Simon and the others took the oxen out this morning to clear away some brush," Drew told her. "And Beth turned out the goats, horses and pigs." He glanced around at the harnesses and tools hanging from the walls, the rough-hewn troughs of fresh water.

Catherine opened the lid on the large bin near a square of planked floor that somehow seemed out of place. The bin was empty, but it smelled of something dry, nutty.

"That's the grain bin," he told her. "And the threshing floor beyond it. But Simon and the others help with that. With all of us around, Ma generally doesn't need to come out here anymore. I can't see how anything in the barn could have made her sick."

He sounded puzzled again, but something else simmered behind the words. Frustration? She was certain he wanted to learn what had caused his mother's illness. Did he disapprove of Catherine's methods?

"I don't see anything dangerous in here, either," she agreed, closing the lid, "but it's wise to check all possibilities when it comes to your family's health."

He snapped a nod and stalked deeper into the barn.

Mystified, Catherine lifted her skirts out of the dirt and followed. "Really, Mr. Wallin, this search is important." She detoured around a suspicious-looking clump on the floor. "Do you want one of your brothers to sicken? Beth to grow ill?"

"Of course not." The words sounded as if they had been bitten off. "But I've been keeping them safe for years. I don't know what's changed."

He'd stopped at the end of the barn, where another set of wide doors led out into the forest. The breeze carried the scent of damp wood and new growth. She could hear birds calling from the shadows. Yet Drew stood a silhouette against the light, neck stiff, shoulders braced.

Catherine lay a hand on his arm. "Forgive me, Mr. Wallin. I never meant to imply any of this was your fault. You cannot know everything about medical science. It's constantly changing! What we were certain of last month will be challenged as folklore tomorrow. I merely wish to help."

His hand came down on hers. "Thank you."

The two simple words, said with conviction, warmed her more than she'd thought possible. Or perhaps it was the feel of his calloused palm pressed against her skin. She couldn't help remembering the scars she'd seen yesterday. This was a man who had earned his place, whose physical efforts kept his family fed and clothed and housed. A man who took the health of his loved ones as seriously as she did as a nurse.

She traced the vein of puckered skin across the back of one hand. "How did this happen?"

He did not pull away from her touch. "A saw snapped. The end whipped free and caught me. I was just glad it missed my face."

So was she. She swallowed at the thought and dropped her hand.

He was gazing down at her, face in the shadow, hair a golden nimbus of light. She waited, expecting a word, a movement.

The touch of his lips to hers.

"Do you hear that?" he asked.

She didn't think he meant the birds outside. Now that she wasn't so focused on him, she did hear something else—a rumble and a snort that sounded somehow familiar.

Drew grabbed a long iron pole from the wall and poked it up into the hay stored loosely above their heads in the mow. Someone yelped, and a moment later, Levi's curly-haired head popped into sight.

"What are you doing up there?" Drew demanded. "I thought you were with Simon."

Levi slung a leg over the nearby ladder and clambered down to drop beside his brother and Catherine. Hay stuck out at odd angles from his curls, clung to his flannel shirt and poked from the suspenders holding up his rumpled trousers. "Simon thought you might need help with Ma."

Drew towered over him, voice deepening. "And you thought the best way to help Ma was to sleep in the hay?" He pointed out the door. "Git!"

Levi dashed out of the barn.

Drew shook his head as he and Catherine followed. "Can't turn my back for a minute."

"It was only a lark," Catherine said. "But if you're concerned, you can always find better things for him to do."

Drew cast her a glance. "Good idea. Levi! Show Miss Stanway to the spring."

Levi led her to where the ground sloped upward between the barn and the main house. A deep, stone-lined basin followed the curve of the hill; a wall of mortared stone about three feet high enclosing the water filling it. At the back of the pool, overshadowed by the firs, water bubbled, cool and clear. A wooden weir on the west side allowed the spring to overflow in a stream that ran away from the house down to the lake. Just inside the pool, a stone lip provided space for cooling food like milk and cider. Iron rings driven into the ground around it served as anchors for the ropes that held several wooden buckets for accessing the water.

Catherine picked up one of the buckets. The wooden staves were worn, the iron binding them turning red from prolonged exposure to water. "How often do you clean these?" she asked.

Levi rolled his eyes as if he thought she was being too fussy. Drew frowned as if thinking. "Since we only use them to draw fresh water, would they require cleaning?"

Catherine ran a finger around the inside of the bucket and held it up for him to see the green smearing it. "Moss will grow with damp and dark. Scrub them out at least twice a year."

He nodded, brow clearing. "I will."

How easily he believed her. It was refreshing, and she felt herself drawing in a deeper breath, her shoulders settling.

Levi was clearly less impressed. "Never heard of moss making a body ill," he scoffed.

"You never heard of keeping the windows open, either," Drew reminded him. "And Ma is better for it."

He stuck out his lower lip, as if considering the matter.

"I doubt the moss caused your mother's fever," Catherine said, "but it is a sign that things could be more sanitary." She leaned over the lip and gazed down into the dark pool. The sun filtering through the trees turned the water to amber. She sniffed the cool air.

"Does that smell odd to you?" she asked Drew, straightening.

He leaned over beside her, his broad shoulder brushing hers. She could feel the warmth radiating from him and had to fight the urge to hug him closer. He gave a perfunctorily sniff as if he doubted her senses. Then he frowned again. "I smell something. Could be from the barn. We are downwind."

"Let me take a gander." Levi stuck his head over the wall, then straightened and shrugged. "I don't smell anything."

Drew reached across to cuff him on the shoulder. "That's because you've been avoiding a bath for weeks."

"Have not!" The youth's cheeks were turning crimson. "I jump in the lake on a regular basis."

Catherine hid her smile as she peered in the pool again. "I'm sure there's an odor, and I doubt it's coming from your brother. Could something have fallen in?"

"With the lake so close, there's generally no need for an animal to risk trying to scale that wall," Drew reasoned. "But the best way to be sure is to put someone into the water." He turned to his brother. "I'll hold the rope, Levi."

"Me?" His brother scrambled back, dark blue eyes widening. "I'm not going in there."

"Surely there's some other way," Catherine protested. She could not imagine it was safe or sanitary to let the youth enter the drinking water.

Drew had pulled up one of the buckets and was untying it from the rope. "No other way I know," he said, tugging on the line as if testing its strength. "We could wave around a lantern, but if that smell's caused by firedamp, we'll only cause an explosion."

"An explosion!" Catherine cried, hands pressed to her chest.

Levi turned white. "You can't put me in there, Drew. I won't go."

Drew shrugged, coming around the wall toward his brother. "You're the logical choice. You're light enough to brace easily and strong enough to take care of yourself. Besides, you'll know what you're looking for."

Levi shook his curls off his forehead and pointed at Catherine. "She's light. Make her go."

Catherine felt a moment of panic, but Drew waved away the suggestion with one hand. "You can't send a woman in a dress into a pool that deep. The weight of her skirts would pull her down, and you'd never get her out. The idea is to fix the spring, not plug it up."

Catherine nearly choked. *That* was his reason for not putting her in the pool?

Levi wavered a moment longer, then stalked up to Drew and held up his arms. "Fine. I'll go. But you owe me."

"Is this safe?" Catherine asked as Drew knotted the rope around Levi's waist. "How deep is that pool?"

"About six feet," he told her. "He's not the best swimmer in the family, it's true, but if the rope fails and he can't reach the side easily, it will only take me an hour or so to locate Simon to help get him out."

Levi stared at him. "An hour!"

Catherine frowned at Drew. For someone so careful of his mother, he seemed to have little regard for his brother's well-being. But as Levi slung his leg over the edge of the wall, Drew winked at Catherine. What was he up to?

He braced his feet on the stones and nodded to his brother. Levi leaned back against the rope and slowly edged into the pool. Drew played out the rope, and his brother shuddered as the cool water inched up his legs, then his torso. Catherine watched, fingers clasped, until only his curly blond head showed above the top.

"We've never had an issue with firedamp," she heard Drew murmur beside her. "I'll only keep him in a moment, but maybe he'll think before jumping into things in the future."

Catherine managed a breath and nodded. It seemed Drew Wallin knew his brother better than she'd thought.

"Report," he called to Levi.

"Moss," Levi replied, twisting in the water. The eddies around him told Catherine that Levi was moving his arms and legs to stay afloat. "And something darker over there." He bobbed toward the far side of the pool, closer to the trees.

The rope tightened beside her. Catherine glanced up and caught her breath. Drew stood, arms stiff, shoulders hard. Surely King Arthur must have looked like that when he'd pulled the sword from the stone.

"Get me out!" Levi shouted, and Drew hauled, muscles bunching. Catherine shook herself and held out her hands to grab Levi's arms and help him up onto the wall. His hands were covered in something black. At first she thought it was mud, but Levi thrust a finger under her nose, and she recoiled at the potent smell.

"Manure," he said, shaking off his hands and shaking his head at the same time. "Just a little. If there was more, it probably flushed out by now. Someone must have dumped it into the pool by mistake."

Catherine felt ill. "Surely everyone knows that isn't healthy."

"Everyone knows." Drew's words were no less forceful for their quiet. He dropped the rope and tugged his brother upright. "No one in my family would do this, mistake or otherwise. Someone tried to poison the spring. I want to know who, and I want to know why."

Chapter Eight

Drew fought down a rising temper. He'd heard tales of cattlemen and farmers fighting over grazing rights and poisoning each other's water supply, but that had been in other territories. No one he knew bore any grudge against him. Why dump manure in the spring?

"We should call back Deputy McCormick," Catherine said. "Surely this is against the law."

Drew focused on her. Her head was high, her eyes narrowed to blue chips of ice. She looked ready to fight anyone who would dare to threaten the health of her patients. Despite himself, he felt a smile forming.

"McCormick mentioned some of the other farms out this way had been harassed," Drew told her. "There may be a pattern. I'll report the matter when I take you back to town. In the meantime, we'll keep a closer eye out for strangers."

"It was probably just a mistake," Levi protested. "It's not as though we need to mount a guard or something."

Was the boy determined not to do an honest day's work? Drew forced himself to take a deep breath before answering, "If we all lend a hand, it won't be a burden on anyone."

Levi's lean face was turning red. "I never said it was a burden. But all you think about is working! Having a little fun isn't a crime, you know!"

His vehemence seemed too strong, even for his mercurial personality. Drew eyed his brother. "Do you know who did this, Levi?"

"Me?" He took a step back. "No! Of course not! I'm just upset they made more work for us." He turned and stalked off to the barn.

"Surely he wouldn't poison a spring his family uses," Catherine said, her tone unusually gentle. Drew glanced back at her to find her watching him as if to gauge his response. "He may not appreciate the importance of good health, but he must realize he'd have to drink the water, too."

There was that. But something was bothering his brother. "I doubt Levi dumped manure in the spring," he told her. "But I wouldn't be surprised if he hadn't angered some other young bucks who thought this was fair retaliation. I'll let him cool down a bit before I talk to him again. I won't tolerate this kind of nonsense."

"Agreed," she said with a nod. "In the meantime, what do you intend to do about the spring? Levi is right about one thing. Your mother became ill at least two weeks ago, so the manure was added before then. Very likely the bulk of the contamination was flushed out with the rains, but obviously some remains."

"I'll have Levi clean it out," Drew said. "We'll only draw from it for the stock until we know it's purified. We can use the pumps on my claim and Simon's for the house. It's farther to go, but they're capped. It wouldn't be easy to dump anything down them. Beth can show you how to work my pump."

She frowned at him. "Are you leaving?"

"I need to find my brothers," he said. "They'll want to know about this. I'll leave Levi in case you need an extra hand."

"I'm sure he'll be quite helpful."

He could hear her sarcasm. "He will if I have to beat it into him."

She blanched. "Please, Mr. Wallin. There's no need to strike the boy."

Did she think him a brute? Many saw his size and immediately assumed his temperament was as large.

"It's only a matter of speaking, ma'am," he replied, turning away. "I've never had to raise a hand to any of my brothers to get them to obey." With a nod, he set off for the woods.

Once he'd reached his brothers, he filled them in on the day's events. They were glad to hear that Ma was feeling better but irate that anyone would damage their main water supply. Unfortunately, no one could determine a reason.

"What about that prospector who sold you your fancy waistcoat?" Simon asked James as the brothers finished clearing away the smaller trees that might damage the spar when it fell. "Could he feel cheated?"

"I don't see why," James replied, swinging his ax into a sampling. "I paid him well enough for it. If anyone is aggrieved, it should be me." He paused a moment to lay a hand on his heart and bow his head.

Drew ignored the melodramatics. "Deputy McCormick said there's been other harassment out this way. We'll just have to keep a closer watch."

None of his brothers looked amused by the thought. Between the main farm, their own claims and the logging, they had more than enough to do.

Still, he couldn't deny a sense of peace as he returned to work for the first time since he'd started nursing his mother. There was something about the feel of the ax in his hands, the weight of its swing, the sound as it came into contact with the tree, the vibration up his arms. Although accidents could happen at any time, he knew to his sorrow, the work was predictable and productive. And when the tree was down and the land was cleared, he could see his accomplishments and knew he'd done well. He only wished raising a passel of brothers and a headstrong sister was as simple.

After Drew left, Catherine returned to the house. She agreed with him that his brother's actions were suspicious, but she hated to think that a group of boys would take matters so far as to poison a neighbor's water supply. They had to know this prank could have had dangerous repercussions.

"So what do you think?" Beth asked when Catherine rejoined her and her mother upstairs. "Was something wrong with the spring?"

Mrs. Wallin was sitting up in the bed, and the sock and needles resting in the lap of Beth's blue gingham gown told Catherine what the girl had been doing while she waited. The two women listened as Catherine explained what she and Drew had found. She purposely omitted any mention of Levi's possible involvement, but Beth hopped to her feet, face reddening, tumbling the sock to the floor.

"Oh, that Levi! I will skin him for this!"

"Elizabeth Ann Wallin," her mother scolded. "I can't believe your brother would do such a thing."

Catherine was watching Beth, whose color was only darkening. "Why do you suspect your brother, Beth?"

She bent to retrieve the sock and needles, voice muffled. "I shouldn't. Ma's right." She set her things on the chair, then caught up a bit of hair and twisted the golden strand around one finger. "It's just that he's made no bones about the fact that he thinks we should have taken a claim closer to town. He says when it's his turn, he's not choosing acreage this far out."

"And that is his decision," her mother said, voice firm though her face was pale. "Just because his brothers lined up their claims along ours doesn't mean he must."

"Yes, Ma," Beth said. "If you'll excuse me, I'll just go start the baking." She headed for the stairs.

Catherine knew she shouldn't interfere, but something about Beth's reaction told her there was more to the story. "I'll come with you," she said, following her. "I need to explain what we're doing about water now."

Mrs. Wallin wiggled deeper under the covers. "You do that. I think I'll just take a nap."

Catherine caught up with Beth at the foot of the stairs. As if Beth had guessed her purpose, she paused and lowered her voice. "I'm sorry, Miss Stanway. I should never have spoken that way about Levi. It's just that he makes me so mad! All Pa did, all Drew and the others have done to build us a home, make our own community... I hear him sneak out sometimes, going off at night when he thinks Drew and the others are asleep. He doesn't seem to value anything Drew taught him!"

"Maybe he just wants to go his own way," Catherine said, remembering her brother with a pang. "Boys often do at his age."

"Well, I'm glad I'm not a boy, then." Beth started for the back of the house. "I'm not abandoning my family when I turn eighteen."

Catherine hid a smile at the defiant tone, spoken with such authority by one who had seen so little of the world as yet. "You never know," she told Beth as she joined the girl in the back room. "More and more professions are open to women, and Seattle will have many opportunities as it grows."

Standing by the iron tub, which seemed to serve for both laundry and bathing, Beth grinned at her. "At least you didn't tell me it's a woman's duty to wed and have babies." She stuck up her arm and pointed to the ceiling as if calling the Lord as a witness. "By golly, young lady, don't you know that's how the West was won?" She dropped her arm and giggled.

"I would be the last one to tell you that you must marry," Catherine assured her.

"Then you're the only one." Beth sighed. "I may cause the West to be lost, but I've already had my fill of cooking and cleaning for a mess of men. Now, what do I have to do differently to keep us all healthy?"

Catherine and Beth spent the rest of the day planning what needed to be done and setting it into motion. Drew and his brothers must have had chores or timber that needed cutting, for she saw nothing of them. She and Beth aired the ticks and washed the linens and hung them to dry on tree limbs around the clearing. They washed and hung out Mrs. Wallin's nightgown and underthings, as well.

Levi helped whenever they managed to catch him,

and always with such a martyred expression on his face
that Catherine wanted to send him to the corner. Unfortunately, he was past the age where such discipline
worked, and she didn't have the authority in the house
for that sort of thing anyway. She was merely glad Mrs.
Wallin and Beth were willing to listen to her suggestions.

Beth had dinner on the stove, and the sun was dip-
ping low when Levi brought in another load of firewood. Catherine had noticed a raised crib, sheltered
under the eaves of the barn, where they must set the
logs to cure.

"Will the others be coming home soon?" Catherine
asked as she helped Mrs. Wallin to the table. Her patient had felt well enough that Catherine was willing
to allow her to eat with the family. Just the trip down
the stairs had taken its toll, however, for Mrs. Wallin's
hands were shaking as she tried to sip from the cup of
cool water Beth had handed her. Catherine couldn't help
remembering the strength of Drew's arms as he'd carried her across the clearing last night. Surely he could
help his mother back upstairs after dinner if needed.

"Oh, we have to call them," Beth said from behind
the hearth. She hooked her stirring spoon over the edge
of a steaming pot and headed for the back door.

"They're close enough to hear us?" Catherine asked
with a frown.

Levi grinned. "In a matter of speaking."

"It's something their pa dreamed up," Mrs. Wallin
explained. "Levi, go fetch Miss Stanway the plates we
use for dinner. None of that tin on my table."

Levi was returning with some delicate-looking pink-
and-white-patterned dishes from the sideboard when

a gun roared outside. Catherine nearly jumped out of her skin and found her own hands shaking as the gun barked again. Levi started laughing, but a look from his mother silenced him.

"Two shots means you're needed at home," Mrs. Wallin told Catherine. "One shot means come a-running, now."

Beth poked her head in the door. "They should be here shortly."

She was right. Catherine had barely set the last china plate on the table when boots thudded across the boardwalk of the house. John was the first through the door. His face was smeared with dirt, his red plaid shirt darkened by sweat. His smile brightened when he saw their mother, and he went to peck her cheek before taking a seat farther down the table. James, an elegant silver-shot waistcoat wrapped around his lean frame, had a similar reaction, though he went to wash his hands before joining them.

Simon approached his mother more cautiously. "Should you be up?" he asked her, his gaze seeking Catherine's as if for confirmation.

"Nurse Stanway approved it," his mother assured him with a smile to Catherine. "Besides, having my family around me is the best medicine, if you ask me."

Catherine didn't meet her gaze. It was the best medicine in her mind, too, although she thought her father might have once argued the matter.

Drew was the last one through the door. His damp hair clung to his head as if he'd dunked it under the pump. His face was clean, though an evening's stubble lay like gold across his jaw. He took his seat opposite his mother at the foot of the table, then bowed his head and asked the blessing. Male voices punctuated by Beth's and Mrs. Wallin's sopranos rumbled the amen.

Catherine wasn't sure what to expect from a family of rough loggers, but the Wallins were polite in their eating. Platters and plates passed in orderly fashion up and down the table and, except for an occasional lunge for a particular goody, everyone took turns serving themselves. There was ham, molasses clinging to the edges; mashed potatoes with salty gravy; biscuits and carrots. Though the fare was plain and simple, she couldn't remember enjoying a meal more.

As they ate, she monitored Mrs. Wallin. The lady partook sparingly, but her color was good and her eyes sparkled at the stories her sons were telling of their day in the timber.

"John was nearly carried away today," James reported, helping himself to another biscuit.

John rolled his eyes, but his mother smiled. "Do tell."

"Was it a bear?" Levi demanded, fork stilled a moment in his hand. "I saw some fearful tracks down by the lake earlier."

"Not a bear," James said. "And no cougar, either. It seems fair John surprised an owl up in the tree and the beast nearly took his head off. I figured that, seeing he was so wise, our friend the owl thought to carry him off for its own."

His brothers chuckled, and Mrs. Wallin shook her head at his jest. John leveled his spoon at his brother.

"If you'd bother to open a book once in a while, you might be just as wise. Besides, at least I caught a few quills for writing later." He nodded to Beth. "I'll give you one."

"Thank you!" Beth beamed at him.

The stories continued over a dried-apple pie that seemed to disappear in one bite. But Catherine noticed she wasn't the only one watching her patient. Every time she glanced in Drew's direction, he was eying his mother.

Indeed, he didn't enter into the teasing with his family. He seemed to stand aside, like a massive oak, shielding them from any harm. Although his protection was noble, she couldn't help wondering whether it was a lonely vigil.

"What about a game tonight?" Levi asked, slinging a leg over the bench where he, James and John were sitting.

"Kitty in the Corner," Beth said with a clap of her hands before reaching for the empty pie plate.

Levi made a face, but Drew spoke up, hands cradling his tankard of cider. "We should have music tonight in honor of Ma coming down to dinner."

This time when Mrs. Wallin smiled, Catherine could see the effort it took. "Perhaps one tune. Simon, would you play for us?"

Simon climbed off the opposite bench from beside Catherine. "Whatever you want, Ma. Just give me a moment to fetch my fiddle."

Drew stood and came around the table to lift his mother. "Miss Stanway," he said, gazing at Catherine over his mother's shoulder, "please join us. The rest of you, clear up."

With good-natured grumbling, his brothers rose to help.

A short while later they were all seated around the hearth. Mrs. Wallin had settled so contentedly in the bentwood rocker that the dark wood seemed curved to her frame. Beth sat at her feet, legs curled up under her gingham skirts. Levi, James and John lounged on the rug before the fire. Catherine felt like a queen seated on one of the ladder-backed chairs. Drew braced his shoulders against the log wall and crossed his arms over his chest. Catherine could feel his gaze roaming over his family; her cheeks warmed when she felt it resting on her.

She told herself to focus on Simon, who had moved to stand before the fire. He held a well-polished violin and bow. Since arriving in Seattle, she'd heard a number of fellows scrape out a tune with many a protest from the instrument and prepared herself for a similar performance.

"Something gentle, I think," Mrs. Wallin said, leaning back in her chair. "Something to calm the spirit."

"Gentle it is." Simon put his bow to the strings and out drifted a lilting song. The notes danced and skipped about the room, like young lambs in the spring. Catherine felt a smile forming.

Mrs. Wallin was smiling, too, as were most of her sons. Beth had her lips pressed close together as if to keep from laughing, but Levi went so far as to snicker.

Drew pushed off from the wall. "Very funny, Simon. Try something else."

Simon inclined his head, and the tune changed. It was slow, serious, nearly mournful. Beth frowned as if she had never heard it before. Mrs. Wallin sighed and seemed to hunch in her chair.

The sounds spoke to Catherine of loves lost and friends parted, yet hope rising through it all, whispering of new life, fulfilled purpose. Around her, the men quieted and stilled. It was as if the very forest was holding its breath and listening.

Simon urged one final note from his violin and lowered it.

Mrs. Wallin managed a smile. "Well done, Simon. You surely inherited that skill from your father. He'd be proud."

Simon shrugged as he set down the instrument, but Catherine could see the faintest of pink in his lean cheeks.

Mrs. Wallin rose then, saying good-night to her family. Catherine watched as each of her children went to kiss her or give her a hug, wishing her sweet dreams, promising they'd see her in the morning. The love glowed around them as surely as the light from the lamp. Catherine felt as if she stood in a circle of darkness.

Then Drew looked her way, and the glow seemed to expand, to encourage her closer.

She could feel her heart responding. Would it be so wrong to give in to its urging?

Chapter Nine

Drew moved to Catherine's side. He didn't think she knew what his brother had just done with his playing, but for a moment she had looked almost stricken. Once more, he'd wanted to gather her close. He had to settle for helping her instead.

"Let me," he said when she took his mother's arm to assist Ma up the stairs. He lifted his mother and carried her up. Catherine and Beth followed.

"That Simon," Beth said with a tsk. "I hope he didn't offend you, Miss Stanway."

Drew tensed, but Catherine's voice held its usual composure. "Not at all," she assured Beth as they reached the top of the stairs. "He plays beautifully."

Drew couldn't help himself. "He ought to pay more attention to his selection than his tuning." He set his mother down on the bed and stepped back to give her room to settle herself. He didn't like her pallor. It was obvious to him she wasn't as well as she wanted them to think.

But despite her evident weariness, her eyes were bright. "Why, what do you mean, Andrew?" she asked innocently. "I like to hear the songs from the old country. I thought the wedding march and the christening song fine selections."

Fine selections for a man who was courting. He wasn't. Drew bit back an answer and turned to Catherine before she could question his mother. "I'll take first watch tonight."

She raised her head, as if he'd challenged her capabilities. "Nonsense. You've labored hard all day. My place is at your mother's side."

So was his. But even as he opened his mouth to say as much, he felt weariness tugging at his sleeve, urging him to take the opportunity to rest.

Beth settled the matter for him. "No, I'll watch first," she insisted. "I'm not sleepy. You and Drew have a lot to talk about, I'm sure."

There they went again. He could see the way his mother and sister exchanged glances. So could Catherine if the set of her mouth was any indication.

Oh, no! He wasn't about to let himself focus on her lips again tonight.

"Miss Stanway has had a long day, as well," he informed his sister. He turned to Catherine. "If you're ready to retire, I'll walk you to the cabin."

"Surely there's no need, Mr. Wallin," she protested. "I believe I know the way by now."

"Oh, but Miss Stanway," Beth interrupted, "the moon's out tonight. There's nothing finer than a stroll in the moonlight."

Catherine did not seem to agree. Indeed, she was turning nearly as pale as Ma in the firelight.

He put a hand to her elbow. "Are you all right?"

She pulled away from his touch. "Fine. Just tired, as

you noted. I'll see if one of your brothers can walk me to the cabin. I'll be expecting your knock after midnight, Miss Wallin."

She turned and descended the stairs as if a bear was at her heels. With his mother and sister glaring at him, he knew just how she felt.

John agreed to escort Catherine across to the other cabin. She felt as if she was running away, but the idea of strolling in the moonlight with Drew had raised such a longing inside her that she'd known retreat was her best choice. She was merely glad John showed no interest in the silvery light bathing them.

"I find your approach to healthful living to be inspiring, Miss Stanway," he said as they neared the cabin. "Especially the different foodstuffs you advised for Ma." He opened the door and peered in. Did he think someone else had wandered into the house while she was out?

"Perhaps you can suggest a book on the subject," he said, returning his gaze to hers. "I hear Mrs. Howard has started a lending library. I may be able to persuade her to order a book for me."

"My father was rather fond of *Culpeper's Complete Herbal*," Catherine told him. "I'll see if I can find a copy for you."

He nodded his thanks, made sure the fire and lamp were burning and left her.

Despite her reaction to Drew, once more sleep came easily, the air so cool and crisp she could almost taste it. A few hours later Beth woke her as promised, rousing Catherine from a hazy dream in which she ran through the woods, searching for something she couldn't name.

"Though I'm not sure you're needed, as Ma's sleeping just fine," the girl reported as she walked Catherine back across the clearing. Both the trip with John and now with Beth had gone remarkably smoothly. Had Drew really needed to carry her the previous night?

But as Catherine settled herself in the chair next to Mrs. Wallin, she almost wished she had stayed in bed. There was nothing to keep her mind from the memories that crept up on her like a woodland mouse.

Her father teaching her brother to ride.

Nathan so proud in the uniform she'd helped sew for him.

Her standing by their gravestones, lined up clean and bright next to the church.

She rose and stoked the fire, then traveled to the far window and peered out. The moon was riding high; she could see a reflection of silver on the lake, brightening the shore. For a moment, she thought she saw a shadow slipping along below the house, but she blinked to focus her weary eyes and it was gone.

Drew or his brothers must have found food elsewhere, for no one disturbed them. The sun had already risen when she yawned and reached for the water bucket. Drew had left them plenty of wood, but she thought Beth might need most of the water for breakfast. Perhaps she could ask Levi to fill this bucket for her so she could help Mrs. Wallin wash up.

Unfortunately, she found his bed empty, seemingly undisturbed from last night. Well, she'd simply have to fend for herself. She took the bucket downstairs, intending to fill it from Drew's pump. She stepped out on the porch.

And froze.

There were men everywhere. Some had curled up along the boardwalk of the house, heads pillowed on their bent knees. Others camped under the eaves of the barn. All lay still, the silence broken by the occasional snore.

What had happened? Why were they here? Had she been wrong about Mrs. Wallin's illness? Was this the start of an epidemic?

She dropped the bucket and ran into the yard. Crouching over the closest fellow, she felt for a pulse at his wrist. It was beating strongly.

His eyes popped open, a bleary blue in his grizzled face. "Glory be, it's true! There *is* a woman in the woods."

Catherine was so surprised she fell back on her skirts. Even as he scrambled to his feet, other hands grabbed her under her arms and hauled her upright.

"There now, ma'am," a man dressed in fur skins said with a smile that revealed several missing teeth. The burned smell of badly tanned leather coiled around her before he released her. "Don't you mind Old Joe. He don't got the manners of a flea."

"But I do." Another man in a fine wool suit, starched collar lifting his shaven chin, pushed forward. He whisked out a snowy white handkerchief and attempted to dust off her skirts. "There you go, missy. All set to marry me."

"Marry you!" Catherine sputtered, shaking out her skirts.

Old Joe shoved him back into the muddy yard. "Hey, I saw her first!"

"But I got here before any of you lot," declared the man in fur. "I paid Mercer a pretty penny for a bride, and none of them hoity-toity misses in town will listen to me. By rights, this one is mine."

He shouldered aside Old Joe, who pushed him right back. The two wrestled to the ground, grappling, mud squelching with each grunt. What were they doing? They couldn't be fighting over her! Even the chickens fluttered about in their coop in protest.

She backed away from the struggling men as the rest of the strangers in the clearing roused at the sounds of raised voices and began standing. As a crowd, they shambled toward her, gazes as bright as if she were a cool drink of water on a hot day.

"Stop, right now!" she ordered them, pointing an imperious finger. "I'm marrying no one."

Old Joe managed to fend off his comrade and struggled to his feet. Wiping muck from his face, he turned toward her with a determined glint in his eyes. "Course you are. That's what you Mercer gals came for. I couldn't get into town before most of them was spoken for, but when I heard one was here with the Wallin boys I figured I stood as good a chance as any of them."

That seemed to be everyone's opinion, for they were all nodding and smiling as they converged on her, arms outstretched as if to shake her hand or grab her closer. Heart pounding, she lifted her skirts and dashed for the boardwalk.

"Won't do no good to run," one shouted after her. "You'll only get caught and brought back."

Her breath was what was caught. All this because they wanted a wife? Had they no moral grounding, no sense of propriety? She felt like the baby in the tale of Solomon's wisdom, about to be cleaved in two to settle a dispute.

She couldn't run into the house and expose Beth and Mrs. Wallin to these men. Who knew where Levi might be or whether he'd be any use at all. If Drew and his other brothers hadn't heard the commotion by now, they must already be out in the trees. They had no way of knowing an army was besieging their little castle on the lake.

And then she remembered. She reached the back door a good few yards before any of the men and snatched up the rifle hanging from a hook. She'd never fired a gun in her life, but it seemed obvious what she should do. Whirling away from the door, she held it out and put her finger in the little loop at the base of the barrel.

The men following her skidded to a stop. One put up his hands as if surrendering.

"Now, you just set that down, little lady," Old Joe said, taking a cautious step closer, eyes narrowing. "We wouldn't want anyone to get hurt."

"She don't know what she's doing," another muttered, with an elbow in the side of the man next to him. "Look at how her hands are shaking."

Catherine could feel it as well, and she could see it in the way the barrel bobbed. *Help me, Lord!*

She stiffened her spine and glared at the mob surrounding her. If they wanted her for a wife, they should know what they were getting.

"I may be shaking, sir," she told Old Joe, "but I know exactly what I'm doing." She raised the gun and fired.

Chapter Ten

Drew heard the shot echoing through the woods and lowered his ax. Simon must have heard it as well, for he paused, too. The two of them and James had been working behind Simon's cabin, cutting away some of the brush that had sprung up in the spring rains before heading out deeper into the woods for the fir they'd chosen for Captain Collings's spar. John and Levi were out notching the tree in preparation for cutting it down.

"Was Beth planning a big breakfast?" James asked, venturing closer from where he'd been dragging the brush into a pile. He must have been expecting the work to be light, for he'd elected to wear the silver-shot waistcoat of which he was inordinately proud.

Now they all listened, tensed, waiting for the second shot that would assure them all was well.

No shot came.

Drew ran.

His brothers were right behind him, axes down and at the ready. They weren't far from the clearing, but each step seemed a mile. Had a cougar wandered too close and threatened the stock? Had the enemy who'd poisoned the spring returned for more? Had their mother taken a turn for the worse? Was Catherine in danger?

He careened into the clearing and skidded to a stop at the sight of more than a dozen men surrounding the main house. Some were peering in the lower windows. Others were pounding at the back door. One was trying to climb up onto the roof.

"Hey!" Simon shouted, the first one out of the woods behind him. "What do you think you're doing?"

The men at the rear of the crowd glanced the brothers' way, and the fellow on the eaves dropped to the ground. Two turned and ran off into the woods. James made to follow, but Drew called him back.

"No! We need you here. You and Simon take the right. I'll take the left. Use your axes only if you must and handle for the blade."

With grim nods, his brothers started forward.

More men peeled off as they approached. Some looked apologetic; others glared belligerently. But no one raised a hand or stammered an explanation.

By the time Drew reached the back door, only a few remained. One was begging at the panel.

"Oh, come now, missy! You can't hide in there forever. We're all fine fellows. Just tell us which you prefer, and the rest of us will go home peaceful-like."

Drew frowned at the statement, but Simon evidently understood its meaning, for he lowered his ax as he joined Drew on the porch.

"You're too late, boys," he said, smile cocky. "We already decided she's marrying one of us."

The man at the front turned to him with a frown, but the door of the house jerked open. The remaining men scattered from the fury on Catherine Stanway's face.

She marched out onto the porch like a colonel leading a battalion into battle.

"Oh, *you* decided, did you?" she said to Simon. "Just like that. No need to consult the lady in question. You're as bad as this bunch!"

His brother was paling, but he had the good sense not to argue with her.

Drew stared around him in amazement. "You all came here to court Miss Stanway?"

"No, siree." A prospector Drew knew was called Old Joe stretched his suspenders as if he were quite proud of himself. "I didn't come to court. I came to marry."

"You came to make a fool of yourself." Catherine leveled her stare at him. As his head dropped, she met each gaze in turn. Most lowered, too, or glanced away.

"Where I was raised," she said, voice as crisp as a winter's afternoon, "a gentleman courts a lady, and they mutually agree that marriage is the best course. I will not be coerced or bullied into marrying. And anyone who attempts to force his way into my affections will rue the day he was born."

Drew raised his brows. Simon took a firmer grip on his ax as if expecting her to pounce on him any moment. From the back of the crowd, James grinned at her.

"Well, she's a shrew," someone muttered. "Think I'll take my chances with one of them tamer ones in town."

Several others nodded, backing away or turning.

Enough was enough. Drew pushed his way to the front and faced the last of her suitors. "You heard the lady. Clear off. If you've a mind to marry, you'll have to find another partner."

His brothers joined him, lining up beside Catherine,

and more men left, shaking their heads and grumbling. Soon only two remained.

One approached, cap in hand. He was a short man with a thick mustache, highly waxed, and a precise part down the center of his dark hair. Drew recognized him from town.

"Miss Stanway," he said, "I'm Jonas Cooper. I work for Mr. Yesler at the mill. He'll vouch that I'm a tidy, sober man. I attend church every Sunday, and I tithe ten percent to the poor. I've had some education, and I've managed to put money aside for a house in town. I don't cuss, but I do enjoy a fine cigar from time to time. I'd be honored if you'd consider allowing me to court you properly."

Drew's fingers tightened on the ax. Catherine had every right to choose a fine man, and Cooper was about as upstanding as they came. Yet Drew felt a sudden urge to go dunk the fellow's perfectly combed hair in the lake.

Not to be outdone, the other man swept in front of Cooper. Drew had never seen him before. He had black hair, a neat goatee and a definite twinkle in his dark eyes. James was already eyeing his coat, which was trimmed with velvet. Instead of a handkerchief at his throat, he wore a fancy cravat held in place by a gold stickpin mounted with a green stone that looked suspiciously like an emerald.

"Nay, fair maiden," he said, voice hinting of a foreign shore, "consider my suit instead. I'm Gulliver Ward. I made my fortune in the gold fields of California, and I'm set to build a playhouse in Seattle, where only the finest theatricals will be performed. My wife will be gowned in silks and satins and fed on oysters and caviar. She will be one of Seattle's first ladies, when the money starts coming in, of course. With your beauty and my wit, no door would be closed to us. Allow me to win your heart."

Drew stared at him. What was he doing, laying his life at her feet? He'd never even met her!

"Out!" he shouted, raising the handle of his ax. "You have five minutes to get off my land. James, escort these fine fellows."

His brother started forward. So did Catherine, but this time her fury was turned on Drew, and he found himself backing away from it.

"And there you go, Mr. Wallin," she said, eyes sparking fire, "deciding my future just as surely as the rest of these men. *I* will decide who I court, if I court. Have I made myself clear?"

Drew nodded. "Clear enough. But may I remind you that you shot the rifle. I thought you wanted my help."

She took a deep breath as if to calm herself. "I did. But I am quite capable of making my own decisions." She turned to the two men. Drew steeled himself to hear her answer. If she accepted that gussied-up Ward, he thought he'd have to go soak his own head in the lake.

"Mr. Cooper," she said, voice as precise and calm as it usually was when she spoke about clinical matters, "I appreciate your thoughtful assessment of your worth as a matrimonial candidate. Allow me to reciprocate. I am headstrong, opinionated and outspoken. We would not suit. I suggest you look more closely at the ladies still in Seattle."

Drew felt as if the air was sweeter as Mr. Cooper stared at her in surprise. Catherine turned to her other suitor.

"Mr. Ward, you certainly have a way with words. I predict you will go far."

Drew couldn't help it. He took a step closer to the fellow, but Ward's gaze did not waver from Catherine's.

"I'm glad we are of a common mind, my dear," he said, inclining his head. "Allow me to escort you away from this rustic hovel. You shine like a diamond even here, but I know you will positively glow in a more suitable setting."

Drew could feel his teeth grating on each other; he was surprised Catherine couldn't hear them. Simon was smacking the handle of his ax into his palm as if he couldn't wait for an excuse to use it.

"You are too kind," Catherine said with a smile that raised gooseflesh along Drew's arms. "But I have work here. You might look up my friend Miss O'Rourke in Seattle. She has a particular fondness for silks and satins. I do caution you, however, that she may be just as loath to spend her life as a decoration for a man's arm. Good day." She turned and entered the house, closing the door decisively behind her.

Drew wanted to howl at the sky in triumph. She'd turned them down!

Cooper had a harder time believing it, for he shook his head. "They said she was cold, but I wouldn't believe it. You had better think twice before taking that one to wife, Wallin."

"You, sir, are blind," Ward said, stepping down from the porch. "A man can go far with the right woman at his side. I'd heard Miss Stanway was the best of the lot."

"How did you know she was here?" Simon asked, lowering his ax.

"'Twas a tale told over a friendly hand of cards," Ward assured him. "When a lady is so lovely, word will get around. And the fact that she was willing to sojourn with you all indicated her taste in men might not be overly finicky."

Simon frowned. "Did you just insult us?"

"Not with that accent," James joked.

Ward swept them a bow. "I meant no harm, gentlemen. My own past is no less humble. That hasn't stopped me from reaching high, even in a bride." He glanced at the door and sighed. "Ah, well. Back to the city for this lad. Farewell, gentlemen." He turned and strolled out into the woods, where Drew assumed he must have a horse waiting.

"Reprobate," Cooper said with a shake of his head, as if he hadn't also just tried to marry Catherine at first sight like the fancy Ward. He turned to Drew. "Sorry to have troubled you. Mr. Yesler sends his regards and hopes you will have more timber for him soon."

"Maybe we would," Simon said, "if we weren't so busy defending what is ours."

Cooper reddened. Stammering another apology, he, too, headed for the trees.

"I'll just make sure they've all gone," James said, "and ask that Ward fellow where he purchased his coat." He set out toward the edge of the clearing.

Simon shook his head. "I warned you, Drew. If you won't marry Miss Stanway, someone else will."

"You heard her," Drew snapped. "She refused to marry any of them."

"So she said," Simon agreed. "But what I want to know is why she looked at you every time she said it."

* * *

Beth had come down from upstairs and stood by the stove as Catherine closed the door behind her, hands still shaking. The girl's eyes were wide in her round face, her fingers twisting at the material of her pink gingham gown.

"Who were those men?" she cried. "Was that Simon I saw outside? Where are Drew and the others? Should I fetch a rifle?"

Catherine only felt confident answering the last question. "No need for the gun. I think the other men have gone. I'm sorry if I frightened you when I fired."

Beth took a step closer and put out a hand as if she needed to be certain Catherine was safe. "When someone fires one shot around here, we notice. What happened?"

The chair by the hearth beckoned, but Catherine couldn't sit, not when her heart was hammering as furiously as her temper. She had to smother these emotions. She paced to the stove, a cast-iron series of steps into the fireplace with a fat-bellied oven in the center near the fire and burners on top. Reaching above it, she pulled down a copper teakettle from a hook on the wall, talking as she worked. "We had company this morning, a great deal of company. And they were not the sort of men I wanted to introduce to you."

As if she disagreed with Catherine, Beth scrambled to the window and peered out, blond hair brushing the pane. "I don't see anyone. Were they the ones who poisoned the spring?"

About to lift the bucket of water by the stove, Catherine stilled. Was it possible? Whoever had thrown manure into the Wallin's pool had been bent on making trouble. Was this simply more of the same?

But no, the water had been contaminated before Mrs. Wallin had fallen ill, which was long before Catherine had arrived. If those men were truly here because of her, they could have had nothing to do with the spring.

"I don't think so," Catherine said, pouring water into the teakettle.

Beth wheeled away from the window. "Oh, good! Drew's coming in. Maybe he'll have answers."

Catherine's fingers tightened on the wooden handle of the kettle as the door opened. Although she was grateful Drew and his brothers had come running at her shot for help, she didn't appreciate the way they'd presumed to know her mind. Like her neighbors in Sudbury, they seemed certain her only course was marriage. Had she gained nothing by traveling across the country?

Drew came in and shut the door behind him. His mouth was set in a firm line, and his eyes were narrowed as if he wasn't sure of his reception.

In truth, she wasn't sure how to receive him, either. She busied herself setting the teakettle on the stove. The movement was stiff enough that metal clanked on metal.

"What was all that?" Beth demanded as he came into the room, boots thudding against the worn boards of the floor. "Who were those men?"

"Apparently a pack of fools," he replied. He crossed to Catherine's side and lowered his head and his voice.

"Forgive me if I offended you," he murmured. "I just didn't like the idea of those men pushing themselves on you."

Neither had she. In truth, she'd panicked, something she'd always thought beneath her. She was an intelligent, well-educated, skilled woman. She'd never been in a situation she couldn't master, until her father and brother had died. Even then, she'd fallen back on reason and logic, walling off all the emotions that troubled her.

But those men had demanded that she marry one of them, as if she were no more than a commodity. How did reason prevail?

"They have no excuse for their behavior," she said, pulling down the tea canister from the shelf at the top of the sideboard along one wall. Her hand was still shaking as she scooped up some of the leaves, and she forced her fingers to still. "Wilderness or big city, there are conventions on how one goes courting."

"Courting?" Beth ventured closer, head cocked. "You mean all those men came here for you, Miss Stanway?"

"As I said, they are a pack of fools," Drew answered. He caught Catherine's hand and held it as if to stop her trembling. "You were wise to call us. I never dreamed something like this would happen. I heard there was a lot of nonsense when the Mercer belles had first arrived, but I'd thought that had died down by now."

Catherine shuddered, remembering. "This sort of thing followed us the entire trip. From Brazil to Chile to San Francisco, men flocked out to greet us as if they'd never seen a woman before. When we arrived in Seattle, men lined the shore, claiming they'd paid our passage to be their brides."

"Oh," Beth said, obviously fascinated to the point her usual banter failed her.

"I paid my own passage," Catherine informed her. "As did most of the ladies aboard. It certainly isn't our fault Mr. Mercer made promises he couldn't keep. I won't be held accountable for that man's larceny. But what I don't understand is how those men knew I was here."

"That fellow Ward said something about a card game," Drew told her, his hand still cradling hers. "Perhaps McCormick reported on your whereabouts when he returned to town."

Possibly, but most of the men seemed to have come from the area, not Seattle. She hadn't seen the smoke from a single homestead when she'd ridden north with Drew. Where had these men come from?

"Deputy McCormick was here?" Beth cried, turning pink. "Why didn't someone tell me? Oh, I miss all the excitement!"

"Be thankful for that," Catherine said. She knew she should pull back her hand and finish preparing tea, but the warmth of Drew's touch spread through her body, relaxing tense muscles and calming frazzled nerves. She'd never thought she'd be one to need a man to feel safe, but she could not deny that his presence was unaccountably comforting.

"It doesn't matter," he said. "What's done is done. James and Simon will make sure those men leave, but I'll stay nearby until you've returned to Seattle. You have no need to fear."

Fear? That emotion had long since fled. Catherine forced her fingers out of his. "It wasn't fear that made me so angry. It was your brother's statement that you've all decided one of you is going to marry me. I heard you talking with your brothers the other night. You didn't disagree, then or now."

Color was creeping into his cheeks, like the sun rising over a mountain. "Simon can speak all the nonsense he likes. He can't tell anyone how to feel."

She drew in the first deep breath since she'd seen those men in the clearing. "No, he can't. Nor can he dictate my actions. I think I've made myself clear. I'm not planning on marrying. I have a calling, a vocation, and certainly one Seattle sorely needs. I intended to stay another day, but if you all can't understand my position, then perhaps I should leave now."

He met her gaze, and this time she had no doubt the emotion flickering in that expanse of blue-green was regret. She felt it, too, just as she felt herself leaning toward him, as if her body vied with her mind as to where she belonged.

Beth spoke before he did. "No, you can't go, Miss Stanway. Not until Ma's well."

"Your mother is on the mend, Beth," Catherine said, drawing back though her gaze refused to leave his. "We've determined the cause of the illness, and your brother has already isolated it. There's nothing more for me to do here."

She waited for him to argue. She wasn't sure why she expected it. Some part of her believed him when he'd said he didn't wish to wed, either. If he truly did intend to court her or marry her to one of his brothers, he ought to protest her leaving. And if he actually cared about her…

She shut that thought away. She had never been one of those girls who collected beaux like frosted candies, turning this one aside when that one struck her fancy. She didn't want Drew to care about her.

Because that meant she'd have to care about him more than she already did.

Chapter Eleven

She was determined to leave. Drew could see the challenge in those cool blue eyes. She'd had her fill of his family, and who could blame her? Between Simon's demands and Beth and Ma's collusion, Catherine had to feel surrounded. And their unexpected visitors this morning had only made matters worse.

Still, he ought to argue. Ma was a great deal better, but who was to say she wouldn't have a relapse? And he would have liked to sit by the fire with Catherine, quiz her on what more he could do to keep his family healthy, hold her hand, cuddle her close.

What was he thinking? Maybe it really was time for her to go.

He snapped a nod, breaking their gazes at last. "I'll hitch the team to the wagon and we can take you back to Seattle right now."

She stepped away from him as if he'd ordered her to go. "Very well. I'll check on my patient one last time." She picked up her skirts and swept from the room.

Her patient, she said, as if Ma were no more than one of the stock, an ax that needed sharpening. Ma and his brothers clearly meant nothing to her. They were his responsibility only.

The kettle began to hiss. Beth went to lift it off the stove.

"Well, you made a great hash of that," she said, disgust evident in each syllable. "You need lessons in courting."

Drew shook his head and turned for the back door. "I'm not courting."

"Not like that, you aren't!" She dropped the kettle on the sideboard with a clatter, ran after him and grabbed his arm before he could open the door. "For pity's sake, Drew! You can do better. You always told us if we set our minds to something, we should keep trying until we won it."

Perhaps that was the problem. He couldn't set his mind to courting Catherine, despite his family's urging or the murmur of his heart. As much as he had taken an instant dislike to that Ward fellow, Drew could not argue that Catherine seemed destined for greater things than Wallin Landing.

From her fancy dress to her proper ways, Catherine seemed cultured. Certainly she was better educated than most people he knew, even the ever-studious John. She ought to be somewhere she could use those skills, not just doctoring his family. That was his job.

"Leave be, Beth," he told his sister. "This is for the best."

She released him with a scowl. "Whose best? Not yours. Not ours."

"No," Drew said, yanking open the door. "Hers. Tell her I'll have the team out front when she's ready." He left before his sister could launch into the tirade he saw building in her eyes as sure as the steam from the hot teakettle.

Simon and James were still out in the woods as Drew stalked across the clearing, but he heard a cheery whistle coming from the opposite direction. Not another would-be suitor! He almost pitied the fellow, for Drew was in no mood to be conciliatory. Turning, he planted his feet and brought up both fists.

John strode out of the trees, ax over one shoulder and rifle in the other hand. Spying Drew, he stopped and dropped his ax. "What have I done?"

Drew lowered his fists and narrowed his stance. "Nothing. We had some excitement this morning."

"I thought I heard a shot!" He hurried to Drew's side. "I'm sorry, Drew! I was so far out I couldn't be sure. And I knew Levi was headed this way, so I figured he'd come back for me if I was needed."

Drew frowned. "You sent Levi home?"

John nodded. "Early this morning. The dunderhead forgot the wedges. Honestly, Drew, sometimes I wonder whether we dropped that boy on his head a few too many times when he was a baby."

"We never dropped him," Drew said. "We wouldn't have dared. He was Ma's favorite until Beth came along."

"Sometimes I think he's still Ma's favorite," John said, no rancor in his tone. "That's the only reason I can see for why she wants him around so much. I take it he was too busy helping you to bring back those wedges."

"He never returned to the Landing that I saw," Drew replied.

Now John frowned. "Did you check the barn? It's his favorite place to nap."

So Drew had discovered yesterday. "If he slept through the chaos this morning, I'll make sure he doesn't sleep tonight," Drew promised, turning for the barn.

John paced him, and Drew took the opportunity to explain what had happened with Catherine's surprise callers.

John whistled as they came into the barn. "It seems Simon was right. She is valuable."

"Her value has nothing to do with the fact that men rush to court her," Drew said. His tone must have been hotter than he intended, for the chickens flew out of their roost at the sound.

John set the ax and rifle by the door. "Oh, I wouldn't say that. I understand a woman's allure is an important part of what she can accomplish. Look at Helen of Troy."

"Never met her," Drew said. He grabbed the iron pole and poked it up into the straw. "Hey! Levi! Wake up!"

No curly-haired head appeared.

"Am I the only one who reads in this family?" John complained, climbing the ladder to make sure his brother wasn't up in the haymow. His voice drifted down to Drew. "Helen of Troy was a beautiful woman in ancient Greece. Thousands of men sailed to her rescue when she was stolen away."

Drew shook his head. "That's a story."

"That's a legend," John corrected him. "There's a difference." He craned his neck to glance around the loft, then looked down at Drew. "Empty."

Drew's sigh was forceful enough to set the chickens to clucking again. "This is ridiculous. He knows we have work to do."

John hopped down beside him. "He's a loafer, but I've never known him to abandon us in the middle of a job."

The barn seemed darker. "Something's happened, then," Drew said. "Find Simon and James. We're going hunting."

John went for his rifle.

Catherine stepped out on the porch, Beth at her heels. Neither Wallin lady had taken her decision to leave well.

"I'm not convinced of my recovery," Mrs. Wallin had said, going so far as to cough into an embroidered handkerchief. "What if the fever comes back?"

"Beth knows what I did for you," Catherine had assured her, refusing to sit on the quilt-covered bed beside her patient lest Mrs. Wallin hug her close. "She has the skills to be a fine nurse."

Beth had shaken her head so violently her hair had come undone and spilled about her shoulders. "No! I don't know half of what you do, Miss Stanway. Please don't go."

"It's for the best," Catherine had made herself say. "I have other patients in town who need me."

Mrs. Wallin had caught her hand. "Ah, but do you need them?"

Catherine couldn't seem to look away from those kind green eyes. Of course she didn't need any specific patient. That was not a nurse's role. A friend of her father's had once commented that a doctor's goal was to work himself out of a job by making his patients well. Unfortunately, she'd found there were always more sick or injured people.

She'd set Mrs. Wallin's hand down on the covers and

pulled back her own. "Truly, I must go. Send word if you need help later. I'll see that someone comes out."

Mrs. Wallin's face had crumpled, but Catherine had turned and walked away. She knew how to comfort those who had been cut or bruised; she knew how to bring down a fever. She didn't know how to heal a wound she was feeling herself.

Now she stood beside Beth, surveying the clearing. The goats were munching in the closest pasture, horses and oxen farther out. She could hear the chickens clucking and the grunt of a satisfied pig. There wasn't a wagon in sight.

"They're clumsy, my brothers," Beth murmured, rubbing a hand up the sleeve of her gown. "They don't do what they should, and they say what they shouldn't. But they're nice when you get used to them."

"I'm sure that's true," Catherine replied. The problem was, she wasn't willing to get used to them. This family, this place, was already growing in her heart, like a seed planted in fertile soil. If she didn't weed out these feelings now, they would only overpower her just as they had when her father and Nathan had died.

Beth, however, was warming to her theme. "Take Drew," she said, pushing her hair back from her face. "Everyone says he's just like Pa, always working, always trying to make things better for us. He spent last winter carving me a hope chest. Roses on vines. Would another fellow even have thought of that?"

"Very likely not," Catherine had to admit. It was a kind thing for Drew to have done, an acknowledgment of impending womanhood in a predominantly male household. At times, she'd thought Nathan and her father would have found it decidedly more convenient if she'd been born a male.

If she'd been male, perhaps they'd have listened to her and stayed home. If nothing else, she might have fought beside them.

Just then Simon and James came striding out of the woods, John beside them. She'd never seen their faces so set. Even the ever-teasing James was frowning. Were they about to lecture her, too?

She raised her head, determined that logic would prevail this time, but they merely nodded to her and Beth before converging on the door of the barn. Drew came out, and four heads, ranging from coppery red to golden brown, bent together.

"What are they up to?" Beth wondered, speaking Catherine's thoughts aloud.

Whatever it was, they seemed to have reached an agreement, for Simon and James headed in one direction, and Drew and John crossed the clearing to the porch.

"Forgive me, Miss Stanway," Drew said, "but our trip to Seattle will have to wait. Levi's gone missing."

Beth clamped her mouth shut as if she couldn't find the words, but Catherine's heart skipped a beat. "Missing? I thought his bed didn't look slept in."

"He didn't sleep in the house last night?" Drew glanced at his brother. "Was he bunking with James?"

John shook his head. Though Catherine knew he was a lean fellow, he seemed all the smaller compared to Drew's brawn, or perhaps it was his concern for his brother that made him look so tense.

"He didn't sleep in Simon's cabin, either," he replied. "But he was in the barn when I went to fetch the ax this morning, and he came with me to the tree. I sent him back to the house for some tools, but he never returned."

"Surely if he'd reached the Landing he would have come to help us," Catherine reasoned, growing colder every minute. "Something must have happened along the way."

The look on Drew's face told her he agreed with her.

"He's probably just loafing off somewhere," John assured her.

Beth nodded. "You'll find him eating the honey from a comb behind some bush."

"Very likely," Drew said.

Catherine didn't believe him. An assurance was building inside her. Levi wasn't trying to avoid work this time. Just as when her brother had met unexpected cannon fire, something had gone wrong. But this time, she had the power to fix it.

"Take Pa's rifle, and stay in the house," Drew was telling Beth. "We'll send word as soon as we know anything."

"All right," Beth agreed. "Be careful."

Drew nodded, then stepped back from the porch. His gaze lingered on Catherine as if he thought it might be the last time he'd see her.

The look propelled her to his side. "Take me with you."

Chapter Twelve

Catherine was certain Drew would refuse her request. His brows were drawn down, and the muscle under her hand was unyielding. Still, his voice when he spoke was as gentle as a caress.

"If there's something dangerous enough in the woods to take out a seasoned young man like Levi," he said, "I don't want it anywhere near you."

How could she argue with that? Besides, he had to wonder why she'd changed her mind. One moment she had been ready to walk out of their lives, the next she was determined to ride to the rescue.

"I appreciate your concern," she said. "But my thoughts right now are for your brother. If he's hurt, I can help."

"If he's hurt," Beth put in, "she can do more than help. She might save his life."

Drew's head came up. She should have known that, where his family was concerned, the more help, the better.

"Very well," he agreed. "Simon and James are circling along the lake in case Levi decided to take a swim instead of working. John and I are tracking back through the trees. This way."

She fell into step beside him. Though her heart was beating rapidly at the thought of Levi in danger, she forced herself to walk as calmly as if they were strolling to church on a sunny Sunday morning. She would not allow her inexperience with the wilderness to hinder their search.

Unfortunately, it was tough going almost immediately. He and his brothers had apparently hacked a path to the tree they hoped to fell, but they had hardly designed it to accommodate a lady in full skirts. Drew and John had to slow to help her over logs and push back encroaching limbs. All the while her mind kept bringing up the picture of Drew's brother lying on the ground, life ebbing.

Not Levi, Lord! He's so young. He doesn't even understand how life works yet.

"And you're confident this is his most likely route?" Catherine asked as she ducked under a low-hanging branch.

"It is the shortest way from the tree to the Landing," Drew replied, spreading a clump of saplings that had been reaching out to clutch at her sleeve.

"Not that he's ever been known to favor the shortest route," John said. He took his ax to an encroaching shrub. "Levi has always had his own way of doing things. Drew, remember when he announced he wanted to be called Matthew on account of it being more biblical?"

Drew slapped a fly off his cheek and smiled at the memory. "He renamed us all. Simon wasn't too fond of being dubbed Cephas."

"Cephas?" Catherine tugged her skirts out of the grip of a thorny blackberry vine. "Why Cephas?"

"Pa named us for the first disciples," John explained. "By order of their calling. Andrew, Simon…"

"James, John and Levi," she finished. "Very clever."

Drew frowned as if he thought his father had taken the matter too seriously, but John grinned as he used his ax handle to push back a set of brambles. "James always says we should be glad Beth was born, or we might have ended up with a Judas Iscariot, and no child should have to be saddled with that name."

Despite her fears, Catherine felt laughter bubbling up. By the similar smile on Drew's face, the sound had warmed him, as well.

Ahead, something rustled in the bushes. John dropped the ax and aimed the rifle. Before Catherine could think, Drew had shifted around her, blocking her path. He was like a sturdy stone wall between her and the danger.

"Oh!" a higher-pitched male voice exclaimed. "Didn't know you were in the woods this morning."

Drew relaxed his stance enough that she could peer around him. Half tangled in blackberry vines was a youth about Levi's age. In other circumstances, she might have wondered at the state of his worn, wrinkled and stained shirt and trousers and the matted thatch of his brown hair, but what caught her attention now was the blood tricking from his crooked nose.

She pushed past Drew. "You appear to have broken your nose, sir. I'm a nurse. Let me help."

He took a step back, vines snagging his sleeve and fingers going to his nostrils. "It ain't broke. It just naturally looks that way."

Catherine didn't believe him. She'd seen any number of noses through the years, and that lump near the bridge and the sideways cant were decided clues that something was wrong. She was only surprised there was no sign of swelling.

"Miss Stanway," Drew said, voice a warm rumble behind her, "meet Scout Rankin. His pa has the closest claim to ours to the south. And he doesn't look any different to me than he did the last time I saw him."

So the break had to be old. Then why the blood? As if to remove any trace, Scout rubbed his nostrils with the back of one hand and sniffed. "Nice to meet you, ma'am. I'd best be going."

He started to ease around John, but Drew put out a hand to stop him. "What are you doing up this way, Scout?"

"And does it happen to have anything to do with Levi?" John added.

Scout froze like a squirrel started by a carriage, brown eyes wide. "Levi? Are you all looking for Levi?"

"We are," Catherine told him. "Do you know where he is?"

His hands were starting to shake. He must have noticed her watching him, for he shoved them behind him. "Saw him up by that tree you all are working on," he said, gaze avoiding hers. "If you find him, tell him I sent you that way."

It was an odd thing to say, but he darted past Drew, branches clutching at his clothes, and dived into the bush for all the world as if he expected the Wallins to hold him captive otherwise.

"Is there some disagreement between your family and his?" Catherine asked Drew.

He shook his head, but more at Scout's behavior than at her question, she thought. "Not that I know of," he answered.

"They're not the friendliest sorts," John said, lifting the ax once more. "Ma tried to be hospitable when they first took over the claim a few years ago. Scout used to come up for lessons in reading and arithmetic. It doesn't seem to have done much good." He, too, shook his head as he turned toward the path once more.

Catherine fell in behind him. She had her suspicions as to why Scout Rankin might have trouble learning, but she could not voice them without more evidence. Given where Scout and the Wallins lived, any number of accidents might explain why a child would receive a broken nose in the past and a bloody nose now.

But so could something other than an accident, such as a beating. She made herself a promise to find a way to look in on the boy in the future once they had Levi home safe and sound.

Drew pushed back a clump of wild grapes to allow Catherine to move ahead. Perhaps it was the cock of her head, the filtered sunlight sparkling off her pale hair. Perhaps it was the fact that she'd grown silent, the only sound the swish of her blue skirts against the rough path. Either way, something about their meeting with Scout seemed to have troubled her.

It troubled him, too. There was no reason for Scout to be on their land so far from the house. And he'd seemed surprised to find them in the woods, when some set of his brothers could always be expected out among the trees any day but Sunday. Then again, Scout had known right where to find Levi. What were those two up to?

"And here we are," John announced, lifting a branch out of the way for Catherine. Ahead lay the area Drew and his brothers had cleared in preparation for removing the graceful fir destined for the deck of the *Merry Maid*. The tree reached for the sky, the floor surrounding it covered in a thick carpet of shed needles and dotted with the leafy fronds of ferns.

Drew didn't spot Levi right away, but Simon and James must have made good time along the lake, for they had beaten Drew and the others to the tree. James was crouched near the base, and Drew sucked in a breath when he realized Levi lay still on the ground next to him.

Simon came to meet them at the edge of the cleared area. His face told Drew the news before he spoke.

"He must have missed John on the way back," Simon said. "It looks like he went up the tree to clear some branches. You know how he is about widow-makers, Drew."

The words felt like a punch in the gut to Drew. He knew how Levi felt about the broken branches higher up. Every Wallin understood that a loose branch had killed their father.

"How bad?" Drew asked.

Simon was paling. "He isn't conscious."

Drew felt ill.

"It may have been the jar from hitting the ground," Catherine said. "I won't know until I examine him."

She stood beside him, head up and one hand fisted in her skirts as if to give her freer movement. All he could do was nod.

Simon reached out and took her free hand. "Thank you, Miss Stanway. This way."

Levi was spread out not far from the base of the fir. Either James or Simon must have pulled a branch off him, for it was bent off to one side. Their brother's shirt and trousers were rumpled, as if he'd hit a few branches as he fell, and his pale face was bruised and swelling. Beside him, James met Drew's gaze, his usual humor fled. John went to his other side as Catherine knelt next to Levi, skirts belling out among the needles.

Drew could see her head turning as she surveyed his brother's form. As if Levi felt the look, his eyes opened. He stared at the branches overhead, then focused on Catherine.

"How'd you get here?"

James leaned back with a chuckle that was all relief. "You kidnapped her, remember?"

Catherine ignored him. "You seem to have met with an accident, Mr. Wallin. Should we be concerned?"

To Drew's surprise, Levi's face darkened. "No, ma'am. I'm sure I'll be fine." He started to lever himself up with his elbows, then gasped and dropped back onto the ground, eyes tearing.

"Easy," Simon advised. "Looks as though you fell out of the tree going after a widow-maker."

"The tree?" Levi blinked as if recognizing the branches above him for the first time. "The tree. Right. I fell out of the tree." He turned his head and met Drew's gaze. "Don't be mad, Drew." He coughed, and blood trickled out of his mouth.

"We'll talk about it later," Drew said, throat tight. "Right now, we need to get you home."

"No." Catherine put a hand on Drew's arm as if to hold him in place. "First we need to know exactly what we're dealing with."

She didn't wait for Drew to respond, turning instead to his brother. "I'm going to ask you some questions, Levi, and then I'm going to touch you. I want you to tell me what you feel."

His gaze darted between her and Drew, as if he sought permission.

"Do as she says," Drew told him.

"Just think what a lucky fellow you are," James said, his usual teasing tone strained. "Lying there while a pretty lady gives you all her attentions."

Levi managed a weak smile.

Catherine set her hand carefully on his chest. "Can you breathe? Swallow as good as usual?"

Drew could see Levi's Adam's apple bob as if he was testing. "Yes."

Relief washed over Drew, but he knew he could not trust it, not yet.

"That's good," Catherine encouraged the boy. "Does anything hurt a lot?"

He sighed as if too much hurt. "I can't rightly tell. Everything is sort of sore right now."

"Well," James said with a grin, "that does tend to happen when you fall out of a tree. A shame you didn't just land on your head. That's hard enough to absorb anything."

Levi glared at him.

Catherine's smile was prim. "Perhaps we should test your brother's theory, Mr. Wallin. I have a feeling your legs are more sturdy than he thinks." She rested her hand on his right thigh. "Can you feel that?"

Levi nodded. "Yes, ma'am."

Thank You, Lord! Surely the fact that his brother could feel sensation in his leg was good news. Yet

Drew's body couldn't seem to relax. He watched as Catherine moved her hand to Levi's knee.

"Here?" she asked, watching him.

"Yes." Levi's face was brightening. He wiggled on the ground as if he thought he could jump right up, then sucked in a breath and blanched. Drew felt as if he was the one who'd fallen.

"Where does it hurt?" Catherine asked.

"Left leg," he grit out. "Below the knee."

Gingerly, she reached across him and touched his calf. Levi jerked.

"Hold him down," she ordered Drew.

How could she be so calm? Drew blinked sweat out of his eyes, though the day was still cool. His stomach was a knot; his hands shook. While James kept an eye out for trouble, all merriment gone, Simon held Levi's shoulders and John leaned over his brother's hips. Drew grasped Levi's ankles, anchoring him to the ground.

Catherine never hesitated. Levi grunted as her hands passed down his leg and over his ankle-high boot. "The leg's broken," she reported as if relaying the expected weather for the day. "I can feel the crack, but I see no blood, so I don't think it's come through the skin. Still, I need to set it and splint it before we move him anywhere."

"Drew," James murmured.

He wasn't sure why James would protest, and he wasn't in the mood for one of his brother's jests. Drew released Levi and leaned back. "I'll find sticks for a splint. John, help Miss Stanway."

"Drew." James said his name more forcefully this time. Glancing toward him, Drew saw that his brother's face was nearly as white as Levi's.

"What is it?" Drew demanded as Simon, John and Catherine frowned at James.

"Cougar," James said as if the word would barely leave his lips. "In the tree over your right shoulder. And he looks annoyed we're about to deprive him of a meal."

Chapter Thirteen

Catherine saw the blood drain from Drew's face as she stiffened. The big catamounts were the stuff of legend in town. Men talked in hushed tones of the nine-foot-long monster an early pioneer had shot. Massive footprints were still seen along the edges of the community. Cougars devoured stray calves and colts, and they sometimes stalked people. Maybe this one had heard Levi's fall and come to investigate.

"Won't it be frightened by so many people?" she murmured to Drew.

"Bears run from noise," Drew said, back straight and hands stilled. "Nothing scares a cougar intent on prey." He glanced at Simon, James and John. "Whatever happens, we protect Catherine and Levi. Agreed?"

Catherine knew she should protest. He had his family to consider. But she could feel her legs starting to tremble, and she knew she'd never be able to outrun the big cat in her skirts.

Simon and John nodded, faces determined.

"I would love to be included on that list," James said. "But agreed."

"What do we do?" Catherine said. "We can't run with Levi in this condition."

Levi glanced among his brothers. "Leave me. I'm the least important person in the family. All I do is cause trouble."

Drew jerked as if the youth had struck him. "No one is running. We go together or not at all."

"Besides, running would only encourage it," James said cheerfully.

"But if you leave me behind, it won't follow you," Levi protested.

Had he hit his head on the way down so he didn't know what he was suggesting? The idea of abandoning the boy raised bile in her throat.

"That is entirely enough of that sort of talk," Catherine told him. "No one is leaving anyone, not even for a splint." Still, she had to do something. She had no doubt Drew could carry his brother, but jostling that leg could turn a simple fracture into a compound one. There had to be something nearer to hand that she could use, something stiff enough, firm enough.

She eyed James. "Mr. Wallin, remove your waistcoat."

James glanced down at the garment that covered his cotton shirt. Catherine suspected it was made from heavy brocade and probably lined with satin. It was certainly stiff enough to stand on its own, and the firmest piece of fabric among them.

James fingered the collar. "I paid a pretty price for this."

"Is it worth more than your brother's life?" she challenged.

He began loosening the silver buttons.

Drew's head was turned as he watched the carnivore. "It hasn't moved. What do you have in mind, Catherine?"

Did he realize he'd used her first name twice now? Every time he said it, she felt as if he'd run his hand against her cheek in a caress.

"We'll wrap the waistcoat around Levi's leg and use the laces from his boot to secure it. Then one of you can carry him on your back while the others protect us from the cougar."

She waited for him to disagree with her plan. What did she know about surviving in the wilderness? But he merely nodded and rose. "I'll carry Levi. James and Simon, keep your rifles at the ready. John, the ax is yours."

The plan made, they set to work. John unlaced Levi's boot, fingers moving with quick efficiency. Levi clamped his lips shut as if to hold back sharp words as Catherine tied up his leg. Then she and John helped him climb to his good foot, and they hefted him onto Drew's back. Above them, dark clouds obscured the blue of the sky as if in sympathy with their plight.

"Try not to jiggle him," she told Drew as he adjusted his hold on his brother. "We don't want to make the break worse."

"Oh, I don't know," James said, gaze on the tree where he'd spotted the cougar. "A little hobble might give him character."

Behind them came a soft thud. James stiffened. "It's jumped down."

For the first time, Catherine looked toward the brush at the edge of the clearing. Through the thicket of bracken and blackberries, she made out the shape of something long, sinuous and tawny. Baleful amber eyes met hers, unblinking. It was as if she were being evaluated for her best parts.

"Walk," Drew advised. "John, lead the way. Simon, take the rear. James, keep an eye on that cat."

"The blond Cat or the tawny one?" James quipped, but Catherine could feel him behind her as John started for the trees.

He hacked away a bit more of the brush as he went, trying to make a path for the others. Simon remained between the rest of them and the cougar, James at his side. Drew used his shoulders to widen the path and carry Levi through, Catherine right behind him.

"I'm sorry, Drew," Levi said, clinging to his brother's shoulders as his feet stuck out on either side. "It's all my fault. I should never have left John."

"No, you shouldn't have," Drew agreed, stepping over a log. "You know we agreed no one would go up a tree alone. You should have waited until someone else was near in case you needed help."

"We don't make the rules to annoy you, you know," James added from behind Catherine. "Though that is a nice benefit."

Catherine wanted to smile, but she felt as if those fiery eyes were watching her every move. She chanced a look back around James and Simon and saw the cougar slipping from sunlight into shadow, tail looped up behind its body, less than twenty feet back.

She spun forward again. "It's following us."

"That it is," James replied. "Sorry, I assumed everyone knew that." He reached out to lift a branch so that Catherine could cross under it.

"It will follow until it sees whether we'll give it an opportunity to strike," Simon said.

Drew hitched Levi up, and his brother grimaced. "Cougars tend to pick off strays," Drew explained to Catherine. "We won't allow that. We stay together."

Catherine nodded, drawing in a breath. She couldn't help moving a little closer to him. Drew's strength seemed to radiate out from him as they walked, his steps firm and back barely bent under Levi's weight. His gaze was focused ahead, as if he was determined to make the Landing at all costs. Once again, he reminded her of a knight, intent on his noble quest, determined to prevail.

"Still a good fifteen feet back," James reported. He started whistling as if he hadn't a care in the world. Rain began to fall, pattering down softly on the boughs over their heads.

Catherine wished she could be so calm as to whistle. She'd faced with equanimity mothers crying in fear as their babies struggled to be born, men with wounds spurting blood. That was her profession, her duty. This was something else entirely. The thought of that big cat leaping on Drew or his brothers made her chest hurt. She couldn't seem to stop the panic from rising.

Was this how Nathan felt when he heard the roar of the cannon, Lord? I hate being so helpless! There must be something I can do!

"You know what might help?" James asked, pausing in his whistling. "Singing. You can sing, can't you, Miss Stanway?"

Catherine swallowed. At the moment she barely trusted herself to speak. "I'm not sure now is the time, Mr. Wallin."

"The best thing with a cougar," John told her, glancing back over his shoulder, "is to act as if you are not prey. I must admit I've never known prey to sing." He swung the ax and hacked off the top of a fern as if to prove to the big cat he meant business.

Catherine couldn't help glancing back again. There was no sign of the cougar, but she felt as if something was watching her, waiting for her to fall, to fail. She turned front and raised her head.

"Do you know 'Wait for the Wagon,' Mr. Wallin?" she asked.

"That I do," James replied. His baritone burst out, strong and sure. "'Will you come with me, my Catherine dear, to yon blue mountain free?'"

"It's Phillis, not Catherine," Levi complained, but John's voice joined his brother's.

"'Where blossoms smell the sweetest, come rove along with me.'"

Now Drew's bass and Simon's tenor chimed in, as well.

"'It's ev'ry Sunday morning, when I am by your side. We'll jump into the wagon, and all take a ride.'"

Their confidence was contagious. Catherine found herself joining in the chorus, her higher voice melding with their deeper ones, the rain drumming a counterpoint.

"'Wait for the wagon, wait for the wagon, wait for the wagon, and we'll all take a ride.'"

They sang the song through three more times before she saw the brighter light of the clearing at Wallin Landing ahead through the trees. Beside her, Drew sucked in a breath. His hair was damp against his forehead, turning the gold to brown. She didn't think it was just from the rain, for his face was darkening, as well.

"Holler," he said as if the song had taken the last of his strength.

"You-halloo!" John obliged. "Beth, bring Pa's rifle! Cougar!"

The horses must have sensed the cat's presence, because now Catherine could hear the frightened neighs coming from the field.

Beth met them at the edge of the wood, cloak wrapped about her, hood surrounding her worried face. "What's happened? Did it get Levi?"

James answered for Drew. "Alas, no. He fell out of a tree. The cougar is stalking us."

Simon turned, cocked the gun and swept the path. "We're ready. James, stay with me."

"Right." With a nod to Catherine, James dropped back.

John stepped closer to Drew. "Can I help?"

"Just…steer…me…to the porch," Drew said, panting. Catherine took one elbow and John the other, and together they managed to reach the broad boards with Beth hurrying along beside them. John helped Levi down, and he and Beth assisted the youth into the house. Drew bent a moment and gulped in air.

Catherine put a hand on his damp back. "Are you all right?"

He nodded, straightening. Catherine knew she should tend to Levi, but her concern at the moment was more for the man standing in front of her.

"That was heroic," she said. "You may well have saved your brother's life."

Instead of smiling at the praise, he shuddered, the

muscles rippling under her hand. "That's one, at least. Do you need my help with him?"

Catherine lowered her hand. "Beth can help me. You should rest. You're in no condition to fight off a cougar."

He pushed away from the porch. "I'll be fine. Watch over Levi." He lifted the ax he'd left behind when they'd set out earlier and started after his brothers.

As the rain turned to mist, Drew followed James, John and Simon a little ways into the woods. His back ached and water ran down his face, but his breath grew stronger with every step. Once more thanksgiving raised his spirits and lifted his head.

Thank You, Lord.

"Any sign of it?" he asked when he caught up with his brothers.

Simon nodded into the bush. "It came close enough to get the scent of the stock, then headed off toward the lake."

"No doubt it was our singing," James said. "All we needed was Simon on his fiddle, and we could well have frightened it over the mountains to Walla Walla."

Simon shook his head.

"We're safe for the moment, at any rate," Drew said with a warning look to his irrepressible brother. "With any luck, it will find easier prey along the water and forget about us. But just in case, we'll leave someone at the Landing for a while to protect the stock."

"And our little Cat," James agreed as they turned for home. "She seems to attract any number of predators."

"That's enough," Drew said.

James danced out of reach as if he expected Drew to

try to cuff him. "Are we a bit concerned for Miss Stanway? Methinks the gent is smitten."

What sane man wouldn't be? If it had been Beth out in the woods, Drew would likely have had to carry her back, too. Even his mother had been known to freeze at the sight of a bear or a cougar. But Catherine had been all business, focusing on how to bring Levi home. She'd sung that song as if she'd been standing in service on a Sunday, best bonnet on her head, prayer book in her hands. Some men might quibble about her unflappable nature, but Drew could only be thankful for it.

"Miss Stanway deserves our respect," he said as they neared the house. "I won't have her teased or bullied."

"Miss Stanway, eh?" James jumped up onto the porch ahead of Drew. "I was certain I heard you call her Catherine in the woods. No doubt it was the strain of the moment."

"No doubt," Drew returned, hearing his voice deepen.

John shook his head. "Now you went and made him mad, James."

"I'm not mad," Drew growled.

"Yes, you are," Simon corrected him. "I wasn't ten before I understood what that set face meant. The problem with having brothers is that we know you too well."

"The problem with having brothers," Drew countered, "is that you all talk too much."

John didn't follow him onto the porch. "I'll take first watch, Drew. Send someone out to tell me how Levi's doing." He loped toward the barn.

With a chuckle, James shouldered his way into the house.

Simon caught Drew's arm before he could follow.

"A moment. You may not like talking, but I need an answer."

Drew nodded, pausing on the porch. Simon glanced in the door, then shut it carefully behind James. Drew felt his wet scalp tingle in foreboding. "What's wrong?"

"Nothing." Simon leaned his rifle against the wall of the house. "I told you the other night that the best thing for this family would be for one of us to marry Miss Stanway. From what I can see, this episode only proves that."

Drew shook water off his face. "We had this conversation this morning. Why do you persist?"

"Because we need her!" Simon's eyes narrowed as his gaze bore down on Drew. "Why can't you see that?" Though they had disagreed on any number of topics over the years, he generally deferred to Drew in the end. Not this time, Drew thought.

He glanced in the window, watching as Catherine carefully unwrapped James's prized waistcoat from Levi's leg. "I can see it. But she isn't a heifer needed to build the stock or a new plow to open more acreage. She's a person, Simon. She has wishes and needs, too. She won't be content to stay out here."

"Maybe she just hasn't heard an offer she likes," Simon countered. "So I'll ask you straight out—are you going to court her?"

Something leaped inside him at the thought. He could imagine walks along the lake, sitting on the porch holding hands under the stars, her head on his shoulder by the fire at night as he listened to her tell him all that was in her heart. He could build her a dispensary where she could treat any who came to her for care. He could see himself at the head of the table, her at the foot, and ranged between children with her beautiful hair and stunning smile.

But those were crazy thoughts. If she stayed, there'd be more days like this, worse days, living in terror that something would yank her out of his arms, send her to the grave and leave him powerless, broken. That thought, more than any of the others, set his gut to churning. Catherine might praise his strength, and his brothers might rely on his arm to swing an ax, but when it came to losing someone he loved, he feared even his strength would fail.

"No, I won't court Miss Stanway," Drew said to his brother. "I have enough to do around here without looking out for a wife."

Simon was watching him as if doubting his word. "Then you won't mind if I give it a try."

His hands fisted, but he forced his fingers to relax. "You do what you must, Simon. You always have."

Simon shook his head. "You have an odd way of encouraging people, brother. But you're right. I tend to look at the practical side of things. There are too many opportunities for us to get hurt or sick out here, and it takes too long to bring people to town for tending. We need a doctor or nurse. I doubt we can hire one, so I plan on marrying one, whether you like it or not."

Chapter Fourteen

It was nearly dinner before Catherine had Levi settled. First she and the others had to dry themselves from the rain. Although she had toweled off her hair with a cloth Mrs. Wallin provided, the only way to dry her dress was to stand and turn in front of the hearth like a chicken on a spit, careful not to get too close lest a stray spark catch her skirts on fire.

She used the time to direct James how to shave kindling to her specifications for Levi's splint and to send Beth for the other supplies she'd need. Then she splinted the leg properly and added a stick at the end that could be twisted as needed to provide traction.

Levi generally cooperated with few protests, and Beth peppered her with questions. But by far the most helpful was Drew. Once she had Levi positioned on one of the benches near the table, he sat at his brother's head, hands braced on Levi's shoulders as both a warning not to move and a deterrent when the youth had second thoughts.

"You'd make a fine nurse," Catherine commented at one point when she'd finished setting the bone.

"I'll leave that to the professional," Drew answered, but his smile warmed her more than his words.

When she finished, Levi gave the splinted leg a wiggle, then yelped at the pain the movement must have caused. "How long do I have to wear this?"

"Weeks if you're careful," Catherine said, rising and shaking out her skirts. "Months if you're not. Despite what your brother said about hobbling, limping for the rest of your life is best avoided if possible."

The boy grumbled, but his pallor told Catherine that some part of him would heed her warning.

Mrs. Wallin had been sitting nearby. Now she shifted to be next to her youngest son. "You listen to Miss Stanway, Levi. And to your brothers, as well. What would you have done if they hadn't come back for you?"

"Died and rotted," James said cheerfully, and Beth smacked him on the shoulder with one hand.

Catherine drew back, watching as James and Beth teased Levi until the youth's cheeks bloomed red. John had returned to the house a while ago, with Simon out spelling him on watch. He, too, joined in the fun.

Catherine wished she could joke about it, but the entire time she'd been working on Levi, her family had kept intruding on her thoughts. What if someone had gone back for Nathan on the battlefield? Would he be alive today? Where were the men her father had tended when the medical tent had been shelled? Had none of them gone to see if he could be saved?

Levi's wounds weren't as serious, and for that she was thankful. But something about his injuries nagged at her, and she wasn't sure why.

Drew rose and came to where she stood by the stairs.

"I didn't want to ask you in front of Levi," he murmured, "but I need to know. How bad is it?"

"It was a simple fracture," Catherine assured him. "From the lack of swelling, I'd say nothing was damaged internally, and externally, as you saw, he's fine."

Drew nodded, but she wasn't sure he accepted her explanation.

"I know from experience as well as education," she told him. "I've seen someone fall out of a tree before."

His eyes widened.

"Oh, he wasn't up as high as Levi, I'm sure," she said with a smile. "But my brother, Nathan, climbed a sycamore in our yard once, going after a wayward kite. He managed to free the kite, but he lost his balance on the way down and tumbled out." She shook her head, remembering.

"Did he break anything?" Drew asked, watching her as if the story had given him hope.

"No, but you should have seen his face and hands. Scratches everywhere! One took stitching up. Oh!" She stared at Levi.

Drew had stiffened at her explanation. "Forgive me. I didn't mean to bring up bad memories."

"It's not that." Catherine shook her head to clear it as Levi ducked under James's hand to avoid his brother's teasing. "I've been trying to determine why your brother's injuries trouble me, and I think I know why." She turned to Drew. "There isn't a scratch on him."

Drew frowned, glancing between her and Levi. "He looks pretty beat up to me."

"He is, but that's my point. Falling through a tree, you don't generally think to protect your face, and if you did, the backs of your hands would bear the brunt of the damage. Levi's face and hands are clear."

"Perhaps he hit his chest instead. He coughed blood. Did he break a rib?"

Catherine shook her head. "He isn't any more sore there than anywhere else. And the blood in his mouth came from a split lip."

Drew cocked his head. "There's that bruise around his eye."

"Indeed," Catherine replied. She glanced at Drew. "Exactly as if someone had struck him."

Drew's shoulders tightened, raising him higher above her. "You think someone beat him? Broke his leg?"

She knew it sounded far-fetched. Why would anyone be so cruel? Besides, Levi had confessed to climbing the tree. Yet she also had had suspicions about Scout. Could the two have been fighting?

"I don't know," Catherine admitted. "But I'd talk to him about the matter if I were you."

He growled something under his breath about that being his life's work, and she thought it best not to ask him to repeat himself.

Beth hopped up just then and hurried toward the back room and the stove. A moment later, she was in the doorway, beckoning John to help. Simon came in the door and set down his rifle before wandering over to Catherine and Drew. She thought he might ask about his brother's situation, but instead he pulled a little leather-bound book from his coat pocket.

"My father was partial to poetry, Miss Stanway," he said, offering the book to her with a smile that didn't quite light his green eyes. "I wonder, would you be willing to join me in a reading for the family tonight?"

She glanced at the title, picked out in worn gold on the slim volume: *The Courtship of Miles Standish*. "My father was partial to Longfellow as well, Mr. Wallin. I'd be delighted to help."

"Please," he said, eyes lighting at last, "call me Simon. It's far too confusing to have all of us be Mr. Wallin."

Drew shifted beside her, calling her attention to the difference between him and his brother. Though Simon was a match for him in height, Drew's younger brother was more slender, a willow to Drew's cedar.

"Very well," Catherine said. "Is there a particular part you'd like us to read tonight?"

"Try page thirty-three," Simon said. With a nod to Drew, he strolled back to Levi's side.

"Poetry," Drew muttered under his breath, as if the very idea was ridiculous.

Catherine frowned at him. "Do you have something against lyrical language, Mr. Wallin?"

He shook himself. "Forgive me, Catherine. This argument is between Simon and me. We both have the same goal, to keep this family safe. We just disagree on how to go about it. If you'll excuse me, I need to go check that the barn is closed up properly."

Catherine nodded, and he strode out the door without another look to his brother. She couldn't help noticing, however, that Simon watched him go.

Curious, she opened the book's well-worn pages to the section Simon had indicated. The Pilgrim hero John Alden had just called upon the lovely Miss Priscilla Mullins on behalf of the colony leader, Miles Standish, and the young lady was protesting that if Mr. Standish was too busy to court her, he was likely too busy to be married to her. This was what Drew's brother wanted her to read?

"Excuse me, Miss Stanway." She looked up to find that John had finished helping Beth and stood beside Catherine. She snapped the book shut and met his gaze.

"Yes, Mr. Wallin? What did you need?"

"Perhaps you could call me John," he said with a soft smile. The closest in age to Levi, she could see that he resembled his mother the most, for his straight, thick, neatly cut hair was a reddish-gold, and his eyes were the greenest of all the brothers. "I merely wanted to thank you for your excellent work on Levi's leg. I've always been fascinated by the human body's ability to heal after great trauma. Is there some secret to how you treat a break like that?"

He looked so earnest, eyes intent on her face, wiry body poised forward, that Catherine found herself prosing on about fractures and sutures and dressings. He asked probing questions, offered suggestions from things he'd read and praised her knowledge so much that she was in an uncommonly good mood when Beth called them all to dinner.

John offered her his arm to escort her to the table. Simon pulled out the chair Drew normally sat in for her, and James presented her with a bouquet of wild flowers, which earned him a glare from Simon.

"There's no need to thank me," Catherine told them as Beth and Mrs. Wallin took their seats at the table. "I was only doing my duty in helping your brother."

"But with considerable style," James assured her as he sat. He elbowed Levi, who had been propped up next to him on the bench, leg straightened out before him. "Isn't that right, Levi?"

Not waiting for the blessing to be said, Levi spooned a mass of mashed potatoes onto his plate and shrugged. "I suppose."

James shook his head.

Catherine glanced to the window overlooking the yard. "Isn't your eldest brother going to eat?"

"Drew's busy with the stock," John said, seating himself on the bench nearest her and pushing Simon father down as he did so. "We can send something out to him when we're done."

"If there's anything left," James agreed, reaching for a biscuit.

"Boys," their mother chided. "Just because I'm not up to taking him a plate doesn't mean one of you can't do it."

Catherine found herself on her feet before she'd thought better of it. "I'll go."

Immediately Simon was on his feet, as well. "Allow me, Catherine."

James stood so quickly he set the bench to rocking, raising a protest from Levi. "I probably owe him the next shift. I'll go, as a favor to you, Cat."

They were all entirely too thankful for her intervention with Levi. "Catherine," she corrected him. "And truly, gentlemen, there is no need. You've worked hard most of the day. It will only take me a moment."

"I insist," Simon said, grabbing Drew's plate and throwing on a biscuit. "We can't impose on a guest."

"Quite right, Simon," James said, lowering himself back onto the bench. "I'll just stay here and keep Catherine company."

"Catherine isn't the only one at this table, you know,"

Beth put in. Her mother patted her hand as if to quiet her, a smile hovering about her mouth.

John nodded. "She's right. You both can go out and help Drew. I've already taken my shift, and I'm perfectly capable of keeping Catherine company."

What was wrong with them? Now all three were glaring at each other, while Beth shook her head and Mrs. Wallin's smile broadened. Levi kept shoveling food into his mouth as if he suspected someone would take his plate next.

"We'll all go," Simon announced, lobbing on a dollop of mashed potatoes and splashing it with gravy.

James rose once more. "Fine," he said, grabbing a cup.

"Fine," John agreed, snatching up a fork. They bumped each other's shoulders on the way out the door.

Mrs. Wallin laughed. "How nice to see my sons so helpful. Would you care to say the blessing, Levi? I believe you have the most to be thankful for."

Levi dropped his fork, face reddening, then bowed his head and clasped his hands.

Catherine bowed her head as well, listening to his simple prayer of thanks for the food and the family around them. She couldn't understand what maggot had infested the Wallin men's minds, but it almost seemed as if they were trying to court her despite her warning from this morning. Were all the men in Seattle mad? Was it something in the Puget Sound waves? In the air? She knew brides were at a premium, but this was ridiculous.

She was highly tempted to dose them all with Peruvian bark and send them to bed before they infected anyone else!

* * *

Drew was shutting the horses in for the night when three of his brothers entered the barn. They stalked up to him, each trying to walk faster than the others. Simon thrust out a plate. "Here. Catherine thought you might be hungry."

James held out a cup from which half the cider had sloshed, if the shine on the side was any indication. "She sent us with your food."

"Actually," John said, handing him a fork, "Simon and James made fools of themselves trying to be gentlemen, and we all decided it was wiser to retreat to the barn for a while rather than confess our shortcomings to Catherine."

Simon stared at him, then shook his head, chuckle tumbling out. "He's right. Peace, James." He offered his hand.

James shook it with a grin. "Peace. For the moment. It never lasts long in this family."

Drew balanced the cup on the edge of the plate and eyed his brothers. "Let me get this straight. All three of you made a fool of yourselves over Catherine? Are you all trying to court her?"

James shrugged as he released Simon's hand. "Can you think of a better way to keep her in the family?"

"I believe there's good historical evidence that women generally frown on being kept captive," John pointed out. "You have only to look to the Romans to see that."

They were mad, the lot of them. Drew motioned them over to the bench his father had built along the stalls and sat with the plate in his lap. "It isn't easy adding a wife, you know," he told them as he forked up some of the mashed potatoes, gravy dripping. "She's your partner in all things. Remember how Ma and Pa used to act?"

Simon nodded as he sat beside him. "Every decision, every action taken together."

James raised his brows as he leaned against the wall. "That's a tall order. Based on some of the married folks I've seen in town, not every marriage is such a joyful union."

"But it should be," John protested, glancing among them. "'Therefore shall a man leave his father and his mother and shall cleave unto his wife, and they shall be one flesh.' That's what the Good Book says."

"That may be what the Bible says," Simon answered, leaning back on the bench and crossing his arms over his chest, "but Adam only had to worry about Eve. We might as well face facts. There aren't many women like Ma."

"Isn't that why Asa Mercer brought all those ladies?" John asked, frowning.

Simon eyed him as if he suspected his brother had been reading too many books. "The women Mercer brought out seem more interested in town life than helping make a home in the wilderness."

"And you think Catherine is different?" Drew challenged.

Simon dropped his arms and straightened. "Yes, I do. I haven't seen a thing about our lives to quail her yet."

"Neither have I," James agreed. "And we've thrown our best at her—cougars, wild men, John's cooking."

John picked up Drew's biscuit and threw it at his brother. James caught it and popped it into his mouth with a grin.

Drew set aside the cold remains of his dinner, no longer hungry. "Then you do intend to court her."

Simon eyed James, and James eyed Simon, then both looked to John. As if in concert, all three nodded. Drew felt as if the food he had just eaten might come back up.

Simon turned to him. "No, we aren't going to court her. She clearly favors you."

Drew blinked, feeling as if he'd missed a moment of the conversation. "What?"

"You heard me," Simon said, eyes narrowing. "You're the one to court Catherine Stanway, and we're going to help you do it."

Chapter Fifteen

The things he did for his family. Drew led his brothers back across the clearing for the main house, the stock safely enclosed for the night. He didn't agree with his brothers' logic that everyone in the family would perish without someone like Catherine to help them. He'd done pretty well keeping them all safe until now. He didn't agree with their assessment that she favored him. At times, he wasn't sure she even liked him. He certainly didn't agree that he needed their help to court a woman. As Beth had pointed out, once he set his sights on something, he was as apt as their mother to achieve it.

But if anyone in the Wallin household was going to court Catherine Stanway, he knew he'd go mad if it wasn't him.

The ladies had cleaned up after dinner and returned Levi to a chair next to the fire. Catherine sat nearby as if to keep an eye on him. Her gaze brushed Drew's as he entered, her smile lifting briefly before she looked away. Was this odd feeling in his stomach what other people called butterflies? Maybe he should have eaten more dinner.

Ma was seated in her rocking chair, a basket of mending beside her, needle and thread in hand. Flitting from one brother to another, Beth seemed to be trying to avoid their mother's gaze lest she be put to work, too. His youngest brother brightened as Drew and the others let themselves in.

"There you are, Simon," he proclaimed. "Go get your fiddle, and let's have a song."

"Because you're in such good condition to dance," James teased, coming to tweak the stockinged toe peeking out from Levi's splint. Levi scowled at the reminder.

"I have something else planned for tonight," Simon said. "Catherine, are you ready for that reading?"

She rose and went to retrieve the book from the mantel, where she must have set it before dinner. "Perhaps, but I do have a question about the selection you chose, Mr. Wallin."

Drew couldn't help but chuckle. His brother may have asked her to use his given name, but either she chose not to or the gesture meant so little to her she'd forgotten his request. She came to their sides and held out the open book. "Are you certain you want to read this part?"

Simon took the book from her and gazed down at it. "Hmm, perhaps not. I'll find something better. Give me a moment." He turned away, flipping the pages.

As if they knew what to expect, the others settled themselves around the room, James and John on the floor near Levi's chair and Beth, likewise, curled up at Ma's feet.

Drew knew he needed to say something to Catherine, who stood waiting patiently beside him. Simon would have been polished, James playful and John profound.

For the life of him, he couldn't think of an appropriate comment. He could hardly compliment her gown; she'd been forced to wear the same one for the past three days, and the blue skirts were beginning to sag from their adventures. She must own a mirror, so it made no sense to tell her that her hair was as soft as moonlight. And he refused to talk about her lips being as red as the wild woodland strawberries, for when he looked at her now he wondered what it would like to taste them.

Oh, but he was in trouble.

Annoyed with himself, he went to stand by the stairs.

James glanced over his shoulder as Drew passed. "You know Pa built those very well, brother. You don't need to hold them up."

Some help he was.

Catherine followed him. "Everything all right in the clearing? Any sign of the cougar?"

At least that was a safe subject that didn't remind him of what his brothers expected. "Everything seems quiet. My biggest concern was Levi, and he's doing surprisingly well."

She laughed, and the sound bathed him in light. "It would take a great deal more than a broken leg to unsettle your brother." She cast him a glance from the corners of her eyes. "But I do wish you'd tell your other brothers to cease fawning over me."

He nearly choked. "Oh, I expect the fawning has stopped for now."

She frowned as if she wasn't sure what he meant, but Simon called her just then, and she excused herself to move to his brother's side by the fire.

Drew couldn't deny that they made a fine-looking couple, with Simon all angles and Catherine all soft curves. But he'd never noticed how tiny his brother's eyes looked when he squinted at the words on the page. Did Catherine notice? Did she mind? Did she think Drew's eyes were squinty?

Please help me master my thoughts, Lord!

"I found just the thing," Simon was saying to Catherine, head bent as if to be closer to her. "I'll read the man's part, you the lady's." His large hand cupped hers as they held the book open together. Drew could imagine holding her hand that way, cradled in his. She'd smile that brilliant smile of hers, and the day would brighten.

As if Simon was as affected by her touch, he cleared his throat. Then he released her and stepped away.

"On second thought, I'm not sure I'm the best one to do this justice," he said with a rueful shake of his head. "Drew, come read."

Everyone turned to him, looks ranging from surprised to amused. The hint of a smile played about his brother's lips. He wasn't sure what Simon was doing, but he decided to go along with it.

Though Catherine's brows were up, she did not protest as Drew went to take his brother's place at her side.

Drew offered her a smile, then slipped his hand under hers. Her fingers were warm and supple, strong, he thought, from her work as a nurse. Yet he could feel the slightest tremor in them. He ran one hand farther up her wrist to steady her and heard her suck in a breath.

Now his hands were trembling as well, and he had a sudden urge to run for the door. Best to plow ahead. Glancing down, he looked to see where Simon had directed them to read. And then he very much feared he'd have to kill his brother, if the reading didn't kill Drew first.

"Right there, Mr. Wallin," Catherine said, her other hand coming to point to the stanza as if he might have mistaken his way.

Drew's smile was tight. So was his throat. "'He was a man of honor, of noble and generous nature,'" he began reading.

Levi snickered and was hushed.

"'Though he was rough, he was kindly,'" Drew continued. "'She knew how during the winter he had attended the sick, with a hand as gentle as a woman's.'"

"That's our Drew," James called out, and this time both John and Levi laughed.

"Let him be," their mother scolded. "Go on, Andrew."

He would never make it through this. Drew cleared his throat. "'Somewhat hasty and hot, he could not deny it, and headstrong. Stern as a soldier might be, but hearty and placable always. Not to be laughed at and scorned, because he was little of stature.'" He glared at his brothers to keep them from commenting. "'For he was great of heart, magnanimous, courtly, courageous. Any woman in Plymouth, nay any woman in England, might be as happy and proud to be called the wife of—'"

"Drew Wallin!" Levi yelled.

"'Miles Standish,'" Drew thundered.

Catherine did not so much as wince at his raised voice. Her tone was firm and polished as she took up her part.

"'But as he warmed and glowed, in his simple and eloquent language, quite forgetful of self, and full of the praise of his rival, archly the maiden smiled, and, with eyes over-running with laughter, said, in a tremulous voice, "Why don't you speak for yourself, Drew?"'"

Drew blinked. His father and mother had read them this poem countless times. The name should have been John, and he'd expected his younger brother to make much of it. Had Catherine really just said Drew's name instead?

He glanced out to find that everyone in the family was staring at Catherine. So he hadn't mistaken her.

She must have realized her gaff, for she was turning crimson. Her mouth opened and closed, as if she was trying to continue reading, but no words came out.

James hopped to his feet. "Here, let me take the next stanza. I'd be delighted to read, at length. In falsetto."

Levi cringed.

"Have pity on us, Catherine," Ma said with an encouraging smile. "Your voice is so much better than James's."

James threw up his hands. "And you claim to be my mother!"

"Hush," Beth scolded. She had scooted forward on the rug. "I want to hear more."

But Drew didn't think Catherine could take any more. He could hear the breath hissing out of her as if she was having trouble controlling it.

"John," he said, taking the book from her and closing it. "You've always been good for a puzzle. Come up with one of your twenty-question posers."

John grinned. "Delighted!" He rubbed his hands together. "Now, let me see…"

Levi and Beth leaned closer as if determined to guess what was on his mind. Ma cast Drew a glance before doing likewise. Simon and James, however, were frowning at him.

Drew turned his back on them, blocking their view of Catherine.

"It's all right," he said. "It was only a poem."

She nodded, fast and hard. "Yes, a poem. Just a silly poem. Thank you for pointing that out. If you'll excuse me, I should retire. It's been a long day." She started around him, and Drew turned with her.

"I'll walk you to the cabin."

"No!" She must have realized how firmly she'd spoken, because her color faded as all gazes returned to her again. "That is, there's no need for you to leave your family on my account. I'm perfectly capable of walking across the clearing."

"You forget," Drew said, taking her elbow and finding it tense. "There's a cougar prowling about. Until we're sure it's left the area, no one goes anywhere without a gun or escort."

She pulled back and glanced around the room until her gaze hit Simon. "Mr. Wallin, would you accompany me? Surely we have imposed on your brother enough today."

What did she think was an imposition? Carrying Levi back from the tree? He'd recuperated from that in less than a half hour. Had the slip of her tongue truly so overset her? Where was her commendable composure?

Simon straightened away from the wall. "Of course." He nodded to James. "We should turn in, as well. Come along, James."

Simon picked up the rifle, James a lantern. Then he went to open the door for Catherine. She paused beside Beth and Levi.

"If you need me tonight, come find me," she told them.

"I will," Beth promised.

Without another look in Drew's direction, Catherine exited.

John left Beth and Levi arguing over the answer to his riddle and joined Drew by the fire. "That didn't go as well as it should have."

"No, it did not," their mother put in, setting aside her mending. "Andrew Wallin, if you intend to court that girl, you'll need to work harder than that."

John met his gaze, and Drew thought his own must be just as panicked. The last thing they needed was for their headstrong mother to throw herself into the fray.

"No one said I was courting, Ma," he started, but Beth clapped her hands, hopping to her feet.

"Oh, you decided to court her after all!" She seized Drew's hand. "I have so many ideas."

Perhaps a young lady's opinion would help. His sister was entirely devoted to that society magazine after all. "Oh?" Drew said. "Such as?"

Beth's eyes glowed. "You could take her for a picnic by the lake."

"There's a cougar running about," John reminded her.

"All right," Beth said, undeterred. "A picnic in the barn, then."

"The barn?" Levi rolled his eyes. "What girl wants to be sweet-talked in a barn?"

"There will be no sweet talk," Drew said with all the solemnity he could manage. "Anywhere."

Beth shook her head. "Oh, Drew, there has to be some. That's what courting is all about."

"I thought you never wanted to court," John challenged.

"I don't want to marry," Beth corrected him. "That doesn't meant I don't want to be courted. Every girl wants to be courted."

Drew frowned. "Why?"

She stared at him as if appalled he had to ask. "Because it's wonderful! That's what that entire poem is about—the beauty of courting. Pretty words and longing looks and sweet sighs. Walking hand in hand, holding the prayer book together in church, sharing secrets." She peered closer at her brother. "Haven't you ever wanted to do those things?"

"No," Drew said. The panic he'd felt when he'd considered his mother's interference was nothing to the fear that bubbled up at Beth's outlandish ideas. "I appreciate everyone's help, but I'm capable of courting a woman on my own."

"If that was your best effort," Beth said, wrinkling her nose, "I don't believe you."

"That's enough, Elizabeth Ann," Ma said, gathering up her sewing. "I think it's time we all went to bed. Tomorrow will be another day, another opportunity." She smiled at Drew. "And I know you will make her a marvelous husband."

Drew only wished he had his mother's confidence. For he feared with all the demands on his life, he'd make a terrible husband for any woman, especially one as sought after as Catherine.

Catherine hurried across the clearing for the cabin, mist wrapped about her like a damp towel. Simon paced her on one side, rifle in the crook of one arm; James walked on the other side, lantern held high to light their way. Though the glow pushed back the darkness, she felt as if her escorts were walls closing in on her.

Why? Simply because she'd all but asked Drew to propose to her.

Where was her mind? Why had she slipped and used his name? The word *John* had been clearly written on the page. Her brother, Nathan, had once read the poem aloud to her and her friends over tea. She knew her part.

Why did her heart persist in offering Drew's name instead? Had she no control where he was concerned?

"I hope we didn't offend you, Miss Stanway," James said, twisting his head as if to see more of her face. "I didn't mean any harm."

"No offense taken, Mr. Wallin," she said, detouring around a rocky patch. "It was simply time for me to retire."

From inside the barn came the neigh of a horse and the fluttering cackle of chickens.

Simon's hand shot out to stop her. "Something's wrong."

Catherine felt as if the lantern had dimmed. "What should we do?"

He glanced back at the house, and then, as if deeming it better to keep her near, he nodded to his brother. "Stay close to James and follow me."

Together they set out for the barn. James pulled open the big door with a rattle of metal, setting the chickens to clucking again. The lantern's glow only reached the first few feet of the space, making Catherine feel as if they had entered a cave. As they ventured down the main aisle, she could see that the horses were backed up in their stalls, shifting and bumping against the wood.

Their eyes showed white. Nearby, the oxen lowed a warning, and a pig let out a squeal. James hung the lantern on a hook and went to quiet the beasts as Simon moved through the building.

Doubting she could be of any use in this instance, Catherine sat on a bench near the lantern, rubbing one hand up her arm. It did nothing to stop the chill that was overtaking her.

"James," Simon called, and his brother hurried to his side, bringing the lantern with him.

Before the darkness could swallow her, Catherine rose as well and went to join them by the rear door. On the ground outside, something lay in a heap that glistened in the light.

"What is that?" Simon demanded.

James climbed out onto the ground and bent over the mass, then raised his head and stared at his brother. "It's meat. A haunch of venison, I think. I don't remember John or Drew hunting today."

"They didn't," Simon said, head turning as if he was looking for someone or something in the darkened forest. "And neither did I."

Now James was looking around as well, and Catherine peered deeper into the shadows, fearing that she might see those amber eyes looking back at her.

"It's not like a cougar to leave its kill uncovered," James said, voice thick in the mist.

"I don't think it was the cougar." Simon cocked his rifle. "Someone left that there on purpose. Trying to draw in the cat, I'm guessing."

James jerked upright, lantern flashing with the movement. "You think someone meant to bring the cougar into Wallin Landing?"

"The same someone who poisoned the spring," Catherine murmured. And perhaps had beaten Levi?

Simon glanced her way. "Very likely. Come get the spade, James, and bury that thing."

James complied, scrambling back into the barn and handing the lantern to Catherine before going to find the shovel.

"I'll cover you," Simon promised, watching him. Before his brother could leave the barn again, Simon turned to her, face grim. "I'm sorry, Catherine, but I think you'd better sleep in the house with Ma and Beth tonight."

She wanted to argue. Return to the house? Face Drew and answer the questions she'd seen in his eyes? Meeting the cougar or their unseen enemy in the dark almost sounded easier.

Almost.

"Very well, Mr. Wallin," she said. "Your plan is sensible. But I hope you intend to explain all this to your brother." That might keep Drew busy enough that he'd have time to forget her mistake.

And give her enough time to convince herself she wouldn't repeat it.

Chapter Sixteen

Inside the house, Drew made sure Levi and their mother were situated for the night.

"You don't have to hover over me like a mother hen," Ma said as he tucked her in the big bed she'd once shared with his father. "I'm much better!"

She was, and he was so thankful for that fact. *If nothing else comes from this association with Catherine, Lord, thank You for sending her to help Ma.*

"Perhaps I just like to make sure," Drew told her, bending to kiss her forehead. "Humor me."

"I suppose I should be patient," she said, snuggling under the covers. "But it's not a trait I ever possessed. I was very proud of you for being so patient with your brothers and sister growing up. Don't lose that ability now."

Drew straightened so fast he nearly banged his head on the ceiling. "If I've been impatient with you, ma'am, I apologize."

His mother shook her head, nightcap brushing the pillow. "Not with me. But you and your brothers seem to think all you need to do is show Catherine a little courtesy, and she'll swoon at your feet." She narrowed her eyes at Drew. "A wife worth the having is a wife worth the wooing."

So she was still plucking at that string. "I'm not going to follow after her like a moon-sick calf."

"And who asked you to act so foolishly?" she challenged, flattening her fingers on the quilt. "Your pa liked to say we fell in love at first sight, but the truth is that it took time and proximity for love to grow." She reached out and took Drew's hand in hers, her gaze touching his. "Show her the man you are. If she can't appreciate that, then she's not the woman for you."

Drew nodded and pulled away, but the sound of the door closing downstairs made him pause. Footsteps crossed for the stairs, and he turned to see Simon leading Catherine up. His brother's face was tight, but Catherine's pallor struck Drew in the chest.

He was moving to their sides before they had reached the top. "What's happened? Are you hurt?"

Simon held up one hand. "She's fine. I think it best she spend the night up here. We need to talk." He nodded to Catherine before starting back down, as if assuming Drew would follow him.

Drew couldn't seem to move. He had no idea what had happened, but those same feelings he'd been fighting since he'd first met her wrapped around him, demanding action. He wanted to hold her close and promise to protect her no matter what.

As if she knew it, she managed a smile. "Go with your brother, Drew. I'll be fine."

"She can share my bed," Ma called, patting the covers and smiling in welcome.

Drew had to touch Catherine. He ran his hand up her

arm, then rested his fingers a moment on her shoulder. "I'll be in with Levi later if you need me."

She ducked under his hand and went to join his mother.

Downstairs, Simon explained what they'd found. "James is keeping an eye on the barn. I'll take the next watch, and John can take the watch after that. You stay with Ma."

Normally Drew might have bristled at his brother's high-handed tone, but now he could only agree that the best place for him was in the house.

"There's something else you should know," he told Simon. "Catherine suspects Levi didn't fall out of that tree."

His brother frowned. "How else would he have earned those injuries?"

Drew felt himself tensing just thinking about the possibility. "Someone beat him.

Simon's head snapped up. "Why? And why wouldn't he name the bully? That makes no sense."

Drew couldn't argue with him. "James might say he's annoying enough to have earned it, but I share your doubts. Let him sleep for now. We can ask him when he's had a chance to heal."

"Oh, we will," Simon promised. He turned to head back outside.

But when Drew returned upstairs and bunked down near a snoring Levi, he couldn't seem to get to sleep. Instead of the troubles that plagued them, his mother's words occupied his mind. She seemed to think it was easy to win a woman's heart, that all he had to do was be himself. He hadn't thought he'd been anything else, and Catherine didn't seem enamored.

He listened, trying to isolate her breathing among the other soft noises coming from the opposite side of the hearth. He could imagine her lying next to Ma, face relaxed in sleep, lashes fanning her cheeks. She was beautiful, she was talented, she was clever. Any man would be proud to marry her.

So how did a man show a woman he was interested in matrimony? Catherine didn't seem impressed by James's wit, and she didn't bloom under effusive praise. Not being married to her, he had only so many opportunities when it was appropriate for him to hug her, and it wasn't proper to give her expensive gifts even if he could find them readily in Seattle.

He thought back to how his parents had behaved. Pa always seemed to sit or stand close to Ma when they were done with work for the day, hand on her shoulder or arm about her waist. He'd thank her for what she'd done, even if it was her usual chores of cooking, laying in stores for the winter, washing, sewing or mending. At times, they'd work shoulder to shoulder, clearing a field, building a fence, raising a barn, raising a family. And Pa had always chosen the dirtiest work, the hardest labor, if that meant sparing her from it.

He could do that. He already valued Catherine's skills as a nurse. He could make sure she knew that. And while she was at the Landing, he could share every burden, even if that added to his own.

Maybe actions really could speak louder than words.

He rose the next morning prepared to tell his brothers that he didn't require their help in courting Catherine. But, as usual, his family had other plans.

The first person he saw when he came downstairs was James. His brother wore a black frock coat over his reclaimed vest, and carved leather boots peeped out from under his wool trousers. He adjusted his stiff collar, then pointed a finger at Drew.

"You, sir, are shabbily dressed to appear before your Lord."

Drew glanced down at the shirt and trousers he'd slept in. "I didn't plan on meeting my maker today."

James clasped his hands together. "None of us ever does, brother. Can I get an amen?"

"Amen," John obliged, coming in from the back room. He, too, wore a coat and trousers, but he'd wrapped one of Ma's aprons about his waist, and the smell of frying ham told Drew he was making breakfast. "Did you forget, Drew?" he asked. "Today's Sunday."

In truth, he had forgotten with everything that had been happening. Both his father and his mother had insisted that Sunday was the Lord's day, a time for worship and rest. Basic chores like cooking and feeding the stock had to be done, of course, but there'd be no logging or other major tasks started.

"I'll be back for breakfast and service," he promised his brothers before heading to his own cabin to clean up and change clothes.

When he returned a short time later, wearing his one good suit of brown wool, all his brothers had gathered around the table. Beth was digging a hole in the braided rug as she paced from the table to the stairs. His sister wasn't old enough, Ma insisted, for a fancy dress just yet, but she'd tied a ribbon at the waist of her blue gingham gown, and curls swung from either side of her face.

Maybe Catherine really did know her way around a curling iron as Beth had hoped.

Still, her agitation concerned him. "Is Ma all right?"

he asked, catching Beth's eyes as she swung past the table.

Her nod was a jerk of her head that set her hard-won curls to bobbing. "Fine, fine. And I want you to know, Drew, that it was my idea, and Ma loved it."

He thought she must be talking about the curls, but before he could tell her they looked nice on her, she stopped to glance up the stairs. Following her gaze, he caught himself staring.

Catherine was descending, hands carefully holding up the skirts of the dress his mother had given her to wear. He'd seen it any number of times over the years, but always packed away in a trunk. The elegant scooped neck with its lace collar topped a bodice that drew down in a V at the narrow waist, the blue-and-green-striped cotton brushed to a shine that rivaled the gleam of Catherine's hair.

It was the dress, his mother had told them, she'd worn to her wedding, and she'd never found a good enough reason to use it again, until now.

Drew felt his chest rising with the emotions inside him. Simon stood up from the table as if to escort Catherine, but Drew beat him to the foot of the stairs.

"Catherine," he said, offering her his arm.

"Andrew," she replied with a smile as she accepted. "Your mother said you all dressed in your Sunday best, but I hardly expected all this."

He heard the benches scrape the floor as the rest of his brothers climbed to their feet. Even Levi wavered on his splint.

"I am blessed with the company of a fine set of gentlemen," Ma said, following Catherine down the stairs in her favorite green wool gown. "And now two lovely ladies, as well."

Beth wasn't the only one to blush at her praise.

John's breakfast of ham, eggs and corn bread with honey was quickly consumed, and the dishes were put in the washtub to soak. Simon had already brought over his fiddle, John the family Bible. They all gathered in the front room for Sunday service. Drew made sure to position chairs near the hearth for Catherine and his mother, then took a spot not too far away.

"We've rarely had a minister come out this far," Ma was explaining to Catherine as they sat. "So we've had to improvise when it comes to worship."

"Today we're reading in Matthew, I believe," John said, moving another of the chairs closer and jerking his head to Drew as if he wanted his brother to take a seat.

Drew stayed where he was.

"Or should that be Levi?" Catherine asked with a smile to Drew before looking at her patient, who was sitting on a bench with his leg propped up again.

Levi stared at Drew. "You told her?"

James settled next to his youngest brother. "What can we say? You are an endless source of amusement."

"You're not," Levi retorted.

James pressed his hand to his heart as if gravely wounded.

Normally, Drew took the first reading, but he found himself strangely tongue-tied with Catherine watching him. Simon seemed to take pity on him, for he, too, directed Drew to the seat next to Catherine and read the passage himself. Still, Drew couldn't seem to focus, even when John followed with one of their father's favorite psalms.

"'My flesh and my heart faileth, but God is the strength of my heart, and my portion forever.'"

He ought to rest on the second part of that promise, but too many times he felt the first part. This family had a way of tugging at his heart, challenging his strength. Today, however, he had another concern about praying.

And how did a man pray for the strength to go courting?

Catherine felt as if the room warmed with each reading. God had been the strength of her heart. He'd seen her safely around the country, through months at sea, and now was helping her prosper in this new land. She was so full of thanks that when Drew's hand reached for hers, she did not pull away. The touch felt right, pure.

Hand in hand, they listened as Simon played a series of hymns, the last of which had the whole family singing. Something seemed to be rising in her heart like bread dough in the morning, and it took her a moment to realize it was joy.

Dangerous, a voice whispered inside her. Where one strong emotion bloomed, others would follow. But surely there was no harm in praise. It had been an eventful few days, and she was grateful God had brought them all through it safely.

But apparently others needed help as well, for Drew and his family had barely said "Amen" when there was a knock on the door, fast and furious. James, closest to the panel, jumped up to answer it as the other brothers rose to their feet, Drew once more putting himself between her and possible danger. But then, what else would she expect from a knight, even one in a brown wool suit that stretched across his shoulders?

James threw open the door, and to Catherine's surprise, Old Joe hobbled into the room with a nod to Drew and his brothers.

"Gents," he greeted. "Ladies. I'm right sorry to interrupt, but I got an itch I can't stop scratching."

Drew's voice was a warning rumble. "I'll not have Miss Stanway bothered. She's already refused your suit."

Beth wrinkled her nose. "*He* was one of those suitors?"

Around Drew, Catherine could see the prospector grimace. "Didn't come courting this time. Came for some doctoring." He yanked up on the sleeve of his shirt. "See?"

Beth and her mother recoiled from the puffy red flesh. Catherine rose and pointed to the door. "Outside, sir. I'll do all I can to help."

"Much obliged, ma'am." He hurried back to the door, fingers pressed against the rash. "It drives me so crazy at night I can't hardly sleep."

"Excuse me," Catherine said to the room at large. "I'll be back shortly."

Only Drew followed her out. She thought perhaps he still didn't trust Old Joe, but instead he looked to her as they paused on the porch. "How can I help?"

Catherine smiled in thanks. "Let me examine the fellow and then I can tell you what we'll need to ease his discomfort."

It took her a few questions to confirm what she'd suspected on first sight.

"Is poison ivy or oak prevalent in the area?" she asked Drew, who had remained at her side as Old Joe sat on the porch and Catherine stood over him.

"Not that I've noticed," Drew replied, rubbing his chin with one hand. "But there's a good-size patch of stinging nettles between here and the Rankin claim. Beth picks them sometimes and boils them for greens."

"You must have brushed against them without realizing it," Catherine told their visitor. "If you can get into Seattle, ask Doctor Maynard for some calamine lotion. If not, I've heard him say that the backs of bracken ferns can be rubbed against the rash for some relief. You might try that."

"You bet," Joe declared, slapping his hands on his dusty trousers. He rose and eyed Catherine. "Sure you won't reconsider, miss? You'd come in right handy during an influenza outbreak."

"She comes in handy all the time," Drew corrected him.

Though she had never trusted such praise, his sounded so heartfelt she blushed. "Good luck to you, Mr.... What is your last name?"

"Holzbrinkdannagermengin," he supplied with a grin. "And now you know why they'd rather call me Old Joe."

He started away from the porch, then glanced back at Catherine. "Might be a few other gents in need of doctoring in these parts. Mind if I send them your way?"

"Not at all," Catherine replied with a smile. "But warn them I only plan to stay another few days at most. After that, they'll have to come into town to help."

Old Joe shook his grizzled head. "Shame, that. Body could die between here and town. God bless you, miss."

Catherine waved as he walked toward the woods.

"He's right, you know," Drew said quietly beside

her. "A man could die trying to reach town for medical help."

Darkness seemed to be creeping up on her, as surely as the clouds building over their heads. "A man can die trying to do his duty, as well. That's what happened to my father and brother."

He touched her chin, drawing her gaze to his. "You would have saved them if you could have. I know it."

Tears burned her eyes. "I would have. Oh! I would, Drew. But I never had the chance."

"So now you help others. I will always be grateful for what you've done for my family."

His head dipped lower, and she thought he meant to kiss her cheek. Instead, his lips brushed hers, tender, sweet. Her eyes drifted shut, and for a moment, all she did was feel.

He raised his head and lowered his hand. "Will you walk with me?"

At the moment, she would have gone to the ends of the Earth had he asked. "Of course."

She wasn't sure where he meant to go with a cougar possibly nearby, but he returned to the house long enough to retrieve the rifle. Beth's face appeared at the window, grinning, before she ducked back.

Drew shook his head. "This way," he said, stepping down from the porch.

He led her on a wide track that descended past the house to the lakeshore. Today the waters were as gray as the clouds, but she spotted blue sky in the distance and something else.

"What is that?" she cried.

Drew grinned. "The mountain's out. That's Rainier."

Where she lived in Seattle she'd never gotten a good

look at the mountain, obscured as it often was by clouds or hidden behind tall trees. Now it rose in snow-capped majesty, as if it sat at the end of the lake itself. Gulls wheeled past with shrill cries like courtiers begging a boon.

"Pa loved this place," Drew said, gaze traveling across the water as if he could see his father even now. "He had big dreams—first a homestead, then a town site."

Catherine glanced around, then pointed to the upper curve of the lake, where a knoll thrust out into the water. "Along there, I imagine, with fine houses."

"And wide streets," Drew agreed. "Fit for riding or promenading." He chuckled. "Funny. Pa never struck me as the promenading sort. He was always busy working."

"Like you," Catherine said, watching him. "I get the feeling your mother's illness is the only thing that slowed you down, and then not by much."

"By too much," he said. "Fields need seeding, and we should bring in another load of timber for the mill to pay for a plow."

"You'll have time soon," Catherine promised him. "You can see how she's improving. And Levi should mend quickly. Things will return to normal."

"Normal." He snorted. "There is no normal out here. Every day can be a challenge."

Catherine smiled. "My friend Allegra calls it an adventure."

He turned his gaze on her, the blue-green as alive as the forest around them. "Do you like adventure?"

Once, no. She had been rather pleased with her life in

Sudbury. But then the war had come, and her father and Nathan had gone. And she'd sailed around a continent.

And into Drew's arms.

"My work is adventure enough, Mr. Wallin," she said. "Perhaps we should go back. I'd like to check on your brother."

He nodded and turned from the lake, but not before she saw his face sag. He'd wanted another answer.

So had she. She just wasn't sure she was ready to give it.

Chapter Seventeen

He had made progress. Drew told himself to be satisfied with that. But the feel of Catherine's lips against his had opened a window, flooding him with light. He didn't want to return to the dark.

They spent the rest of the day in family pursuits, playing chess, looking through Beth's sketches of gowns she wished to sew one day, making plans for the week to come. He knew Simon wanted to quiz Levi further on his injuries, but their younger brother looked so sore and worn out Drew advised Simon to wait another day. He couldn't see how digging for information now would help any of them.

And he didn't want to do anything that would spoil the day. His brothers, Ma and Beth were all teasing each other and laughing, with Catherine joining in as if she'd always been part of the family. Was he wrong to hope she might soon be?

Beth and Ma must have been enjoying her company as much as he was, for they begged her to sleep with them again that night. She cast Drew a smile as she retired upstairs.

"I hear the church bells ringing," James predicted, lacing his fingers behind his head and leaning back in his chair.

Drew only wished he heard them, too.

But tomorrow was another day, as his mother often said. So long as Catherine remained at the Landing, he stood a chance.

"That tree has to come down today," Simon said the next morning over a breakfast of dried venison, leftover biscuits and honey as the brothers minus Levi gathered at the table before dawn. "Captain Collings isn't going to wait much longer."

"Agreed," Drew said. "Can the three of you handle it?" He was having a hard enough time following the conversation. He'd made the mistake of peering into the ladies' half of the loft this morning, candle brightening the space. Catherine had been curled up on one side, hair loose about her face. The vision was going to make work challenging today.

"We need you," John answered him, joining them at the table, tin cup of coffee in one hand. "It will take two on the saw and another two with the oxen."

He knew his brothers depended on his skill with an ax and saw to bring down the big trees. But with a cougar around, he could hardly leave Catherine alone with Beth, his ailing mother and an injured Levi.

"It will have to wait, then," he said. "Someone who knows how to handle the rifle has to stay here."

James and John exchanged glances.

"That's easily settled," Simon said, licking honey off his fingers. "Teach Catherine to shoot."

"No," Drew said. He realized he'd just crumbled his

biscuit to powder, and dusted off his hands. "Out of the question."

"Why?" John asked with a frown. "She already understands the rudiments. She proved that when she fired to call us back."

"And being a good shot will only make her more attractive to her future husband if you fail to come up to scratch," James reasoned, popping the last biscuit in his mouth and talking around it. "She can bag the game, dress it and cook it. I'd marry a woman like that."

"That's the most ridiculous thing I've heard in a long time," Drew started, but Simon shoved to his feet and reached for the dirty dishes.

"It's settled, then. After Drew teaches Catherine to shoot, he can meet us at the tree." He glanced over his shoulder as he headed for the sideboard. "Unless you'd rather I spend the next hour or so with my arms around her, helping her hold the gun."

John's brows shot up as if he'd never considered teaching from that angle, but James grinned as if he approved of the technique.

Drew pushed back the chair. "I'll do it. But you'd better watch yourselves, because when Catherine learns to shoot, I wouldn't want to guess how she'll use that gun."

Catherine had spent the night next to Mrs. Wallin, sharing the big bed in the ladies' half of the upper floor. She could hear Levi's snoring and the snort as he stopped when Drew must have nudged him. After spending such a lovely day together, having Drew just on the other side of the hearth made it difficult to sleep. She kept remembering the faraway look on his face as he'd talked about the town his father had hoped to build. She'd been captivated by the image.

More, though, she was captivated by the man. Those large hands could swing an ax and bring down a massive tree, yet his touch to her chin had been soft, tender. He might argue with his brothers, but she could see the love between them. They all relied on him.

But she couldn't allow herself to rely on him. She didn't want to listen for his voice in the morning, the sound of his boots on the stairs. She didn't want to inhale the scent of him, feel the strength of his arms. She didn't want to look into his smile and feel herself trembling.

And she certainly couldn't spend time with this family without missing her own. When Levi grinned, she saw Nathan. When James teased, she heard her brother's voice. Even Mrs. Wallin's gentle correction reminded her of the way her father had taught his children.

She'd already had one family pulled away from her. She couldn't bear to lose another. And the thought of losing someone as close as a husband made her want to jump into the lake and swim for the far shore.

The sooner she left Wallin Landing, the better.

She woke to Mrs. Wallin's yawn. Sunlight brightened the room. Beth was humming to herself as she laid a cream-colored cotton gown dotted with blue forget-me-nots on the bed. Catherine thought it must be for her mother, but Mrs. Wallin nodded toward the dress and smiled at Catherine.

"That's for you," she said, green eyes crinkling in pleasure. "I thought you might like something else to wear today."

First the beautiful gown yesterday, and now this.

She felt a little guilty how happy the dresses made her. When she'd agreed to join the Mercer expedition, she'd known she would have to leave most of her clothing behind. Her single trunk and bandbox had carried only five gowns, one of which was a blue silk evening dress; several white aprons for her role as nurse; a warm wool cloak; a paisley shawl; and a supply of undergarments. But when Levi had abducted her five days ago, even those precious few belongings had remained behind in Seattle, and she'd been wearing her blue dress until yesterday.

Five days? Was that all it had been? She felt as if she'd known the Wallins her entire life.

"It's beautiful," she told Mrs. Wallin and Beth, holding up the simple dress against her frame. The bodice was gathered at the collar and waist, the lower part of the skirt cut on the bias to give it more flounce. The cotton was worn but clean, the blue flowers sprinkled over the cream material bright and cheerful. She'd have to belt the skirt with her apron to compensate for Mrs. Wallin's greater height, but otherwise it would fit. And she wouldn't need nearly as many petticoats to fill the narrower skirts. She felt positively buoyant as she came down the stairs.

Drew was waiting for her, leaning against the wall at the base of the stairs. His damp hair was combed in place around his heart-shaped face; his smile broadened when it met hers. The admiration in his eyes made her cheeks warm.

"Good morning, Catherine," he said, pushing off the wall. "I trust you slept well."

Manners. Being polite. Those things she could manage this morning. "Quite well, thank you. I looked in on Levi, but he was sleeping so soundly I didn't have the heart to wake him."

"Let him sleep," Drew advised. "He can take the day off. Tomorrow, I'll think of things he can do while sitting to keep himself busy. Simon and the others ate up the biscuits, but I can fry some eggs if you're hungry."

Him serving her? That she could not handle. "I'll just make some tea. I'm sure you have work to do."

He nodded, but he accompanied her as she headed for the stove. "When you've finished, I'll teach you to shoot."

Catherine stopped on the rug. "Shoot? I heal people, Drew. I don't maim them."

"No one says you ever have to aim at a person," he promised, pausing beside her. "But my brothers and I have to work today. Ma and Levi aren't as mobile as I'd like, and we need someone besides Beth who can handle a rifle in case the cougar returns."

She could hardly argue with that. Every time she thought about the woods she remembered that powerful body slinking through the shadows, eyes watching her hungrily.

"Very well," she said.

After a quick cup of tea, she and Drew ventured out into the clearing. The day was gray and overcast; she expected they'd see rain shortly. The mist rising from the lake drifted through the trees, leaving the clearing hushed and pebbling her skin with dew.

"The oxen are out at the tree we're cutting," he explained to Catherine, stopping not far from the spring. "The horses and goats are out to pasture. I moved the chickens to a pen by Simon's cabin, so it won't hurt anything if you aim at the barn." He nodded to where someone, probably him, had sketched a circle on the gray wood. "To start, we'll see if you can put a bullet inside that ring."

That shouldn't be so hard. Catherine took the gun from him and held it out as she'd seen Simon do. She remembered firing the other day, but the morning had been such a blur that she wasn't sure she could repeat her performance now. The wood of the stock felt worn under her hand, the barrel cool and slick. But the weight was no different than holding the porcelain-coated cast-iron tray of instruments while her father operated.

Of course, that porcelain pan hadn't propelled deadly bits of metal.

Drew pointed to the gun. "Pa brought this with him when he came West. There aren't too many like it. See the circular chamber? The gun will fire six times before you have to reload."

He sounded proud of the fact, so it must be a good thing. "How handy," Catherine said.

"It can mean the difference between life and death if you're shooting at something as big as a cougar or bear."

Something she hoped never to have to do. She thought he'd explain further, but he positioned himself behind her.

"Keep the barrel up," he murmured, putting one hand on her elbow. "Look down it to where you want the shot to go. See that little knot near the end? That's the sight."

Catherine squinted down the barrel, spotting the bump at the end. She pointed it at the circle. "Very well."

"Now," he continued, other arm coming around her as his breath caressed her ear, "put your finger on the trigger." He hooked her finger over the curved metal. "Hold your breath, and pull."

Hold her breath? She couldn't even find it! With his arms around her, she was held in his embrace. She could feel him behind her, the length of his body, the breadth of his chest, the strength of his arms.

"Catherine?" he murmured. "Is something wrong?"

Yes, but she refused to admit it. She swallowed and pulled.

The gun barked, bouncing upward and pushing her back against Drew. His arms tightened to steady her. But she wasn't steady. Her heart was hammering in her ears.

"Close," he said as the smoke cleared.

Blinking, she saw that a small nick had appeared on the edge of the circle.

"Now you know the gun pulls to the right," he said. "How would you compensate?"

How could he be so calm? Was she the only one affected by their proximity? She took a deep breath and raised the rifle again. "I imagine I aim farther left."

"Exactly." Was his breath hitching, as well? She didn't dare look at him. Once more, his arms came around her and positioned the gun. She pulled the trigger and felt her body press into his. Closing her eyes, she breathed in the scent of him.

"Better," he said.

Opening her eyes, she saw a hole closer to the center of the circle. Grinning, she glanced back at him. Sweat stood out on his brow as if he'd run a race, and his eyes were wilder than Puget Sound waves in a storm. They stood there, no more than a foot apart. She couldn't move. She wasn't sure he was even breathing.

Beth came out on the porch and started flapping out her dust rag. "I saw you from the window. I'm so glad you're learning to shoot. How's she doing, Drew?"

He stepped away from Catherine, and the air felt cold, her limbs too heavy to possibly lift the gun. "Just fine. Try it alone this time, Catherine."

She knew women who would have pretended to misfire, just for the chance to be back in his arms. She wasn't that kind of woman. She lifted the rifle, sighted down its length, accounted for the pull and fired, rocking back with the recoil. Raising her head, she nodded in satisfaction at the hole in the center of the circle.

Beth applauded before darting back inside the house.

"Well done," Drew said, making no move to close the distance between them. "Beth can show you how to load it. You remember the way we call?"

"Once for danger, and twice for dinner," Catherine said.

That earned a smile from him. "Couldn't have put it better myself." He finally took a step closer, smile fading. "If you need anything, call. I'll come."

She nodded. She didn't dare do more than that. For if she opened her mouth she might just tell him how much she was beginning to need him.

And then he might never let her go.

Chapter Eighteen

The rest of the day, Drew waited for the sound of a shot that would send him careening through the forest to rescue Catherine. He imagined men circling the house, demanding her hand in marriage. He envisioned the cougar prowling up to the back door and scratching its way inside. He thought about whoever had poisoned the spring and left the haunch of venison returning to set fire to the house with her inside.

He was, in short, a mess.

"What are you planning to do, brother?" James teased him at one point after they'd felled the tree and set about removing the limbs. Drew had sat on a log to sharpen his ax and discovered the sun was suddenly much farther along its track.

"Any sharper," James warned when Drew looked up, "and you can give Simon a nice close shave."

Simon arched a brow and continued chopping at the branches.

He at least could focus. But how could Drew put himself into his work when all he could think about was Catherine? The brush of her hair against his chin when she was in his arms, the warmth of her body when the recoil had pushed her back against him, the deepening blue of her eyes as they'd stood gaze to gaze, the touch of her lips yesterday—how could any man forget?

Lord, You made us male and female, but did You have to make the female so deadly?

John slung a leg over the log and perched beside Drew. "Courting, as I understand it, is supposed to make a man giddy, not grumpy. But then again, we are talking about you."

Drew shook his head, lowering the ax. "I'm not grumpy, John, or if I am, it's no more so than usual. I know what you all want me to do, but I'm still not convinced I can do it."

John cocked his head, reddish hair falling against one cheek. "So you don't actually care for Catherine."

Drew's hand tightened on the handle. "I never said that."

"Ah, then you don't think she cares about you."

In truth, he'd doubted, but the way she'd reacted to being close to him said she wasn't entirely adverse to his company. "I'm not certain."

John cuffed him on the shoulder. "And that's why you court! It's an adventure. Enjoy it."

Catherine hadn't been keen on adventure yesterday. He couldn't blame her.

"Cougars, poisoned springs and abductions, and you think I need more adventure in my life?" Drew challenged, though he felt himself smiling.

John stood. "Every man needs the right sort of adventure, Drew. You're the one who has to decide whether that's Catherine. You know what Pa used to say."

"Pray about it before you talk about it," Drew replied. "Maybe I should."

"No maybes about it." John bent and picked up Drew's ax. "Why don't I help Simon, and you sit and think? You aren't much good to us right now anyway." With a good-natured smile, he strolled off, ax slung over one shoulder.

Drew leaned back on the log. Thinking, he had a feeling, was only going to get him into more trouble. But he'd never been the sort to hear the Lord's voice in answer to prayer. Then again, he'd never been one to pray overly much.

He had the notion he was supposed to close his eyes, but doing so in the middle of a busy logging group seemed foolhardy in the extreme. Instead, he raised his gaze heavenward, through the canopy of the forest, through the misty air.

Lord, I seem to remember a verse in the Bible about it being good if a man chose to stay unmarried. You know the work I have set before me. Won't a wife just get in the way of that?

"Hey!" Simon shouted. "James! Fetch me that saw."

Drew dropped his gaze to watch his younger brother trot across the cleared space with the tool Simon needed. They were a team.

A husband and wife could be a team.

It was an odd thought, yet he felt the truth of it. Certainly his mother and father were proof of the fact, and he'd seen how some of the wives in town were assets to their husbands.

But Catherine, Lord? She's not a hardy woman like Ma. She was born and raised in the city. She's used

*to finer things. She has a calling. Could she be happy
clear out here?*

That question didn't get answered until the evening.
He and his brothers had finished the day's work without the sound of a single shot. They had been picking
up their tools when the rifle called. Drew tensed, but
the second shot was almost immediate.

"Dinner is served," James quipped, and they all
headed back to the house.

Everything seemed to have gone well. Ma was helping Beth with dinner. Catherine had Levi's leg propped
up on pillows on the near bench of the table and was
sitting beside him. Ma must have given her some of the
scrap clothing, because she was cutting it into lengths
and Levi was rolling them up.

"Bandages," he said when Drew wandered closer.
"She seems to think I might need them."

Catherine smiled. "It never hurts to be prepared,
Levi."

"Except if you're digging your own grave," James
said on his way to the door with the bucket for more
water. "Someone might think you're ready to go and
happily oblige."

That reminded Drew of a conversation he needed to
have with Levi. He slung a leg over the bench and focused his gaze on his youngest brother.

"Do you expect to need more bandages any time
soon, Levi?" he asked. "Are you planning to fall out
of another tree?"

His brother busied himself winding up the strip of
cloth. "No, siree. I've learned my lesson. I'll be more
careful in the future."

"That's the thing," Drew said, leaning closer. "You've

always been good up in the trees. It's not like you to fall."

Catherine was watching him, lips compressed as if determined to let Drew lead the conversation. Levi shrugged and kept winding.

"You did fall, didn't you, Levi?" Drew pressed.

The bandage shook in his brother's grip. "Of course I fell. You don't think I'd break my own leg to get out of work, do you?"

"The thought had crossed my mind," James said, stopping beside them, water from the now-full bucket sloshing on the floor. "Either that, or you finally annoyed your friends sufficiently."

Catherine met Drew's gaze, but Levi shoved the bandage at her. "I have no friends."

"What about Scout?" Beth asked, bringing a pile of plates to the table. "You're always running off somewhere with him."

"He was the one who pointed us to where you fell," Drew told him.

Levi shifted on the bench as if he wanted to run off right then, but Drew knew his injury kept him from escaping their questions. "Scout Rankin is no friend of mine. He talks about being independent, being his own man, but he's the first one to do whatever that pa of his wants, even if it's…"

He swallowed and reached for the material Catherine still held in her hands. "Here, Miss Stanway. Let me tear that."

"Even if he what, Levi?" she asked, holding on to the old shirt.

"Doesn't matter," Levi said, head once more down. "I'm getting tired. Are we eating soon?"

Drew would have liked to question him further, but Ma and Beth put dinner on the table then. It wasn't until after the dishes had been cleared away and washed that Drew had a moment to talk, and then it was with Catherine.

Simon, James and John had headed to Simon's cabin to finish some chores there. Levi and Beth were playing the chess game their father had carved. Levi had never enjoyed the pastime, so Drew guessed he was trying to fend off more questions. Ma sat in her chair, the family Bible open in her lap. Catherine knelt next to Drew and started to add a log to the fire.

"Let me do that," Drew said, taking the rough wood from her hands.

He'd meant to do her a service, but she immediately bristled. "I'm perfectly capable of adding fuel to the fire, sir. I can even walk and talk at the same time. Some women are that talented."

Drew grimaced. He dropped the wood into the fire, and flames shot up the chimney. "I didn't mean any disrespect, Catherine. It was only a courtesy."

She sighed. "Is it a courtesy to do something someone could do for themselves?"

"Certainly." He sat on the floor beside her and crossed his arms over his knees. "Why do men open doors for women, help them up into wagons? It's a sign of respect."

"A sign of respect or a sign of dependence?"

Drew frowned. "Respect. Who'd want a dependent woman?"

She cocked her head, eying him. "You are a singular gentleman, Drew Wallin. Do you know that?"

He must have sat too close to the fire, for his cheeks

were getting hot. He shifted away. "I take it everything went well today."

"No sign of the cougar, no noise from the barn and Levi is healing nicely," she reported. "What did you think of his excuses before dinner?"

Drew glanced to where Beth was gloating as she took Levi's queen. "They sounded like just that—excuses. It seems he and Scout Rankin had a falling-out."

Catherine frowned. "To the point of a broken leg? Young Mr. Rankin hardly seems strong enough."

Drew shook his head. "It was probably an accident. Either way, Scout has to know I won't tolerate bullying."

"So does Levi," she said. "Perhaps he prefers to fight his own battles."

There was that. He'd be the last to stop his brother from taking responsibility for his actions. "I'll keep an eye on him."

She settled on the floor, skirts spread around her. "That shouldn't be hard for the next few days. Can you fell that tree without him?"

He wasn't about to admit his own lack of effort had kept them from finishing the job today. "We're nearly there. We should have it to the ship tomorrow."

"And when it's down? What next?"

He hadn't thought beyond the tree. "There will be more trees needed, for houses in Seattle, for businesses in San Francisco. There are always trees."

"Until there aren't," she countered. "One day you'll have this entire area cleared. What then, sir?"

He smiled. "Then we build Wallin Town, where men can turn timber into something more than log houses— ships and furniture and works of art."

She returned his smile. "And I'm sure you'll include

a fine hospital, with a staff willing to help women and children. It is a sad fact that some doctors neglect their needs or fail to take them seriously."

"Of course. And schools and churches and a civic hall for music and theatricals."

She tapped her chin with one finger. "And a library for John."

He chuckled. "For John and the rest of the community. Free for all."

"A noble calling, Mr. Wallin," she proclaimed. "I could see Wallin Town even eclipsing Seattle one day as the finest city in the Territory. You'll have your work cut out for you, but my father always said it was wise to plan for the future."

Perhaps that was his problem. He was so used to thinking about the present, counting heads, counting limbs, making sure everyone was fed and clothed and educated. His father's dream had been a distant thing, urging him on.

Perhaps it was time he started planning his own future, with Catherine.

Catherine was thinking about the future as she came down the stairs the next morning. To her, it seemed clear that her work at Wallin Landing was ending. Mrs. Wallin was up doing chores, cooking and cleaning for her family, and though she still tired easily, the danger was obviously past. Levi, as Catherine had told Drew, would heal quickly. A day or two more to make sure there were no complications, and then she could return to Seattle.

What she didn't expect was for Seattle to come to her.

Mrs. Wallin and Beth were tending the garden behind the house, Levi propped up on the porch with the rifle to keep watch. Catherine had insisted on helping them, bending and tugging out the vine-like weeds that seemed to flourish along with the carrots and peas. The day was still overcast, the sky a leaden gray above them. Birds called from the wood and swooped low over the lake.

"I've been meaning to ask you, Catherine," Beth said as she trained her peas up the lattice of sticks John had made for her. "Do the ladies really wear those big metal cages under their skirts like they show in *Godey's*?"

"Silliest things I ever saw," Mrs. Wallin said, pausing to adjust her sunbonnet. She'd given Beth and Catherine ones to wear as well, and Catherine was thankful for the long material at the back and sides that protected her neck from the little bugs she could see swarming down by the lake.

"I like them!" Beth protested, straightening. "I imagine they make you feel ever so graceful."

"They do indeed," Catherine replied, yanking out a weed from the rich, dark soil. "And they allow you to have the fullest skirts without the need for layers and layers of petticoats."

Beth nodded as if vindicated.

"Of course, they make it frightfully difficult to go through doorways," Catherine continued. "And sometimes, if you aren't very careful, they flip up and show your underthings to the world."

Beth look positively horrified. Mrs. Wallin laughed.

Levi climbed unsteadily to his feet. "Someone's coming." He aimed the rifle down the track leading south.

Rather inhospitable. Who did he think was head-

ing this way? Then she remembered about the spring
and the carcass behind the barn and took a step closer
to Mrs. Wallin.

A wagon and team pulled into the clearing, tack jin-
gling.

"There, are you seeing what I mean now, Mrs. Howard?" Maddie proclaimed from the back of the wagon.
"Sure'n but she's working much too hard."

Catherine smiled as her friend Allegra raised a hand
in greeting from the bench. In the lap of her fashionable
full-skirted gray dress, her four-year-old daughter, Gillian, wiggled in her eagerness to be free, golden curls
tumbled about her face.

Deputy McCormick jumped down and began un-
threading the reins from the horses' harnesses. "Mrs.
Wallin, Miss Wallin, Miss Stanway," he greeted with a
tip of his black broad-brimmed hat. His eyes narrowed
on the porch. "Levi."

Levi sat with a thud and lowered the gun.

As the deputy helped Allegra and Gillian down,
Maddie climbed to the ground, shook out her cinnamon-
colored skirts and hurried over to give Catherine a hug.

"And how is my Catie-girl?"

Her Catie-girl couldn't help noticing how Beth was
turning as pink as her gown, gaze on the wagon and
finger twirling the tie of her sunbonnet. She couldn't
be bashful of meeting new people, not after all her talk
of socials and such.

Catherine glanced at Mrs. Wallin, who was smiling. "Any friends of Catherine are welcome," she told
Maddie. "Why, I might not even be here if it wasn't for
this dear girl."

Catherine thanked her, then introduced everyone

around as Allegra, Gillian and Deputy McCormick came to join them.

"I'm only sorry my husband couldn't come with us," Allegra told her. "He had pressing business in town. I was simply glad Deputy McCormick agreed to accompany us."

McCormick glanced at the porch again. "I had a reason to travel out this way."

Beth's color deepened. Levi's fled.

Mrs. Wallin invited them all into the house for cider. Only Levi demurred, claiming a need to keep an eye on the horses Deputy McCormick had let into an open patch of pasture. Though Mrs. Wallin looked disappointed in his response, Catherine thought Drew's mother took special delight in serving the rest of them from her pink-and-white dishes.

Catherine took more delight in the bandbox Maddie had brought with her.

"My clothes!" she cried, clutching it close.

"I feel the same way," Beth said with a grin.

Maddie had also brought a loaf of spice cake with her, the scent of cinnamon and cloves drifting up as Mrs. Wallin sliced off pieces.

"Oh, but my boys will be sorry they missed this," she said as she poured Deputy McCormick another cup of cider.

"And how many sons would you be having, then?" Maddie asked.

The question was polite, but Catherine could see the light in her friend's brown eyes.

"Five," Mrs. Wallin answered, pride evident in the height of her chin.

Gillian perked up from where she sat on the bench next to Allegra. "Can I play with them?"

Mrs. Wallin smiled at her. "I'm afraid they're a little too old. Drew is nearing thirty, Simon is twenty-eight, James is twenty-five, John is twenty and Levi is eighteen. But I'm sure Beth would be happy to play with you."

"Mother!" Beth dropped her gaze and gripped her teacup so hard Catherine thought the handle might snap. "I'm not a child!"

Mrs. Wallin frowned. "Who said you were?"

Deputy McCormick rose from his place at the end of the table and held out a hand to Gillian. "Come along, urchin. There's a goat or two around here somewhere that needs petting, if I remember correctly."

Beth hopped to her feet so fast her cup rattled in its saucer. "I'll be happy to show you."

McCormick nodded. "Much obliged, ma'am."

As the three set out, Mrs. Wallin stood, as well. "Now, you ladies just visit. I want to bring Levi some of this cake. He's taking this guard duty so seriously." Plate in hand, she moved toward the rear door.

Maddie slid along the bench until she bumped into Catherine. "And what about you, Catie, me love? Are you taking your duty seriously?"

Catherine sipped from her cider before answering. "Mrs. Wallin is feeling much better, and I am convinced the youngest Mr. Wallin will heal nicely from his injury." She was just as convinced he'd stayed outside to avoid having to talk with Deputy McCormick.

Maddie tsked. "And was your nursing the duty I was meaning?" She lowered her voice. "How are you and the eldest Mr. Wallin getting along?"

Catherine broke off a bit of the moist cake with her fork. "He has been very helpful in the nursing process."

Maddie glanced at Allegra with a frown, then returned her gaze to Catherine's. "Has he sung you no songs? Tried to steal a kiss under the moonlight?"

Catherine felt her face coloring as she remembered the kiss they'd shared. It hadn't been under the moonlight, but she'd still felt moonstruck. "Certainly not," she told Maddie.

Allegra blew out a breath that stirred her dark hair. "Well, what's wrong with the fellow?"

"Nothing," Catherine protested, and Maddie crowed.

"You see? Wasn't I telling you that, Mrs. Howard? There's not a thing wrong with the fellow, at least nothing marrying a good wife wouldn't fix."

"That's quite enough," Catherine said, picking up her teacup with two fingers. "Mr. Wallin and I are both quite indisposed to courting."

Maddie picked up her own cup and pointed her little finger at Catherine, nose in the air. "La-di-da, but aren't we above such things, now?"

Allegra shook her head with a smile. A slender beauty with coal-black hair and stunning blue eyes, she had been one of the leaders among the women Asa Mercer had brought to Seattle. She'd organized a school aboard ship so that they'd all know everything they could about their new home, and she ran the town's lending library from her home near the territorial university.

"No one says you must marry, Catherine," she replied now. "But it seems you couldn't choose a finer fellow. I asked around town, and everyone I talked with holds Mr. Wallin in the highest regard. He always fills his contracts on schedule, and he and his family have been very generous in donating wood for civic and church projects."

That did not surprise her. Drew was so conscientious about his responsibilities to family. It seemed he extended that responsibility to his neighbors, as well.

"Sure'n but he's a pillar of the community," Maddie agreed. "Especially as he's as sturdy as a pillar. Why, I can't imagine a thing that would ever threaten the man."

Catherine blinked, then set down her cup. "But something has." She went on to tell her friends what had happened at the Landing, including her suspicions about Levi's injuries and his response that even Scout Rankin was not his friend.

Maddie made a face. "Rankin. I've heard his name in town. There was a scrawny lad wandering about trying to interest gentlemen in stopping by his father's property for a good chicken dinner. I thought he might be needing a cook or cleaning woman, so I asked Mrs. Elliott, who has the running of our boardinghouse. She advised me to stay away from the man. Said he could drink Puget Sound dry."

"That could be nothing but gossip," Allegra reminded her. She slid off her end of the bench and stood. "I'm sorry to cut our time together so short, Catherine, but we'll need to go soon if we want to reach Seattle by dark. I'll fetch Gillian. Why don't you tell Deputy McCormick your concerns?"

Should she? She didn't want to give the lawman more to consider when it came to Levi. Drew had enough on his hands. But if Deputy McCormick knew something that could help Drew protect his family, wouldn't Drew want to hear it?

Chapter Nineteen

Drew dunked his head in the spring pool and shook the water from his face. It had been a long day. They'd sheared off the last of the branches and dragged the fir down to the stream. Bracing the log by ropes and poles, they'd worked the oxen to maneuver it down into Salmon Bay, where sailors from the *Merry Maid* were waiting to take it to the ship. A carpenter was already aboard to help them varnish the mast, step it into place and rig it properly. One more job done, and no one hurt.

John came out of the barn where he'd penned the oxen. He took one look at Drew and shook his head. "That is no way to approach a lady." He pulled a comb from his hip pocket and handed it to Drew. "We want you neat and tidy to court Catherine."

Drew accepted the carved wooden comb, another example of his father's handiwork, but his annoyance must have shown on his face, for John stepped back with a grin. Either that, or Drew looked even worse than he thought.

"And smelling nice," James agreed, joining them by the pool. He took a sniff near Drew and reared back, waving a hand before his nose. "Where's that cologne Simon bought from the tinker?"

"Gone," John informed him. "I used it to start that pile of wet wood burning last week."

Drew pushed away from the spring. "I'm fine. If Catherine can't appreciate a man who works, she's not the bride for me."

"Drew?"

The looks on his brother's faces would have told him who had called him even if he hadn't recognized the voice. James stepped aside, and Drew saw Catherine standing just behind him. The pink of her cheeks suggested she'd heard at least part of their conversation.

Drew nailed a smile on his face. "Good evening, Catherine. We were just about to join you for dinner."

James and John murmured their agreement and hurried for the house, James with an arch look to Drew.

"I hoped to catch you," she said, taking a step closer, "before you went inside."

He didn't think it could be about anything good, but he made himself lean a hip against the stone wall of the pool and say, "Oh? About what?"

She blew out a breath as if she wasn't sure how to tell him, and he tensed for the worst.

"Deputy McCormick was here today," she said, one finger rubbing another in front of her gown, which was the color of the lilacs that grew in the wood. She hadn't had it with her before, and the wide skirts and fancy white piping along the bust and waist told him the dress didn't belong to his mother, either. Had McCormick brought her clothes? Was he courting her, too, now?

"Why?" he asked. "More trouble?"

"He said it was a social call. He brought my friends Miss O'Rourke and Mrs. Howard to visit."

Drew relaxed a little. So that was where the dress had come from. A shame his brothers hadn't been here to meet the feisty redhead.

"I don't think he was telling all the truth," she continued. "He seemed inordinately interested in Levi. And he didn't seem surprised to see him in a splint."

Drew frowned. McCormick was as hard as the cedar Drew felled, but he couldn't see the lawman beating his brother. "Did he have words with Levi?"

"Not that I noticed. He seemed more interested in observing. But I thought he should know about the troubles you've been having, so I told him." She closed the distance between them, gaze turned up to his. "I hope you don't mind."

"Why should I mind?" Drew replied. "You were looking out for my family. What did the deputy make of it?"

"He said our problems were similar to what's been happening at the other farms between here and town. Only no one's been hurt there."

"So whoever is behind this singled out Levi," Drew said, hearing his voice deepen.

As if she heard it, too, Catherine laid a hand on his arm. "There's more. My friends mentioned a Mr. Rankin. I take it he's the father of Levi's friend Scout."

Drew nodded. "But you saw Scout. I'm having a hard time imagining him beating Levi."

Catherine cocked her head. "Or perhaps looking the other way while his father did it?"

Drew didn't know what to believe. "Why shield someone, even an old friend, who treated you so badly?

No, something else is at the bottom of this. Did McCormick have any suggestions as to what we can do, how we can protect ourselves?"

"Just to be vigilant," she said with a shrug that spoke of her own frustration at the vague advice. "He said he'd do the same. I'm sorry, Drew. I wish I had something more for you."

Drew shook his head. "You tried, and for that I'm grateful."

He'd followed such a statement with a kiss before. It seemed only natural to do so again. But this time when his lips met Catherine's, emotions exploded around him like Mr. Yesler's fireworks on the Fourth of July. He couldn't think, could only feel. He wrapped his arms about her and cradled her against him. She clung to him, arms coming around his waist, hands pressed to his back, as if she wanted him closer. The world fell away, until all that was left was Catherine.

Nearby, a rifle roared.

Drew's head jerked up, and he put Catherine behind him, sheltering her, fists up and at the ready.

Levi stood on the porch, gun in one hand. "Do I need to fire again, or do you get the message?" he asked, face tight.

Drew wiped his lips, still tingling from the kiss. "We'll be right in."

Levi nodded, hung up the rifle and hobbled inside.

Drew turned to Catherine. She looked as though she wasn't sure whether to laugh or cry.

"Drew, I…" she started even as he said, "Catherine, I…"

He smiled at her. "Go ahead."

She seemed to take him literally. "Thank you. Excuse me." She hurried for the house.

Drew followed more slowly, trying to master his emotions. He'd thought her so calm, her feathers never ruffled. But there was a fire inside her. He could feel it calling to him. Was this how his father had felt about his mother?

Not for the first time, he wished his father was there to ask. Drew had managed to figure out everything else the past ten years, from how to weld his quarrelsome brothers into an effective logging team to where to plant vegetables during a chilly spring.

But when it came to falling in love, he hadn't a clue.

Catherine found it hard to eat dinner that night. Levi had surprised a fat hare in the garden, and the stew was savory with the tender meat. But every time her spoon touched her mouth, she remembered the pressure of Drew's lips, his fierce embrace and the way she'd reacted. All she'd wanted to do was hold him closer and sway with the emotions he raised in her.

She could not be in love. She'd shut the door on feeling. She had to remember her calling, her purpose. Anything else was not to be borne.

So she refused to be alone with Drew the rest of the evening. That was surprisingly difficult, given that they were sharing the main room of the cabin with six other people. She started by offering to help Mrs. Wallin with her mending. Drew's mother agreed with a smile, and Catherine took a chair next to hers and accepted the red flannel shirt from her former patient.

"Such a time they have working," Mrs. Wallin said with a shake of her head that made her red-gold hair catch the light from the fire. "They're forever ripping or tearing something. That one's Drew's—a hole in the sleeve."

Catherine felt as if the fabric warmed in her hands. She set it aside and rose. "Would you care for some water? I could do with a cup."

Across the room, Drew had been leaning against the wall while his brothers sat at the table, Simon whittling, James rubbing linseed oil into an ax handle and John reading. Now James elbowed his younger brother.

"Did you hear that, John?" he said, overly loud. "Catherine wants water."

John eyed Drew. "Someone should fetch it for her."

Drew straightened away from the wall.

Panic pushed Catherine to the other side of the room. "No need. I'm fine." She collapsed on a chair next to Beth. "What does *Godey's* have to say about the new hemlines, Beth?"

The girl grinned at her. "That the more narrow silhouettes are very becoming. I was thinking about making a new dress, a nice one for church and socials and such."

"And taking tea with the governor's wife," James teased.

Beth ignored him, rising from her chair. "I'll go get my sketches and show you." She glanced around the room. "Drew, why don't you keep Catherine company until I return?"

Again, he straightened off the wall, and Catherine racked her brain for a way to avoid him.

This time she had an unexpected ally. "My leg's paining me," Levi announced. "Maybe you could have a look at it, Miss Stanway, if you're not too busy with other matters."

Catherine hurried to his side. "Of course I'll take a look, Levi. That's what I'm here for." Not to fall in love and risk her heart.

Levi had been sitting on the bench of the table, leg straightened out in front of him. James vacated his chair for Catherine, and she sat and examined the splint. Everything seemed in place, and she could detect no sign of swelling.

"Where does it hurt?" she asked Levi.

To her surprise, he glared at his hovering brothers. "Can't a man have a little privacy?"

"In this family?" James asked with a grin. "No." But he allowed John to lead him over to the fire. Simon went to sit beside his mother. Drew relaxed back against the wall, though Catherine could feel him watching her and his youngest brother.

"What's troubling you, Levi?" she asked.

He lowered his voice. "I saw you talking with Deputy McCormick. What did he say about me? What did you tell Drew?"

So that was the problem. Catherine kept her voice lowered as well, fingers skimming the wood of the splint. "We talked about the other accidents that have happened recently. I believe Deputy McCormick sees a pattern."

"Then he's smarter than he looks," Levi muttered.

Catherine eyed him. His face was paling, and he'd crossed his arms over his chest.

"What do you know about this, Levi?" she asked.

He narrowed his eyes. "Why do I have to know anything? Why is it always my fault?"

"No one said it was your fault," Catherine argued. "But if someone hurt you or threatened your family, you must tell us."

"I don't have to tell you anything. We did just fine on our own until you came along."

Catherine recoiled from the anger in his voice. "If you ask me, Mr. Wallin, it's not your leg that pains you. It's your conscience."

"And if you ask me, you ought to go back to Seattle where you belong!"

His voice had risen, and everyone in the room glanced their way. Beth, returning with her sketches, paused on the stairs. Drew moved to his brother's side.

"That's enough, Levi. Your injury may explain your temper, but you should apologize to Catherine."

Levi was breathing hard, as if the air had grown too thin. "Sorry," he muttered. "I want to go to bed now. John, will you help me?"

"Surely," John replied, coming to join them. He put an arm under Levi's and helped him to his feet. Together, they moved toward the stairs.

"I'm sorry, Catherine," Drew said, and for a moment she wasn't sure what had made him apologize, his actions earlier or his brother's now.

James returned to their sides. "Am I getting old, or was brother Levi testier than usual tonight?"

Simon ventured over, as well. "What did you expect? He's a young man with nothing to occupy his thoughts or utilize his energy. Something was bound to snap."

Was that it? Sometimes she thought Nathan had gone off to war because he couldn't bear being left behind by his friends and father. Was Levi acting out because Drew hadn't given him enough responsibilities?

"Perhaps he should come with us tomorrow," James said. "We'll keep him busy."

Catherine shook her head. "I fear a logging camp is no place for healing."

Drew eyed her. "Have you ever seen men log?"

"No," she admitted. "But I'm certain it's hard work."

"No argument there," James said. "Sometimes I positively grow faint." He collapsed back against Simon, who pushed him up with a grimace.

"It might surprise you what we have to do, Catherine," Simon said. He glanced at Drew. "I say we bring her out with us tomorrow morning. Watching us work should give her a fair idea of whether it's a suitable place for Levi."

It was a logical suggestion. She really couldn't determine what was safe for her patient otherwise. Yet some part of her was more curious to see Drew in his element.

He glanced around at his brothers, his eyes narrowed, as if he suspected treachery of some kind. Finally, he sighed and nodded. "Very well. If you're willing, Catherine, we'll need you to be ready by dawn."

She was willing and ready at the appointed time. She'd dressed in the flowered cotton gown Mrs. Wallin had loaned her, deeming it far more practical than her fuller skirts. A sunbonnet shielded her hair from the cool morning mist.

James set out first toward the west, ax poised over his shoulder. Simon and Drew carried saws and a burlap sack each that clanked as they walked. John bore the rifle, gaze shifting around the brush as they traveled along a well-worn path through ferns and thick green bushes where white flowers burst in clusters. Someone in town had told her they were called rhododendrons.

"Have you seen any more of the cougar?" she asked Drew, who was walking beside her. His checkered shirt was tucked into dusty trousers, which in turn were tucked into heavy boots. By the way they sucked at the mud, she thought the bottoms might carry spikes.

"Only some tracks down by the lake yesterday morning," he said. "We're hoping it headed for better hunting."

So did she. She glanced around the forest. The mist obscured the trees, touching her skin with soft fingers, but she could see a brighter patch to the east where the sun was trying to burn through.

At length they reached an area where the trees had been cut away, stumps like teeth jutting up through the wild grape and blackberry vines. A single tree remained in the center. Catherine gasped at the sight of it.

James grinned. "Why, Catherine, don't you like our little sapling?"

"Sapling?" she sputtered. "It's huge!"

John went over and patted the rough bark. "And several hundred years old, a mammoth of the forest." He sighed. "A shame it's come to this."

Catherine felt a similar sorrow. The tree soared into the air, so high she had to hold the bonnet to her head from craning her neck. Birds darted among the upper branches, and lichen clustered around the base.

"Must you cut it down?" she asked Drew.

"That's our job," Simon said as he passed, long-toothed saw bouncing over one shoulder.

Drew pointed up the bark. "See the holes? They were made by woodpeckers seeking bugs. The tree's sick,

Catherine. If we don't fell it, it could infest all the trees around it."

"Not to mention knock half of them to the ground when it falls in the next windstorm," James said cheerfully, going to help Simon.

John held out the rifle to Catherine. "If you wouldn't mind? With Levi at home, we're a man down."

She took the gun gingerly from him. Though she felt confident she could shoot it now, she still didn't like the idea.

"That's something for Levi," Drew said. "He could keep watch for danger. Most animals shy away from the noise of the axes, but a few get curious enough to come too close for comfort. Holler if you see any that concern you."

She nodded, and he went to join his brothers at the tree.

Now that she looked closer, she could see where they'd notched it earlier, the cuts of the ax pale against the weathered bark. John and James hacked away on the opposite side, then Simon and Drew drove in wedges with a sledgehammer to hold the back cut open.

James brought over the big saw and positioned it along front cuts. Simon joined him on one side, while Drew and John took up the other. Slowly, then gathering speed, they rocked the metal through the wood, the blade humming.

Catherine could see their muscles strain under the cotton. Soon sweat darkened their necks, and the shirts clung to their backs. They were a testament to strength and power, their bodies moving as one with the song of the blade.

And Drew was their leader, the commander of this

little army, directing his brothers, encouraging them. His was the voice that rose above the noise, the head that never bowed with the effort. The sun broke through the mist and turned his hair to gold. She could not look away.

Beside her, something rustled in the brush. She tore her gaze from Drew and aimed the rifle at the spot, but whatever it was must have had its curiosity satisfied, for she saw no movement and heard nothing more.

"Scatter!" John's voice echoed through the clearing. "Widow-maker!"

All four brothers dropped the saw and dashed away from the tree.

"What is it?" Catherine cried, clutching the gun.

Drew was frowning up the tree as if trying to spy the danger himself.

"There," John said, pointing. "I thought I saw it shift."

Now Catherine saw it, as well. Halfway up the tree, a massive branch had broken off. Right now, it lay wedged between two other branches, its tip pointing down, but the vibration of the saw could easily have sent it plummeting.

Right onto Drew and John. She shivered at the thought.

"I'll go," Drew said. "Brace the cut and rig the rope." His brothers moved to comply.

"What are you doing?" Catherine asked with a frown.

He offered her a grim smile as he walked away from the tree to give his brothers room to work. "Removing a danger before it removes one of us."

John and James put more wedges around the big

saw to keep the tree from shifting while Simon began swinging a weighted rope. Up it went, over one of the larger branches not far from the broken one. He tugged down on the weight and went to wrap the rope around a stump. Once he was certain it was secured, he brought the other end to Drew.

Catherine stared at Drew as he looped the rope around his waist. "You aren't going up there."

"One of us has to," Simon said, coming to tug on the rope as if to make sure it would hold his brother. "He volunteered."

James and John came to join him, spitting on their hands before taking hold of the rope. They were going to haul Drew into the tree!

"Are you sure this is safe?" she asked, feeling a tug of panic as strong as their hold on the rope.

"Safer than leaving that up there," Drew answered.

"Never fear, Catherine, dear," James said. "We hardly ever drop anyone."

Catherine choked. "Hardly ever?"

"He's teasing," Drew assured her. "We've done this many times, and we've never been hurt."

"Ever since Pa was killed by a falling branch," John explained, "we tend to take such matters seriously."

Catherine took the matter just as seriously. She wanted to order them all back to the house and lock them inside. As if Drew understood, he took a step closer.

"Trust me, Catherine," he said. "We know what we're doing."

She felt as if the mist had returned to clog her senses. "Promise me you'll be careful."

He smiled. "I promise. I'll be back by your side before you know it." He touched her cheek. The warmth only pushed her panic higher.

She shoved the fear down. He needed to focus, not worry about her. "Good luck," she made herself say.

With a nod, he turned to the tree.

Drew positioned his spiked boots against the trunk and nodded to his brothers, who began pulling back on the rope. One hand braced on the rope, the other on his ax, Drew leaned back and took a step higher. In a moment, he was nearly perpendicular to the tree, moving slowly upward, one step at a time.

Simon, James and John kept hauling, their own feet braced on the damp ground, hands tight on the rope. Catherine tilted back her head and watched as Drew reached the branch and swung his ax. Each time the blade fell, his body jerked against the tree, and she was certain she felt the tree tremble. She trembled along with it. Then one more cut, and the branch broke free. Drew pulled back one boot and kicked the branch away. It twisted in the air to fall.

Right on the rope.

Simon, James and John stumbled forward with the weight as Drew was jerked higher.

"Get it off!" Simon shouted, and John released the rope to scramble forward, yanking at the massive limb.

"It's no good! We need at least two of us to cut it." He stared at Simon, and Catherine felt his fear.

Simon looped the rope around his waist, then pulled a knife from his belt and drove it hard into the ground as if to help anchor himself. "Go," he told James, who released the rope.

James had taken two steps toward their axes when

there was a snap as loud as a gunshot, and the rope whipped upward.

Catherine cried out, then threw up a hand even though she knew she couldn't reach him, as Drew tumbled down the tree.

Chapter Twenty

The world reeling around him, Drew clutched the rope and tried to dig his heels into the bark. The spikes on the bottoms of his boots refused to find purchase. He felt every bump on the way down. He was going to die.

Lord, protect Catherine and my family!

He was a few feet from hitting the ground when he jerked to a stop, the rope burning against his chest. Blinking, he looked up to see the line tangled among the branches.

John reached him first, knife out and sawing at the cord. "Are you all right?" he begged.

He was alive and in one piece, something he hadn't believed possible a few moments ago. *Thank You, Lord!* The rope snapped, and he dropped lightly onto the ground to suck in a breath.

"I'm all right," he started to say, but Catherine had beaten his other brothers to his side and was thrusting the rifle at John. She put her hands on Drew's shoulders and peered up into his eyes, her own smoky with fear.

"Where does it hurt?" she demanded. "Can you breathe? Speak, man!"

Drew tried to smile at her. "Only a nurse would ask a man to breathe and speak at the same time."

Simon and James, who had also come running, pulled up beside her. He could see them frowning at her, but he could feel her body shaking.

"You hit eleven branches on your way down," she informed him, as if she'd counted each one. "And you struck your back at least twice. You could be bleeding internally, have fractured a dozen bones..."

He caught her close and held her in his arms, thankful he still could. "I'm all right," he repeated against her hair. "You have no reason to fear."

She clung to him a moment before pushing away. "I'm not afraid!" she cried. "I am furious! What sort of antic was that? How could you risk your life? Don't you know your family depends on you? Do you want to leave them orphaned?"

Her words hit harder than the tree, and his breath rasped out of him.

"He isn't our father," Simon said quietly. "We can take care of ourselves."

"Can you?" Catherine whirled on him. "I didn't see you volunteering to climb that tree. And you," she turned to James as Simon reddened. "You take nothing seriously. How can your brother rely on you? And you," she turned to John, who dropped the gun and held up his hands as if surrendering. She threw up her own hands. "I have no opinion about you."

James grimaced, but John looked stricken at being an afterthought.

"You asked me out here to determine whether it's safe for Levi to return to work," she continued, undaunted, gaze stabbing each in turn like the flash of a knife. "Of course it isn't safe. It isn't safe for any of you. If you want my advice, you will find another line of work, immediately!" She turned and stalked out of the clearing.

"Go with her," Drew told John. "She finds you the least offensive."

"Small comfort," John muttered, retrieving the gun. "Apparently I have so little personality I failed to make any impression." He jogged after Catherine.

Simon blew out a breath. "Forgive me for demanding that you court her, Drew. She is obviously not the bride for a lumberjack."

"Oh, I don't know," James said, scratching his chin. "She could probably fell a tree by pointing out its shortcomings. It would certainly make this job easier."

"Enough," Drew said. He threw off the last of the rope, wincing as his sore muscles protested. Catherine had been right about one thing—he had bruises on bruises. "She's trained to heal. You can't blame her for objecting to someone getting hurt. To her, it must look as if we take chances intentionally."

"Wild men that we are," James agreed, bending to loop up what was left of the rope. "Still, Simon is right. This is how we make a living. People need this wood for houses, for ships, for furniture. We can't just stop working because it looks dangerous."

"It doesn't just *look* dangerous," Simon said. "It *is* dangerous. Any woman who can't live with that fact has no place in the wilderness."

"Clear off the branch," Drew said. "I'm going after Catherine."

Neither of his brothers protested as he limped away. Catherine must have kept going at a goodly clip, because Drew didn't catch up to her and John. And it took him a little longer than usual to reach the Landing, given his injuries.

On the way, he kept thinking about what he would say to her. She was right on all counts—Simon didn't like to take chances, James treated the world as if it were designed for his entertainment and John would crawl inside a book and stay there if Drew allowed it. But they were all good men and would make fine husbands one day—for the right woman.

And she was right about their work, as well. When the saw had whipped past him years ago, he'd been fortunate to walk away with a lacerated hand. His father hadn't been so fortunate. Every year loggers were crushed by falling logs or trampled by oxen. What they did was dangerous.

The past few days had been particularly challenging with the cougar and Levi's injury, but even on the best of days accidents could happen, people could get sick. He did everything he could to keep his family safe and healthy. What more did she want from him?

He had nothing left to give.

At last he reached the Landing and hobbled out onto the grass. He didn't see Catherine right away, but John met him at the edge of the clearing.

"She's in your cabin," his brother reported, face pinched as if he'd been the one to fall down a tree, "and she asked Beth to help her change into one of her gowns. She wanted to know whether I'd drive her back to town or whether she had to walk."

"Go help James and Simon," Drew said. "I'll talk to her."

He started across the clearing, but his mother came out of the main house to wave at him from the porch.

"Everyone all right?" she called.

"Fine, Ma," he said, gritting his teeth to saunter up to the cabin as if he hadn't a care in the world. No need to worry his mother when Catherine was worried enough for all of them.

"But why must you go?" Beth protested as she watched Catherine finish buttoning up her dusty blue gown. Mrs. Wallin's pretty dress lay draped over a chair, along with the sunbonnet. Nothing looked out of place in the cabin. It was as if she'd never been there.

She drew in a shaky breath. It was for the best. Her work here was done. Mrs. Wallin was well; Levi was healing. Drew said he was fine, although she'd seen the pallor on his face and watched the skin darken on his hands where he'd hit them against the tree. She feared the number of ways he could be hurt, but felt equally certain he'd never allow her to treat him. If he and his brothers were determined to risk their lives, she didn't have to stay and watch them die.

But she couldn't say that to Beth. The girl had to live out here with her brothers; it was probably a kindness that she didn't realize how close to death they walked.

"Doctor Maynard needs me in Seattle," she told Beth, knowing the statement for the truth, as well.

"We need you here, too," Beth argued, hands worrying in front of the apron on her pink gown. "What if Ma gets sick again or Simon pushes James out of a tree?"

Catherine's stomach flip-flopped. What if one of them got hurt? Who'd tend their wounds? Who'd nurse them to health?

*Lord, You can't ask me to stay. You know the need
is greater elsewhere.*

"You all survived before I arrived, Beth," Catherine
said, moving toward the door. "And if Simon pushes
James out of a tree, maybe it will knock some sense
into him."

"You don't mean that!" Beth followed her to the door.
"Please, Catherine, don't go! It was so nice having another girl to talk to. I never got to show you how to make
flapjacks or milk the goats. We could have had fun!"

Living here was hardly fun. Being around the Wallins hurt deeply. And the thought of losing Drew made
her physically ill.

"You can come visit me in town anytime you like,"
Catherine offered, pausing at the door. "You'll most
likely find me at the hospital." Where she could deal
with patients on a purely clinical level.

She opened the door to find Drew on the porch. His
hair had fallen into his face, and a bruise darkened one
cheek. She had to fist her hands to keep from reaching out to him.

"You don't have to go," he said. "I'm fine."

But he wasn't. She didn't have to lay her hand on his
forehead to see that he was sweating. She could hear
his breath coming fast, as if it hurt to draw anything
deeper. He should be lying down, putting a cold cloth
on his bruises, being examined for broken ribs.

But not by her. She knew if she put her hands on him
now, she'd be holding him close and never letting go.

"All the more reason for me to leave," she said, picking up her bandbox and stepping around him. "There
is nothing more for me here."

As if the very earth disagreed, Wallin Landing

seemed to leap toward her, surrounding her. Everywhere she looked, she saw memories: sending Levi into the pool, firing the gun to bring Drew and his brothers a-running, sitting by the fire and listening to his dreams, being so sweetly held and kissed.

She straightened her spine and cast him a glance.

"No John, I see. Very well. I'll start walking."

Drew's arms came around her. For a moment, she closed her eyes and gave in to the feeling of warmth, of safety. But it was all an illusion. He could be taken from her at any time.

"You don't have to walk," he murmured. "I'll drive you. Are you certain this is what you want?"

He leaned back and gazed down at her. She could feel herself slipping into the blue-green of his eyes. *Stay*, some part of her urged. *Take whatever life gives you and enjoy it while it lasts.*

But she couldn't. Her heart wasn't strong enough. Already she felt as if she were shattering into a thousand pieces.

"This is for the best," she made herself say. "I'll wait while you harness the horses."

He let her go and headed for the barn.

Beth touched her arm, blue eyes swimming. "Please, Catherine, I know Drew cares about you. I thought you cared about him."

Catherine watched him cross the clearing. His shirt was torn where a branch must have caught it. Though he tried to hide it, she could tell he was limping. He was a battered, tattered fellow, yet he had never looked more honorable or more dear.

"I do care about your brother," she murmured. "That's why I have to leave."

* * *

Maddie at least was glad to see Catherine when she walked into the boardinghouse late that afternoon. She took one look at Catherine's face and hugged her close.

"Is there a fellow I should be scolding?" she murmured, "for putting such a look on your face?"

"No," Catherine said, drawing back. "I'm the one who should be scolded, for putting myself in such a position."

She could not forget the silence between her and Drew as he'd driven the wagon back to Seattle. She'd heard every creak of the wheels, each thud of the horses' hooves. He'd kept his gaze ahead, as if she weren't sitting beside him, wishing him to speak, praying he'd stay silent.

"Ma and Beth will miss you," he'd said at one point, and she nearly asked whether he'd miss her, too. But she didn't want to know. Oh! She didn't want to know.

Now Maddie followed her upstairs to the room they shared. All she wanted to do was change out of this dress into something fresh, something that might not remind her of how she'd spent the past few days. But the room with its twin beds covered in bright wool blankets and its window overlooking Puget Sound felt tighter than she remembered. It was as if even the air in town wasn't as clear, as deep.

"What happened?" Maddie asked as Catherine pulled out her trunk from under the bed and drew out her favorite brown dress. "I left you with a handsome man. Could you not be bringing him back with you?"

At least Maddie hadn't changed. "I sent you a handsome man," Catherine countered, rising to begin unbuttoning her gown. "Did a Mr. Ward call on you?"

Pink crept into Maddie's cheeks. "Mr. Ward, the thespian? Oh, he's as charming as the day is long, so he is. But I'm not sure I'm the lass for him."

"Oh?" Catherine glanced up with a frown. "Why?"

Maddie twisted her fingers around each other, avoiding Catherine's gaze. "Well, two Irish people? You know what everyone will say—there they go a-breeding! And a man with ideas about acting and such. No, no. If I marry, sure'n it will be to a man with gold in his pockets and the respect of the community behind him, someone I can be proud to stand beside."

Money and position. Catherine knew many women back East who had married for those reasons. "I always thought a marriage required more than that," she told Maddie as she pulled off the blue gown. "Love, for one thing."

"Oh, now don't you be getting on your high ropes the moment you get back, Catie, me love," Maddie warned her, flopping down on her bed. "Isn't position why you refused that lumberjack out in the wild?"

Catherine tossed the gown on her bed. "Mr. Wallin never asked me to marry him. And it's not his position that troubled me."

Maddie cocked her head. "Was he such a gadabout, then, courting any woman who took his fancy?"

She couldn't leave her friend with that impression. "Not at all," she said as she drew the dress over her head. The fine brown wool was fitted, the skirts narrow and it said the wearer would brook no nonsense.

"A more faithful fellow you'll never find, I'm convinced," she told Maddie. "But what he does for a living, where he lives, there are so many dangers, Maddie. I don't think I can bear it."

"Ah," Maddie said, straightening. "You want a husband who will treat you like a fine porcelain doll, keep you safely wrapped in pretty blankets."

"Certainly not!" Catherine shuddered at the image. "I wouldn't stand for such treatment. I've worked too hard at my profession to want to give it up. I help people, Madeleine. Sometimes I give them back their lives."

Maddie stiffened. "Begging your pardon, me darling girl, but only the Lord gives life. I've seen you be His hands. Yet doesn't the Good Book say that any act done without love means nothing?"

Catherine marched to the little table near the window, picked up her brush and began attacking her hair. "So simply because I don't engage my heart with every patient who walks in the door, you would have it I've done nothing worthwhile. I don't believe that."

In the mirror over the table, she could see Maddie watching her. "I'm not casting aspersions on your work, Catherine. I'm questioning your motivations." She gentled her tone. "Sure'n you can't bring back your father and brother."

"No," Catherine said, hand stilling on the brush. "But I do my best to see that no one else suffers such loss."

"And you can keep yourself from suffering, I'm thinking," Maddie said, rising from the bed and crossing to her side, "by making sure you never let anyone close enough that you start to care."

The words slammed into her, piercing her chest. She shut her eyes, but she couldn't shut out the truth.

"Very well. I don't want to hurt like that again. I don't think I'm strong enough. Is that what you want to hear?"

Maddie's arms came around Catherine, and she

opened her eyes to meet Maddie's gaze. "No, me darling. I want to hear that you realize love is worth the risk that you might be hurt again."

Tears were coming. She could see them sparkling in her eyes in the mirror, along with Maddie's mournful smile.

"I'm sorry, Maddie," she murmured. "I'm not sure I believe that."

Maddie gave her a squeeze before releasing her. "Well, that's progress, isn't it, now? Once you would have told me you didn't believe it at all."

Catherine smiled at her friend through the tears. "Only you would see my doubts as progress."

Maddie nodded as if the matter were settled and picked up the brush to run it through Catherine's hair, the strokes gentle and calming. "Doubt can be good if it brings you to the truth. And if it's that Mr. Wallin who's made you wonder, I'll be saying a prayer for you both. Now let's get you prettied up so you'll be ready when he comes back for you."

Something inside her leaped at the thought, but she couldn't let her friend hope in vain. "He isn't coming back, Maddie."

"Oh, he is," Maddie insisted, twisting up a hank of Catherine's hair and pinning it in place. "I saw his face as you came to the door. He's hurting as much as you are, so he is. A man like that isn't going to give up. I'd say he'll be back within the week, so you better decide what you'll say when he proposes. And if it's anything less than yes, you and I will have words, me darling."

Chapter Twenty-One

Drew returned to Seattle three days later. He hadn't intended to. They didn't need supplies. The days were warming as May went by, and the leafy tops of Beth's carrots were already waving in the garden. They didn't need medical help. Ma was back to her regular routine, Levi was hobbling around on a crutch that John had made for him, and Drew's bruises were fading.

At least, the bruises on the outside of his body.

No, the reason he had to return to Seattle was because he'd never know peace otherwise.

"You let her get away?" James had protested from his place on the rug when they'd all gathered in the front room the night Catherine had left. "And you call yourself a man?"

His mother, seated in her rocking chair, had tsked as she'd worked on knitting a new pair of socks. Beth at her feet had looked from one brother to another.

"I thought things were going so well," she'd protested. "Levi said you kissed her."

James had hooted as if he quite approved, but Ma had silenced him with a look.

"If she let you kiss her, I don't see how you could have lost her," John had said from his place beside James. "You've never failed to bring in a deer or bring down a tree you set your mind to."

They'd had no idea what they were talking about. Wait until they fell in love. Leaning against the stairs, Drew had shaken his head. "Catherine is hardly a tree."

From the opposite wall by the window, Simon had crossed his arms over his chest. "But the same principles apply. You determine your objective, plan your approach, gather your supplies and act. You knew the objective was to keep a nurse in the family. We gave you a plan and offered our help. You had all the supplies you needed." He'd pointed a finger at Drew. "You didn't act."

"For shame, Simon Wallin," Ma had said, frowning at him over her knitting. "I never taught you to think of a lady that way. Why, you make falling in love sound like a battle!"

Simon had colored as he'd lowered his hand. "Apologies, ma'am, but I tend to think of courting that way."

"Another reason I'm still waiting for a daughter-in-law." She'd set aside her knitting and risen to come to Drew's side. Her green eyes had been solemn. "What happened, Andrew? I was under the impression you cared for Catherine."

Drew had pushed off the wall. "I care. She doesn't want to be part of this family. That's all that matters."

His mother's face had softened. "How she feels about us is less important than how she feels about you. A lady can put up with a great deal for the right man."

"Then apparently, ma'am, I'm not the right man."

He had felt the protest building around him, shining

in his sister's eyes, shouting from his brother's tensed shoulders. He'd had enough.

"This topic of conversation is closed," he'd told them all. "I wish you a good night."

He'd felt their surprised gazes follow him as he'd crossed the room and left the house.

Returning to his own cabin had seemed like the best way to remove himself from the criticism, but even there he'd found no rest. Catherine had seemed to linger in the air. One chair had been out from under the table, and he'd fancied he could still feel the warmth of her against its back. His quilt had held the scent of lemon and lavender he'd come to think was hers alone. And one pale blond hair had gleamed in the moonlight on the wood floor. He'd bent to retrieve it, stroking one finger down the length.

Oh, but he was lost.

What do You expect of me, Lord? She hesitates to fire a gun, she hates our work, she's as bossy as the day is long.

And despite what he'd said to his mother, he'd known then and now that Catherine sincerely cared about his family, maybe as much as he did.

In the end, her love for his family wasn't what had driven him back to Seattle. No, he had come for Catherine. For all her propriety and high ideals, there was something vulnerable about her. Spending time with her, watching her ply her trade, holding her in his arms, he'd caught a glimpse of her heart, and he wanted more.

He found her at the hospital, as he'd expected. Several people sat or stood along the white walls of the dispensary, waiting for Doc Maynard to see them. One man cradled his arm; another rocked back and forth, moaning. Catherine moved among them, speaking softly, laying a hand of encouragement on shoulders, offering advice on how to deal with the illness or injury. She was wearing a dress of a warm brown. The color contrasted with her pale hair, and the tailoring outlined her figure. With her apron wrapped about her, she looked competent, confident.

So beautiful he couldn't look away.

He took off his wool cap and held it in his hands as he paused in the doorway. Now that he was here, he couldn't think what to say to her. How did one family compare to the needs of the many here in town? How could his feelings vie with her calling?

Before he'd even taken a step, she looked up and met his gaze. Her eyes widened as she straightened, then she hurried toward him.

"Drew, what's wrong? Did Levi's leg fester? Did your mother have a relapse?" She clutched his arm. "Please tell me Beth's all right. Simon? James? John?"

"Fine," he assured her before she could ask after the stock, as well. "We're all fine, or at least they are. I came for me."

She pressed her fingers to her lips as if offering up a prayer. "Oh, no! Your fall must have been worse than I thought." She gripped his hand and towed him to the nearest chair, pushing on his shoulders to make him sit. "You should have had one of the others drive you in," she scolded. She ran a hand up his arm as if checking for injuries, and his heart started hammering.

"Where does it hurt?" she asked. "Your arms? Your legs? Your back?"

Drew caught her hand and pressed it to his chest. "My heart."

Catherine gasped, and he thought she must have understood him, but she jerked her hand away. "Doctor Maynard!" she cried, dashing for the door. "We need you!"

As the other waiting patients stared at him, Drew stood. "No, Catherine, you misunderstand. I'm fine."

Doc Maynard strode into the dispensary. His white apron was speckled with a dusty red. "One more life in this world. What's wrong?"

Catherine drew in a deep breath. "Apparently nothing. Please forgive me. And give my congratulations to Mrs. Stevenson."

He nodded, then smiled at Drew. "Come to steal my nurse again, Drew?"

He was about to deny it when inspiration struck. "Actually, yes," he said. "I'd like her to come out and take a look at Ma and Levi. I'll return her tomorrow."

Maynard waved a beefy hand. "Certainly. We can make do a day or two without her this time. But not much more." He turned to the man waiting nearest him and began asking questions about his condition.

Catherine moved back to Drew's side. "I thought you said everyone was fine at the Landing."

"They are," Drew replied, "and I'd like to keep them that way."

Catherine's eyes narrowed. "As you can see, we have a great need here."

Though he felt like a selfish oaf for asking her to abandon these people for him, he couldn't very well talk about their future in such surroundings. He needed her somewhere they could discuss matters, reach some agreement.

Where he could hold her in his arms and tell her how much she meant to him.

"Come with me, Catherine," he urged. "I know everyone will be glad to see you, and you can make sure Levi's leg is healing straight."

Still she eyed him. He thought she might be holding her breath. He was holding his. Finally, she nodded. "Very well. But this time we stop by the boarding-house before we go so I can alert Maddie and bring a few things."

Relief coursed through him, and air rushed into his lungs. She was going to give him a chance. Perhaps on the drive or at the Landing, he could convince her to think differently about him.

"Anything you want," he told her. "And thank you."

She should have refused him. By his own admission, everyone was fine at the Landing. What good could she do there? Her heart would only break when she left him again.

She'd had a hard enough time the past few days. Each time the door opened at the hospital, she'd expected Drew to walk through it, coming to tell her something horrible had happened. Or Simon to tell her Drew lay dying from the injuries she'd chosen to ignore. How could she claim to be a nurse and leave the man she loved in pain? Why had she let fear rule her better judgment?

Yet how could she go back and beg his forgiveness when she still wasn't sure how to deal with those fears?

Now she glanced over at Drew as he drove the team along the track out of town. He had been quite the gentleman, escorting her to the boardinghouse and waiting on the porch while she'd told Maddie the circumstances and packed her bandbox. She'd let him carry it to the wagon for her while Maddie had supervised from the porch.

"What's this?" he'd asked as Catherine had handed him a book.

"Culpeper's Complete Herbal," she had told him. "I promised John a copy. I simply wasn't sure when I'd see him again to give it to him."

His smile had been warm as he'd placed the book behind the seat. Very likely he'd thought she'd been hoping he'd come for her.

He wasn't entirely wrong.

"You be taking all the time you need, now, Mr. Wallin," Maddie had called in encouragement as he'd lifted Catherine onto the bench. "Sure'n Catherine could do with a change of scenery, and I'm thinking you have some fine scenery up where you live."

Catherine had frowned at her, but Maddie had merely laughed and waved a hand as they'd set off.

If Drew noticed Catherine's scrutiny at the moment, he didn't show it. More than anything, she wanted to know why he'd made the trek into town to fetch her. He'd said something was wrong with his heart. Was he truly hurting as much as she was, as Maddie had claimed? Why didn't he say something, explain his reasoning, share his feelings?

Tell her he loved her too much to let her go.

"Have you had many patients lately?" he asked.

Polite conversation again? Once she would have welcomed it or sought her own safe topic. Now her disappointment was like bitter medicine in her mouth.

"Enough to keep us busy," she replied, shoulders of

her dress brushing a red-throated rhododendron as they passed. "There's a rumor another doctor may be coming on the next ship from San Francisco."

"That's good news."

In the silence that followed, she could hear the horses' hooves sucking at the mud of the track. She couldn't go on this way. *Lord, help me. Give me the words to tell him what's in my heart, what I fear.*

"Drew, I..." she started, even as he said, "Catherine, I..."

He smiled. "Forgive me. What did you want to say?"

Catherine couldn't look at him. How did a woman tell a man she cared for him so much it frightened her? She fixed her gaze ahead, into the trees, then frowned. "Is that smoke?"

Drew had been looking at her. Now his head whipped around. Rising above the towering firs was a plume of gray, growing larger every minute.

"Something's on fire," he said, and he slapped the reins to urge the horses faster.

Not the Landing! But even if it wasn't Drew's home, the fire looked too close for comfort. How fast did a fire travel among the trees? Could it outrun a person? A horse? How many would be harmed if it wasn't contained?

As if her fears had infected him, Drew called to the team, pushing them forward. Catherine clutched the sideboard as the wagon careened down the track. The forest was no more than a green blur on either side. Something leaped across their path, and she realized it was a deer, fleeing the flames.

Lord, please protect Beth and Drew's brothers. Protect dear Mrs. Wallin. Please keep them all safe!

They rattled into the clearing, and Drew hauled back on the reins to bring the horses to a stop. Flames licked up the side of the barn, darkening the white circle Drew had drawn for Catherine to practice shooting.

The Wallins had formed a line from Mrs. Wallin and Beth working the pump outside Drew's house to Simon closer to the barn, and were passing buckets of water toward the fire. Drew looped the reins around the brake and put his hand on the sideboard to jump down. The team reared in their traces, whinnying in fear, knocking him back beside Catherine. She put out her hands to steady him.

"I'll calm them," he promised as he straightened. "Take Ma and Beth to the lake. You'll be safe there."

"I'm not leaving you!" Catherine insisted, but he was already climbing down, speaking to his horses. A moment later, he was running toward his cabin.

She wasn't sure how she could help fight a fire, but she knew she could ease his mind about his mother and sister. Gingerly, she picked up the reins, then had to pull as the excited horses tried to plunge forward.

Beth ran to the wagon and climbed up beside Catherine. "Drew and the others are going to keep fighting the fire," she reported, face flushed. "He wants us to protect the stock."

James and John had dropped their buckets and raced into the barn. Now they reappeared through the smoke, each leading two goats, some chickens nearly smothered in their arms.

Beth gathered the frightened hens into the back of the wagon while her brothers loaded in the bleating goats. Catherine couldn't catch sight of Drew. Where was he? What was he doing? Would he be safe?

Mrs. Wallin had gone to the house and returned to dump an armful of her quilts at Catherine's feet. Handing her husband's daguerreotype to Beth, she climbed up beside Catherine and cried, "Go!"

Still, she couldn't see Drew in the smoke that billowed about the clearing. She had to trust him to make it through, to come back to her. Just as he trusted her to keep his mother and Beth safe.

It was the hardest thing Catherine had ever done, but she slapped down on the reins and left him.

Chapter Twenty-Two

With Mrs. Wallin on one side and Beth on the other, Catherine guided the team through the trees, following the track she and Drew had walked on Sunday. Nathan had taught her how to drive years ago. He'd thought himself so clever to be better than her at something, the teacher rather than the pupil at last. She'd humored him, though she'd known the skill wasn't critical. Where she'd lived she'd either walked or traveled with friends or family. Besides, her father rarely surrendered the reins to his son, let alone Catherine. Now she blessed Nathan for teaching her, for the knowledge allowed her to bring the horses down the hill and onto the shore by the lake.

If she looked out over the blue water, cresting in places in a rising breeze, she could almost pretend everything was normal. Birds darted back and forth across the lake: gulls with their black-tipped wings, swallows with their mouths open. Mount Rainier rose in the distance, like a mother watching over her children at play. Only the hint of smoke in the air told of the fight going on among the trees behind them.

Beside her, Mrs. Wallin had her hands clasped in her lap, and her lips moved presumably in prayer. Catherine sent up a prayer as well, but it felt so small against five lives, three homes and the work of two generations.

She hated not knowing, not doing more. A part of her had always wondered whether there might have been something she could have done if she'd been there with her brother and father on the battlefield. Was God giving her a chance to help now?

She rose from the bench. "Wait here. I'm going back."

"No, don't!" Beth clutched Catherine's skirts. "Oh, please, Catherine, don't leave us. What if the cougar is still around?"

"Then I won't be much use to you," Catherine replied. "We don't even have a gun."

Mrs. Wallin touched her daughter's hands. "It's all right, Beth. Let her go. She knows her mind." She nodded to Catherine as Catherine climbed down to the ground. "Help them. We'll keep the stock safe. You save my boys."

Save her boys. What faith she had in Catherine.

As she lifted her skirts and started up the hill for the Landing, Catherine knew she didn't have that kind of faith. She wasn't sure why the Lord didn't keep some people, like her father and brother, safe, why some had to die so young or when so needed. Despite her best efforts, things just seemed too chaotic, too out of control.

These things I have spoken unto you, that in me ye might have peace. In the world ye shall have tribulation, but be of good cheer. I have overcome the world.

She drew in a breath, feeling as if the truth of the remembered verse had touched her physically. The Lord had made no promises that life would be safe and secure. He'd only promised to be with her through it all.

And that was a promise she could keep for Drew.

She hurried through the trees and out into the clearing at the edge of the Landing. Though Drew's brothers continued to throw water at the fire, their faces grimy from the smoke, the blaze was beginning to gain the upper hand. Tongues of flame licked greedily through the slats on the barn. The oxen had been let free and were running from one side of the clearing to the other in their fear, the rumble of their hooves accompanying the crackle of the burning wood.

Above the noise rose the bang of metal on stone.

Catherine spun to face the pool. Drew stood, one leg in the water, the other straddling the wall. He lifted a massive sledgehammer over his head, muscles straining, and brought it down. Stone and mortar flew from the blow. He was trying to break open the pool, and she saw in an instant his purpose. If he flooded the barn, he'd cut off the fire at its base and hinder its progress. He raised the hammer again, shirt taut across his chest, gaze fixed on the wall as if it were his enemy. Once more he was a knight, going to battle for king and country.

For all he held dear.

She wanted to cheer him on; she wanted to speed his work. She glanced around, looking for some way to help, and her spirits plummeted.

The woodpile was smoking.

The towering mass of logs, raised on a platform and braced by a pair of struts at either end, all but covered the side of the barn closest to the pool. When Drew battered down the wall, the wave might put that fire out in the pile, but the water would never reach the underlying flames in the barn. And neither Drew nor his brothers was in any position to move the wood.

But she was. She might not be able to hack through a wall or carry off dozens of chunks of wood, some as big around as her waist, but she knew how to break through a strut.

Glancing around, she spotted any number of axes on the grass, dropped, most likely, when their owner had run to join the bucket brigade. A good many she wasn't sure she could even lift, much less swing. But there, stuck in the wood of the porch, she spied a hatchet!

She ran and yanked free the tool, then dashed across the clearing for the woodpile. The movement must have caught Drew's attention, for she heard him call her name, his voice strained. No time to respond, no way to quickly explain, and she needed all her strength. She drove the hatchet into the wood at an angle, as she'd seen Drew's brothers do at the tree, pulled it free and drove it in at the opposite angle. Again and again she struck, watching, praying, as the little V widened.

"Catherine!" Drew's voice was like distant thunder.

"It's all right," she called, pulling back the hatchet. "I'm almost there." She swung it into the strut.

The wood snapped, peppering her with splinters. She stepped back as the pile began to shift. With a rumble, the logs started tumbling out onto the ground.

Something wet sloshed into her shoe, and she slipped. Turning her head, she saw a wave of water churning toward her. The pool was breached, water pouring across the land. She was caught between it and the falling wood.

She struggled to gain purchase in the mud, skirts heavy with water. A log bounced off her foot. She gasped, and strong arms wrapped around her, lifted her, carried her out of the way.

Cradled her close and kept her safe.

Drew set her on the porch, and she had to force her fingers to release her hold on his shirt.

"Stay here," he said, backing away, face drawn and eyes wild. "If anything happened to you, I'd never be whole again."

Catherine reached out a hand to him. "I know. I feel the same way. Let me help!"

A cry went up from the barn. Drew turned, and Catherine saw James dash out into the light. He splashed and kicked up his heels in the remaining puddles as the wave of water spread out across the Landing.

"Yee-haw! You did it, Drew! It's out!"

Catherine sagged against the porch support, clutching the rough wood. *Thank You, Father!*

Levi, who had been manning the pump, hobbled closer to the barn as if to make sure. Now Catherine could hear Simon and John calling to each other as they beat back the last of the flames.

Before her, Drew's shoulders sagged, the past few moments apparently having taken a toll. Catherine climbed down from the porch and put a hand to his shoulder. "You did it, Drew. Everyone is safe."

He took her in his arms, held her close and buried his head in her neck. His damp hair caressed her cheek.

"We did it," he murmured. "I saw the fire starting in the pile, but I couldn't leave the spring to stop it. But if those logs had fallen on you, Catherine, if the water had knocked you under it…"

She felt him shudder. She rubbed his back. "It didn't. I'm safe. Your family is fine."

He raised his head and gazed down at her, eyes haunted. "This time. What about the next time or the time after that? I can't be everywhere, with everyone."

Catherine gave him a squeeze. "That's God's job. And I'm learning we should do our best and leave the rest to Him."

"And His helpers." James grinned as he approached them. "Very nice work on the woodpile, Catherine. Remind me never to leave my hatchet out when you're angry."

"Hatchet, sir?" Catherine answered with a smile. "I have my sights on an ax, two handed, perhaps."

"Better watch out for this one, Drew," James said. "She thinks big."

"One of the many things I love about her," Drew replied.

Catherine could not make herself move from his embrace. Love? Oh, yes, she felt it, too, bright and pure and strong. But though she was beginning to wrestle with her fears from the past, she could see he was still consumed by concerns for the ones he loved. Would he be willing to add her to the list?

Love. He hadn't sought it, had not earned it, but he could see it shining in Catherine's eyes and feel it in the touch of her hands. There was so much he longed to say to her, things they needed to work out, but once again, his brothers had other ideas.

Simon and John strode out of the barn, tossed aside their shovels and crossed to Drew's side. Grime striped their faces, and Simon's green eyes looked pale in their red rims.

"It's out," he announced. "But what I want to know is how it started."

Drew released Catherine, but kept one arm about her waist. He couldn't seem to let her go completely.

"None of us would be so careless," John said. "If Beth hadn't called us when she smelled the smoke, the fire could easily have spread to the forest and threatened dozens of farms before it was through."

Catherine nodded toward the barn. "I think Levi may have an answer for you."

Drew looked to where his youngest brother was walking toward them, leaning heavily on his crutch. His face was white under the smear of mud. He stopped a few feet from his brothers, as if afraid of coming too close.

"It's my fault," he said, voice cracking. "Someone started the fire on purpose, and I know why."

"Surely even you couldn't make someone this mad," James teased. He clapped his brother on the shoulder, nearly oversetting him on his crutch. "Although you must admit that you have the unique ability to annoy a body without trying."

Drew was interested in how Levi would respond. His brother shifted on the crutch as if he'd like nothing better than to run away again. "Oh, I annoyed someone, all right. I didn't intend to. But I may owe someone money."

"May?" John frowned as Drew felt his shoulders tighten. "Either you owe it or you don't."

Drew couldn't remain silent. "Why would you owe anyone anything?" he demanded. "You have all the food, clothing and shelter you need."

"And maybe I wanted more!" Levi's head came up,

and he glared at Drew. "Maybe I wanted something of my own, something I earned all by myself."

Drew reared back from his brother's vehemence, but Simon leaned closer.

"What have you done?" he demanded.

Levi turned his glare on his second-eldest brother. "It was just a friendly game of cards. Scout goes into town and rounds up folks to join his father. I thought, why not me? I'm grown now. I can enjoy a hand of cards or a good cigar if I want."

"I imagine a bottle of gin was involved, as well," John said with a shake of his head. "I've heard there's plenty of that rotgut stuff at the Rankins."

"I didn't drink," Levi said, as if that would be any worse than what he'd already confessed. "I kept my head. And I was winning a lot. I was good at it." Suddenly, he sagged. "Only then I wasn't. Mr. Rankin said I could pay him back when I won, but I couldn't stop losing."

Drew couldn't seem to grasp the idea. "You chose to gamble away what little you earned from logging? When did this happen? You've had plenty to do here."

Levi shrugged. "I did, until Ma got sick. Then you sent me back to the Landing. I was bored, and Scout needed help rounding up clients. Besides, Mr. Rankin hosts his games at night. It wasn't hard to slip away... until she came." He nodded at Catherine.

Anger licked up Drew. Did Levi dare blame Catherine for his shortcomings? She evidently had as little liking for the comment, for her eyes narrowed.

"Then it's a shame I didn't come sooner, Mr. Wallin," she said.

She was getting all prim and proper again, but Drew

couldn't blame her. He felt the same way. He'd thought he'd raised his brother better than this. He wanted to strangle Levi and lock him in the house for safekeeping at the same time.

One of the oxen thudded through the mud, head low and call plaintive. The last of the smoke drifted from the barn. As much as Drew would have liked to question his brother further, they had bigger concerns at the moment.

"We'll settle this later," he said. "For now, there's work to be done. Simon and James, fetch back Ma and Beth and the stock. John and I will make sure all the sparks are out and get the oxen penned again. Levi, start supper. I don't know whether anyone is in the mood to eat, but I want something on the table just in case."

As his brothers scattered, Catherine touched his hand where it rested on her hip. "How can I help?"

"Keep an eye on Levi," he said. "It seems someone has to."

He watched as his brother stumped up the porch, head bowed.

"We'll help him," Catherine said, watching Levi, as well. "He's lost his way, but he's not lost."

Drew could only hope she was right and that he could reach his brother.

And Catherine.

Chapter Twenty-Three

It was a solemn dinner that night. Though Levi had managed to put together a stew with dried venison, carrots and potatoes, as well as a pan of biscuits, no one seemed interested in eating. Simon had returned with Mrs. Wallin and Beth, and the men had built a makeshift pen for the stock until they could repair the fire damage to the barn.

Simon must have told their mother about Levi's confession, for the first thing she did when she returned was to cup her youngest son's face in her hands.

"What's done is done," she'd said, green eyes meeting blue. "Now you must make things right."

Levi had nodded, blinking back tears.

Although Catherine knew Mrs. Wallin was wise to counsel action, she wondered how the boy would go about settling the matter. It was clear to her he was in over his head and up against people with no regard for life or property.

Of course, she knew something about feeling out of control. Despite her best efforts, she had come to love this family. Especially the man who held them all together.

Drew sat at the head of the table, gaze traveling from one sibling to another as if he were counting heads, making certain everyone was safe and fed. He didn't eat until their plates were filled, didn't rest until they were dreaming. And if their sleep was peaceful, it was because they knew he was standing guard. A prayer for him came easily.

Father, they called You the Good Shepherd. I had forgotten that until I met Drew. He thinks he's doing what his earthly father asked, but I think he's doing what You expect and more. Show me how to help him.

Mrs. Wallin and James had cleared away the dishes and were in the back washing up when Drew spoke to Levi again. "How much do you owe?"

His brother seemed to shrink in on himself. "Two hundred."

"Dollars?" Beth asked with a gasp as Simon hissed in a breath.

Catherine felt her stomach drop. It had cost her three hundred dollars to sail from Boston to Seattle, money she'd saved from the sale of her father's house. Two hundred would surely be a huge burden to this family.

"Where did you lay your hands on so much money?" John asked with a frown as if he could not make the sum add up in his head.

"I told you," Levi snapped. "They let me play on credit."

"Knowing your family would make good on your debt," Simon said with a shake of his head.

"I never asked you to pay my debt," Levi protested,

clutching his crutch as if he wanted to swing it at someone. "I told Scout I'd pay his father back. They just didn't like waiting."

Catherine felt ill. "If they torched your family's barn and beat you because they disliked waiting, I shudder to think what they'll do once they know you can't pay."

"We'll pay," Drew said, voice low and hard. "This harassment must end before anyone else is hurt."

"But we can't let them get away with it," John argued. "What they did is wrong."

"Not to mention potentially deadly," James said, coming back into the room with a towel slung over his shoulder. He lay a hand over his heart. "Not that I hold it against them, seeing how Levi so abused their trust."

"'Vengeance is mine, saith the Lord,'" Mrs. Wallin quoted, following James back to the table. "I don't like what Mr. Rankin's done, but I won't see more of my boys hurt because of it."

They were missing the point. Why was this their fight to begin with?

"Surely this is a matter for the sheriff," Catherine said, glancing around at them all. "Deputy McCormick said there had been other harassment out this way. Levi can't be the only one to fall into the Rankins' trap. If we tell Deputy McCormick our suspicions about Mr. Rankin and his son, he'll have enough information to at least warn the man off, perhaps even jail him."

"But suspicion is all we have," Simon reminded her. "McCormick isn't going to arrest anyone unless he has proof."

Catherine lay her hand on Levi's shoulder. "And Levi's word and injuries aren't enough?"

Levi cast her a quick glance. She thought he looked surprised that she considered his word important.

"He claims to have fallen out of a tree," John pointed out.

"And he hasn't actually been the most trusted and respected of citizens," James added.

Levi slumped under her hand. "I really mucked it up this time."

"Yes, you did," James agreed. "But never fear. We still need an annoying little brother to make the family complete, so you might as well keep playing the role. Unless we could get that Gulliver Ward fellow to stand in last minute." He glanced around at his family, as if seeking approval.

Beth shook her head at his silliness, but Catherine felt Drew's sigh.

"Levi made a mistake," he said, and she thought he took it personally. "Rankin made a bigger one by destroying property and threatening lives. But the fact of the matter is that Levi owes him money. Like it or not, deserved or not, the debt must be paid."

The conviction in his voice seemed to build her strength, as well.

Simon did not seem to share it. He leaned forward. "And just how do you intend to pay it? You don't have two hundred dollars."

Drew's jaw tightened. "I'll go to Yesler, offer him a contract on timber for his sawmill and ask for an advance."

John snorted. "Yesler doesn't pay on time even after we deliver the wood. I doubt he'll give us money ahead of receipt."

Now Drew's shoulders were tensing, as well. He was trying to protect his family, as he always did.

"I'll find a way," he insisted. "I refuse to see this family endangered."

"And you think the rest of us will sit by contentedly?" Simon asked. He rose from his seat, gaze on Drew's. "I heard Pa that day. He made you head of this family. I know the sacrifices you've made to raise us all. Your clothes wore out, but you made sure ours didn't. You were the first one out in the fields in the morning, the last in at night."

So he saw it, too. What Catherine couldn't understand was why he sounded so angry about it.

Simon bent and braced both hands on the table so that he and Drew were eye to eye. "You did your job, Drew. We're grown men. It's time you started letting us have a say in how things go around here."

Catherine leaned back from him. She still disliked his tone, but she realized that he was right. If Drew's brothers took more of a hand in keeping Beth and Levi safe and supporting their mother, it would surely ease Drew's mind. Maybe enough to start the family his mother hoped for him.

Perhaps with her.

Drew was watching his brother. "I never told you to hold your peace," he said. "Not about family matters."

"No, but you act as if we're all your responsibility." Simon straightened. "When something threatens one of us, it threatens us all. I have sixty dollars saved from my cut of the timber. That can go against Levi's debt."

"I have forty," John put in. "I can do without a few books for a time."

"I brought you *Culpeper's*," Catherine offered, and he beamed.

James fingered his shirt. "I have thirty, but I owe twenty at the mercantile." He shrugged. "Mr. Howard has commented more than once on my taste in clothing. I could probably get him to pay twenty for my waistcoat."

Sacrifice, indeed. Not to be outdone, Beth took a deep breath.

"I have three dollars from gifts," she said, twisting a strand of hair around one finger. "I was saving it for my social dress, but James is right. When will I attend a social?"

Catherine touched her hand. "Sooner than you think."

Levi glanced around at them. "I can't take your money. I don't deserve it."

"You certainly don't," James said. He patted his brother's shoulder. "I believe that's why it's called a gift."

"That's one hundred and thirty-three," Simon said. "If we put in the hundred from Captain Collings, we've more than enough."

"But that money was to go for a plow," John protested. "And we'll need lumber to repair the barn."

Catherine clasped her hands together on the table. "I am paid two and a half dollars a week at the hospital. I've saved five dollars, and I have it with me. You are welcome to it."

They all stared at her.

James spoke first, tugging down on his smoke-stained shirtsleeves. "If you had told us you were such an heiress, Catherine, I might have tried harder to wedge my way into your affections."

Drew's hand came down on hers, warm and firm. "Thank you, Catherine." He looked to his brothers. "It seems we're all in this together, then."

Together. A family. Oh, but that was what she hoped they soon might be.

They set out the next morning. Drew wasn't sure what to expect at the Rankins', but he'd agreed that Catherine should come with them. She'd fought for her place at his side when they'd laid out their plans around the table last night.

"Having a lady with you may make him think twice about his behavior," she'd insisted, eyes bright with fervor.

Levi had snorted. "You've never met Mr. Rankin."

"You're right," she'd admitted. "I haven't had the pleasure."

"Believe me, it's not a pleasure," James had assured her.

"He's proved he cares about nothing but money," Drew had agreed. "He could have killed us all or damaged acres of timber by torching the barn. It's not safe for you to come with us, Catherine."

"Then it's not safe for you to go, either," she'd insisted. "You cannot expect me to sit idly by while you are in danger."

His brothers should have done more to help him counter her logic, but instead they had all grinned at her.

"I've always admired a woman willing to fight for those she loves," James had said. "That and one with a good head of hair."

She had ignored him. "And Scout. I promised myself I'd look in on the boy. I'm convinced his father is
beating him."

That might be, but the thought that Catherine might
fall under those fists as well had made his back stiffen,
his fingers tighten. He'd wanted to argue further, but
she'd laid a hand on his arm. "If anyone is hurt, Drew,
I want to be there to help."

As always, that logic he could not defeat. So Catherine was walking in front of him when they left at first
light that morning.

"Be careful," she murmured as they started into the
trees. "You don't know how Mr. Rankin will react. If he
gambles all night as Levi said, he may not take kindly
to visitors so early in the morning."

Drew was counting on it.

Only an old game trail, heavily overgrown, led between the two claims. They went single file, Simon at
the head, Drew at the back. James held the bushes so
John could help Levi and Catherine could come through
with her wide brown skirts. The boy had tried to remain behind, worried that his injured leg would slow
them down.

"You started this," Simon had told him. "It's only
right you be there to finish it."

Now they moved quietly, his brothers with axes in
their hands and knives at their waists. James carried his
rifle, but Drew had warned everyone use their weapon
only for protection. Catherine carried her bandbox,
which she'd packed with the bandages Levi had rolled
and some medical supplies she had brought from town
this time. Drew only hoped she'd have no call to use
any of them.

The Rankin cabin was set near the shore of the lake, drowned trees lying like giant needles in the mud all around it. Scout had once bragged that his father let the water do his clearing for him.

But it didn't look as if Rankin had worked on his land in any other way. Blackberries had overtaken the vegetable patch, and a few chickens pecked among the weeds of the yard. The log cabin looked nearly as deserted, standing silent as they approached.

The Rankins had never bothered to install glass in their windows. Shutters closed up the house like the shell of a turtle. Only smoke trickling from the chimney, rising to meet the gray clouds, said someone might be home. But a new hitching post had been built in front of the house, resin still dripping from the timber, and the dirt around it had been packed solid, as if any number of horses had waited for owners busy inside. Somewhere near to hand, Drew caught the acrid scent of fermenting grain.

As his brothers fanned out across the yard, Catherine behind Simon for her protection, Drew nodded to Levi, who limped up to the door and banged on it. "Mr. Rankin? It's Levi Wallin. I have your money."

Inside came thuds and a raised voice before Benjamin Rankin yanked open the weathered door. A large man with ample folds around his thick neck and a protruding belly, his eyes squinted against the light. The sneer on his flabby face quickly vanished as he spied Drew and the others in the yard.

James raised the rifle, but Drew thought Catherine's glare was far more effective in making the man take a step back.

"We don't want any trouble," Drew assured Rankin. "Pay the man what you owe, Levi."

Levi shoved the sack of silver and gold coins at the man. "Two hundred, just like we agreed."

Rankin spat a stream of something yellow into the yard, as if the sight of the money left a bad taste in his mouth. "You forgot the interest."

Drew stiffened. So did Catherine and Levi.

"Interest?" his youngest brother cried. "You never said anything about interest."

Rankin shrugged with a roll of muscle and fat. "Didn't think I had to. Goes without saying that there's interest on a loan. You get to use my money. I get a consideration." He opened the sack and dug a thick finger into the coins, making them clink against each other. "I see no consideration here."

"How very inconsiderate of us," James quipped. "What do you say, Drew? Shall we pay Mr. Rankin back the same way he paid Levi?"

Simon smacked his ax handle into the palm of one hand.

To Drew's surprise, Catherine strode forward, eyes flashing. "Levi already paid your interest, Mr. Rankin, with his blood. And so, I believe, has your son, Scout. I demand that you show us the boy."

"You demand?" Rankin laughed, the sound like the creaking of a badly oiled door. "You have no rights on my property. A man can treat his boy any way he likes."

Catherine looked him up and down, standing tall and trim in her tailored brown wool. "And he can treat himself as he wishes, as well. You certainly have. Veined nose and bloodshot eyes—the effects of too much alcohol. Ample girth, too much food of the wrong sort.

Shortness of breath and wheezing laugh, indications of an asthmatic condition brought about by excessive exposure to tobacco smoke. If you do not mend your ways, Mr. Rankin, I predict you will shortly die of heart failure."

Drew took a step closer, fully expecting Rankin to light into her verbally, if not physically. Instead, the man squinted his eyes at her. "Who are you?"

"Catherine Stanway," she replied. "Trained nurse and assistant to Doctor Maynard. And I strongly suggest you take my advice and see to your diet and surroundings immediately."

Rankin glanced between her and Drew. "Is she crazy?"

Drew smiled. "Not in the slightest. Ma nearly died of a fever. She nursed her back to health in a couple of days."

"Took care of Old Joe's rash, too," James called. "For which we are all grateful." He shuddered, as if even the recollection of the puffy skin was painful.

Scout crept up beside his father, one hand tugging at the man's sleeve. "She knew about my nose, Pa, before I ever said a word."

Rankin frowned, rubbing one finger against his own nose. "So what it is you want, ma'am?"

Catherine lifted her chin, gaze still militant. "You will cease striking your son. I suspect you'll need his goodwill should something horrid happen to you."

Rankin glanced at Scout as if he'd never considered that possibility before.

"You will drink at least eight glasses of water a day," Catherine continued, "and take a turn around the yard three times, rain or shine. You will watch your diet, choosing vegetables over meat for a time. And you will stop drinking alcohol."

Rankin grimaced. "I ain't no teetotaler."

"If you wish to live," Catherine said, "you will be."

Drew took another step forward, towering over them all. Pride for Catherine vied with anger over what Rankin had done to his family. "And your business with us is over, Rankin. You leave the Wallins alone."

"And the Wallins will return the favor," Simon added.

Rankin looked from one of them to another. He must not have liked his chances, for he squared his shoulders. "I don't like your attitude, Wallin. Sheriff might have something to say about this bullying."

Bullying? And this from a man who had perfected the art? But another voice spoke from behind them.

"As a matter of fact, the sheriff has quite an opinion on the matter."

Rankin turned white as Deputy McCormick stepped out from behind a tree, rifle resting in the crook of his arm. He nodded to Drew.

"Wallin. We saw the smoke from out this way yesterday, but I couldn't come investigate until this morning. Thought I'd better check on all the farms in this neck of the woods. Any trouble here?"

Drew glanced at Rankin, who had all but disappeared into the shadows of his cabin, leaving Scout on the step, blinking at the light.

"Our barn caught fire yesterday," Drew told the deputy. "You might ask Mr. Rankin if he knows anything about that."

Rankin's piggy eyes were bright in the darkness.

"Shame when hay just catches fire by its own self. Been known to happen."

Scout dropped his gaze.

"True," McCormick mused. "Funny how so many fires have sprung up out this way, though. Maybe you and your boy ought to move into town, where we can keep an eye on you."

"A fine suggestion," Catherine agreed. "It might improve your health, Mr. Rankin."

Rankin's smile turned oily. "Thank you both for your concern, but we're doing just fine out here. I think Mr. Wallin is right. His family and I are finished with our business for now." He gazed up at Drew. "Any interest on that loan is forgiven, seeing as how young Levi is such good friends with my boy, and your lady friend here is so helpful about my health. And you're all welcome at my table anytime."

"Don't hold your breath," Levi said, turning away.

"Actually, do hold your breath," James suggested. "For say ten or twenty minutes. I guarantee it will improve the neighborhood immensely."

Rankin slammed the door on them, leaving Scout standing on the step. Catherine immediately drew him aside, and Drew heard her start to question the boy about his own health.

McCormick waited as Drew and his brothers gathered around him, then spoke with a low voice as if mindful of Scout and Catherine not too far away. "I take it you have reason to believe Rankin burned your barn."

"Among other things," Drew murmured. "But we have no proof to offer you. It's our word against his."

McCormick's smile was grim. "No question in my mind which a judge would believe. I'll keep watch here for a while until you get home. And the sheriff and I will be keeping an eye on Rankin." He glanced at the house and shook his head before returning his gaze to Drew's. "That's some lady you have there. Never thought I'd see any miss who could stand up to Rankin."

"I never thought I'd see a lady who could stand his smell," James added. Simon cuffed him on the shoulder.

"I expect she'll need to return to town soon," McCormick continued, ignoring them. "Do you want me to fetch Miss Stanway back with me?"

His brothers were all watching Drew, waiting for his answer.

"Not just yet," Drew said. "First, I need to propose."

He wasn't sure which of them had the biggest grin.

Chapter Twenty-Four

The air smelled cool and sharp as Catherine walked back through the wood with Drew and his brothers. Rain would be here soon, but she didn't mind. She felt as if they'd achieved a victory, both in removing Mr. Rankin's threats from over Levi's head and in letting him know they would brook no further nonsense.

She glanced back over her shoulder where Scout Rankin walked just behind her. Seeing her look, he straightened from his slouch and managed a smile. She'd thought it best to keep the boy at Wallin Landing for the day to give his father time to calm down and think about what she and the others had said. And perhaps he and Levi could mend their differences. The boy had already confessed that he'd tried to stop his father, to no avail.

Beyond him, Drew smiled at her as well before she turned front again, cheeks heating. He looked as if he wanted to say something to her, but this walking single file through the woods certainly wasn't conducive to conversation. She could hardly wait to return home.

Home.

Her smile deepened as the woods opened up to reveal the cabin and barn, the horses trotting about the pasture, the chickens pecking in their yard. Mrs. Wallin had set the large cast-iron kettle on a fire in the clearing, and the pile of shirts and trousers next to it said she was about to start the laundry.

Beth had made her own path from the tub to the ruined wall Drew had opened in the pool, where the spring bubbled below the level of the break. The way her face brightened at the sight of her brothers told Catherine how little she'd liked waiting. Catherine knew the feeling. She'd waited for her father and brother to come home, and they never would. This time, she'd been the one to help.

Lord, I thought I was the healer, but I've been blind. Everything I've done was to try to take control because I doubted You. You didn't send my brother and father to their deaths—they chose to fight. You didn't force me out of Sudbury—I ran. I can see You've given me a chance with Drew. Please help me find a way to tell him how much he's come to mean to me.

She glanced back again and caught her breath as Drew moved into the sunlight. His head was high like the trees he felled, his smile brighter than the spring sun. Something fluttered in her stomach, and she let Scout pass her so she could wait for Drew to reach her side.

He came to a stop beside her and lowered his ax. She couldn't look away as he bent his head to hers. "Thank you," he murmured before he kissed her. His arms came around her, fierce, protective, as if he'd never let her go. She nestled against him, returned his kiss and trembled with the joy that tumbled through her.

"Ahem."

Catherine blinked and realized James was standing next to them, hands clasped behind his back. Seeing he had her attention, he wiggled his blond brows.

"It appears, Miss Stanway, that you have compromised my brother's reputation, and I want to know what you intend to do about it."

Catherine glanced at Drew even as her cheeks heated.

Drew frowned at his brother, but she saw merriment in his eyes. "You better hope she doesn't need a gun to get me to the altar, because we both know her aim is questionable."

"Oh!" Catherine cried in indignation. "I can hit the broad side of a barn."

James snorted, then hurriedly turned the sound into a cough.

"I'm not worried," he told Drew when he'd recovered. "I figure Simon will be the one standing up beside you. I'll be safely in the throng of well-wishers."

"No throng would be safe with you in it," Drew countered. "Now, go on. Catherine and I weren't finished talking."

"Oh, talking he calls it," James said, but he bowed and sauntered back to where his other brothers were telling Beth and Mrs. Wallin about their reception at the Rankins.

Drew had kept his arms around her, and she did not mind. His warmth seeped into her heart like water on parched earth.

"Deputy McCormick wondered if you wanted an escort back to Seattle," he murmured. "I told him I had something I needed to ask you first."

Her heart started beating faster. "And what would that be?"

He pulled back to meet her gaze. "Catherine, nothing would make me happier than for you to agree to be my wife. But I've long known that whoever marries me marries into this family. Ma has her way of doing things. Beth could talk the paint off a wall. Simon must have the last word, James the last laugh. John thinks he knows everything, and Levi hasn't realized how little he knows. We're not the easiest bunch to get along with."

"You're not the most difficult, either," she countered. "You love each other, support each other."

"Argue with each other, fuss at each other."

"Work together toward a common goal. I envy you that. But as much as I love your family, Drew, I cannot marry you for them. That wouldn't be fair to you."

He released her. "Is there nothing I can say, nothing I can do, then, to win your heart?"

Catherine cocked her head. "Do you want to win it, Drew? I know the burden you've put on yourself to keep this family safe. Even with your brothers taking a bigger role, are you willing to add more to the family—a wife, perhaps someday children? Are you willing to speak for yourself, Drew?"

That was, of course, the key question. He wasn't sure why he was surprised she'd asked it. Certainly his family thought nothing of him taking a wife. Look how they'd campaigned on Catherine's behalf.

He knew every argument against her, every reason a marriage wouldn't work. Yet when he tried to imagine life without her, the future looked dark, empty.

"I want to speak, Catherine," he told her. "But I feel

like that Miles Standish fellow. I'm not the most eloquent man. I can't play a love song like Simon or quote from some book like John. But if it's pretty words you want, I'll try."

She took his hands, fingers spreading to wrap around the edges of his. "Then perhaps I should go first, before I lose my courage."

Anything that scared her ought to terrify him. "All right," he managed to say.

She took a deep breath and met his gaze. "You know I love this family, Drew, but everything that's happened over the last week has proved something to me. When we were all in danger, it scared me to think of losing my family. But what truly made me fearful was the thought of losing you."

She squeezed his hands. "What I'm trying to say is that I love you, Drew Wallin. You are a fine, noble, honorable man. Any woman would be proud to stand beside you."

She seemed to think he should just smile and nod in agreement. But his brain had seized on one statement and wouldn't let go.

She loved him.

Against all odds, this clever, talented, amazing woman loved him. He finally understood what James meant about it being a gift, for he knew he could never earn her love, but would always be grateful for her.

He was pretty sure a smile and nod was not the appropriate way to respond to such feelings. He pulled her into his arms and kissed her.

Catherine closed her eyes, glorying in the feel of Drew's arms around her, his lips caressing hers. The sound of the Landing, the clamor of her heart, the lingering smell of smoke faded away, until he filled all her senses. He had not said the words, but she could feel his love in the way he cradled her against him, hear it in murmur of her name. She had traveled thousands of miles to find a new life, and the journey had led her home, to him.

Slowly, he raised his head, and she smiled at him. She thought it must be a besotted sort of smile, a bit crooked and trembling about the edges. His matched it.

"I promised myself I would do things properly this time," he said, "but I seem to have a hard time being proper where you're concerned."

Catherine laughed. He released her to go down on one knee on the ground, gaze lifted to hers.

"Catherine Stanway," he said, deep voice echoing around the clearing. "I love you. Will you do me the honor of becoming my wife?"

"Say yes!" Beth cried, and was quickly hushed.

Drew's cheeks darkened. Catherine cupped his face with her hands, feeling the hint of stubble peppering her palms. "Yes, Drew. Yes. A thousand times yes. Nothing would make me happier."

He rose and gathered her close once more. "I'll fix up the cabin, whatever you want. And I'll build you a dispensary so you can nurse from the Landing. Someday, when we have a hospital, you can lead it. You have a gift, Catherine, and I want to see you use it."

He might not be a poet, but he'd just found every word she needed to hear. "Thank you," she murmured. "For understanding, for making me part of your family. I'll be a good wife for you, Drew. I promise."

He smiled. "How could you be anything else?"

"Simon!" James called. "Fetch your fiddle. Methinks I detect cause for celebration."

Catherine glanced over her shoulder at her new family and found them all grinning at her. Mrs. Wallin wiped a tear from the corner of her eye.

Beth rushed up to them. "Oh, a wedding! You must let me help. We'll need flowers and a cake and a special dress. I saw the latest prints in *Godey's,* yards of lace and long veils of the sheerest net."

"Beth," Drew started.

"And a quilt! Ma has to make you a quilt. I'll help. It might take a few months."

"Beth," Catherine warned.

She was patting the tips of her fingers together, eyes bright. "Oh, there are so many people to invite—all the Mercer belles and Mr. Yesler and Doc and his wife. We'll need to talk to Mr. Bagley, of course. I wonder if the brown church will be big enough. Maybe we'll have to see if they'll let us use the white church."

"Elizabeth Ann Wallin," Mrs. Wallin said. "Leave them be."

With a blush, Beth hurried off, humming to herself.

Catherine shook her head. "It seems we'll have no trouble planning a wedding."

Drew chuckled. "I had no idea it was such an undertaking. Months, she said. I hope you'll have pity on me, Catherine, and not make me wait that long."

Catherine smiled. "You speak to the Reverend Bagley and see how soon he can fit us in. So long as our family is around us, I'd be happy to be married at any time."

And so, two weeks later they gathered at the brown church. After being at the Landing, Seattle looked crowded to Catherine, the muddy streets teeming with people, but perhaps that was because she had so many attendants at her wedding. She still found it hard to believe—her, marrying a brawny lumberjack. It was nothing she could have imagined and everything she'd ever wanted.

She stood at the back of the church, pews of carved dark wood stretching on either side, beams open above like the boughs of a forest. She wore Mrs. Wallin's blue-and-green dress, which she now knew had served as the lady's own wedding gown more than thirty years ago. The skirts might be narrower than she was used to, but the fine material and love behind it made it the most beautiful dress she'd ever worn.

Maddie, wearing a jade-green dress she'd sewed for the occasion, was standing between her and the altar. Behind Maddie stood Allegra in a similar gown, Doctor Maynard's wife, Susanna, in darker green, then Beth in her first social dress, paid for courtesy of Maddie's laundry earnings. Waiting at the front, Drew stood with his brothers beside him, hair slicked down, all in dark suits and high collars. Only James looked comfortable in them.

It was most likely the largest wedding party Seattle had ever seen, but she would have had it no other way.

Next to her, Doc Maynard squeezed her arm. "I'm honored you chose me to give you away, Catherine." His eyes twinkled. "But then, I seem to be always giving you away to these Wallins."

Catherine smiled. Doc had already packed up a number of supplies and instruments for her to take with her to the Landing for her dispensary.

"A lady should have family beside her when she

weds," she said now. "And I am blessed with the most wonderful family, even if we don't share the same mother and father."

"Ah, but the good reverend would remind us we do share the same Father," he replied with a wink. "And I think we've kept Mr. Bagley and your charming groom waiting long enough."

Catherine nodded. They started down the aisle, the congregation standing as they passed. She spotted Sheriff Boren and Deputy McCormick, boardinghouse owner Mrs. Elliott and all the women who had come with her on the Mercer expedition, some married and some, like Maddie, determined to remain single.

Unless You send them someone like Drew, Father. Someone who can find the way to their hearts. Thank You for being patient with me, for helping me understand. My family chose to leave me. I can choose to stay.

Reverend Bagley beamed at her as she reached the front of the church. "Who gives this woman to be married?" he asked, adjusting his spectacles on his thin nose.

"I do," Doc Maynard said. "And if you don't recognize me by this time, Daniel, I'd say you need to polish those glasses."

The minister frowned at him as the congregation laughed.

As the room quieted again, Drew moved to Catherine's side. Looking up into his eyes, she felt as if his arms, and his love, were holding her even now. Her heart was so full she barely heard the words of the ceremony.

Thank You, Lord, for this gift. I will never take it lightly.

"I now pronounce you man and wife," Mr. Bagley said. "You may kiss the bride."

Drew took her in his arms and pressed his lips against hers, sealing their promise. Her husband, his wife, forever, no matter what happened.

A cheer went up behind him. As he broke the kiss with a smile, Catherine could see James and John clapping each other on the back, Simon actually grinning from ear to ear and Levi doing some sort of dance with his crutch along the front pew.

The reverend coughed as if trying to remind them of proper behavior in church, then gave it up and grinned as he raised his hands in benediction.

"Ladies and gentlemen, friends and family, I give you Mr. and Mrs. Wallin."

Their guests clapped and cheered as Drew and Catherine made their way down the aisle.

"You are my hero," Catherine told him. "I didn't think I would ever be this happy again."

They stepped out onto the porch. Seattle rain fell softly like a blessing. Drew's brothers spread out on the steps, demanding the right to kiss the bride on the cheek.

"Go ahead," Drew said, moving aside. "Just remember one thing. I know the trouble you went to to make sure your brother courted his bride. I think the best Catherine and I can do is return the favor."

James, who had just pecked Catherine on the cheek, straightened. "You mean you're going to marry us off?"

Catherine bit her lip to keep from laughing at the shock on his face.

"Yes, I do," Drew said. "Turnabout is fair play. I think we should start with Simon."

Simon raised a brow. "You can try, brother, but I haven't seen a woman yet who can meet my criteria for a bride."

"Sure'n that's because you've been looking in the wrong places, me lad," Maddie said, nose in the air as she passed. She twitched her jade skirts to one side. Then she seized Catherine's hand. "Come along, me darling girl. Toss your bouquet, and let's see who's next to wed."

The other women hurried past to gather at the foot of the stairs, faces alight as they gazed up at Catherine. She caught James and John eyeing them appreciatively.

She turned her back and tossed the flowers over her shoulder. Then she whirled to see who had caught the bouquet.

Most of the women looked downright disappointed to see the flowers nestled in Beth's hands. Beth was staring at Maddie.

"You threw it at me!" she accused.

Maddie's brown eyes were wide, though her cheeks were turning pink. "Sure'n it bounced off my fingertips."

While the others congratulated a confused Beth, Drew put his arm about Catherine's waist. "Perhaps we should add your friend to the list of those needing help finding a match."

"Perhaps," Catherine agreed. "But you surprise me, Drew. I never took you for a matchmaker."

"With the right teacher, a man can learn anything," he said, holding her closer. "And starting right now, I aim to learn all the ways I can show my wife how much I love her."

Catherine smiled up at him. "An admirable goal. And I intend to show my husband my devotion, as well. I predict the process will take a lifetime."

And it did.

* * * * *

LOVE INSPIRED

Stories to uplift and inspire

Fall in love with Love Inspired—
inspirational and uplifting stories of faith
and hope. Find strength and comfort in
the bonds of friendship and community.
Revel in the warmth of possibility and the
promise of new beginnings.

Sign up for the Love Inspired newsletter
at **LoveInspired.com** to be the first
to find out about upcoming titles,
special promotions and exclusive content.

CONNECT WITH US AT:

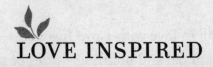